Praise for Meg Benjamin's
Don't Forget Me

"Benjamin is an extraordinary storyteller who melds sizzling spice, flirty fun and lively laughter to entertain the reader with every word. Three-dimensional characters leap off the pages, captivating readers for an engaging read. This sixth book in the Konigsburg, Texas, series is escapism at its best."

~ *Romantic Times*

"The characters in this series have been strongly developed and you feel you could step on the streets of Konigsburg and spot them one by one. The suspense elements do a great job of providing motion to the plot, and touch of mystery to keep you guessing. I thoroughly enjoyed Meg Benjamin's *Don't Forget Me*. I haven't read the entire series but I enjoyed book 6 as a stand alone. After meeting the characters throughout the novel, I know I'll be looking for the first 5 books very soon. Recommended Read."

~ *Guilty Pleasures Book Reviews*

"*Don't Forget Me* is a wonderful timeless contemporary romance that hits all the right notes—humor, passion, suspense, and love."

~ *Sizzling Hot Book Reviews*

Look for these titles by
Meg Benjamin

Now Available:

Konigsburg Texas Series
Venus in Blue Jeans
Wedding Bell Blues
Be My Baby
Long Time Gone
Brand New Me

Don't Forget Me

Meg Benjamin

SAMHAIN
PUBLISHING

Samhain Publishing, Ltd.
11821 Mason Montgomery Road, 4B
Cincinnati, OH 45249
www.samhainpublishing.com

Don't Forget Me
Copyright © 2012 by Meg Benjamin
Print ISBN: 978-1-60928-815-0
Digital ISBN: 978-1-60928-825-9

Editing by Lindsey Faber
Cover by Valerie Tibbs

First Samhain Publishing, Ltd. electronic publication: December 2011
First Samhain Publishing, Ltd. print publication: November 2012

Dedication

To my family, Bill, Josh and Molly, and Ben. To my editor, Lindsey Faber, and my agent, Maureen Walters. And to the Nine Naughty Novelists who helped to keep me sane: Juniper Bell, Kate Davies, PG Forte, Kinsey Holley, Kelly Jamieson, Skylar Kade, Erin Nicholas, and Sydney Somers.

Chapter One

Nando Avrogado was hiding. Granted, the Dew Drop Inn didn't provide much in the way of cover, although it was dark enough to make identifying anyone pretty challenging unless you were less than six inches away. Granted, Nando himself, at six three and a hundred eighty-eight pounds, was somewhat difficult to hide, even when he wasn't in uniform (as he wasn't at the moment). Nonetheless, he was hiding. From Francine Richter, five three and a hundred five.

It was embarrassing. It was nothing a mature adult male of twenty-eight should be doing.

He should just get over it. He knew that. He should just head down the street to the Faro tavern, where he usually hung out, and take his punishment, whatever that punishment turned out to be—tears, curses, possibly violence. It wasn't exactly his fault that Francine hadn't understood the meaning of their goodbye date the way she was supposed to. It sure wasn't his fault that she'd been leaving messages on his voice mail for the past two days.

Except that it was his fault. Sort of. He'd tried to make it clear throughout their handful of dates that nothing more serious was on the horizon for them. That they weren't going to hook up for the long term. That they were just having some temporary good times.

And in reality, the times hadn't even been all that good after the first couple of dates. He had to admit that, for the most part, he'd just been going through the motions. Francine was okay. She didn't natter too much. She looked good. She was...a decent kisser. Not bad exactly, but not good either.

Nando sighed, taking a sip of his lukewarm beer. If he were honest, it wasn't Francine who'd been the real disappointment. He was the one who wasn't measuring up to expectations, Francine's for sure, but his own too. Given his lack of enthusiasm, maybe it was just as well that they'd never progressed beyond a few hot make-out sessions on Francine's couch.

Of course, if he were honest he wouldn't be sitting in this dive, drinking beer that tasted like dishwater. He'd be down the street with his friends at the Faro, drinking some honest brew and dealing with Francine when and if she showed up.

He rubbed his eyes and fought back the impulse to groan in frustration. God, he was tired. And it wasn't just the hours from his job as a Konigsburg cop. During the last few months he'd seemed to fall into a rut that just got deeper and deeper. Same people, same problems, same everything. When had this feeling started anyway? And why? He'd gotten all the things he'd once thought he wanted in his life—full-time appointment to the Konigsburg police force, a decent place to live away from his parents (sharing an apartment with his brother Esteban, but doing that wasn't such a bad deal), an active social life without being tied down to anybody.

Yeah, right. It was that "active" social life that was the problem. Maybe he should try deliberate celibacy rather than the unintentional kind for a while. See what it felt like to *not* hit the clubs on his night off. The whole excitement-of-the-chase thing was getting very old. And truth be told, the chase hadn't been that exciting for a long time. Eighteen months, in fact.

Don't go there. It's over. No matter how much you wish it weren't.

"Geez, where'd you hide the body? You look like a man at a wake." His brother Esteban slid onto the stool next to him, waving a hand toward Ingstrom, the bartender. "What are you doing here anyway? I thought you did your drinking at the Faro these days."

"I could say the same thing about you." Nando took a disgruntled pull on his beer. "I don't think I've ever seen you in this dive before."

Esteban cleared his throat. Ingstrom, who owned the Dew Drop Inn as well as being its bartender, was standing across from them behind the bar. He scowled at Nando before turning to his brother. "You want beer or wine?"

"Lonestar," Esteban said hastily. He was the assistant wine master at Cedar Creek Winery, which meant he routinely avoided the wine-in-a-jug served by the Dew Drop Inn. "You still haven't explained why you're here," he continued as Ingstrom headed back down the bar. "I haven't seen you in the Dew Drop for a couple of months. Why aren't you at the Faro watching Deirdre Brandenburg serve beers like every other red-blooded man in town?"

Nando shrugged. "Deirdre's attached to Tom Ames. If I start ogling Deirdre, he's likely to put Ipecac in my beer. Besides, the Dew Drop's closer to home. I didn't feel like walking."

Esteban smirked. "Yeah, those three blocks will really do you in. Especially with the temperature hovering in the high seventies."

"Get stuffed," Nando muttered, but his heart wasn't in it.

Esteban turned, resting his elbows on the bar behind him as he surveyed the room. "You trying to avoid your latest fling? I'd say that's a heavy price to pay for romance gone wrong."

Nando studied his younger brother with hooded eyes. Esteban looked like a linebacker, which he'd been in high school, or like someone who bench-pressed wine barrels, which he also did frequently. He wore his hair almost as short as Nando's, even though the management at Cedar Creek wasn't as stiff about hair length as Chief Toleffson was at the cop shop. But he made up for the hair with the luxuriant moustache that curved around his mouth. His skin was darkened from working in the vineyards—just like their father.

"What would you know about romance gone wrong?" Nando grabbed a handful of peanuts. "I haven't noticed you tearing up the town with anybody since you broke up with Dawn Benavidez. And that's been over three months, bro."

Esteban shook his head. "Nice try, but we're not switching the subject of this conversation to me. Are you or are you not trying to avoid Francine Richter?"

Nando blew out a breath. "Maybe."

"Right." Esteban shook his head. "You don't think that's a little pathetic? Hiding out in a joint like the Dew Drop just to avoid a woman you dated for a couple of weeks?"

Nando ran his glass through the circle of condensation on the bar. "I can drink where I want, bro. Who knows? Maybe I'll check out the talent around here this evening." There had to be some. Even at the Dew Drop.

Ingstrom set Esteban's draft on the bar with a clink. "Stay away from my barmaids, Avrogado, they got work to do." He stomped back to the other end of the bar.

Nando took a quick survey of the Dew Drop's barmaids, the most prominent one anyway. Ruby looked more like a biker chick than usual. Tonight she had on a leather vest that was zipped partway up

11

her sizeable chest and blue jeans that showed a roll of white flesh at the waist. Her magenta hair was caught in a banana clip that looked perilously close to slipping out. Every man in the bar was trying not to look down her cleavage, knowing the instant retribution that followed. As if she sensed she was being watched, Ruby caught Nando's eye. Her lip twisted in a world-class sneer.

"Now going after that really would be pathetic," he muttered.

Esteban nodded. "True that. So why can't you just tell Francine it's over? Fun while it lasted, time to move on and so forth."

Nando grimaced. "Because I'd rather not get into one of those discussions where you end up either making somebody cry or making somebody mad enough to bean you with her purse. If I stay out of her way long enough, she'll get the message."

"And that way you just come off as a jerk instead of a sleaze."

Nando gritted his teeth. "You could put it that way."

"You know, bro, sooner or later all this bad karma you're building up with women is going to come back and bite you on the ass." Esteban took a long swallow of Lonestar.

"What are you, some kind of wine-making Buddhist now?" Nando shook his head. "This doesn't qualify as bad karma. So I don't like talking about 'relationships' with women. Name me one man who does."

Esteban shrugged. "I'm just saying if all the women you've screwed around with over the past few months ever got together, you'd be a dead man."

Nando rubbed his eyes again. The vision of all his recent exes getting together, possibly with automatic weapons, was not altogether comfortable. "Yeah, well, I'm thinking of cutting back. Maybe putting the brakes on the relationships for a while. Take a breather from women."

"You?" The corners of Esteban's mouth curved up. "You're giving up women? Maybe I should spread the word. I could sell tickets."

A slight prickle of unease slid down Nando's spine. He wasn't that much of a womanizer, was he? He never used to think of himself that way. Of course, that was before the major fuck-up of his love life. "Do *not* spread the word." He gritted his teeth again. "This was just between the two of us. And I haven't decided for sure what I'm going to do. Just thinking about it."

Esteban nodded, still grinning. "Right."

Nando drained the rest of his beer. *Screw it.* "I'm going down to the Faro, see what's going on. You want to come?"

"Maybe later." His brother peered toward the far corner of the bar where Britney Collins was seated with a couple of her girlfriends.

Nando rolled his eyes. Clearly, he wasn't the only Avrogado who had females on the brain. "Good luck with that."

He dropped a handful of bills on the bar, then pushed back, dodging around a couple of protruding rear ends to get to the door. Among other things, the Dew Drop was short on open space, particularly since Ingstrom had added some extra tables in the middle of the room. Nando ran through the bar's very own obstacle course, then opened the door to the street.

It took a minute for his eyes to adjust to the early evening light. People still strolled down Main, ducking into the few open stores. Mid-March wasn't a great tourist time in Konigsburg, but they got some families who filled up the motels and bed and breakfasts for Spring Break. He settled his Stetson on his forehead and started up the street toward the Faro.

Ahead of him the crowd parted for a moment and he saw a swing of long dark hair reaching down below a woman's shoulders. *Nice.* For a moment, he concentrated on her as she walked up the street in front of him, wondering what she'd look like when she turned around. You could never predict exactly how attractive someone's face would be based on her back side.

Nando grimaced. He really needed to stop ogling women. Particularly if he wanted to take the whole celibacy thing seriously. Besides, if anyone ever heard him talking about faces and back sides like that, he'd be banned from the female sex for life. *Which you would richly deserve, and which might not be such a bad thing.*

A couple walking in front of him turned in to one of the candy stores and he got a better look at the woman up ahead. Silken dark hair, slender waist, long, long legs that showed off well in her white Capri pants. Nando finally gave in and checked her behind. *More than respectable.* The whole package was superlative, in fact. Always assuming the face matched.

What the hell are you doing? You're supposed to be giving this up. You know it won't go anywhere.

13

Nando shook his head. Going cold turkey was going to be a lot harder than he'd thought. On the other hand, he couldn't go on indefinitely moving from woman to woman like some deranged honey bee, could he? Time to start being selective. Time to learn how to pace himself.

Time to grow up. More than time, if he were honest. He grimaced. That one hurt, largely because it was true.

Ahead of him, the woman slowed alongside Docia Toleffson's bookstore. Slowed and then stopped, staring in the window. After a moment, she waved at someone inside. Nando let his own pace slow down so that he wouldn't pass her just yet. He really wanted to see her face.

The door to the bookstore flew open, and Docia Toleffson herself stepped out, all six feet of her—maybe seven feet if you counted that pile of red hair on top of her head. She grinned at the stranger and then extended her arms to give her a hug. As she did, Nando got his first look at the woman's face.

His heart stuttered and then promptly dropped to his shoes. *Oh god, of course. I really had this coming.*

"Kit," Docia was saying. "Kit Maldonado. Where have you been keeping yourself? Allie said you were coming back this week. Oh, it's so good to see you!"

Kit said something back, but Nando didn't hear it. He was too busy stepping backward into the doorway of another shop where he'd have some cover. The last thing he wanted right then was a conversation with Kit. Hell, he didn't even want her to see him just yet. Not until he figured out what exactly he was going to say to her. And how he was going to say it. And what it would mean.

Kit Maldonado. Here. Back in Konigsburg.

For a moment he swore he could almost hear Esteban laughing. The force of karma had just sunk its teeth firmly into his ass.

Thank god for Docia Kent Toleffson. Kit headed back up Spicewood toward her Aunt Allie's house. Before Docia had come barreling out of her shop to give her a massive hug, she'd almost been ready to head back to San Antonio.

She hadn't really meant to start her job search today. She was going to take the afternoon to get reacquainted with Konigsburg. But people she knew had told her about a couple of possibilities, and she'd decided to check them out. Finding the right job on her first afternoon in Konigsburg would be great luck. It would have given her self-confidence just the kind of boost it needed.

It was also impossible. The hotel in the restored cotton warehouse shop complex had already filled their assistant manager position, although they'd taken her résumé and told her they'd keep her mind if they had any more openings. Then she'd talked to Jess Toleffson about maybe taking over as manager at the Lone Oak B and B, a job Jess had once held, only to discover that the owner, Nedda Carmody, defined the manager as the person who cleaned the cabins and brought the breakfast rolls around from Sweet Thing rather than as someone who actually managed the place. And Mrs. Carmody's payment consisted largely of free lodging, which Kit didn't need, thanks to Aunt Allie.

It had been enough to make her wonder if her decision to strike out on her own hadn't been a little hasty. She could still have her job at Antonio's Fine Mexican Cuisine for another six weeks or so. And her father would have helped her find another job somewhere else when the restaurant closed. Or anyway, he would have tried. He knew everybody in the business, particularly the ones on the west side of town. But without her family around, San Antonio wouldn't have felt the same.

And it was time to move on now anyway. Papi and Mami couldn't prop her up forever. She had to make it on her own. Somehow.

Kit shook her head. San Antonio wasn't a possibility, not really. Of course, since she was living with Aunt Allie, Konigsburg might not really qualify as being on her own, but it was still a step away from the house where she'd spent the first twenty-three years of her life. Plus, after fifteen years on the front lines, she was really tired of restaurant work. She had a degree in Management with a minor in Hospitality Services from UTSA, along with a very nice résumé, thanks to her internship at that hotel on the River Walk. Surely somebody in the hotel business would want to hire her. She'd just started looking, after all.

Still, she'd been feeling pretty low until she saw Docia. Docia Toleffson's smile would warm anybody up, plus seeing her helped to remind Kit just why she'd decided to try Konigsburg for her first post-college job in the first place. After San Antonio, Konigsburg felt most like home. She had Aunt Allie, Aunt Allie's fiancé, Steve Kleinschmidt, Docia and all the other Toleffsons. The town was full of friends.

And, of course, acquaintances who weren't exactly in the *friend* category, like Nando Avrogado. Kit's jaw tightened. Nando Avrogado was the reason she hadn't looked for a job at Cedar Creek Winery, where she'd once been assistant manager of the tasting room. She liked Cedar Creek and she had a good relationship with Morgan Barrett Toleffson, who was the marketing director. But the Avrogado family were part owners. She'd see Esteban and his parents every day out there, and inevitably, she'd see Nando too. She wasn't really ready to face that—not quite yet, anyway.

She was over him. So over him. Really. Over him.

For a moment, just a moment, she had a flash of memory. Dark brown eyes, a swing of dark hair across his forehead. His hands. Rough and gentle at the same time.

Over him. Damn it, she was.

She blew out a breath as she turned into Firewheel Lane and headed down the block toward Aunt Allie's forties-style bungalow. Aunt Allie was only nine or ten years older than she was, more like a big sister than an aunt in a lot of ways. But Kit had a big sister already and she really preferred having an aunt.

Right now, Aunt Allie was sort of living with Steve, whom everybody called Wonder Dentist for reasons Kit had never understood. But Allie wasn't completely living with Steve. She still had half her pots and pans and kitchen gadgets in her own kitchen. Considering that she was a professional chef and baker, one of Konigsburg's most celebrated, leaving her All-Clad copper core skillet at her own house instead of taking it over to Steve's had a lot of symbolic significance.

Kit started to pull out the key Allie had given her, then realized that the kitchen lights were on. Her aunt must be home after all.

She pushed open the front door. "Hey."

Allie glanced up from her cup of coffee and her copy of the *Konigsburg Herald-Zeitung*. Across from her, Steve was finishing a piece of what looked like blackberry pie.

"Hey." She smiled absently. "Any luck with the Cotton Palace?"

Kit shook her head. "They're fully staffed. Said they'd keep me in mind, but I'm not holding my breath, not in this job market."

Allie shrugged. "You'll find something. You've got a good degree in Management, and lord knows you've got hospitality experience."

Steve gave her a wry smile, pushing his horn-rims up his long nose. "Given the number of lame waiters I've run into lately, I'd say you're just what this town needs."

Kit sighed. "Right." She flopped into a chair opposite her aunt. "I'd just as soon not go the waitress route, thank you very much."

"Have you tried the hotels yet? I heard they're redoing the Millsberger Building into some kind of ritzy bed and breakfast." Steve shoveled in the last bite of his pie. Judging from his expression, he was considering licking the plate.

Kit shook her head. "I'll start doing the hotel rounds tomorrow. I don't think the Millsberger project is very far along, though. Some of their backers are supposedly getting cold feet."

Steve's jaw tightened. "Seems to be a persistent problem around this town."

Allie glanced at him, then folded her paper in a flurry of rustling pages. "There's some leftover lasagna in the refrigerator or you can make yourself a sandwich if you're hungry."

"Maybe I'll head on home." Steve pushed himself to his feet, then gave Allie a long look. "Care to join me?"

Allie shook her head, keeping her gaze on Kit. "Not tonight. There's also some potato salad in the plastic bowl."

"Okay." Kit moved to the counter where she had a better view of the action. Or non-action in this case. She pulled a jar of mustard out of the refrigerator along with bread and cheese.

Steve sighed, still staring down at Allie. "All right then. See you tomorrow." He leaned down and kissed her lightly on the lips.

For a moment she held his hand, then she gave him a tight smile. "See you tomorrow."

Kit watched him walk out the door and down the drive as she smeared mustard onto the seven-grain bread on the cutting board. *Something definitely not right there.* She turned back to Allie as she added slices of ham and American cheese.

Her aunt picked up Steve's plate and carried it to the sink. "So what's new in San Antonio?" she said in a voice that sounded overly bright. "How's Tony? I haven't talked to him for a month or so."

Kit cut her sandwich into precise triangles. "Papi's fine. Mami's fine. Arturo is fine. Everything's fine."

A moment of silence stretched between them, then Allie cleared her throat. "Okay, that sounds a little like overstatement. Care to explain?"

Kit took a deep breath. "He's selling the restaurant."

Allie blinked. "Tony? His restaurant? How could he..." She put a hand to her throat, her voice suddenly tight. "He's not sick, is he?"

"Papi? He's fine. I mean, he's tired but he's not sick. So far as I know."

"Then why?" Allie's forehead furrowed. "Why would he sell the restaurant? It's been the center of his life. I mean...besides Lara and you kids."

Kit managed not to grimace. Sometimes Antonio's Fine Mexican Cuisine had seemed to be the only center of her father's life. "He got an offer he couldn't refuse."

"Who from?"

"The Romano Group." Kit took a quick bit of her sandwich. "Sal Romano's company. They want to expand into Mexican food."

"And Tony sold?" Allie shook her head. "People have been trying to buy him out for years. What made Sal different?"

Kit shrugged. "Timing, I guess. This time Papi was ready." She managed to keep her tone light. *Good for you, Catarina.*

"But what are Tony and Lara going to do?"

"They're moving to South Padre Island." Kit ran her fork through the potato salad, pretending to take a bite. "They've got a condo north of town. Near Pat and Rodolfo and the grandkids."

Allie's jaw dropped. "They're moving? Selling the house? Leaving you kids?"

Kit nodded, eyes on her plate. "Papi was afraid if he stayed around, he'd want to keep an eye on the restaurant. So he decided the best thing to do was just to leave."

"What about you?" Her aunt narrowed her eyes. "Is that why you came up here, Kit?"

Kit shrugged. "Partly, I guess. I might have come up here anyway." *But probably not, given everyone who lives here.*

18

Allie leaned forward, putting her hand over Kit's on the table. "I'm glad you're here, sweetheart. No matter why you came."

"I am too." Kit forced the corners of her mouth to turn up. "Really."

And you're sure you mean that, Catarina?

Kevin Brody took a long look down Main Street. Konigsburg. He hadn't set foot here in years, and the last time he'd been moving too quickly to pay much attention. He wondered now if he'd realized that was the last time he'd see the place. Probably. At any rate he'd hoped it would be, since at the time, going back again would probably have meant being in handcuffs. All in all he hadn't been that sorry to leave.

Now he studied the unchanging contours of the main drag. Still as wide as it had been when the first settlers had moved in. Streets meant for cattle drives and the occasional stage coach. Looked like the town had continued to use diagonal parking down most of Main. He would have argued against that if he'd been able to stick around. Made the place look like some Podunk Center. Plus it made for traffic problems at what passed for rush hour. They needed a parking garage or a municipal lot somewhere.

He started down the sidewalk past the German beer garden on the corner of Milam and Main. New shops were scattered all around the streets. Fewer T-shirt shops. More wine stores, boutiques, even a place that looked like it specialized in fancy stuff for dogs. He shook his head. *Tourists. Buy anything you put under their noses.*

A couple of men lurched out of the Dew Drop Inn a few yards down from where he stood, and he fought the impulse to duck his head. He'd lost weight since his last time in town. His hair was grayer and longer. And he wore jeans and a T-shirt, clothes far removed from the ones he used to wear. Plus his face had never been particularly distinctive. People weren't inclined to remember him. Even if the men had known him from before, they wouldn't know him now.

Still, it was risky coming into town like this. He couldn't afford to do it too often. He wasn't inclined to take unnecessary risks this time around. Not after what had happened last time.

He slowed his gait slightly to let the men get to their cars, pretending some interest in the shop windows along the street. Ahead of him a folding sidewalk sign indicated Brenner's Restaurant, which had been around when he'd been in town before. Nice place from what he could remember. Not that he'd ever gone there to eat. Too expensive. Too high class for his tastes, or the tastes he'd indulged when he'd lived here.

He glanced in a few more windows, then stopped. Kent's Hill Country Books. His jaw tightened. Now there was a place he remembered all too well, unfortunately. He wasn't exactly surprised to see it was still around, but during the years he'd been gone he'd hoped that it might have gone out of business. Occasionally, he'd pictured Docia Kent broke and on her way out of town, but of course she'd always have the Kent family money to back her up.

He flexed his shoulders, fighting the tightness in his chest. He didn't have time for useless emotions like anger. He had a job to do, and once it was done, he'd be gone and never set foot in Konigsburg again.

Still, Kent's Hill Country Books. He took a long look at the window, then shrugged. Time enough to figure things out. He had a few weeks at least until he had to act. It might be interesting to see exactly what he could come up with to entertain himself in Konigsburg.

Particularly if that entertainment helped him do what needed to be done.

He turned and headed back toward his truck. Time to get out of town for now. He'd be back again soon enough.

Chapter Two

Nando sat at his desk in the Konigsburg Police Station, trying to finish some paperwork while nursing his throbbing head. He'd gone straight home after seeing Kit outside Kent's Hill Country Books. Fortunately, he hadn't run into anybody who wanted anything from him since he wouldn't have been able to hold a coherent conversation. Fortunately or unfortunately, depending on how you looked at it, he'd had an almost-full bottle of Jim Beam at home. Said bottle was now half empty and Nando's head was close to splitting in two.

At the front desk, Helen Kretschmer gave him a quick, assessing glance, her lips spreading up in a faintly sardonic grin. Helen was maybe on the near side of fifty, steel gray hair in a tight frizz around her head, pale green eyes that could pierce body armor. Chief Toleffson had made her a full-fledged officer of the Konigsburg Police Department, which allowed her to wear a uniform. Once she finished her mandatory training with the state, she'd also be given a gun. After that happened, Nando figured every hood in town would be heading down the highway toward Kerrville as fast as their jalopies would move. One look at Helen with a Glock on her hip would send the most hardened criminal packing.

He blew out a long breath, massaging his aching forehead. At least the coffee she'd given him had made a slight dent in his agony. Realistically, he'd known he'd have to run into Kit Maldonado sooner or later. She visited her Aunt Allie regularly. But he'd hoped he could put it off for a while, possibly a long while. Maybe until he'd forgotten just how shapely those legs of hers were, or how her hair fell in an unbroken curtain of black silk when she raised her head to look at him. Or how she felt when...

His head gave a particularly vicious throb and Nando gritted his teeth. He'd been an idiot in his relationship with Kit Maldonado, but thinking about it after all this time was pointless. Sooner or later he'd run into her face-to-face and they'd get that first awkward conversation over with. Then he could go back to whatever the hell it was he was going to do with his life from now on. Both celibacy and debauchery looked pretty bleak at the moment. Hell, consciousness looked pretty bleak at the moment.

The front door of the station slammed, which sent his head to a new level of pain. He squinted toward the front desk where Helen was glaring at the doorway.

Ham Linklatter was hanging his hat on the rack.

"Christ on a crutch, Linklatter," Nando muttered. "Do you have to slam the goddamn door?"

Ham shrugged. "Wind took ahold of it. Couldn't stop it." He dropped into his desk at the front where Helen could keep an eye on him. The general consensus of opinion was that Ham couldn't do much damage as long as Helen made sure he was working on whatever the hell he'd been given to do, assuming that wasn't a major task.

Nando closed his eyes briefly. Better Helen than him.

"What are you doing here at this time of the morning anyway, Linklatter?" Helen growled. "You got night duty this week."

"Got something to take care of."

Linklatter turned on the computer near his desk, leaning back slightly from the keyboard as if he thought it might explode. Given his general level of competence with electronic equipment, he might not have been far off. He smoothed a hand over his thinning blond hair, flattening it against his skull. It looked a little like blond seaweed straggling across his boney forehead.

According to town gossip, Ham had gotten back together with Margaret Hastings again. Nando had had no idea Margaret was so hard up.

He heard the door open one more time and glanced up to see Chief Toleffson gathering the mail from the inbox. He nodded at Ham, then narrowed his eyes at Nando. "You look like death badly warmed over."

"Just a headache," Nando muttered, rubbing his eyes.

"Okay, take an aspirin and come on back. I've got some things to go over with you." Toleffson headed down the hall toward his office. He looked more like a cop than any man Nando had ever known, like he should be on a recruiting poster for the forces of Truth and Justice. Since he was also six foot five or so and built like a Corinthian pillar, messing with the forces of Truth and Justice in Konigsburg was not a good idea. Between Toleffson and Sheriff Friesenhahn at the county level, evildoers tended to give the town a pass.

Nando swallowed three more aspirin. At this rate he'd probably reduce his stomach to Swiss cheese before anything could put a dent in the Headache From Hell. He pushed himself up from his desk and headed down the hall after Toleffson, aware of Ham's baleful glance as he did.

Ham had never quite gotten over not being promoted to Konigsburg Chief of Police, and he kept hoping the City Council might reconsider its decision to hire Toleffson instead. Nando figured Ham had a nice little bungalow in the Land of Denial.

Toleffson gestured toward the chair in front of his desk as he read through a couple of bulletins from DPS. "Are you as hungover as you look?" he asked without looking up.

"More, probably." Nando rubbed his eyes again.

Toleffson narrowed his eyes slightly. Everybody knew he didn't drink. Nando wasn't sure whether he was a former alcoholic or not, but he was currently as upright as they came. Also thoroughly married and devoted to wife and family. All in all, an annoyingly decent man. The chief narrowed his eyes. "Can you handle duty?"

"I'll be fine once I drink a pot of coffee." Nando profoundly hoped that was true.

"Okay." Toleffson leaned back in his chair, tossing the bulletins into a tray on his desk. "Here's the deal. I finally managed to hire a replacement for Peavey. He's supposed to get here this morning. I want you to show him the ropes."

Nando blinked. Curtis Peavey had retired a couple of months ago. It had taken the chief some time to get the authorization to hire a replacement, particularly with the town's tight budget, but apparently once the authorization had come through, he'd moved with the speed of a diving red-tail hawk. "Who is it?"

"Kid named Clayton Delaney. Know him?"

Nando shook his head. "Doesn't ring any bells. He from around here?"

"Sort of. Folks live outside Johnson City. He went to ACC. Took courses in Criminal Justice. Seems like a smart kid."

Nando leaned back in his chair. "Good. Curtis was smart, too, but he didn't have much stamina left. He couldn't run anymore. Be a nice change to get somebody who's smart and fit."

Neither of them mentioned Linklatter. Ham's level of cluelessness was a given, but he'd been with the department longer than either of them, and getting rid of him would be more trouble than it was worth.

Toleffson nodded. "Okay. Take Delaney out with you today and show him how things work. Give him a ride around town. I don't imagine it'll take him much time to get focused, but you can keep an eye on him for a couple of weeks or so."

"No problem." Nando pushed himself forward as a preface to getting up. "Anything else?"

Toleffson leaned back, steepling his hands on his chest. "Yeah. Got some interesting news at the City Council meeting last night."

Nando sat still, his muscles suddenly tensing. News from the City Council was rarely good.

"A while back I suggested a new position here, Assistant Chief. We've got a growing population. We need somebody to take up some of the slack, oversee all the special policing for fairs and festivals and liaise with DPS. Plus it would give us two people on call for emergencies like that night when the Faro got hit and I was out of town. City Council's decided to go along with it."

Nando stared at him, trying to understand what was happening here.

"Not much additional money for salary, but some. And an office when we get around to reorganizing the station. And some travel money," Toleffson continued. "Like I say, not much but some. I gave them my recommendation last night and they accepted it."

Nando's jaw tightened. Several interesting possibilities occurred to him. "Are you posting the position announcement today?"

Toleffson shook his head, his gaze sharpening. He leaned forward again, resting his hands on the desktop. "I don't have to. I already made my decision. You're it. Delaney's just come on, Helen's not eligible until she finishes the damn training courses, and Ham's, well, Ham. Congratulations, et cetera."

"Thanks." Nando's chest clenched. Maybe it was the hangover, but something about Toleffson's explanation made him uneasy. "Why do I sense a *but* coming up here?"

The chief gave him a dry grin. "Because there is one. And you know it already. *But* there's still some sympathy for old Ham around town and on the council. Nobody much wanted him to be chief except our departed crook of a former mayor, but a lot of people felt sorry for him when he got passed over even though they were glad he didn't get the job. Felt like he got his feelings hurt."

"So he should be assistant chief because of his hurt feelings?" Nando's headache gave another vicious throb.

Toleffson shook his head. "Not necessarily. I said people feel sorry for him, but he's still an idiot, and everybody knows that too. Most people in town know you're the only logical choice for this. The thing is, though, the Council wants a probationary period as part of the deal. Six weeks. Just make sure you don't do anything stupid for the next couple of weeks. I'm talking Dudley Do-Right, Nando. No screw-ups. No massive hangovers."

Nando nodded slowly. "I can do that."

"Yeah, knowing you, I figure you can. It would also help if you could save a couple of drowning puppies or help some old ladies across the street or catch somebody on the Ten Most Wanted list, but even if that doesn't happen, keeping your nose clean would be a very good idea."

"Right. I understand." Nando nodded again.

"Good." Toleffson blew out a long breath. "Now go wait for Delaney. I have to tell Linklatter and Helen about him and that you're the new Assistant Chief."

The chief gave him another dry smile as he stood, ushering him out of the office. Nando limped back to his desk. He figured when he was feeling like a human being again, he'd probably be real happy about this whole deal.

Kit sipped a cup of coffee that was the best thing that had happened to her thus far on her trip to Konigsburg. Deirdre Brandenburg's coffee shop smelled like what the celestial realms would smell like if the angels were all heavily into French roast, as Kit figured they would be. She gathered that Deirdre ran the coffee roaster in the morning so that the smell had time to dissipate before the dinner hour at the Faro Tavern next door. But that smell alone had been enough to draw a shop full of coffee drinkers who were almost weeping with pleasure.

Now the morning rush had begun to die down and Deirdre was gathering up cups and swabbing down tables as she talked to Kit. "I've got an opening for a barista during the morning rush," she explained, "but it's basically just pouring coffee, and I'm afraid it's only part time. I'm doing all the managing myself, and I'll go on doing it for the foreseeable future, although that could change if we keep doing the business we're doing now."

Kit figured Coffee Delight, Deirdre's shop, would be doing this much business until all of them were old and gray unless somebody decided to pass a law against coffee. "I'd like something full time, but I'm not sure how much luck I'll have in finding anything in this market. Could I maybe let you know about the job in a day or two?"

"Sure. I can hold it open for a while. I haven't even advertised it yet. I guess you heard about it from Docia."

Kit nodded. "She suggested I talk to you. She said your coffee business was booming."

Deirdre gave her a dazzling smile, which demonstrated just how gorgeous she really was. Deep blue eyes, ebony hair, pale, flawless skin with the slightest blush around her cheekbones. Deirdre looked like something out of Hollywood, but amazingly enough, she didn't seem to be conscious of it at all, a beautiful woman completely unaware of her beauty.

Kit had been aware of her own beauty since elementary school. She knew she looked very good, and if she put some effort into it, she could look stunning. She sometimes used her looks to charm people, as she had when she'd worked in the tasting room at Cedar Creek Winery. More often she simply ignored the whole thing.

"This is great coffee," she said, draining her cup. "I'm not surprised you've got people lined up around the block."

"Well, I wish I had something better to offer you in the way of a job. I'd love to hire someone with your qualifications." Deirdre sighed. "Of course, Tom's always looking for another barmaid at the Faro, but I'm guessing that's not what you had in mind either."

Kit smiled at her, a little dryly. "Not exactly, although I may need to check that out, too, if none of my other possibilities pan out." At least the tips at the Faro would probably be good. She got to her feet, carrying her coffee cup to the counter at the back of the shop. "I've got a few more people to talk to today. I'll try to get back to you later this afternoon."

Deirdre shook her head. "Don't worry about it. Like I say, I'm doing okay for now. Good luck with the job search—I remember what that's like."

Kit sighed as she headed to her car. A part-time barista job wasn't much of a fall-back, but given the number of people she'd talked to over the last couple of days who had no openings at all, serving coffee for Deirdre might turn out to be her best bet.

She checked her handwritten list of business names once again. Only a couple were left. She thought about doing eenie meenie but decided to just go for the nicest location, even if it was outside Konigsburg proper.

She drove up Highway 16 for a mile or so, then turned onto the road to Oltdorf, a wide spot in the road about ten miles from Konigsburg. Early bluebonnets dotted the dark green on either side of the road, along with the occasional deep red of winecups. A few cows wandered through patches of prickly pear cactus, detouring around limestone outcroppings. The hills wore the olive green of spring. Kit was enjoying the view so much she almost missed the large white sign with its elaborate script letters: *The Woodrose Inn.*

She turned onto a graded gravel road that was surprisingly smooth. The inn appeared around the first bend, sprawling across the hilltop, a three-storey, white wood-frame building with blue shutters. Wide galleries stretched around the first and second stories and wide stairs led down from the front door to a white gravel walk that twisted among the live oaks on the front lawn. Kit thought it looked like a stage set: Texas elegance and charm personified.

The parking lot had the predictable mix of Suburbans and Mercedes, with the occasional pickup looking wildly out of place. She found a spot under a live oak that could shade her Civic from the afternoon sun and headed for the front entrance. Beyond the parking lot, the inn's event center perched on a rolling hillside. With its white limestone walls and tin roof, it was classic South Texas architecture with what looked like a spectacular view from its plate-glass windows.

Aunt Allie had suggested she try the Woodrose, based mainly on restaurant gossip. Resorts Consolidated, an international hotel chain, had just bought the place, and a new chef had taken over a month ago after the previous chef had been fired for letting the Woodrose's four-star restaurant go to seed. Nobody had heard exactly what was going on at the place, but the word was the inn was looking for new people. Kit figured she was qualified for something at the lower management level. Plus a job at the inn with its solid reputation would look great on her résumé.

She'd already spoken to the manager, a Ms. Morgenstern, about an interview. Morgenstern hadn't exactly given her an appointment, but she'd said she'd be willing to talk to Kit if she dropped by during the afternoon. Kit didn't know if that was good news or bad, but at this point she was ready for almost anything.

The desk clerk looked to be around sixteen, but Kit figured that might be because of the red stretch jersey worn maybe a half size too small and the bright blue Capri pants. Her dark hair was spiked with acid green tips, and Kit could see the edge of a tattoo curling around the back of her neck. If this was the best the Woodrose could come up with for greeting guests, the inn really must be in trouble.

"Can I help you?" the clerk asked her, without much interest.

"I'm here to see Ms. Morgenstern," Kit said crisply. "Is she in?"

Capri Pants raised a pierced eyebrow, but picked up the house phone. "Ms. Morgenstern? Somebody to see you."

The woman who came out of the office behind the desk had Dress For Success written across her chest, at least figuratively. She wore an electric blue knit jacket over an ivory shell and black skirt, with at least four silver chains wound around her neck. Her black patent stilettos rose a good three inches. Kit momentarily regretted that she hadn't worn the four-inch platforms she'd scored at the last Nordstrom's sale. At least she was wearing her best gray business suit with the silk blouse she'd bought at Neiman's Last Call.

Do not get competitive with the potential employer. Kit stepped forward. "Ms. Morgenstern? I'm Kit Maldonado. We spoke on the phone earlier."

Ms. Morgenstern's brow furrowed briefly before she gave Kit a blinding smile. "Oh yes. I remember. Won't you come into my office? Her voice was remarkably warm for someone she'd just meet, sort of like dripping honey.

Kit followed her around the desk clerk, who had already turned back to her computer screen. Kit caught a glimpse of something that looked like Facebook.

"Darcy dear," Morgenstern said, her voice a shade less warm. "Have you checked the reservations?"

Darcy raised one shoulder in a sort of half shrug. "Yeah, but we've only got a couple of people coming in. Luella should be able to handle it."

"Did you remember to tell Luella which rooms had been reserved?" Morgenstern was still smiling, but it looked more like she was gritting her teeth.

Darcy shrugged again. "I'll check."

"You do that, sweetheart," Morgenstern said in a level voice, then turned back toward her office at the side of the hall. Kit followed her.

One wall of her office was taken up with a pair of French doors that opened onto the gallery at the side. Kit could see a man on a riding mower clipping the green expanse of lawn stretching down to the glass-enclosed event center at the bottom of the slope. Even the office views were spectacular. Morgenstern walked behind her desk, gesturing to a chair in front for Kit.

"Please have a seat, Ms. Maldonado," she said. "Now tell me what kind of work you're looking for."

Kit took a copy of her résumé from her folder, handing it across the desk. "I'm interested in hospitality management. As you can see here, I have a degree in Management from UTSA, and I've worked in the hospitality industry for most of my life. My family owns restaurants in San Antonio and Brownsville, and my aunt has a restaurant here in Konigsburg. I interned at the Gunter Hotel in San Antonio, and I've worked for Cedar Creek Winery in their tasting room."

"So—" Morgenstern's forehead furrowed slightly as she glanced at the résumé, "—mostly food service."

Kit gritted her teeth. She'd known this would come up. "I've worked in various parts of the industry. My internship at the Gunter was largely hotel management."

Morgenstern put the résumé down on the desk. At least she hadn't handed it back. "Well, dear, as a matter of fact we're in need of someone with hospitality experience at the moment. There's been some...turnover in the kitchen of The Rose, our restaurant. I'm looking for someone to manage The Rose, in fact. Would you be interested in that?"

Kit licked her lips. Not hotel work, exactly, but not waiting on tables either. "Of course. The Rose has an excellent reputation."

Morgenstern's brow furrowed again. "It certainly did once. We're trying to bring it back to what it was."

"That sounds intriguing." Kit's pulse quickened slightly.

"Oh, it is." Morgenstern nodded. "You'd definitely be in on the ground floor. It's just, well, the kitchen staff can be somewhat temperamental."

Kit let herself smile. "I've worked with cooks since I was a child. I know how they feel about their work. Does the manager work with the chef on ordering supplies?" She'd done that at Antonio's. Or rather she'd helped Papi when he'd done that at Antonio's.

Morgenstern shook her head, her smile sliding to sympathetic. "Oh my, no. All the purchasing goes through my office. We do the accounting for the hotel."

"What about wait staff? Hiring servers?"

"Well, of course you'd handle the applications and the job interviews, but I approve all the actual hiring and firing." Morgenstern gave her another sunny smile. "It's better to keep everything in one office, you know. Keeps the accounting simpler."

Kit felt a cold lump of apprehension tightening her chest. "What sort of thing does the manager do then?"

"Oh, you know." Morgenstern waved a vague hand. "Reservations. Seating guests. That sort of thing."

"Hostessing." Kit managed to keep the disappointment out of her voice.

"A very important job," Morgenstern said. "We're trying to rebuild the Rose's reputation. There have been a few...problems over the last few years."

"I see." Kit forced a smile. "So this would be for lunch and dinner?"

Morgenstern shook her head, her smile sympathetic again. "Oh no, dear. We're only open for lunch at the moment. But you'd have several hours before and after the serving time. And, of course, overtime for extra hours, at least at first."

Kit's heart fell to her toes. "It's an hourly job."

"Oh." Morgenstern's eyes widened. "Of course. We don't have

many salaried positions here, dear. The salary is eleven-fifty an hour. But, as I say, you'd get lots of hours."

Kit refrained from grinding her teeth. She'd probably make more money as a barmaid at the Faro, given that she wouldn't get any tips as a hostess.

"Well, Ms. Maldonado, you're certainly qualified for the job. And we'd be so lucky to have you. Are you interested?" Morgenstern's smile was blinding again.

Kit took a breath, trying to decide just how desperate she really was. The salary was ridiculous, and it was basically just serving as the restaurant hostess rather than any management duties. But she'd have the manager's title, and maybe that would give her some access to the management of the inn. And she'd be on site, with an inside track if something else came available. "I..." she began.

The office door flew open behind her, banging against the wall. "Morgenstern," a voice boomed. "What the fuck have you done with my prep cook? I need her, goddamn it! The freakin' vegetables don't chop themselves."

Kit twisted over her shoulder to see a massive man standing in the doorway. At least six four or so, a good two hundred pounds, wide chest straining his white chef's coat. He had a moustache and trimmed beard that made him look a little like a diplomat. A very big diplomat. As she watched, he pulled off his black chef's beanie, revealing a gleaming shaved head. "What the hell is going on here anyway?"

"Darcy is watching the front desk for an hour or so while Luella took care of an emergency," Ms. Morgenstern said, her smile curdling. "It's good experience for her."

"Bullshit!" the chef snarled. "She's a freakin' culinary school graduate. She doesn't want to learn how to be a desk clerk—she can make twice as much in the kitchen. Plus she's got work to do for me. Don't you go poaching my staff, Morgenstern. They're not your lackeys." He glanced toward Kit, his eyes sharpening, then turned back. "Who's this?"

Kit's lips tightened. She hated being treated as if she wasn't in the room. "I'm Kit Maldonado. Who are you?"

"Joe LeBlanc." The chef's mouth spread in a wide grin. "Maldonado, huh? Any relation to Allie?"

"She's my aunt."

"Great bloodlines there. Want a job in my kitchen?"

Ms. Morgenstern cleared her throat, her face settling into a parody of her earlier sunny expression. "Ms. Maldonado is already applying for a job. As the manager of The Rose."

"The manager? What are you going to let her manage? I do all the ordering for the kitchen. You gonna let go of some of the front of the house stuff? Let her hire enough waiters to run the place right?" LeBlanc's grin deepened, revealing a dimple in one cheek.

Kit took a deep breath. *Just what I want to hear.*

Morgenstern waved her fingers in a shooing motion, giving him a look that was probably meant to be indulgent. "You can take Darcy back to the kitchen if you need her. Now you get out of my office, Joseph. We've all got work to do."

LeBlanc grinned at Kit again, nodding his head. "See you around, kid. Don't let her lowball you on the salary—she needs you real bad right now. Should be interesting."

That's one way of putting it. Kit felt like sighing, but she managed not to.

"So, Ms. Maldonado, about this job. Are you interested?" Morgenstern fluttered her eyelashes like a southern belle magically transported to an executive office. "I might be able to make it fifteen an hour for someone with your experience."

Kit took a breath, then waved a quick mental goodbye to her dreams of a full-fledged management position straight off the bat. "When do you want me to start, Ms. Morgenstern?"

Ninety minutes later, Kit was back in town again, trying to decide if she was happy or depressed. Some of each, as it turned out. At least she had a job, even if it wasn't what she wanted. And at least the Rose looked interesting. She'd never been in at the beginning with a restaurant before. If what the chef, Joe LeBlanc, had said was true, she might have a chance to do some real managing sooner or later, rather than just working the hostess stand.

She pulled into a parking spot in front of an antiques store a half block down from Allie's restaurant, Sweet Thing. The sidewalks had their usual collection of blue-haired elderly ladies and families with rambunctious children. Given that the kids frequently came complete with waffle cones or candy apples, the possibilities for disaster were endless.

Kit started toward Sweet Thing a bit gingerly, trying not to collide with either retirees or ten-year-olds, when something flashed at the end of the next block. She glanced up to see what it was.

A couple of Konigsburg cops were standing next to a parked cruiser talking as the sun reflected off their gold badges. One of them was a stranger—blond and apparently very young. Maybe he was a new officer. There had to have been some turnover since she'd been in town last.

The other was familiar. Kit's heart gave a quick thump as her chest clenched tight. *Very* familiar. Even at a distance she recognized that tall, muscled body, that fall of dark hair. He held his Stetson in his hand, ready to put it on. She caught the quick flash of his teeth as he grinned at something the kid had said. Then he turned in her direction.

She stumbled backward into a doorway, her heart pounding almost painfully. *No, no, no!* She didn't want to see him the first time like this. She wanted to be ready—controlled, collected, maybe even a little amused. *Oh, hi, Nando. Long time no see.*

Right. Like that was ever even a possibility. She peeked around the edge of the display window at the side of the door, trying to see if he'd spotted her.

He still stood where he had before, although she thought he was still glancing in her direction. Then the kid said something else, and he turned back. After a moment, they both climbed into the cruiser.

Kit pressed a hand to her chest, trying to catch her breath. *All right. You're all right.* She wasn't, though, not really.

Over him. So over him.

She wanted to be. She needed to be. But now she had to admit it—she wasn't even close.

Chapter Three

Clayton Delaney made Nando feel like a geriatric case. The kid reminded him of one of those golden retriever pups who'd keep running after thrown sticks until it dropped from exhaustion, only in this case Nando was more likely to drop than Clayton was. He even looked a little like a golden retriever: golden blond hair, shiny white teeth, big brown liquid eyes. Nando half expected him to start panting.

He let Delaney drive the cruiser on patrol. It gave him a chance to rest his eyes while he gave the kid directions around town. Now that he'd consumed a pile of aspirin and a pot of coffee, along with a couple of bottles of water, he felt marginally better.

"How often do we patrol?" Delaney asked. "Do we split the town up into sections or do we all do our thing? I know you're here to keep an eye on me today, but I'm guessing I'll be on my own usually. Or do we ride partners?"

Down boy. Nando rubbed his forehead. "We do it alone. And you can patrol the whole damn town in an hour or so—Konigsburg's not that big. Turn left here, then left again."

They glided by the high school and middle school complex, watching the baseball team practice under a canopy of pecan trees. "I used to come here for games when I was in high school," Delaney exclaimed. He sounded delighted.

Nando sighed. "Yeah, me too." Only of course he'd usually been playing in those games. "Some places in town you need to drive by regularly, like a couple of times every shift. This is one of them." He gestured to the bleachers at the side of the football field. "Kids go there to drink beer sometimes, sometimes smoke pot or worse. Occasionally, you'll get a dealer hanging around. If you come by every once in a while, at unpredictable times, they get the idea that it's not the best place to try selling anything. Then you need to keep your eyes open for where they head next, but at least you don't have the parents on your back."

Delaney's expression shifted instantly to grave. "Yes sir, I understand. Good plan."

Nando winced. Being called "sir" didn't usually bother him, but lately he found reminders of his advanced age sort of annoying. "Kid, I'm twenty-eight and we're both police officers. Call me Nando, for Christ's sake."

"Okay...Nando." Delaney sounded as if he was trying the name on for size.

Nando directed the kid toward the outskirts of Main. Might as well give him the complete tour.

"So what do I do usually?" Delaney asked. "Check in with the dispatcher, then get the keys for the cruiser?"

Nando nodded, hoping his head would stay on. "Duty roster's behind Helen's desk so you can see what shift you're on and what you're slated to do. Most of the time, it's patrol and paperwork unless we've got something going on in town. Then you may end up in the city park or directing traffic downtown. Emergency calls come through your radio in the cruiser."

"And there are only four of us plus the chief?"

"Four of us on full-time, plus a couple of part-timers who fill in any gaps in the schedule and come on full-time whenever we've got something that'll draw a crowd. They also work private security." Nando could remember when they'd all been part-timers except for Ham. But that was before Toleffson had taken over and turned the Konigsburg cops into an actual police department.

Delaney pulled the cruiser carefully to a stop at the light on Highway 16. "So what do you think of the Chief?"

Nando grimaced. Clearly silence wasn't a possibility with the kid. "Toleffson saved the town's ass," he said flatly. "We had a chief of police, Brody, who was a gold-plated crook. He'd been extorting money from some of the groups who came up here for festivals and shit. Then he tried to steal some antique documents. The woman who owns the bookstore on Main, Docia Kent Toleffson, got all caught up in it without realizing what was going on, and Brody tried to kill her. By the time he took off with the Rangers on his tail, the department was in a shambles."

Delaney's eyes were wide. "Was the woman he tried to kill related to Chief Toleffson?"

35

Nando nodded. "Sister-in-law. The chief wasn't here then, though, and she wasn't married to Cal Toleffson yet. There are four Toleffson brothers here in town, plus their wives and kids. You'll get them all sorted out eventually. The guy who took over as chief after Brody was named Olema. Only he turned out to be a screaming incompetent—a dangerous prisoner escaped from the jail because of him. So the city council fired him, and then they hired Toleffson."

Delaney shook his head. "Boy, a lot goes on here, doesn't it?"

Nando sighed. "Yeah, kid, you got that right." He pointed to a shop on the right as they rolled down Main. "That's Angels Unaware. The owner's Margaret Hastings. Brody also attacked her because she saw him committing a burglary. She wound up in the hospital for a while. Also, she dates Ham Linklatter."

Delaney narrowed his eyes. "So this guy attacked a police officer's girlfriend and the current chief's sister-in-law. And he was a cop?"

"He was indeed. That's Docia Toleffson's bookstore over there, Kent's Hill Country Books. Down the street from it, you've got one of the best restaurants in town, Brenner's. Just bring money when you go there."

"How about that other place?" Delaney nodded toward the Dew Drop.

"Do not eat at the Dew Drop." Nando rubbed his eyes. "You probably don't want to drink there either, unless you like warm beer. Got a good dart board, though."

"No pool?" Delaney rolled to another stop light.

"The Faro is the place to shoot pool. It's up ahead there on the right. The shop next door, Coffee Delight, has the best coffee in town, bar none, although the Coffee Corral's okay in a pinch. And the Faro's got a great cook, Clem Rodriguez. The Faro's my recommendation for a place to grab a meal and a beer, if you're looking for one."

"Is that where the cops go?" Delaney's eyes were taking on that puppy gleam again.

"That's where *I* go. The chief doesn't drink and pretty much eats at home, and Ham's dating a teetotaler so he doesn't go anyplace much at the moment. And Helen..." He paused to consider just where Helen might hang out. Probably at the toughest bar in the Hill Country. "I don't know where Helen goes, but my guess would be Rustlers' Roost."

"The biker bar?" Delaney's voice squeaked slightly.

36

"Yep. Sounds like Helen's kind of place."

Delaney pulled into a parking lot at the other end of Main. "So now what?"

"Now we go back to the station to see if Helen's caught anything while we were on patrol, along with all the other crap that usually piles up. I can catch up on my paperwork, and you can fill out all the forms that she's probably got sitting in your mailbox."

The radio on the dash let out with a burst of static and Nando picked up the mike. "Yeah, Helen, what do you need?"

"Possible break-in at the fairgrounds. Manager's waiting for you at the gate."

"Got it." He tossed the mike back in its holder. "Looks like we're in luck, kid. They actually need us to be cops this afternoon."

It wasn't until she'd finished dinner with Aunt Allie and Wonder Dentist that Kit remembered she was supposed to get back to Deirdre Brandenburg about the barista job at Coffee Delight.

Dinner had had her grinding her teeth, and not from the food. Aunt Allie and Wonder seemed to be carrying on some kind of covert warfare—very polite on the surface, somewhat nasty just underneath.

Finding Deirdre Brandenburg so that she could pass on the news about her new job at the Woodrose would also be a distraction from the chunk of ice that seemed to have settled into her stomach after she'd seen Nando that afternoon.

According to what Allie had said earlier, Deirdre still worked as a barmaid at the Faro some evenings. Apparently, she and the Faro's owner, Tom Ames, were a couple. Kit figured she'd wander down to the tavern to see if Deirdre was around. Even if she wasn't, it would give her a chance to get out of the house, away from Allie and Wonder. And besides, she'd never been inside the Faro. When she'd lived in Konigsburg before, it had been a notoriously rough bar that her Aunt Allie had ordered her to avoid. That was one piece of advice from Aunt Allie she'd taken seriously.

The Faro's customers were still mostly men. Kit fielded the usual speculative glances when she walked in around eight, but she knew how to ignore them by now. She wasn't in the mood to fend off potential pick-up lines. She took a seat at the bar, midway between the two bartenders.

The one nearest the door looked like he'd been tending a bar all his life—thinning hair, rounded shoulders, an economy of motion that meant he could pour five drafts in quick succession.

The guy at the other end was, well, yummy. Kit took a longer, appreciative look. Short blond hair, broad shoulders, killer grin.

He was currently grinning at Deirdre. Kit did a quick mental headslap. Tom Ames. Had to be. *Oh well.*

Deirdre caught sight of her and put her tray back on the bar. "Hey, Kit. I was just talking about you a minute ago." She slid onto a stool beside her.

Tom Ames looked her way with a slightly guarded smile. Kit wondered what she'd done to earn "guarded" so quickly. She turned back to Deirdre. "I just wanted to let you know I won't be taking the barista job. I found something full-time. I'm sorry—I really like your shop."

"Where did you end up?" Deirdre pulled a bowl of peanuts between them. "You want a beer? I've got an in with the bartender." She gave Tom Ames one of those dazzling smiles that probably turned his knees to rubber.

Kit shrugged. "A beer sounds good. I found something at the Woodrose Inn. I'll be managing the restaurant. Sort of."

"Oh." Deirdre frowned. "I heard something about them not long ago. I'm not sure what, though."

"New chef." Tom put beers in front of them both. "Friend of Clem's."

"Oh, right." Deirdre nodded. "They just hired a new guy. Clem knew him from somewhere she worked before. She says he's really, really good."

"I'm not surprised. The Rose is a four-star restaurant. Or it used to be, anyway. Aunt Allie said they've had a few problems recently." Kit took a sip of her beer and tasted something mellow and hoppy, a long way from the thin stuff taverns around here usually had on draft. "This is really good! What is it?"

Tom shrugged. "Microbrew out of San Antonio. Texas still isn't as far along with artisan brewing as places like Colorado, but they're trying."

"What were the problems at the Rose, Tom?" Deirdre frowned. "Do you remember?"

"Chef was a drunk. Plus cocaine. Asshole ran the place into the ground."

Kit turned toward the sound of the voice and saw a huge man standing behind her. His long black hair was pulled back by a bandana wrapped around his forehead. A thin moustache angled down on either side of his mouth, and he had a soul patch in the middle of his lower lip. He was the size of a small landslide. She fought the impulse to duck.

Deirdre nodded at him. "Kit, do you know Chico Burnside?"

Kit licked her lips. The man mountain looked vaguely familiar now that she got a good look at him. "I think we met once a while ago."

Chico Burnside frowned slightly. "Kit Maldonado?"

"Right."

He narrowed his eyes as if he were trying to remember her, then his mouth spread in a flat grin. "Yeah. You know my cousin."

"I do? Who's that?"

Chico pointed across the room and Kit turned just as the crowd parted slightly. Enough for her to see the one man she'd really hoped not to see again so soon, at least not until she was ready.

Golden skin, black hair, dancing eyes. A body with slim hips and broad shoulders. If memory served, he also had a light dusting of dark hair across the chest and just the right proportion of muscle to bone, along with a light touch that set her entire body on fire.

Why couldn't fate have given him a beer belly and thinning hair by now? Why did he still look like sin on a stick?

"Nando Avrogado." Kit sighed. "The cherry on the cake of my day."

Nando leaned back in his chair, watching Clayton Delaney shoot pool. The kid was good, a lot better than he would have thought. He had that innocent choir boy look going for him too. Nobody had expected him to be able to clear the table his first time out.

Of course, it helped that he was playing the Steinbruner brothers, possibly the worst players in all of Konigsburg. As Nando looked on, Denny Steinbruner scratched for perhaps the fifth time. Probably a record for a single game.

Nando could see potential for Delaney in the future. If he could convince the kid to play innocent until he actually picked up a cue, they might be able to lay a few bets with tourists who expected all good pool players to look like Chico. Thinking of his cousin, Nando glanced over in his direction.

And felt karma's teeth sink deep once again.

Kit Maldonado was staring at him from the bar, sitting next to the only woman in town who was in the same league with her in terms of looks, Deirdre Brandenburg. He was surprised the two of them side-by-side hadn't reduced the entire bar to a simmering pool of testosterone.

Standing across from her, Chico gave him a faintly sardonic grin. Of course, Chico had been around during the Breakup From Hell, although he hadn't known Kit. By now, he probably knew all the major details. Discretion wasn't exactly prized in the Avrogado family. *Thanks, cuz. Your support is always appreciated.*

Nando drew a deep breath and pushed himself up from the table. Only a jerk would postpone this meeting any longer, and Kit's probable opinion to the contrary, he wasn't really a jerk. He'd even managed to work up a sort of smile by the time he got to the bar. Not that Kit was doing much smiling herself.

"Hey, Kit," he said, trying for something that sounded like enthusiasm. "I heard you were back in town."

She gave him a sort of smile that involved pushing her lips up slightly at the ends. "Hi, Nando. Good to see you."

That was, he thought, a patent lie, but they both let it go. "Visiting Allie?"

"Yeah, I finally finished my degree." She gave a sort of shrug. Her whole body looked tense, almost rigid. He just hoped it was nerves rather than disgust.

"Good." He nodded, trying desperately to think of something—anything—relevant to say. "Good deal."

Kit's face, that glorious, heart-stopping face, looked stiff. She kept glancing over his shoulder, as if something fascinating were happening at the pool tables. He had a feeling everybody at the bar was listening to this conversation. Too bad it was so boring.

"So how long are you staying?"

"A while. I've got a job at the Woodrose."

Somehow he managed not to choke. "The Woodrose Inn? Outside of town?"

Kit nodded, her expression still perfectly blank. "That's the one."

"Oh. Well, great." He felt like moaning. He'd managed to achieve a level of lameitude that exceeded even his own expectations.

"I guess you're still with the police, right?" She picked up her beer, one perfect eyebrow arching.

Nando nodded. "Yeah. I'm on full-time now."

Kit sipped, dropping her gaze to the bar. "Good for you. I know that's what you were looking for."

He tried to think of something else to say, something not totally inept. "Yeah. I guess everything's worked out."

He sensed a slight tensing in the bodies standing at the bar. *Okay, that probably didn't sound the way I meant it.* "I mean, jobwise."

Kit took another swallow of her beer, then set the glass back on the bar. "Thanks, Tom. This is good beer. Looks like you have a nice place here."

Tom nodded, glancing back and forth between them quickly. "It has its points. Come back and see us again sometime."

"Maybe I will. Time for me to walk back home. I've got to get to the Woodrose early tomorrow."

She pushed away from the bar, giving Nando a slight nod and a smile that looked like a brief flex of muscles one step up from a grimace.

"You're walking?" he blurted. "To Allie's house?"

She narrowed her eyes, throwing him a cool glance. "It's not that far. I can walk it."

"It's night. You shouldn't be walking around Main."

"That's ridiculous." She shook her head. "I've walked around Main my whole life."

Tom Ames cleared his throat. "Actually, he's right. Things are a little rougher around here at night. We've had a few problems with drunks over the past month. If you can wait a little while until the evening rush dies down, I can walk with you."

Kit shook her head. "No, don't do that. I can walk home by myself. Really. Don't bother." She turned toward Deirdre. "Tell him to stay here, okay?"

Deirdre shrugged. "He's right, as a matter of fact. There was a mugging in the park last week. It's really not as safe as it used to be, unfortunately." She cast a quick look at Nando. "Not that the police aren't doing a good job, but we've got a lot more people around town now than we did when you visited as a kid."

"But I don't want to take you away from your work, Tom." Kit cast another slightly desperate glance around the bar.

"I'll walk with you," Nando muttered.

Her eyes widened slightly as her lips compressed. She looked as if she'd prefer taking her chances with the muggers.

He held her gaze for a moment, keeping his own desperation to a minimum. "You said it wouldn't take long."

She blew out a breath, then gave him another of those grimace smiles. "I think I can guarantee it'll take no time at all."

Kit wondered which of them would break first as they walked up the street. Actually it was more like a trot than a walk. Clearly, he didn't want to be walking along Main at her side any more than she wanted him to be. Still, talking would probably have been an improvement over the strained silence between them. Except that she couldn't think of a thing to say that didn't sound idiotic.

When they reached the intersection of Firewheel Lane and Milam, Nando turned toward her. "I saw you in town."

She stiffened. So he had seen her that afternoon. She took a breath, trying to think of some way to downplay the whole panic thing. "Oh?"

"Yeah, you were talking to Docia."

Docia. She blinked. "Oh. A couple of days ago."

"Yeah. I should have said hello I guess. I didn't..." He shook his head. "Look, we need to talk."

Kit pulled herself up, wishing she had on heels that would bring her eye-to-eye with him. "About what?"

"We're living in the same small town." He sighed, stabbing his fingers through his hair. "We know the same people. We go to the same places. We're going to run into each other regularly. We need to agree on how that's going to go down, or people are going to start running in the other direction when they see us coming. I mean, you saw how everybody acted tonight—like we were going to explode or something."

Kit's jaw tightened. She wished she could see an error in his logic, but at the moment she couldn't. "So?"

"So how about a truce?" Nando looked at her directly for the first time since they'd left the bar. She'd forgotten the depth of those brown eyes, sort of like black coffee. As she recalled, they turned to velvet when he was aroused.

Pull it together. Now. "A truce involving what?"

"Polite conversation when we have to. Silence as long as we can do it without making other people uncomfortable."

"Works for me." She kept her gaze on his Adam's apple.

He sighed. "All right then."

She glanced up the street toward Aunt Allie's house. "I can go on home by myself from here."

He nodded. "Okay. I guess I'll see you around."

Not if I see you first. She watched him start up the street, trying unsuccessfully to ignore the pinch of her conscience. "Nando."

He half turned back. "What?"

"Thanks for walking me home."

He nodded. In the dimness between the street lights it almost looked like he gave her a small grin. "*De nada.*" He turned and headed back up the street toward Main.

Chapter Four

Kit walked in the front door at Allie's, telling herself she was perfectly okay. She'd seen Nando. She'd exchanged a few sentences. She'd escaped unscathed. More or less. She didn't really feel nauseated. She wasn't really short of breath.

Okay, it hadn't exactly been her finest hour, but she'd gotten through it. And she'd managed not to show anybody how she felt about seeing him again. Her chest tightened, and she closed her eyes for a moment. Surprising how much it still hurt. It had been over a year, after all.

But there hadn't been anyone else during that year, or no one else who made her feel the way Nando did. That mixture of ecstasy and terror, the certain knowledge that nothing that hot could last.

And she'd been right, of course. It wasn't like he'd cheated on her just yesterday. It sure felt like it, though.

"Aunt Allie," she called. "Are you here?"

"Here." Allie's voice drifted down the hall.

Kit saw a light in the kitchen. There was a faint thumping sound. She headed toward it.

Allie was seated on the floor, surrounded by pots and pans. Apparently she was rearranging the cabinets. Which Kit knew for a fact she'd already done only a couple of days ago.

"Hi," she said, tentatively. "Need some help?"

Allie blew a lock of hair off her forehead. "I'd say yes, but I'm not sure what I'm doing yet. The way I set this up the other day just isn't working. I can't seem to get things exactly the way I want them to be." She started rearranging the pot lids on a sliding rack.

"Steve's not here?" Kit settled into a kitchen chair.

For a moment, Allie's jaw tightened. Then she shrugged. "No. He went home for the evening." She went back to rearranging the lids again.

Ooookay. Kit leaned forward on the table. "I saw Janie this morning before I headed to the Woodrose."

"Yeah?" Allie said absently. "What's new with her?" She slid the rack back and forth slightly, narrowing her eyes.

"She says she's got some more pictures of bridesmaid dresses to show you. You're supposed to drop by the bookstore tomorrow when you get a chance."

"What?" Allie stared at her, sliding the lid rack into the cabinet with a sudden clang. "Why? Why would she want me to do that?"

"She said she'd seen some nice dresses in this magazine and maybe they'd work..." Kit's voice trailed off. "Is something wrong?"

Across from her, Allie's hands were clasped so tightly on the floor in front of her that her knuckles showed white. Her eyes looked suspiciously bright. "She's always trying to get me to make decisions on dresses when I'm not ready yet. I just wish everybody would back off on the whole wedding thing. Just back off for a while and give me room to think."

Uh-oh.

Kit leaned forward in her chair, placing a hand on her aunt's shoulder. "Aunt Allie, what's happening? Did you call off the wedding? Did Steve?"

"Call off..." Allie stared at her blankly. "No, of course not. Why would I call off the wedding? The wedding's great. Steve's great. Everything's great. I can't wait for the wedding. Whenever we get around to it."

"Get around to it?" Kit narrowed her eyes.

"Right. Well, I've just been so busy. The holidays, and then I went to that food festival in Florida. And I've got the cookbook coming out." She licked her lips. "I'm sort of behind on my wedding planning. I haven't done as much as I should. But, I mean, why would you think we weren't getting married?"

"Well, I don't know exactly. You just seem so...uncertain about it." Kit swallowed. "And then Steve seemed kind of...upset tonight." And last night. And the night before. She took a deep breath. "Look, Allie, I feel like I'm tiptoeing blindfolded through a china shop here. You're upset about something. I can see that. Is it the wedding?"

Her aunt rubbed her hands across her face, closing her eyes for a moment. Then she shook her head. "No. The wedding is on. Definitely. Honestly. It's just me. All me. I'm off."

"Off how?"

"I can't seem to make any decisions about anything," Allie blurted. "I can't decide where to have the ceremony and the reception. I can't decide what decorations we're going to have. I can't make up my mind about a dress for myself, let alone dresses for bridesmaids. Jesus Christ, I can't even decide on a wedding cake! Me. I mean, I've made hundreds of wedding cakes. Maybe even thousands. And I can't decide what kind of cake I want for Steve and me. Every time I try to work on it, I end up putting it off. I'm a freakin' basket case." She covered her face with her hands, resting her elbows on her bent knees.

"What does Steve say?"

Allie sighed, looking up at her again. "He's getting antsy. He keeps asking me when we're going to get going on the date and the venue. He thinks maybe I'm having second thoughts."

"Are you?" Kit asked slowly.

Allie shook her head so hard her hair went flying. "No. Honestly, I'm not. I'm just... It's everything at once. I can't seem to get it all put together. I can't even get started."

"But, Allie, you do this for a living." Kit frowned. "I mean, I've seen the events you've put together at the catering company. You're a star."

Her aunt groaned. "That's part of the problem. I do this all the time for other people. Now I have to do it for myself. What if I mess up? What if it's not perfect? Hell, what if it's a complete disaster? I'll never live it down."

"But it doesn't have to be perfect. It just has to be what you want. And what Steve wants." Kit took a breath. Clearly, she still wasn't out of that china shop yet. "Couldn't he help you somehow? You know, maybe take over some of the decisions so you don't have so many to make?"

"Steve!" Allie exploded. "His only suggestion so far has been a country and western band to play for the ceremony. Not the reception, mind you, the actual wedding ceremony. Maybe 'Whisky River' for the introit." She shook her head. "I can count on him to show up and to take care of the best man and the groomsmen. And he's already said he'll pay for everything, although I don't think I'll let him do that. I mean, I've got money of my own. But I can't count on him for anything else, certainly not for planning a perfect wedding."

Kit rubbed a hand across the back of her neck, thinking of all the Maldonado wedding bashes over the years. "Why does it have to be perfect?"

"It just... It does. That's all." Allie's lips thinned. For a moment, Kit was afraid she might cry.

"But you're sure this isn't about you and Steve?" she asked carefully.

"It's not. Honestly, it's not." Allie took a shuddering breath. "Honestly. I do love him."

Kit ignored the fainted buzzing of alarm bells at the back of her mind. So what if Allie sounded like she was trying to convince herself as much as Kit?

"Do you have a date you're thinking of?" she asked hurriedly.

Allie nodded. "Sort of. I mean I've got no venue or anything, but I thought maybe in May. Or possibly April. Just not June. That's so passé."

"May. Possibly April." Kit stared at her for a long moment. "You do realize it's the beginning of March right now."

"Yes I realize that. Believe me I'm only too well aware of that." Allie sounded as if her teeth were gritted. Her eyes were tearing up again.

Kit's chest squeezed painfully. Her Aunt Allie's house had been a refuge from Antonio's Fine Mexican Cuisine for as long as she could remember. Allie had gotten her out of all the family drama that inevitably surrounded the restaurant a couple of times a year and let her run wild in the Hill Country as long as she helped out occasionally in the bakery. Allie had showed her that there was more to life than opening and closing the restaurant on time, that cooking could be something to be proud of and something to enjoy. That serving people was an art, and making them happy was a pleasure all its own. Allie was the reason she'd ended up in hospitality management instead of something like nursing. Because she wanted to be like Allie some day. She owed Allie a large chunk of her sanity. She owed her more than that.

"Can I help?" she murmured finally. "With the wedding, that is? Maybe do some of the planning? Find you a venue or something? I'm not as expert at the whole thing as you are. I mean I had a couple of PR classes that covered event planning, but I haven't really done anything on my own. I'd be willing to try if it would make things easier for you, though."

Allie took hold of her hand, squeezing so tightly it was almost painful. "Oh my lord, Catarina, are you serious?"

Kit nodded, ignoring the feeling of panic that made her shoulders clench tight. "Absolutely. I'd be glad to."

"Hallelujah." Allie gave a long sigh. "I'll take you up on it. You have no idea how big a relief that is."

Actually, Kit thought she knew exactly how big it was. The whole load had just landed on her own shoulders, after all. Oh well, at least it would take her mind off anything to do with Nando Avrogado.

Nando didn't bother going back to the Faro after he watched Kit walk up the steps to Allie's porch. He didn't particularly want to answer any questions, and he knew damn well there'd be some, from Deirdre if no one else.

He unlocked the apartment and walked down the hall, only to stop when he reached the kitchen. His brother's cat, Guinevere, was sitting in the middle of the table.

Nando knew nothing about cat breeds. He did, however, know that his brother's cat looked less like a Guinevere than any cat he'd ever seen. She was huge, for one thing, and she had a more than passing resemblance to a bobcat, assuming that bobcat had gray tiger stripes. Her ancestor, Arthur, had been the winery cat at Cedar Creek. Guinevere was a product of some long ago liaison between Arthur and another winery feline. She had Arthur's Maine coon ears and body, but her eyes were pure savagery, a kind of glowing gold that sometimes raised the hair on the back of his neck. Nando tended to avoid her whenever possible. Now, however, his mood was just rotten enough to take her on.

"Hey, you, Bozo," he snapped. "Off the kitchen table."

The cat regarded him with contempt for a moment, then rose slowly to her feet, stretching at the end, toes extended.

"Get down, I said," Nando snarled.

Guinevere moved ponderously to the edge of the table, then jumped to the floor with a heavy thump. She gave Nando another contemptuous look as she stalked past his boots. *See? I did it. So get off my case.*

He grimaced. He was arguing with a cat. But somehow that seemed easier than deciding on a course of action for the future with Kit. Going for an extended vacation somewhere out of state didn't seem feasible, given that he was supposed to be proving himself to the town in his new position as Assistant Chief of Police. No, he'd just have to live with Kit being in town for a while. Surely he could do that. He was a full-fledged adult, after all.

"Right," he muttered. "All of this is a really mature reaction."

"Talking to yourself?" Esteban walked across the kitchen to the refrigerator where he took out a pitcher of tea. "Things may be more dire than I thought."

"What things?" Nando settled into a chair.

The cat was regarding Esteban with an expression of reverence. Clearly, his brother had at least one acolyte.

"I heard about Kit." Esteban leaned down to scratch Guinevere's ears. "About the two of you hooking up at the Faro. I was down there later and Chico told me."

Nando sighed. "We didn't hook up. We had a very brief conversation and then I walked her home so that she wouldn't be on the streets by herself."

"So is anything going on between you and her?" Esteban poured him a glass of iced tea along with his own. "Are you going to try to get back with her again?"

Nando shook his head. "No chance of that. She wouldn't want me even if I tried. The best we can probably do is to be civil to each other. Beyond that, it's mostly a lost cause."

Esteban shrugged. "You could always apologize."

"No I couldn't." Nando's jaw clenched tight. "I tried that before and it didn't work. And after a year, there's not much chance she'd be interested. Best to just let it go."

His brother leaned back in his chair, shaking his head. "Lizzie Farraday."

Nando closed his eyes briefly. "Let it go."

"What did you see in her anyway?"

"Nothing." He sighed. "I didn't see anything in her, and she didn't

49

see anything in me. It was just one of those stupid things."

"She never struck me as much competition for Kit," Esteban mused.

"She wasn't. Not one of my smarter moves."

"Got that right. Did you ever..."

Nando gritted his teeth. "What part of 'Let it go' do you not understand?"

Esteban glanced at him, smiling faintly. "That bad, huh?"

Nando rubbed a hand across his face. "Oh yeah. Definitely that bad. Nothing like having your worst mistake waved in front of your face every day."

Esteban took a swallow of his tea. "So tell me what happened. Everybody in town's gonna be talking about it soon enough. Might as well let me know too."

"You mean what happened tonight or what happened then?"

His brother shrugged. "Then."

Nando closed his eyes. Might as well get it over with. "We had a fight. A big one. Epic. Kit told me to get the hell out and then she walked out too. I went down to the Dew Drop and ran into Lizzie Farraday. That's it. Unless you want the lurid details of us doing the nasty in the backseat."

Esteban frowned. "Whatever happened to Lizzie Farraday?"

"Damned if I know. She took off a few weeks later. Didn't bother to say goodbye. Not that I wanted her to. We didn't have anything much to do with each other after that night."

Esteban grimaced. "Nice story."

"No it's not. But that's what happened."

"You want a beer? There's some Shiner in the fridge."

Nando shook his head. "Not tonight. I'm tired. I'm turning in." He pushed himself up from the table and started down the hall. So what if it was only nine-thirty? If it was a choice between sleep and alcohol, at least this evening he'd be smarter than he'd been the night before.

Behind him he heard the pad of feet. Guinevere stared up at him when he turned back. "Beat it," he muttered. "I don't need company."

The cat stayed where she was, studying him with burning golden eyes. *Bite me, tough guy.*

50

After a moment, he sighed, pushing open his bedroom door. He wasn't even particularly surprised when Guinevere jumped onto the foot of his bed and stretched herself out full length.

Just another female getting her own way at his expense. Seemed to be the way his luck was running these days.

Chapter Five

Nando wasn't altogether surprised when he dreamed about Kit that night. It wasn't the first time it had happened. It wasn't even a new dream—just the one where he saw her looking the way she had the first time they'd made love. Like a ribbon of gold against the white sheets, dark eyes made darker by desire, lips parted slightly to show a glimpse of white teeth, nipples rosy against the golden cream of her breasts. The dream didn't last long, but it was enough to make him wake up aching and sweaty.

Sweet Jesus, is this going to happen every time I see her? If it did, he'd have to come up with some counter measures, like getting a mental image of his eighth-grade math teacher, a dead ringer for Frau Blücher in *Young Frankenstein.*

At least they'd gotten the first meeting over with. Over the long run the best remedy would probably be to find somebody else. Another woman he could spend time with even if he did end up thinking about Kit.

Oh yeah, that's a wonderful idea. It worked so well last time.

He rolled out of bed at six, after he finally gave up on sleep. He might as well go to work early. Helen's coffee was better than his own anyway. He grabbed an energy bar out of the box on the counter and hiked over to the station.

The parking lot should have been empty at that time of day except for the cruiser and maybe Helen's vintage Mustang, although she frequently parked it on the street. Instead, he saw Toleffson's truck parked at the side. He picked up his pace slightly.

"What's up?" he asked as soon as he was in the door.

Helen was frowning at her computer. "Burglary and vandalism," she said shortly. "Over at the bookstore?"

"Docia's bookstore?"

Helen gave him an eye-roll. "You know any other bookstore in this town?"

Nando grabbed the duffel bag with his crime scene kit and headed out the door.

Kent's Hill Country Books was a three-minute walk from the station, which explained why the chief had left his truck in the lot. It didn't explain why Ham had parked the cruiser outside the store, but Nando guessed it had to do with Linklatter's obsession with showing everybody he was on the job. He pushed open the front door of the shop and found chaos.

Books were scattered everywhere. It looked like some had been torn apart, their pages flung around like confetti. One of the bookcases had been pulled loose from the wall. The cash register was on the floor at the front, and the items that had been on the front counter—pens, pencils, bookmarks, flyers—were scattered around it like flowers around a grave.

Toleffson stood at the side of the room with Docia, one protective hand resting on her shoulder. Docia herself looked like she was suffering from post-traumatic stress. Her eyes were wide, her lips trembling. One hand was pressed against her mouth.

The chief saw Nando across the room and waved him over. "Helen catch you up on this?"

"Not really. When did the call come in?"

"I found it when I got here this morning, around six thirty." Docia's voice shook and she swallowed hard. "I was going to get some work done before we opened. Now I guess we won't be opening at all." Her lower lip trembled.

Nando blew out a breath, hoping to god she wouldn't start to cry. He never knew what to do with crying women. "How did they get in?"

Toleffson gestured toward the store room at the side. Nando glanced in. One of the windows had been smashed.

He looked back at the main room again. "Do we know what they were after? Anything obviously missing?"

Docia shook her head. "We don't leave money here. We take the deposit to the bank when we close up each night. There were some ebook readers and MP3 players at the front that are gone. And the books..." She gazed at the carnage spread around her shelves. "I don't know if anything's missing," she whispered. "I don't..." She caught her breath on a sob, and Toleffson stretched his arm around her

53

shoulders.

He turned back to Nando again. "I'm going to take her home. I'll interview her there. You and Ham can do some preliminary processing of the scene. We'll have to get Friesenhahn in on this so we can use the county lab and have their forensics people go over the place. I'll call him after I get to Docia's."

Nando blinked. Calling in the county forensics unit for a burglary and vandalism case seemed close to overkill. But the county sheriff owed Toleffson all kinds of favors, so he'd probably okay it.

Toleffson narrowed his eyes as if he knew what Nando was thinking. Given the circumstances, he decided it was best not to ask any questions.

"Once you get the store locked down for the forensics techs, check around outside to see if the burglar left anything. Then start talking to the neighbors. Maybe somebody heard something."

"You have any ideas about what time it happened?"

The chief shook his head. "Last night. Probably late. Nobody reported any suspicious activity on Main so far as I know."

Nando started to nod, then paused. "I walked by here last night around nine or so."

"Notice anything?"

Hell, he hadn't been thinking about anything besides Kit Maldonado. A battalion could have marched through the bookstore and he might not have noticed. "Not that I remember."

"Talk to the neighbors. Maybe somebody heard him smash the window." He nudged Docia gently toward the back door.

"Right." Nando sighed. This definitely wasn't the time to lose his focus. Kit Maldonado had to be filed away under Past Mistakes until he'd finished his job here.

Processing the scene with Ham mainly meant keeping Ham from screwing up whatever evidence there was. Nando turned back to the room again, pulling his camera out of his duffel bag. The pictures wouldn't be as high quality as the ones the county forensics people would take, but at least it would give them a record of their own at the station.

Ham was standing at the front counter, using an amazing amount of fingerprint powder to dust it. Since most of the people who'd bought books from Docia over the past few weeks had probably leaned on the counter, his chances of getting anything useful in the way of evidence were close to zero. At least he'd pulled on vinyl gloves. Nando pulled on his own.

"Why don't you get started on the interviews?" Nando suggested carefully. "I can do pictures in here until the crime scene techs show up." He wasn't sure how much authority his new job title gave him over Ham, but getting him out of the bookstore before he could mess up any evidence seemed like a good idea.

Ham's jaw firmed. He gave Nando a mutinous look. "Chief said to do preliminary processing. That's what I'm doing."

Nando gave a mental shrug and turned back to the vandalized store again.

He worked his way around the room, snapping shots of everything that looked like the burglar's doing and checking to see if any other trace evidence had been left on the floor. How come he never found helpful things like matchbooks from the criminals' hideout the way they did on TV? Why did real life have to be so messy?

Halfway back, he smelled something. He paused, checking beside the corners of the bookcases.

Ham stepped up behind him. "Smells like their sewer's backed up. Better get a plumber in here."

"It's not the toilet," Nando muttered.

Ham stepped forward and then froze. "Oh for Pete's sake. Is that what I think it is? Smells like poop."

"Smells like what it is." Nando fumbled in his pocket for an evidence bag.

"That's *evidence?*" Ham sounded scandalized.

"There's DNA in feces, just like blood and semen." Nando took a breath and collected the sample, trying not to think about what he was doing as he did it.

"So this guy took a crap in the bookstore and left us a sample of his DNA? Why'd anybody want to do that?" Ham gave Nando and his evidence bag a wide berth.

"My guess is it's a message." Nando deposited the sample in his kit to be handed on to the forensics techs when they arrived, then turned back to the store again.

"A message?" Ham snorted. "What kind of a message is poop?"

Nando shrugged. "Maybe somebody really, really doesn't like books." *Or really, really doesn't like Docia Toleffson.*

Kit's first morning at the Woodrose was spent trying to figure out the computerized reservation software. Ms. Morgenstern have given her a brief introduction and then disappeared, apparently a lot more confident about Kit's computer skills than Kit was herself. She finally downloaded an on-line instruction manual so that she could enter the reservations that had come through on the computer last night before digging through the others that had landed on voice mail.

By mid-morning she'd begun to worry about overbooking— apparently the software had no way to check for availability. She figured she could juggle things around for today, but tomorrow she'd definitely have to figure out something different.

Actually, the more she worked on it, the more Kit became convinced that the whole system needed to be replaced. The Rose should probably have been using a national reservation service rather than trying to limp by with something one step up from email on their web site. She'd discuss it with Ms. Morgenstern, but it seemed like a no-brainer.

At ten, Morgenstern appeared again, brushing the wrinkles out of her beige linen suit. "All right, dear, time to get the dining room set up for the lunch crowd," she trilled. She gave Kit the usual sunny smile, then promptly scuttled back into her office again.

Fortunately, Kit had already taken a peek at the dining room on her way in that morning. Like the rest of the inn, it was elegance personified. The tables were set with pink linen cloths and green napkins, the crystal and silver sparkling in the sun. French doors opened onto a patio with a view of distant green hills. She guessed the patio would provide some great outdoor dining possibilities later in the spring, although it was too cool in the shade at the moment.

She stood in the center of the room now, trying to familiarize herself with the layout diagram she'd found at the hostess station. The French door to the patio creaked open behind her, and she turned to see Joe LeBlanc's massive frame filling the doorway.

"Took the job, I see."

Kit gave him her professional smile. "Yes I did. Now I'm trying to see where the server stations are."

He glanced over her shoulder, then shook his head at the diagram. "That thing's out of date. We don't have five servers anymore."

Kit raised an eyebrow. "For the off-season, you mean?"

LeBlanc gave her a slightly sour smile. "For any season. We got two, and you better hope they both show up. If one of them stays home to nurse a hangover, things go to hell fast."

Kit did a quick calculation. Two servers would be responsible for around fifteen tables each, some of them with seating for six. All of a sudden, she really hoped they weren't too busy at lunch. "What happened to the other three servers?"

"Quit when the restaurant went to shit. Weren't enough customers to justify that many servers anyway, given the stuff coming out of Carville's kitchen most of the time. Now traffic's picking up again, but Morgenstern won't hire any new staff."

Kit's shoulders tightened. "Maybe she's waiting to see the monthly receipts."

LeBlanc gave her a slow smile. "Yeah, well, maybe. Anyway, you got two servers and a busboy to work with. I give everybody a rundown on the specials at ten thirty. We open at eleven thirty."

Kit checked her watch. That gave her fifteen minutes to go to the bathroom, check her makeup, and try to make her pulse rate slow down to something approaching normal.

Fifteen minutes later she stood in the kitchen with what passed for her staff. One of the servers, Elaine, was so young she looked underage for a dining room that served wine. The other, Phillip, was probably in his forties. He was also probably experienced, but Kit wasn't sure at what. His face looked like he'd been through a lot of hell in some capacity.

The busboy was named Gabriel. He was maybe seventeen, but he clearly felt his age was no handicap to his budding career as a lady killer. Kit had told him gently but quite firmly that she didn't get involved with people she worked with. Gabriel didn't look like he was going to let that stop him.

LeBlanc watched her with that same sardonic grin he'd had in the dining room. One of these days she'd tell him just how annoying it was, but right now she didn't have time. He stood in the midst of his own staff. Darcy now wore a chef's coat and beanie. Two other dark-eyed men in white coats lounged against the prep table, looking both exotic and bored.

"Okay, y'all, listen up," LeBlanc intoned in a voice that carried to the back of the kitchen. The servers came to attention. Gabriel reluctantly turned his gaze away from Kit.

"Soup of the day is wild mushroom bisque. Mushrooms are local. Try to mention that—we don't want it hanging around after today. Special is broiled redfish with haricots verts and rice pilaf. Sandwich is a Spanish chorizo and manchego panini. Pasta is penne with Meyer lemon cream sauce and grilled shrimp."

"We got any steak?" Phillip called.

LeBlanc grimaced. "We got some strip. Not much. Expect it to run out early. Push the Panini and the pasta—we got lots of both. And chicken. Always chicken."

"Cooked how?" Elaine asked, eyes wide.

"However you want it, darlin'." LeBlanc grinned at her. "Regular menu stuff. Mostly salads. Staff meal's on the steam table."

Kit watched the waiters and chefs head for the food. Her stomach felt too full of butterflies to squeeze in anything else.

LeBlanc raised a bristling black eyebrow. "You don't like pasta? I can fix you up some of that wild mushroom bisque."

She shook her head. "Not hungry right now. If there's anything left after the lunch crowd, I'll eat then."

LeBlanc peered at her. "You're not nervous are you, darlin'?"

Kit flexed her shoulders. "I won't be after this meal. After I get used to the place."

He shook his head, his sardonic grin returning. "Darlin', this place has been limping along with Mabel as hostess for a month. Anything you do will be an improvement, believe me. Particularly if you actually know what you're doing."

"Mabel?"

"Morgenstern." LeBlanc's mouth twisted slightly. "Ol' Mabel may have a lot of great qualities, but running a dining room ain't one of them. Come to think of it, I'm not real sure what the others might be."

Kit swallowed hard as the butterflies took another pass around her stomach. The Rose was nothing like Antonio's Fine Mexican Cuisine. Her mom wasn't around to pick up the slack if she had any problems, and the customers undoubtedly wouldn't cut her a break if she screwed up. She peeked out the kitchen door toward the hostess station. Four women in Ralph Lauren were staring around the dining room, obviously trying to locate someone who could give them a table.

"Show time," Kit whispered, assuming her best professional smile.

By the end of the lunch shift, Kit had come to two firm conclusions—the Rose could be the best restaurant in Konigsburg with a little work, and two servers weren't enough.

After the first half hour, she'd been dividing her time between seating customers, pouring water, tea and coffee, and occasionally helping Gabriel clear tables, which meant discouraging his not-particularly-subtle passes and avoiding the occasional wandering hand.

After his fifth attempt to impress her with muttered promises of his sexual stamina, Kit's patience snapped. "Listen, kid, I'm old enough to be your big sister," she snarled. "And if you don't stop hitting on me and start doing the work you're paid for, you'll be looking for alternative employment as a boy soprano. Now zip it!"

Gabriel had given her his version of puppy eyes, but Kit ignored him. She didn't have time for hurt feelings. Hell, she didn't have time to breathe!

Ms. Mabel Morgenstern had looked in during the height of the rush, waving cheerfully when she saw Kit with a water pitcher but wisely choosing not to stop for a chat. Other than that, she saw no one but customers and wait staff.

She soon figured out that Elaine was at the beginning of what passed for her food service career. She was sweet and friendly and likeable and only borderline competent. Phillip knew what he was doing, but he wasn't likely to warm up the customers with an expression that made him look like a former serial killer. Still, when a group of six came in, she put them on Phillip's station, although it would bring him close to capacity, since only he was remotely capable of handling a group of that size. She hoped his tips would make up for it.

The rush began to die down around one thirty, although they still got a few groups of four and some couples.

When she'd run the last credit card and watched the last table of four head through the dining room entrance, Kit collapsed into one of the booths near the bar. If this pace kept up, she'd forget about looking professional and start wearing running shoes.

LeBlanc appeared beside her, carrying a bowl and a couple of plates. Apparently he'd been a waiter in some earlier incarnation. He placed the bowl in front of her. "Mushroom bisque. Saved you a bowl. The server corps managed to move the rest of it."

He dropped down opposite her, putting a plate of cheese, bread and fruit in the middle of the table while he set a large Panini in front of himself. "See what you got yourself into, darlin'?"

Kit picked up her spoon. "This is insane. If it's like this at lunch, why aren't we open for dinner? Surely we'd pick up some of this crowd."

LeBlanc's smile curdled. "You got that right. I don't know what the hell Mabel's waiting for. You want a fine dining experience in Konigsburg, right now it's Brenner's. It's taken us a while to build back up from where that asshole Carville left us, but word's gotten out little by little. We could definitely give Brenner's a good run for the dinner crowd."

"Do you do breakfasts too?"

He shrugged. "We buy pastry from your aunt, and either Jorge or Leo comes in early to make omelets. It's mostly for the inn guests anyway."

"What about Sunday brunch?"

LeBlanc glowered again. "I've been trying to get Mable to let us start one, but she's dragging her feet. Hell, brunch makes a shitload of money and it burns off leftovers. What's to lose?"

Kit shook her head. "What leftovers?"

His grin returned. "Piece of advice, darlin'—don't get anything on a brunch table that's served in a cream sauce."

"So no brunch and no dinners." She frowned. "Seems like a waste of a great kitchen and what could be a great restaurant."

LeBlanc grimaced. "It *is* a waste of a great kitchen. Right now the only outside stuff we're doing is catering for groups at the event center. Sooner or later Mabel will get her ass in gear, but right now she's stalling."

Kit took a bite of her mushroom bisque and sat up straight. The earthy, woodsy taste of the mushrooms was bound in a silken sauce of broth and cream. Her taste buds were applauding. "This is wonderful."

His mouth spread in a slow grin. "Well, sure it is, darlin'. I don't do crap."

She didn't bother to comment. Judging from his bisque, his opinion was justified. "No wonder we're doing such great business."

"Yeah, now maybe ol' Mabel will hire somebody who actually knows how to serve food," LeBlanc growled.

Kit sighed. "Elaine's trying. She just needs more experience. I'll work with her—she'll pick it up. And Philip does okay."

"Ol' Phil knows his way around a table. Course he only learned it after Mabel hired him, but he's a quick study."

"He didn't have any experience when he came?" Kit shook her head. "I thought that's why you must have hired him. I mean he's sort of mature for a beginning waiter."

"Hey, darlin', I was desperate. All the wait staff quit when Carville cut their wages. Mabel kept promising me people, but she didn't get around to it. Phil showed up looking for a job and he wasn't fussy about what he did, so I drafted him. Showed him how to be a waiter, so we at least had a warm body in the dining room when we got customers."

"And Elaine?"

LeBlanc shook his head. "She was Mabel's hire. I don't know what she's getting paid, but my guess is Phil gets more. He's worth it too."

Kit rubbed a hand across the back of her neck. "I don't understand. Isn't the restaurant separate from the hotel? Why is Ms. Morgenstern responsible for hiring people in the front of the house?"

"The hotel owns the restaurant, so Mabel can hire wait staff, but the kitchen's mine. I hire the chefs. In a crisis, I'll hire the wait staff too, but we're beyond the crisis now, at least theoretically. You and I need to get on the same page about the kind of wait staff we need. Then we can make the case with Mable. Or try to, anyway. Tell her there are better places to save money than by hiring people who don't know what they're doing because they work cheap. Plus you need to be in charge of stuff like laundry and printing the menus. Maybe it's time for another Come To Joe conversation."

"Sounds like you and Ms. Morgenstern have some issues." She took another spoonful of her soup.

"Mabel doesn't know a mussel from a clam. She's strictly interested in the bottom line. Me, I'm more in tune with the sensual arts." He gave her a slow smile that made her stomach feel jumpy all of a sudden.

Kit blew out a breath. "Thanks for the soup. I guess I'd better run to check the reservations again. I'm still trying to figure out the software."

LeBlanc's faintly sardonic grin returned. She had a feeling he knew exactly what she was really running to, or from. "You do that, darlin'. I'll check to make sure Gabriel got the dining room cleaned up. He's okay, but sometimes he gets distracted."

Kit swallowed hard as she headed for the restaurant office again. She had a feeling Gabriel wasn't the only one who got distracted around here.

Brody put his frozen dinner into the microwave and set the controls. He'd much rather have grabbed a hamburger in town, but that represented one of those unnecessary risks he was trying to avoid. The less he showed his face in Konigsburg, the less likely it was that anyone would recognize him. He did his limited grocery shopping in Johnson City, and even there he was constantly on guard for people who might look at him twice.

His jaw tightened as the microwave timer ticked down. He was still trying to understand the unnecessary risks he'd taken the night before. Breaking into the bookstore had been part of the plan, of course, but he hadn't realized just how good revenge would feel once he got in there. He hadn't originally intended to go beyond knocking some books on the floor and walking off with a few of the more expensive trinkets lying around to attract the tourists. But once he got started, the rest of it just seemed to happen. Each book he'd tossed across the room had loosened something inside his chest until he'd started doing more than tossing. The sound of tearing paper had given him more pleasure than he'd had in years. More pleasure than he'd had since he'd been driven out of Konigsburg, in fact. For once, he'd felt like he was in charge of his own destiny again, the way he should be.

And the final *coup de grâce*, the final gesture of contempt. That had given him a kind of wild satisfaction he'd never thought he'd feel again.

Of course, once he was back at his miserable excuse for a room, he'd realized the stupidity of that final gesture. He'd left them some DNA, although it might take them a while to process it. Then again, he didn't figure he'd wait around too much longer anyway. His plans should be in motion fairly soon, and then he could hit the road for good, never returning to Konigsburg again.

Still, he'd have given a lot to see Docia Kent's face this morning. If he could have figured out a safe way to do it, he'd have waited in town until she showed up at her shop. But when push came to shove, he wasn't willing to trade his safety for the pleasure of seeing her suffer.

At least he didn't think he was. Yet.

Chapter Six

By the end of her first week at the Woodrose, Kit had finally gotten the reservation system to behave (after Mabel Morgenstern had promised to take the idea of a national reservation service "under advisement"), and she'd begun to give Elaine some rudimentary training in the art of waiting tables. And by the end of each workday she was thoroughly exhausted. She pulled into Allie's driveway at six, after she'd gotten set up for lunch the next day. The house was dark, not that she'd really expected Allie to still be around.

Now that her wedding problems had been taken care of by dropping them in Kit's lap, Allie usually took off for Wonder Dentist's around dinner time. Kit hadn't actually talked to her aunt since their last conversation about the wedding a couple of days ago, given that Allie got up at four to bake her breakfast pastries and Kit didn't pull in until she'd finished riding herd on Gabriel and the dishwasher, Morrie.

Allie had told Wonder that Kit was going to take over the wedding. She'd even used the phrase "wedding planner", which made Kit's stomach tie a couple of new knots. She'd managed to pull her aunt aside before she disappeared that evening. "Allie, I don't know much about event planning, let alone wedding planning. I said I'd help, but I figured you'd still be making the major decisions. I mean I've never done anything like this on my own."

Allie shook her head. "You've got terrific taste, sweetheart. You'll figure out what to do, I know it. If I try to do anything, I'm liable to have another panic attack. I'm just going to turn it all over to you."

"But I don't even know what you want to spend," Kit said desperately. "How can I plan anything when I don't know what's in your price range?"

Allie frowned. "That's a good point. Let me put together a budget, then you can work from that. Shouldn't take me long." She gave Kit another bright smile. "I've got confidence in you, kid. And I'm so grateful that I don't have to worry anymore."

Allie's smile was so tremulous that Kit didn't have the heart to make any more objections. But she had a feeling she'd been cornered into doing something that would eat up great chunks of her life for the foreseeable future. Not that she had a whole lot of other things pending at that moment. And, of course, she'd volunteered for this.

You owe her. She did. She really did.

She changed out of her professional clothes, pitching her two-inch heels to the back of the closet. From now on she'd decided to wear flats, possibly even running shoes, even if she didn't look like the hostess of the year. She walked to Allie's kitchen in her bare feet, feeling her arches ache. Her aunt had left a note on the table directing her to the refrigerator for a plate of leftovers. There was also a printout from her spreadsheet. Kit squinted at the figures. Apparently, it was supposed to be the wedding budget. She sank into her chair, rubbing her eyes. She *so* didn't want to screw this up. Any more than she wanted to screw up the job at the Rose. She wasn't sure who she was trying to impress exactly, but she had a sneaky suspicion it might be herself.

She peeked under the aluminum foil at the plate of leftover spaghetti, which was perilously close to what she'd had for lunch, although Joe LeBlanc's sauce was probably more complex. She sighed. What she really wanted to do, she realized suddenly, was have a beer and nachos at the Faro and maybe gossip with Deirdre Brandenburg when she had a minute.

You know Nando will be there, right?

Kit swallowed hard. Well, so he'd be there. So what? She didn't intend to make life difficult for either of them, but she also didn't intend to keep away from places where she wanted to go just because Nando might be there too. They both needed to be adults about this and just get over it. She was ready to show everybody she was a grown-up.

Which was close to a total crock. She sighed. *Oh well, let's just pretend it's true for now.* The Faro had seemed like her kind of place, and she'd find a way to share it with Nando. And if he showed up there with another woman...she'd deal. Somehow.

She grabbed her keys and headed for the door.

The Faro was having a good night, or maybe it was just a normal night. Having only been there once, Kit was in no position to judge.

The tables looked mostly full, the crowd largely male but with enough women scattered around to keep her from feeling uncomfortable. She found a seat at the bar.

Tom Ames gave her a cautious smile. "Hi, Kit. What can I get you?"

"Whatever beer you gave me the other night. It was great." She gave him a smile that she hoped was reassuring. *No drama here—absolutely none. So help me.*

"Kit, you came back!" Deirdre leaned on the bar beside her, grinning as she pushed her tray toward Tom. "Two Shiners and a house red," she called and then turned back. "So how's the Woodrose Inn?"

"Exhausting." Kit grinned back. "I had no idea the Rose was so popular. I haven't had a chance to eat anything since mid-morning. I was hoping you guys were still serving."

"Let's check—Clem's still back there, I think. Let me drop off this order, and then we'll go ask what's around to eat."

Kit wasn't sure who she'd expected "Clem" to be—probably someone large and male, sort of like Joe LeBlanc. She was a little surprised to see a tiny woman with spiked black hair and a side braid, along with a pierced eyebrow and a harassed expression beneath her chef's beanie.

"What's up?" she asked. "I'm not serving anything to those assholes at the pool table. They don't even know what they're putting in their mouths anyway. And I saw Denny Steinbruner put his burger down on the table, right on the felt. Let 'em eat chips."

Deirdre shook her head. "I just wanted to introduce you two and see if you had anything around we could munch on. Kit Maldonado, this is Clem Rodriguez."

Clem narrowed her eyes. "Allie Maldonado's niece? The one working at the Rose?"

"Geez, news travels fast around here." Kit nodded. "That's me."

Clem shrugged. "People in the restaurant trade talk to each other. Joe's a friend of mine. So's your aunt. I saw them both at the market this morning. Sit down." She waved a hand toward a table at the side of the kitchen. "You can finish off the risotto so I won't have to figure out what to do with it. We're not getting many orders for it."

"I need to go wait on a few tables," Deirdre said. "Save me a little and I'll come back for it." She pushed through the kitchen door into the dining room again.

Clem shook her head as she spooned up two servings of risotto. "Sooner or later she's going to burn herself out running Coffee Delight and waiting tables. Tom's been trying to get her to stop, but she likes hanging around the bar in the evening and she can't just sit there for some reason."

"So Deirdre's his significant other?" Kit took a bite of risotto and her tense muscles relaxed. Parmesan, mushrooms, a little hint of sherry. Clearly Joe LeBlanc wasn't the only outstanding new chef around Konigsburg.

"About as significant as you can get," Clem said dryly. "Chico and I have a running bet going about when the wedding will be."

Kit grimaced slightly, which wasn't at all fair to the risotto.

Clem narrowed her eyes. For someone her size, she could look surprisingly menacing. "You got something against them getting married?"

Kit sighed. "Not really. Right now I'm just sort of anti-wedding in general. My Aunt Allie roped me into planning hers, and I don't have a clue about what I'm supposed to be doing. She just gave me her budget tonight and I can't tell if it's realistic or insane."

Clem shook her head. "You mean she still hasn't married Wonder? For some reason I thought that had happened a long time ago."

Kit shrugged. "She kept putting it off, and now she's got some kind of phobia about planning for it. So she's decided I can handle everything, even though I've got no experience doing anything like it. I don't even know where to start."

Clem leaned back in her chair. "Does she have a venue? Go for that first. Once you've got the place nailed down, you can usually build around it."

Kit shoveled in a couple of bites. "What are the usual venues around here? I don't think she wants to get married in a church."

"People used to get married at Cedar Creek Winery," Clem mused, "but they're enlarging their patio right now, so it's not available. If it's a small wedding there's always the party room at Brenner's. Lee Contreras and Ken Crowder are friends of Allie's anyway. They'd probably let her have it for free, or close to it."

Kit frowned. "I don't think the wedding's going to be that small, given all the people Allie knows around town and the size of our family. I mean Aunt Allie and her sisters and brothers alone would fill up Brenner's."

Clem buttered a piece of bread for herself. "Well, kid, if push comes to shove, you're working at the biggest wedding venue in town. That event center at the Woodrose is wedding central."

"Yeah, and it's probably booked for the next five years," Kit said gloomily. Plus it also probably cost more than Allie's entire budget.

"Not necessarily." Clem leaned back again. "They had this really lousy chef, Aaron Carville, for a couple of years. He ran the restaurant into the ground and that started dragging down the rest of the inn too. My guess is they've been scrambling to make up for the damage he did." She took a bite of her own risotto. "Of course, that's going to change fast now that Joe's in charge. He's already taking a major bite out of the lunch trade here in town. It doesn't hit us because we're not in that price bracket, but I've noticed that Kip Berenger at the Silver Spur has been doing a lot more lunch entertainment and special events than he did before."

"Joe's a really good chef. So are you," Kit added hastily.

"Yes, I am." Clem grinned. "But Joe's more high powered than I am. He was sous chef at one of the biggies in New York and head chef at a restaurant in New Orleans. He's definitely the real deal."

"What's he doing here?" Kit shook her head. "I mean, not that Konigsburg isn't a good foodie town, but..."

"But it's not one of the big ones." Clem nodded. "He had some...problems. Personal problems. A few years ago. But now he's pulled himself together again. If anybody can get the Rose back on its feet again, it's Joe."

Clem shoveled in a couple more bites of risotto. Kit considered asking her some more specific questions about Joe LeBlanc's "personal problems", but she figured if Clem thought it was her business, she'd already have told her.

Deirdre pushed back into the kitchen again, tendrils of her dark hair flying around her face. Depressingly enough, she looked even more beautiful when she was messy. "Back again. Did you save me some food?"

Clem handed her a plate. "Sit down. Do not go through that door again. Let Sylvia and Marilyn handle the tables."

"Okay. For the moment." She took a bite of risotto. "Really good, Clem. Up to your standard."

"Yep," Clem agreed. "Now about the wedding food."

"What wedding?" Deirdre turned to Kit, wide-eyed. "You're getting married?"

Kit shook her head. "Aunt Allie and Wonder Dentist. I'm the designated wedding planner, god help me."

Clem continued as if there'd been no interruption. "If you get the Woodrose, you probably won't have a choice—the food will have to come from their kitchen. But Joe would do a great job for you anyway. And he'd probably work with you on price. You should get some kind of discount since you're working there."

"You're going to do it at the Woodrose?" Deirdre grinned. "That's where Docia was supposed to get married. They had the reception there, anyway. All I remember is the champagne, which was first rate."

"Nothing's set up yet," Kit said a little desperately. "I don't know how Aunt Allie would feel about the Woodrose, or who she wants to do the food for the reception."

Clem shook her head. "Doing it at the Woodrose would save you a world of hassles, believe me. If you do it anywhere else, you'll be hip deep in the restaurant wars. Lee and Ken at Brenner's would feel honor-bound to bid for it, and Allie might feel like she should do it herself, and I'd probably put in a bid too." She grinned. "Not that I'd get it, but hey, I'd feel like I needed to stake my claim at least."

"Won't they get mad if Joe does it?" Kit took a quick bite of risotto. "I mean they're competitors."

Clem shrugged. "Like I say, if you do it at the Woodrose, you don't get a choice. And then Lee and Ken can just be guests and Allie can relax."

"Except she'll probably want to do her own cake, and the groom's cake too." Kit chewed her lip. She wasn't sure about that, but since baking was Allie's profession, to say nothing of her pride and joy, she had a feeling her aunt wouldn't want to turn it over to anyone else.

"Not a problem." Clem grinned. "The Rose is already contracting with Allie for pastries and baked goods. Joe hasn't found a pastry chef yet, and he probably won't find one in time for this wedding, assuming he can get the okay to hire one."

Kit leaned back in her chair, frowning. "It can't really be this simple, can it?"

"Sure it can." Clem carried her plate to the sink. "Assuming you can get the event center, you're in."

"Assuming I can get the event center."

"Maybe you could use their wedding planner too. Then you wouldn't have to do everything." Deirdre raised an eyebrow. "Surely they've got one."

Kit considered the Woodrose's wedding planner, one Mabel Morgenstern. "I think I'd rather do it myself, or let Aunt Allie do it once we've got the venue sewed up. It's going to be hard enough to reserve the place. I don't want to push my luck. Thanks for your help, Clem."

Clem grinned. "Anytime. Just remember our catering services when it comes time for the bridal shower."

Kit lowered her forehead to the table. "Oh hell, bridal showers. I have to find out how to run a bridal shower. And here I'd been feeling so good."

Nando lounged on his barstool, nursing his beer. All in all, it was a shitty end to a shitty week, and he used the words advisedly.

They hadn't gotten anything back from the county lab about the bookstore break-in yet, but that would take a while. Given that the county had some more serious crimes in the queue ahead of them, Nando figured they'd be lucky to get anything back in a month or so.

Meanwhile, Ham had actually begun a campaign to undermine him as assistant chief. He should have anticipated that move, of course, but for some reason he hadn't. Ham might be dumb as a post, but he had a certain flair for sneakiness. And he'd clearly decided if he couldn't get Toleffson's job, he'd take Nando's instead.

Unfortunately, so far he was waging a fairly successful campaign, although Nando was willing to bet that success was more accidental than planned. His current problems all centered around the crap sample he'd taken from the bookstore. Ham had spread the story of the sample around town, leaving out the part about DNA, calling him the "poop policeman." Given that most people around Konigsburg had no idea that crap could be evidence, the phrase had definitely caught on.

Nando found himself facing grins where he'd never faced them before, and hearing snickers behind his back from men who were more accustomed to snickering at Ham Linklatter. Maybe he could have explained about the DNA and the importance of the sample, given that they hadn't turned up any other evidence that could identify the perp, but he had a feeling saying anything more about it would just make things worse. He'd perfected an easy grin to mask the acid bubbling in his stomach.

The one saving grace in the whole debacle was the fact that at least Toleffson understood the importance of the DNA evidence. On the other hand, he had a feeling this wasn't exactly what the chief had had in mind when he'd told him to keep his nose clean.

They hadn't been able to find any witnesses to the bookstore vandalism. Nobody had heard breaking glass or seen flashing lights. And nobody was currently living upstairs over the store, so there was nobody there to hear the intruders. All in all, it had been one frustrating investigation.

Now he sat sipping his beer and facing the very sobering possibility that Ham could replace him as the assistant chief if he managed to make Nando look more like a moron than Ham himself. A few weeks ago, Nando would have rated the odds on that happening at near zero. Now it was looking somewhat more possible.

Tom Ames leaned on the counter next to him. "Anything new with Docia's store?"

Nando shook his head. "Not a damn thing. And we've been pounding the pavement for a week now. I don't suppose anybody's mentioned anything in here?"

"You mean other than you and the poop?" Tom grimaced. "Nope."

"The poop was legitimate evidence..." Nando began.

Tom shook his head. "Stow it. I know about the DNA. So does everybody else in town with half a brain. Right now you're getting the grade school playground reaction—you know, 'Dude, he said poop!' Eventually people will sober up and remind themselves what a half-wit Ham is."

"Yeah. With my luck it'll happen after he's pushed me out of the assistant chief's job."

"Don't worry about it." Tom took a breath, polishing a nonexistent spot on the bar. "Kit's here."

Nando stiffened. He'd checked the room carefully when he'd come in, and he hadn't seen her. "Where?"

"Back in the kitchen with Deirdre and Clem. They're bonding."

"Terrific. Does that mean I have to find a new bar?"

"Only if you're tired of my beer." Tom shook his head. "She doesn't seem like she wants to make trouble. I don't see why you can't share the place."

Nando blew out a breath. "Hey, I was here first."

"So we're back to the grade school playground thing again?"

"No." Nando rubbed his eyes. "Okay, I can handle it."

Tom frowned. "What happened between you two, anyway?"

"Momentary lunacy." Nando took a swallow of his beer, hoping that would be the end of it. He really didn't want to get into explanations right now.

He heard the *swish* of the opening kitchen door and saw Deirdre and Kit heading back toward the bar, with Clem emerging a moment later.

As usual, his body kicked into high gear. He figured picturing Frau Blücher wasn't going to have much effect right now. "Evening," he said, keeping his gaze on Kit's left earlobe. Kit seemed to be studying the far wall.

"Hi." Deirdre leaned across the bar to kiss Tom's cheek. "Did you miss me?"

"Always." Tom grinned the grin of a man who was secure in the promise of getting lucky fairly soon. Nando felt like punching him. "What took you so long? I was about to send Chico in there to make sure you were all still around."

"Wedding stuff," Kit explained. "They were helping me."

"Wedding?" Nando felt cold all the way to his toes. Jesus, had she come back to Konigsburg to get married? "Whose wedding?"

Kit looked at him full-on for the first time. "Aunt Allie's. And Wonder Dentist. I've been drafted to play wedding planner."

Tom gave her a dry smile. "I assume just heading for the nearest justice of the peace is out of the question?"

Clem shook her head. "From what I hear, Allie's put this thing off for so long the whole town's getting impatient. People are taking bets about whether it'll come off at all."

"It'll come off." Kit's eyes were steely. "It'll be the best damn wedding this town's seen in years—even if I have to get the entire family to chip in."

"Oh man." Tom grinned. "This is going to be good for weeks of discussion. What's the date?"

Kit shrugged. "I don't have one yet. But I will."

"That can work in your favor." Clem's brow furrowed. "Check to see if they've had any cancellations at the Woodrose. If they've got a slot they have to fill, they might give you a break on the price."

Deirdre frowned. "But if they need to fill it, it would probably be pretty soon. Don't you need time to plan?"

Kit shook her head. "The less time to plan, the less time I have to screw it up. Besides, Allie's had months to pull this thing together. Surely she knows what she wants by now."

Three fists immediately knocked on the wooden counter.

"Here's hoping," Kit muttered. "I need to get home. I've got work tomorrow."

"Let us know what happens at the Woodrose," Deirdre cut in. "Keep us posted. You never know—maybe we can help."

Kit gave her a tired smile. Maybe it had been a long day for her too. "Thanks, Deirdre. I appreciate it." She turned and started toward the exit.

Nando walked out the door behind her.

She came to a quick halt, turning to stare at him under the parking lot lights, her eyes wary. "What?"

He shrugged. "I was going to walk you home. It was time for me to take off too." Maybe the parking lot lights would hide the tension he could feel snaking across his shoulders. He hoped so, anyway.

Kit licked her lips, and he braced himself. "I drove tonight," she said softly. "You all made such a big deal about it not being safe."

He told himself he wasn't disappointed. After all, it was what he'd wanted her to do. "Okay, that's good."

"Would you like a ride?" She raised those astonishing dark eyes to his.

A smart man would say no. A smart man would know better than to take the chance of killing the truce before they'd even gotten started. But he wasn't exactly smart these days. "Thanks," he said. "Where are you parked?"

Kit had no idea why she'd offered him a ride. It wasn't like he needed one. No mugger in his right mind would go after anybody Nando's size. Now she felt like she was in driver's ed class—sitting stiffly in her seat, trying to make sure she didn't break any traffic regulations.

Not that he seemed any more relaxed than she did. He stared out the window, as if he were looking for somebody familiar on the deserted streets of Konigsburg.

"I heard about the break-in at Docia's shop," she said a little desperately. "All the damage. Allie said he destroyed several thousand dollars worth of merchandise and then messed up the store. Why would anybody do something like that?"

Nando winced. She hadn't realized it would be a sensitive topic. "Somebody with a grudge against Docia, I guess."

"But nobody has a grudge against Docia, nobody I know anyway. And I've known her since I was a teenager."

He shrugged. "Some people get teed off and you don't know it until they do something stupid. It could be somebody mad about something that doesn't seem like a problem to the rest of us, like her selection of books or maybe the color of her hair."

"Do you have any evidence that could point to who it is?"

He grimaced again. She wasn't sure what was bothering him, but something about the break-in seemed painful. "Yeah, we've got some evidence. The county lab is taking care of it."

They lapsed into silence again. She forced herself not to look at the sharp line of his profile against the darkened window. After a moment, he blew out a long breath.

"So Allie's getting married to Wonder."

"That's what she says. Assuming I can get everything lined up for her." Kit shook her head. "Deirdre and Clem gave me some good ideas, but I'm still not sure if everything will work out."

"It'll work out."

"I hope so."

"It'll work out," he repeated. "You'll make sure it does."

His smile flashed briefly in the moonlight. She licked her lips. "Thanks. I hope I do a good job for her."

"You will." He glanced out the window. "You can let me out here."

Kit frowned. "Don't you live in that trailer park anymore?"

"Nope. Sold the trailer last year. Esteban and I share an apartment over on Olmos Drive."

"Oh. Well, okay." She pulled her Civic to the curb.

Nando opened the door and stepped out, leaning back briefly as he closed the door. "Thanks for the ride."

"Sure," she murmured.

"Maybe I'll see you at the Faro again sometime."

He turned and walked up the sidewalk before she could answer, but she wasn't sure what she would have said anyway. As she turned back toward Allie's house, it occurred to her that that possibility, seeing him again, wasn't nearly as upsetting as she might once have thought it would be.

Chapter Seven

Before she headed to work the next morning, Kit stopped by Deirdre's shop for a large cup of dark roast. Aunt Allie had a perfectly acceptable coffee maker and a bag of coffee beans that actually came from Deirdre's roaster, but Kit still loved the brew at Coffee Delight. She figured an occasional indulgence wouldn't break her.

The new barista, a boy who looked barely ready for high school, poured coffee and espresso with remarkable élan. Kit was impressed.

Deirdre herself ran the cash register and served up the limited supply of pastries, most of them purchased from Allie's bakery. The number of customers was mind-boggling, but Kit found a seat at the end of the front counter and took a long, welcome sip of fresh-brewed ambrosia.

After a few minutes, Deirdre moved to the counter across from her. "You're up early. Do they actually expect you to show up at the Woodrose at this time of day?"

Kit shook her head. "Just trying to get my thoughts together before I go talk to Ms. Morgenstern about the event center. I figure I need all my ducks in a row."

"Good idea." Deirdre's perfect forehead furrowed slightly. "Do you mind if I ask you something?"

Kit blinked. "I won't know until you ask me, I guess."

"What's with you and Nando? Are you friends? Former friends? Sort of enemies?"

Kit gave her a half smile, staring down at her coffee cup. "We're former more-than-friends. We had a 'thing' going for a while, back during the summer when I worked at Cedar Creek. We broke up when I had to go back to school in San Antonio."

"Broke up amicably?" Deirdre raised an eyebrow.

Kit took a moment to sip her coffee and consider how to answer exactly. "It wasn't amicable. We had a big fight—more like a series of big fights. The closer I got to leaving, the rockier it got."

Deirdre nodded slowly. "You were probably both worried about the big change coming up and what would happen next."

"Maybe." Kit shrugged. "We might have been able to ride it out, but after one of the bigger fights, he went off to the Dew Drop and picked up another girl. Half the town saw them walk out together. He didn't come back that night. It wasn't like I could ignore the whole thing. Particularly when a couple of people called me to fill in the details."

Deirdre blew out a breath. "Ouch."

Kit nodded. "I packed up my stuff the next morning and headed back to San Antonio."

"Did he try to talk to you about it?"

"Sort of. He called. I didn't pick up. He left messages. I deleted them. He sent me an email that said *Sorry, babe, let's talk.* I didn't want to."

Deirdre frowned. "He didn't come to San Antonio?"

Kit shook her head. "I didn't give him any encouragement. I didn't see or talk to him until the other night at the Faro."

Deirdre stared down at the counter, rubbing at an imaginary spot. "He's Tom's best friend, and I like him too. But I want you both to feel comfortable at the Faro. Will you be all right seeing him there?"

"Sure." Kit took a last swallow of coffee. "I'm a big girl now, Deirdre. Moving ahead in the hospitality business. A wedding planner too, no less. Don't worry—I can handle it. He can too." She pushed herself up from her stool. "Speaking of which, I'd better head out to the Woodrose. I need to catch Morgenstern before she locks herself away for the day."

Deirdre smiled. "Come back any time. Beer at night, coffee in the morning. We're a full service stop."

But Kit thought she saw a speculative look in her eye as she headed out the door toward the street.

Great. The last thing she wanted this time around was anybody trying to patch up her love life.

Kit had learned over the days she'd worked at the Woodrose that Mabel Morgenstern was easiest to find before the lunch rush started. Around eleven, she disappeared into her office and seldom emerged again before Kit went home. After the first day, she'd apparently decided Kit could handle the Rose just fine. At any rate, she hadn't made any attempts to supervise, although for Kit, that hands-off policy was actually a plus.

Now, however, she was going to have to track Morgenstern into her lair, which was where the event planning and scheduling software was located. She hadn't bothered to ask Allie for her choice of wedding date. She'd already asked several times, and Allie had done nothing but dither. When Kit had come to the inn that morning, she'd pulled up the daily schedule on her computer. The event center and the inn's meeting rooms had a lot of bookings, although the groups seemed surprisingly small for the space available.

Still, she'd found one conspicuous open night in the middle of next month. Maybe a cancellation, and not nearly enough time to fill it on short notice. The event center was a big revenue generator for the inn. If it was empty, that meant lost cash.

She wiped her suddenly damp palms on her flowered J. Crew skirt and headed down the hall. If Allie didn't like using the event center in a little over a month, she'd have to come up with her own alternative. Kit was fresh out of options. She took a deep breath. Time to go into negotiating mode.

As she approached Mabel's office, she heard voices. Well, at least that meant Morgenstern was already there. Some mornings Kit got to the Woodrose before Mabel did. She peeked in at the side of the open door.

The man standing in front of Mabel's desk wore work clothes, jeans and a denim shirt rolled up to his elbows. After a moment, Kit recognized him as the head groundskeeper, Mr. Didrikson.

"We've got two weddings in the knot garden over the next month," Mabel was saying, "and it looks horrible."

"Half the plants were dead in there," Didrikson explained. "I had to take them out. And there's no budget for anything new. If you want it to look better, given me some money for petunias and lantana. They'll take up the slack for the time being."

Mabel pressed her lips together. "I understood the knot garden was done with perennials."

"It was." Didrikson shrugged. "Even perennials need water and fertilizer. Somebody here let them go to shit."

Kit frowned. She hadn't realized Didrikson was new too. Had Mabel hired the entire staff?

Mabel waved a hand in his general direction. "Just do the best you can. Move some stuff around. Surely we've got plants in the other gardens you can transfer to the knot garden."

Didrikson muttered something that sounded like *poison ivy* as he stalked out, treating Kit as an obstacle to be dodged around.

Mabel glanced up at her, her mouth moving into a parody of her sunny smile. "Yes, Kit? What is it?"

Kit licked her lips again as she stepped into the office. "I had a question about event scheduling."

Mabel's forehead furrowed. "What about it? It's my responsibility. Has someone been asking you about scheduling events?"

"No, well, not exactly. I noticed we've got an open Saturday next month."

Mabel narrowed her eyes. "We had a cancellation. Some kind of problem with a wedding, I understand."

Kit swallowed. Now came the hard part. "I might have an event you could book in there at that time, if it's still available. Although it's very short notice."

Mabel's eyebrow arched. "An event? What kind of event?"

"A wedding. A large one. They've been considering another space, but if they discovered the event center was available, they might be willing to reschedule."

"Reschedule? A wedding?" Mabel's eyes widened. "How can they reschedule a wedding?"

"It's somewhat spur of the moment," Kit improvised a little desperately. "But it's a large group. And they'd have both the wedding and the reception here. Possibly the rehearsal dinner as well. Of course, since it's so last minute, I assume there would be some kind of adjustment in the rental fee."

Mabel narrowed her eyes. "Who are these people? Are they local?"

"My aunt." Kit stared at Morgenstern, daring her to blink. "Allie

Maldonado, owner of Sweet Thing bakery. Her cookbook is currently on the bestseller list at Amazon. And her fiancé is Dr. Steven Kleinschmidt, the dentist."

After a moment, Mabel licked her lips, her glance sharpening. "Your aunt. Allie Maldonado."

"Yes." Kit tried another trump card. "The guests will include all the Toleffson family from Konigsburg. Docia Kent Toleffson is the matron of honor. And of course many of the most prominent restaurateurs in the state will be there, probably including some of the restaurant critics from the metropolitan newspapers and possibly *Texas Monthly*. It would be an excellent way to publicize the new staff at the Rose." She had no idea if any of this was actually true, but she'd do her best to get Allie to invite a few foodies if she could nail down the damn event center. If nothing else, she could guarantee Lee and Ken from Brenner's and the gang from Cedar Creek Winery would be there.

"Docia Kent Toleffson?" Mabel's eyes widened. "*The* Kent family?"

"Yes ma'am." Kit held her gaze. Chances of any of the other Kents besides Docia showing up for the wedding were slim, but it was barely possible. Docia's daddy had always loved Allie's scones.

Mabel's lips moved into something closer to her usual smile. "I'd love to help out, dear, but I'm not willing to give away the event center for free, no matter how prominent the guests are. Even if we did have a cancellation. I have a responsibility to the inn."

"No of course not," Kit soothed. "But a discount might make them more willing to choose the Woodrose over some of their other possibilities." Like Allie's backyard, which was currently the only other place she'd been able to think of.

Mabel assumed an expression that was probably supposed to be canny. "I might be able to offer a five percent discount."

Kit frowned slightly, as she pretended to consider it. "I'm not sure that would be enough. They really were very interested in that new resort outside Marble Falls. Their prices are quite competitive."

Mabel's eyes narrowed. "Perhaps. That is, if you don't mind corporate food and sharing the venue with eight other parties separated by temporary partitions." She stared down at her desk blotter for a moment. "Very well, ten percent, but I can't possibly go below that, even for you, dear."

"Ten percent and the right to supply the cakes from my aunt's bakery."

Mabel shook her head. "Oh my, that would be very irregular. We contract with Bellefleur Cakes in Austin."

Kit shrugged. "My aunt's cakes are famous. She's done weddings all over the state. She's even air-freighted cakes to Los Angeles and Chicago." That some of those cakes were for her nieces and nephews would be a bit of information Kit kept to herself.

Mabel shook her head. "Well, dear, I really don't know. This all seems very...unconventional."

"The wedding will probably rate press coverage on food blogs and the food Web sites," Kit said briskly. "I'm sure they'd want pictures of any cake my aunt baked for herself and her groom."

She could see the moment when Mabel finally caved, possibly the moment she pictured the wedding coverage in the *Austin American-Statesman*. "All right. Ten percent and she gets her own cakes. But we do the rest of the food here."

"Of course." Kit gave her a brilliant smile. "I wouldn't think of using anyone else. I'll work out the details of the menu with Joe myself."

"Yes, why don't you do that." Mabel waved her toward the door. "And of course you can also tell your aunt I'll need a ten percent deposit to hold the date."

"Yes, ma'am," Kit trilled. "I'll get right on it." Right after she went back to her office and collapsed for a few minutes to catch her breath.

Nando wasn't sure why he was heading over to Kent's Hill Country Books again. There wasn't any more evidence to collect. Docia had hired a professional cleaning company to come in and take care of the place. The chief himself had written up the report, listing all the damage. Nothing appeared to have been stolen beyond three ebook readers and a couple of MP3 players, although Nando guessed it would be hard to tell if any of the books were missing, given the chaos the burglar had left behind.

But something about the place kept drawing him back. Maybe it was what Kit had said. *Nobody has a grudge against Docia.* The thing was, while he understood what Kit was saying, he didn't think that was true. Clearly somebody did have a grudge. A serious grudge. And he couldn't say he liked the thought of that much.

Which led him to his next question: who was likely to have a grudge against Docia that was serious enough to lead to this kind of damage?

He knew Docia Kent the way he knew most people in Konigsburg, kind of generally. But he had no idea who did and didn't like her. He'd never heard anybody muttering about her in the bars, which was more than he could say about a lot of the people in town.

He cut up Main toward the bookshop. It still hadn't reopened, but the chief had said it would soon. He peered in the front window, then rapped his knuckles on the glass door.

Janie Dupree Toleffson waved at him through the window and then stepped up with her keys. "Hey Nando, how are you? Anything new about the burglar?"

Nando shook his head. He knew Janie better than Docia since the two of them had gone to school together in Konigsburg. She'd been a year or so ahead of him, but that didn't make as much difference in a small town as it did in a city. "I wish I had something new to tell you, but I don't. We may not have anything concrete until the forensics lab gets through with their analysis."

He saw her quickly suppressed grin and immediately wanted to kick something, preferably Ham Linklatter. "Okay, about the sample of crap, it has DNA in it. It's our best chance for a match with the guy who left it."

She nodded. "I know. And thank god you were here with Ham, because he probably wouldn't have had enough sense to know he needed to collect it. It's still a little weird to think about, though."

"Yeah well, it wasn't all that much fun to do the collecting either." Nando blew out a breath. "When are you going to reopen?"

Janie's smile drooped slightly. "Docia says next week. Frankly, I think we could open now, but she's not ready yet."

"Is she still shaken up?"

She nodded again. "Yeah. Nothing like this has ever happened to her before. I think she's sort of midway between frightened and mad, and she doesn't know what to do exactly."

Nando leaned a hip against the front counter. "Have either of you had any problems with customers lately? Not serious ones, necessarily, but just, you know, people complaining about stuff?"

She frowned, rubbing the back of her neck. "Sure we have. Everybody does. Ask any merchant on Main. You get people who want something you don't have or who don't want to spend as much as you're asking. In here we get damages sometimes."

"Damages?"

Janie pointed to the *No food or drink in store* sign at the front. "We try to enforce that, but we don't always catch people in time. You'd be amazed at the amount of damage a six-year-old with a snow cone can do in five minutes."

"So did anybody get stuck with a big bill lately?"

She shook her head slowly. "It's never more than ten or twenty dollars, tops. Most of the time they mess up the kids' books, which aren't as expensive. Besides, most parents are embarrassed about it. They're madder at their kids than they are at us. People just don't seem to get that mad in a bookstore, at least not a bookstore that stocks a little of everything like this one."

He sighed, rubbing his eyes. "Hell, Janie, there's got to be somebody with a grudge here. Somebody who doesn't like Docia or her books."

"Or me," she said quietly.

"You?"

"I'm part owner." She shrugged. "A lot of people in town still think of it as Docia's store because it has her name on it, but it's partly mine too."

"Okay." He leaned back against the counter. "Anybody been giving you trouble lately? Any enemies in your past?"

"Lots, I guess." She shrugged again. "Nobody goes through life without ever annoying anybody else. There's my ex-boyfriend, for example. But given that he's no longer in Konigsburg and hasn't said anything to me in a couple of years, I wouldn't treat him as a real suspect. I can't see him coming back from Indiana or wherever it was he moved to so that he could mess up the bookstore."

"Otto Friedrich?" Nando shook his head. "I can't see him doing this either. What about your husband? Any recent problems at work? Anybody pissed at him?"

Janie was married to Pete Toleffson, who was Assistant County Attorney. Of all the Toleffsons, he and the chief were the ones most likely to create enemies, although the chief might edge him out in the actual total.

She shrugged. "If anything happened recently, he hasn't mentioned it to me. And attacking the store to hurt Pete seems pretty far-fetched."

"The whole thing seems pretty far-fetched," he muttered.

"It does at that." Her forehead furrowed. "Should we be frightened, Nando? Are we in any danger?"

He stared at the floor, trying to decide how to answer her. "I don't think you're in any immediate danger. But it would be smart not to take any unnecessary risks. Don't work here alone at night, for example. And if you see anything or anybody suspicious—and I mean anything, no matter how small—call 911. Helen can get hold of me or the chief pretty fast."

Janie gave him a slightly shaky grin. "Maybe Helen could just come over herself. She scares the dickens out of me, anyway."

"Maybe she could." He tried for reassuring, although he was afraid the grin looked a little more like a grimace. "And if you think of anybody who might be pissed at you or Docia, no matter how far out..."

"Right. I'll call you or Erik." She picked up her keys, walking him to the door. "Come by next week. We're having a grand reopening sale."

"I'll do that." But as he headed down the street, he wondered if the man who had devastated the shop in the first place would decide to see how well they'd managed to clean up his handiwork. Maybe he'd suggest sending Clayton Delaney over just to keep an eye on things.

As she drove home after finishing up at the Rose, Kit tried to figure out just how to connect with Allie. Their clashing hours had kept them from talking to each other for almost a week. Of course, it would help if Allie actually slept in her own house occasionally instead of at Wonder's place, but that might be too much to ask under the circumstances.

Apparently, though, it wasn't. At least not tonight.

Allie sat at the kitchen table when Kit walked in, a sheaf of invoices spread out on the table in front of her.

"Hi," Kit said carefully. "Anything wrong?"

Allie shook her head. "Just getting all the stuff together so that Lars can do the quarterly taxes. How are you?"

"Fine." She slid into the chair opposite Allie.

"How's the Woodrose?"

Kit took a deep breath. "Actually, that was something I wanted to talk to you about."

"Oh?" Allie stuck her pencil behind her ear. "Problems?"

Kit shook her head. "Not a problem at all. I think we can get the Woodrose event center for the wedding. For a ten percent discount. I checked the calendar and found a cancellation that they need to fill. Only it's a little soon."

Allie folded her hands on the table in front of her, licking her lips. "How soon?"

"About five weeks."

"Oh...well. That soon?" Allie swallowed hard, staring down at her hands. "That's...five weeks."

Kit rushed on. "Allie, it's the perfect venue. Large enough for all your family and friends. And Joe LeBlanc is a terrific chef. Whatever he does for the reception will be absolutely wonderful. You won't have to worry about choosing among your friends for a caterer—since it's at the Woodrose, Joe's the only choice. Oh, and I made sure they'll let you do your own cake."

Allie was still staring down at her hands, clutched tight against the table top. "My own cake."

"I thought you'd want to." Kit frowned. Somehow this conversation didn't seem to be going exactly the way she'd planned. "But if you don't want to, they've got a contract with a place in Austin. You could go with them."

Allie shook her head slightly. "Bellefleur." Her voice sounded slightly stronger. "No way I'd let them design my cake."

"Well then." Kit tried to keep the edge of desperation out of her voice. "You can do your own cake. And once we get the date and the venue set, the rest should fall into place pretty easily. You choose your dress, your attendants. I'll find somebody to do the flowers and the photographs, and somebody to conduct the ceremony. We'll need a band or a DJ for the reception, but that shouldn't be a problem around here with all the musicians in the area."

Allie said nothing, but her knuckles on the table had turned white.

"Aunt Allie." Kit blew out a breath. "What's wrong? You wanted me to do this, and now I've done it. Is there something wrong with the Woodrose? Something I don't know about?"

Allie shook her head. "The Woodrose is a beautiful place," she murmured. "It's perfect."

"All right." Kit resisted the urge to grind her teeth. "Then explain to me what the problem is. Please Allie."

Allie looked up at her, her eyes luminous with tears.

Oh shit! Kit knelt beside her hurriedly, wrapping an arm across her shoulders. "Allie, if you don't want to do this, now would be the right time to tell me that. It's not a problem. Things haven't progressed very far. We can just forget the whole thing."

Allie shook her head vehemently. "I want to do it. I do. I love Steve."

Kit closed her eyes for a moment, trying to reorient herself. "All right then, tell me what the problem is. You were always so good at figuring out what was wrong with me when I was a teenager, now let me help you."

Allie rubbed her hands across her face. "It's just that everything is going to change. I've been putting off all of these decisions—when the wedding will be, where we're going to live, what kind of honeymoon I want, how many attendants. I mean, if I didn't make the decisions, I still had options. Only now..." She sighed.

"Aunt Allie..." Kit paused, trying to figure out how to ask. "You keep saying you want to get married, but sometimes I get the feeling you're not exactly sure that's what you want."

Allie stared down at her hands again, blinking. "I went to culinary school straight from high school. Did you know that?"

Kit shook her head, keeping her gaze on Allie's clasped hands.

"I went straight into my first job after that, working my way up the culinary brigade. It took me a few years to make it to head pastry chef. More years until I had the money for Sweet Thing." She stared out the window, her hands still clasped tight on the table.

"You've done really well," Kit murmured. "I admire what you've done so much."

Allie glanced back at her. "I've been on my own ever since I left home. And now I'm going to give it up and be part of a couple. For the rest of my life."

"But you love Steve," Kit said carefully.

"I do." She nodded. "But it's...a very big step." She sighed again. "I'm sorry, sweetie. I'm a basket case, I know. Thanks for being so patient with me."

Kit gave her shoulders a quick hug. "You're my favorite aunt, and I'll do whatever you want me to do. But if you're going to go ahead with this, it's time to get a move on."

Allie took a deep shuddering breath. "You're right. It's time to put up or shut up. And I want to put up. What do you need me to do?"

"Write a check for the Woodrose so Mabel Morgenstern doesn't give your date to somebody else. Then leave the rest to me."

Allie nodded, wiping tears away from the corners of her eyes. "I can do that. Do you think anybody will want to come to this wedding? I mean it's only five weeks away now."

Kit leaned her forehead against her aunt's dark curls. "Aunt Allie, believe me, the entire family will be here with husbands, wives, children and every significant other they can scare up. To say nothing of all the people in Konigsburg who've been waiting for this to happen. I only hope the Woodrose event center is big enough to hold everybody who'll want to see you and Steve get married."

She had the satisfaction of seeing her aunt smile, which was enough to put the butterflies in her stomach to sleep for the night. But she left the kitchen with the image of Allie, still seated at her kitchen table, staring out into the night.

Chapter Eight

Dream Kit sat across the table from Nando, staring out at the landscape beyond the balcony. He didn't recognize the place—probably some dreamscape his subconscious had pulled out of an old movie. The sun was setting in front of them, turning the ocean waves a glorious scarlet and rose.

"I love you," he said.

Dream Kit didn't look at him. She was wearing something soft and billowing, white against her golden skin. He could see the smooth lines of her body through the fabric. Her profile stood out sharply against the brilliant sunset.

"I love you," he repeated.

Dream Kit's gaze stayed focused on the horizon. Her lips turned up in the faintest of smiles, as if she were thinking of something pleasant. Maybe she didn't know he was there. Maybe she didn't care.

"Kit," he murmured. "Please."

Below them the waves rolled to the shore, the sound distant and rhythmic. Dream Kit ignored him. Maybe he didn't exist after all.

"Catarina..."

Blaaaaaaat!

Nando's eyes flew open. He swatted the top of the clock with the flat of his hand, shutting off the alarm.

Guinevere regarded him steadily from the foot of the bed before opening her mouth in a gaping yawn.

Nando sighed, flopping back against his pillow again. "Morning, Bozo. How did you get in here again?"

Guinevere rose smoothly to her feet, stretching from her haunches to her tail. As usual, she ignored him, thumping heavily to the floor and stalking majestically toward his partially open door.

He still couldn't figure out how she managed to get it open every night. Maybe she was concealing a pair of thumbs somewhere around the apartment.

Right. Thinking about the stupid cat is a great diversion.

He sighed again. He'd had the same damn dream for three nights running now. It always went the same way too. He kept saying *I love you,* and Dream Kit seemed to be totally unaware of his existence.

He had no idea what it meant. All he could say for sure was that it left him both miserable and hard, which was a really shitty way to start the day.

In reality, of course, he'd never told her he loved her. Except in those last panicked messages on her voice mail that she might never have heard. Yet another one of his screw-ups, part of the whole epic screw-up that was his relationship with Kit Maldonado.

He should have told her. At least, he should have tried.

"Hindsight," he muttered. "Always dead on."

He pushed himself out of bed, pulling the spread up over the tangled sheets. Guinevere regarded him impassively from the corner next to the door as she gave herself a quick wash. He also had no idea how he'd come to acquire his very own feline BFF, but for some reason the cat had decided to bond with him.

Oh well, at least one female felt like doing that.

"C'mon, Bozo," he muttered. "Time for breakfast."

Kit stood in the doorway of the Rose, watching Elaine try to take care of a table of four. She got two of the orders mixed up, but the people at the table seemed pretty good-natured about it. And at least this time she remembered to fill their water glasses. Of course, she also forgot to ask the two customers who had ordered wine if they wanted another glass. Kit caught a couple of eye-rolls. She'd have to grab Elaine before she moved on to serving the two-top at the side of the room and then pour the wine before she forgot all about it.

Kit had become the restaurant's de facto sommelier when she'd realized, somewhere around her first day, that Elaine seemed unable to fill a simple wine order without bringing the wrong bottle or misusing the corkscrew. And putting a sharp implement in Philip's hands while he was serving some of his more demanding customers seemed like a very poor idea. At some point, she'd have to show Elaine how to open a wine bottle correctly, but right now it was just easier to do it herself.

At least Elaine was now managing to get her salads to the tables before the entrées most of the time, something Kit had already had to caution her about twice. Philip was putting the food out with his usual stone-faced efficiency. Kit had decided by the end of her first week that getting Philip to smile was definitely not part of her job description.

She sighed, pulled Elaine aside to remind her about the wine, and grabbed an iced tea pitcher to take care of a couple of refills before heading off to find the right wine bottle. Gabriel gave her his usual leer, but she ignored him. His libido fell under the same heading as Philip's lack of smile—not worth her effort to correct.

At least the rush had begun to subside and it hadn't been as hectic as some days. Since Brenner's didn't serve lunch, the Rose had the upscale trade all to themselves, assuming the lunchers in question didn't mind driving half a mile out of town to the inn. Judging from their capacity seating over the past week from eleven thirty until one thirty, most people in town didn't see that as a difficulty.

Kit ran credit cards for Elaine and gave Phillip change, careful to include a lot of small bills in the probably vain hope that they'd leave him a decent tip. She'd heard him grumbling about his take-home pay a couple of days ago. Yet he hadn't seemed to make the connection between his surly demeanor and the amount of money his customers left behind.

The last few diners lingered over their drinks, gazing at the afternoon sunlight dappling the smooth green lawn outside the French doors. By next month the temperature would be spiking into the eighties on most days, but for the moment it was still relatively pleasant. The Rose's gorgeous location was one of its biggest attractions, and she figured they'd start outside seating in another week or so, provided she could convince Mabel to let her hire another waiter.

Kit heard the swish of a door opening, and watched Joe LeBlanc saunter out of the kitchen and through the dining room. A few diners looked after him curiously. Apparently, he wasn't yet as well known to civilians as he was to the town's professional foodie population.

"Hey darlin'," he drawled. "How's things? Lunch crowd happy?"

"Doing well. Looks like the roasted corn chowder was a hit."

"Yes, ma'am." He wiped his damp face with a napkin, leaning forward to rest his elbows on the hostess desk. "Ran out halfway through. Have to maybe move that higher into the rotation. We didn't do as well with the mahi mahi, though. I'm still getting a feel for our customers, I guess."

"I'd say you're doing fine." Kit watched Gabriel clear another table. "We're doing major business, and the crowd is getting bigger every day. I'm going to talk to Mabel about getting another busboy and at least one more server. People should concentrate on the food instead of grousing about the service."

"Yeah, that's the least of what we need—experienced waiters would be a nice change. And we could use a pastry chef too. Maybe we should double-team her—you broach the subject and I'll go in for the kill."

Kit leaned back on the desk beside him. "I also need to talk to you, as a matter of fact."

His mouth spread in a slow grin. "Oh yeah? What about, darlin'?"

Kit grimaced. "About the menu for my aunt's wedding. I just scheduled her into the event center because there was a cancellation. It's at the middle of next month, and I don't even know what we can set up in the way of food when we don't have that much time."

"Miz Allie's getting married?" His smile broadened. "Hell, every foodie in the Hill Country will probably show up. We'll have to do something special for her. And a month's plenty of time to come up with some good stuff, believe me."

Kit felt like a large weight had lifted from her shoulders for the first time since she'd talked to Allie the night before. "Really? That's such a relief."

"I'll do her proud, Scout's honor." He sketched a quick cross on his broad chest.

"I believe you." Kit glanced back across the restaurant with its muted colors, the rolling green hills stretching beyond the French doors. "This has such potential. It's a beautiful location and your food is spectacular. All it needs is a couple of nudges to become a destination restaurant."

She blinked. Where on earth had that statement come from?

LeBlanc narrowed his eyes. "You interested in nudging, darlin'?"

She shrugged. "Maybe. Sometime. Right now I've got a wedding to plan. When can we go over the menus?"

"How about this evening, after everything clears out?"

Joe's blue eyes seemed to darken. Kit felt her own pulse thump. *Danger, danger Will Robinson!*

"Um...okay. You mean look at the menus here?"

"Nope. I usually get out of here as soon as I can." He had that knowing grin again, the one she kept meaning to tell him was annoying.

Kit licked her lips, ready to explain that she couldn't go to his house or his apartment or his trailer, wherever it was.

His grin didn't falter. "How about we go catch some dinner at that tavern where Clem Rodriguez cooks? I've been meaning to check it out anyway."

"You mean the Faro?" She suddenly felt slightly idiotic for assuming he was interested in anything more than talk. Hell, for all she knew he might not be interested in women at all, although given his grin, that was probably wishful thinking on her part. "Sure. That'll be fun. I know the people there."

"All right then. I'll meet you there around seven—got to take care of some business here before I leave."

"Okay, good." She managed a grin that she hoped looked more friendly than relieved. "I'll see you then."

Taking Clayton Delaney to the Faro always made Nando feel a little like he was corrupting a minor. Tom had carded him the first time he'd come in, and he looked like he was considering doing it again.

Delaney, on the other hand, was having the time of his life. The Steinbruner brothers still hadn't figured out that they'd never be able to beat him at pool, and Clayton was finishing off a bottle of Avery White Rascal and cleaning their clocks without a dip in his angelic smile. Once upon a time, Nando might have tried to lay a few side bets, but by now everybody in the Faro knew about Delaney, and of course only someone seriously near-sighted or incurably optimistic would bet on the Steinbruners.

He leaned back against the bar and took a sip of his beer, an IPA with a full body that tasted like you could spread it on crackers. "So where's this one from?"

Tom shrugged, turning away from Deirdre reluctantly. "Colorado."

Nando's stomach gave a rumble, reminding him he hadn't yet gotten dinner. "You got any nachos tonight?"

Deirdre narrowed her eyes. "We do dinner now, you know. Clem's back there cooking up a full menu. If she finds out you ordered pre-made nachos instead of her chicken Acapulco, she's liable to skin you." She grinned up at him. "I can take your order back to the kitchen. Just tell me what you want."

Tom scowled in her direction. "You're not waiting tables anymore, Deirdre. You were up at five to open the roaster. You need to take it easy in the evening."

"Yes, sweetheart, I got the memo." She gave him a dry smile. "But this isn't a table, it's a barstool. And it won't take me any time at all. What do you want to eat, Nando?"

He shrugged. What he really wanted was nachos, but he figured keeping the peace was worth a compromise. "A burger, I guess. That won't get me in trouble with Clem, will it?"

"She'd probably rather serve you her chicken, but she still does great burgers." Deirdre pushed off her barstool and headed for the kitchen.

Tom watched her go with an expression of dazed appreciation that Nando found vaguely annoying. "Why the hell don't you just ask her to marry you and get it over with?" he growled.

Tom frowned. "I already did. We're working on a date. What's got your back up?"

"Nothing." He took another sip of the IPA, wishing he had something lighter. His stomach gave a quick twinge. "Everything. Hell, I'd still rather have the nachos."

"So what's new with the bookstore break-in?"

"Nothing much. I guess they're reopening next week."

"So I hear." Tom turned to fill an order for one of the barmaids.

Nando stared across the room again. Slow night. Nobody around. No Kit, anyway.

As if he'd conjured her up, Kit walked through the door, pushing the silken fall of dark hair away from her face. His pulse gave an unsettling thump, and he wondered if he should do anything about it. Like maybe go over and find a table for her.

She looks tired. Maybe she'd like a beer.

He started to move forward off the barstool, but she stayed standing in the doorway, peering around the room as if she were looking for someone.

A quick shiver moved down his backbone. *Looking for someone.* Maybe if he'd gotten lucky all of a sudden, she might be looking for him. It was always possible. He started to step forward again, as the door opened behind her.

The man who stepped inside was a stranger, a very large stranger. Well over six feet, muscled, wearing a loose jacket over a plaid shirt and slightly rumpled black pants. He had a well-trimmed beard and moustache, and his shaved head gleamed in the dim light of the Faro. Nando thought he saw the glint of an earring.

Kit glanced over her shoulder and smiled at the newcomer.

Nando felt the ache all the way to his toes. *What did you expect? You knew she'd find somebody. You knew it wouldn't be long.* He knew, but he hadn't let himself think about it much.

You knew it wouldn't be you. Yeah, that much he'd definitely known.

Tom leaned back on the bar, glancing toward the doorway. "Who's that with Kit?"

Nando shook his head. "Never saw him before. Maybe he's somebody she knows from the Woodrose."

"Maybe. Clem might know."

"Clem might know what?" Deirdre slid onto her stool again. "Your burger will be out in a minute."

Kit and the big man moved across to a table at the side of the room. Nando fought the urge to check his ID, just on general principles.

"Who the guy is with Kit. Have you ever seen him before?"

Deirdre glanced at the side of the room, frowning. "No, not really." She gave Nando a keen-eyed look that was too perceptive by half.

If he hadn't already ordered a burger, he'd have headed out the door. As it was, he'd lost any appetite he might have had. "I should have ordered fries," he grumbled.

"They come with the burger. Do you want me to find out who that is?"

He shrugged, doing his best imitation of indifference. "Whatever."

Deirdre shook her head, letting him know his imitation hadn't worked, and headed off toward the kitchen. Tom had busied himself at the other end of the bar. Nando wondered if his pariah status would last all night, or just until the guy's identity was nailed down and people stopped worrying that he might pick him up on a fugitive warrant.

Not that he would. Not that he wasn't tempted.

The kitchen door swung open and Deirdre headed back to the bar again, carrying a tray with his burger and fries. She gave him a questioning look.

He closed his eyes for a moment. "Okay, who is it?"

"Joe LeBlanc. The head chef at the Rose."

Nando felt a momentary relaxing of the tightness in his chest. "So they work together."

"Right." Deirdre's smile turned slightly wicked. "Of course, that's what Tom and I used to do. Work together."

He occupied himself with putting pickle and onion onto his burger. At least he wouldn't have to worry about bad breath tonight. The only one who was likely to be around him was Guinevere, and she didn't seem to notice what he smelled like.

He took a savage bite out of his dinner.

Joe made a quick survey of the Faro while he pulled out Kit's chair. Good-sized main room. Pool tables at one side, carved mahogany bar across the opposite wall. Around twenty tables, and it looked like they had a large patio, maybe for performances when the weather was more reliable.

All in all, he was inclined to agree with Clem's claim that the place was potentially a gold mine. Not that they did the kind of food that was his specialty, but it was the type of place where he liked to hang out after hours. He was as fond of a good burger as the next man.

Particularly when that good burger could be shared with a beautiful woman.

Kit Maldonado was, in fact, one very beautiful woman. The most stunning woman he'd seen in a long time. Dark curling hair that fell slightly below her shoulders. Eyes the color of strong coffee, with a faint almond shape. High, sculpted cheekbones and full lips.

He figured she knew how beautiful she was—how could she not? But she didn't seem to be overly obsessed with it. She didn't strike him as a woman who expected tributes, although she probably got more than a few.

He liked her. He'd like to get to know her better. He'd also like to know who the guy at the bar was who looked like he was wishing Joe instant death.

Judging from the way Kit avoided even a glance in his direction, Joe figured there'd been a relationship there at some point. It didn't seem to be current, though. If it had been, he'd have backed off. He hated being somebody's revenge fuck, not that it would be the first time that had happened.

Right now, he was just enjoying the moment, and the fact that he was interested in Kit Maldonado. He'd had a couple of years in the recent past when he wasn't interested in much of anything beyond finding the ultimate white truffle and the ultimate hit of cocaine.

He sighed. "Normality. Ain't it great?"

Kit's brow furrowed, "What?"

He could have kicked himself. No point in dragging her into his drama, even if it wasn't all that dramatic anymore.

The door to the kitchen flew open and a tiny brunette cyclone sped toward their table. "Joe," the cyclone yelled. "Jesus, look at you!"

"Clemencia!" He wrapped his arms around Clem's small waist when she got to his chair. Seated, he was almost the same height as she was. If he stood up, he'd have to bend over almost double to give her a hug.

She dropped into a chair beside him, running her hands through her short, spiked hair. At least she'd gotten rid of the neon-blue highlights she'd had the last time he saw her. She still had at least six earrings in each ear, though, plus another one through the eyebrow.

"So how are you?" She grinned at him. "You're in luck tonight. I've got some ranchero sauce that'll blow a hole in your palate. I've been serving it over chicken, but I can whip up some *huevos* if you want. Fresh queso fresco from a farm up by Mason."

Joe grinned back. Clem had one of those contagious smiles that only a dedicated depressive could ignore "I've got a hard on for one of your burgers, darlin'. You think maybe you could put a little of your ranchero on that?"

She nodded thoughtfully. "Right. And a little quesco fresco on top. Then run it under the broiler for a minute or so."

"Oh yeah. And then lettuce and tomato. Maybe some red onion..."

"Hey, I've got some roasted ancho chilies, too, just to give it a little bite."

He nodded. "Maybe chopped up in the burger."

Clem rubbed her hands together. "Yeah, it'll work. If it doesn't take the top of your head off, I might even add it to the menu."

"Hell, even if it does, it could be worth it."

Clem laughed again. "You want to come back to the kitchen and dish? You can dice the anchos."

Joe shrugged. "Maybe next time."

Clem glanced in Kit's direction. "Hey Kit, I didn't really forget about you, honest. You want a ranchero burger too?"

Kit shook her head, smiling. "Just a regular burger is fine. I need to get to sleep tonight, and I have a feeling that ranchero burger might fight me."

"So what is this?" Clem turned her bright black gaze back toward him again, looking a little like a hungry grackle. "A date?"

Joe managed to keep his smile in place. "You do get to the point, don't you Clemencia?"

She shrugged. "No time to be subtle. I've got burgers to fry."

"We're planning the menu for Allie's reception. I got the event center, just like you suggested," Kit said quickly.

A little too quickly, by his calculations. She seemed kind of eager to make their non-date status clear. All of a sudden he found himself wondering just how recent the relationship with the guy at the bar had been.

"Great." Clem slapped a hand on the table. "Let me go fix you some food and then I can kibitz." She pushed herself up in one quick motion, turning toward the kitchen as she did.

There was a beat of silence at the table after she'd left. "So how do you know Clem?" Kit asked, her smile a little too bright all of a sudden.

Joe shrugged. "From New Orleans. She was an intern at the hotel where I was chef, not in the same restaurant, though. We hung out together some." Actually, it was more that Clem had hung onto him, or tried to. She'd done her best to stop him from sliding down to disaster, but it wasn't a slide she could have prevented. Only he could have done that for himself.

On the other hand, she hadn't treated his slide into the abyss as some kind of spectator sport, the way his other so-called friends had. He owed her for that.

"So..." Kit licked her lips. She looked like she was trying to find a discreet way into the menu discussion.

He decided to cut her off at the pass. "So what brings you here to Konigsburg anyway? Allie?"

She shrugged. "Not exactly. I mean having her here was a draw, but it wasn't what really made me come. I just like the place."

"You're not from here?"

Her lips spread in a cautious grin. "Nah, it's like that James McMurtry song, 'I'm not from here, I just live here'."

He chuckled. "True for most of us, I guess. So where are you from?"

"San Antonio. My family owns a restaurant there, down in the Southtown area. Or they used to, anyway. My dad just sold out to a new owner."

"Was that unexpected?"

She sighed. "It was for me. I thought I might work there for a while, after I finished up my degree at UTSA. I was hoping maybe I could get into front-of-the-house stuff that way. It's probably just as well that I moved on, though. I mean, I started clearing tables there when I was eight. Maybe I needed to widen my horizons a little."

"Best way to learn the business. Be part of it from the ground up."

"Maybe." She glanced at the guy at the bar and back to him again. Definitely something going on there.

"My dad spent his life running that restaurant after he grew up in his parents' restaurant in Brownsville," she explained. "Our whole family sort of revolved around Antonio's Fine Mexican Cuisine. I'm looking for a job that goes in a different direction."

Joe let some of his incredulity show. "Like hostessing at the Rose?"

"Technically I'm managing the Rose." Kit shrugged. "Like I said, the Rose has terrific potential. I'd like to help make it the kind of restaurant it should be."

He narrowed his eyes. "Good luck with that. I have the feeling Mabel will fight you every inch of the way."

A waitress stepped up to the table, pencil and pad in hand. Joe blinked. She was almost as gorgeous as Kit. Holy crap, what did they have in the drinking water around here?

She smiled, upping her bombshell quotient by another twenty percent. "Hi, Kit. Can I get you guys something from the bar?"

Kit smiled back, and Joe suddenly felt as if he were a judge at the Miss Universe pageant. Except that he'd never be able to judge a contest between these two.

"Hi Deirdre, do you know Joe LeBlanc? He's the head chef at the Rose."

The Most Gorgeous Waitress In the Known Universe turned her smile on him, well-nigh frying his synapses. "Hi, Joe. I'm Deirdre Brandenburg. I own the coffee roaster next door. Would you like something to drink?"

"Um...sure." He blew out a quick breath. "Maybe a Coke."

Deirdre turned back to Kit. "How about you, Kit? Lonestar?"

Kit shook her head. "Not tonight. I'm being a wedding menu planner—better keep a clear head or we'll end up with sweetbreads or something."

Joe placed a hand over his heart. "While my sweetbreads have been known to bring grown men to tears, I think I can promise to avoid them for Miz Allie's wedding reception if that's your wish."

"Oh." Deirdre slid down into the chair next to Kit. "You're menu planning. Cool. Can I help?" She waved a hand at one of the other waitresses. "Marilyn? Could you bring over a couple of Cokes when you've got a minute?"

Joe gritted his teeth. "Sure. Join right in."

Clem pushed through the kitchen door carrying a tray and headed straight for their table. She plopped burger baskets in front of each of them and then took the chair opposite Deirdre. "So. Menu planning.

Let's get to it."

Joe picked up his burger. Visions of a tête-à-tête with Kit Maldonado were fast evaporating, but at least he could eat some first class Tex-Mex. He glanced around the table. Deirdre Brandenburg with her heart-stopping eyes. Kit Maldonado with hair like black silk. Clem Rodriguez, not in the same class, but someone you couldn't ignore. How did he end up with three women when he'd come in here hoping to focus on one?

Deirdre flicked a quick glance at the bar and then back, her smile widening, her eyes dewy with innocence. All of a sudden, he had a feeling she and Clem hadn't exactly dropped in by chance. More and more he wanted to know the identity of the guy at the bar.

"Have at it ladies," he growled. "I live to serve. Or to cook, in this instance." He took a bite of his burger. Damn, that ranchero sauce rocked!

Nando was home by ten thirty, cold sober and disgruntled. He'd had a good enough dinner. Deirdre was right—Clem's burgers were superlative. But then he'd had to sit and watch the guy at the table hold court with the three most interesting females in the place. And he said this knowing that Clem's interests weren't fastened on men at all, not that it was any of his business whom she pursued.

He considered getting a bottle of Shiner from the fridge but rejected the idea. Drinking alone every time he saw Kit Maldonado wasn't exactly the path to mental health.

He headed down the hall, pursued by Guinevere, then dropped into bed and managed to get to sleep after a half-hour or so of tossing. When he started dreaming of Kit he wasn't exactly shocked.

He was going through the same *I love you* routine when her cell phone began ringing.

"Answer it," he muttered, but she ignored him.

"C'mon Kit, answer it."

Dream Kit narrowed her eyes. "It's not my phone."

The ringtone finally woke him, and he glanced at the clock. Five. He groaned. What sadist called at this hour of the morning? Outside his window the early morning sunshine leaked lemon-colored light

Don't Forget Me

through the pecan tree in the backyard.

He flipped the phone open, recognizing the number. "Yeah."

"Better get down here," Toleffson's voice rumbled. "We got another one."

101

Chapter Nine

Not the least of the annoyances associated with the newest burglary was the fact that it screwed up Nando's plans for one of Allie Maldonado's breakfast scones and coffee. Of course, it had screwed up Allie Maldonado's plans a lot worse since it was her place that had gotten hit.

Now she stood in the doorway to her café, staring at the chaos littering the floor of Sweet Thing, one of Konigsburg's most popular breakfast and lunch places.

Nando took a quick survey of the two rooms. The damage in the dining area seemed to be confined to overturned tables and chairs, but there wasn't much in that room besides tables and chairs anyway. A few bud vases had been smashed, and it looked like some silverware and plastic water glasses had been tossed against the wall. Still, it could probably be cleaned up in a couple of hours.

The bakery retail section, with the empty pastry cases and the cash register, hadn't fared as well. Several jars of jelly and honey from a display cabinet at the side of the room had been smashed in the middle of the floor, forming a sticky, glutinous mass that smelled vaguely like peaches and sparkled with shards of glass. The cash register had been wrenched away from the wall and tossed into the gummy puddle. A chair from the other room lay on its back in front of one of the pastry cases. Judging from the cracks in the glass, the burglar had tried to smash the case with it.

The door to the kitchen stood open behind the front counter. Nando guessed the situation in there wouldn't be much better.

He turned back toward Allie. "I assume you don't leave money here at night, right?"

She shook her head. "I do a bank run after the lunch crowd leaves. There's no money here after closing. Hell, they couldn't even get any food. We lock the walk-in before we go home for the day."

"So what was taken?"

Allie rubbed the back of her neck. "Looks like some of the kitchen equipment is missing—a stand mixer and a couple of copper bowls. There may be some other stuff gone too. I'll check everything more thoroughly once we can clean the place up, but that's what I can see right now. I can't think of too much anyone would want to take from here, anyway."

Nando sighed, then stepped behind the counter and through the door into the kitchen. The floor seemed to be covered with a fine dust of white powder. Flour, he guessed, although they'd have to check it to be sure. Some pans, spoons, and rolling pins had been tossed around, along with a couple of chef's knives, but the chaos didn't seem to be as extensive, or as destructive, as it had been at the bookstore. He frowned, keeping to the rubber mat that ran alongside the sinks. Behind him, Delaney was taking pictures, the flash catching the gleaming metal surfaces of pots and pans on the shelves.

"He leave any kind of physical evidence this time?" Toleffson's voice rumbled from the doorway.

Nando shook his head. "Not that I've seen. He just grabbed some kitchen equipment, so far as Allie can tell. She's going to go over the place more thoroughly when she cleans up."

"How'd he get in?" Toleffson leaned against the doorway, watching Delaney's careful steps around the kitchen.

Nando nodded at the back entrance. "Broke the glass in the door. Just like he broke the window at Docia's, only this time he stuck a hand through and unlocked the door."

"Fingerprints?" The chief raised an eyebrow.

Nando shook his head again. "I checked. Door's been wiped clean."

Toleffson nodded absently. "Probably won't find anything anywhere else in here either. And out in the restaurant and the bakery, you'll have fingerprints from half the town."

"You want the county forensics lab to come in again?"

The chief took a deep breath, then blew it out. "Doesn't seem worth it. This looks more like a routine break-in, except for him tossing stuff around. Might not even be the same guy."

Yeah, right. Nando kept that opinion to himself. He figured the chief didn't really believe it either.

Toleffson stood again, his expression grim. "You and Delaney process the scene. I'll catch anything that comes in while you're here. Do it right, but see if you can finish by the end of the day so Allie can get her kitchen back."

"Got it." He watched the chief walk back into the sales area. After a moment, he followed him.

Allie still stood where he'd left her, staring around the room with what looked like a mixture of exasperation and disbelief. "What on earth was he after, anyway? It looks like all he did was throw things around."

"That might be most of what he did." Nando shrugged. "Could be simple vandalism. Maybe kids broke in hoping to find some money or something to eat, and then got pissed when they couldn't."

The door to the restaurant opened and Nando turned, ready to send civilian gawkers on their way.

Kit stood in the doorway, her eyes wide.

Nando took a deep breath while his pulse kicked up a notch, telling himself to cool it.

"Aunt Allie!" Kit started to walk toward her aunt, then paused, staring down at the goo-covered floor.

"This way." Nando took hold of her arm, walking her carefully around the edge of the room. Her skin was warm against his hand, her eyes staring up at him, wide and liquid. Like dark, rich coffee.

Do not *go there, asshole!*

"Here you go." He handed her across to Allie.

Kit wound her arms around her aunt, resting her forehead against the smaller woman's temple. "Are you okay?"

Allie took a breath, then turned her face against Kit's shoulder and let out a sob. Nando suddenly felt totally useless.

Toleffson shook his head. "Process the scene. Get pictures. Maybe we'll get lucky and he left something." He turned to Allie. "We'll try to get out of your hair as soon as we can, but you'll probably need to stay closed for a couple of days."

"A couple..." Allie turned stricken eyes toward him.

"Maybe. We'll see. We'll do our best to get out of your way." He tipped his hat hurriedly and stepped out the door, heading for the cruiser.

Nando's jaw tightened as Allie turned those stricken eyes in his direction again. If she started crying, he swore he'd head for the walk-in cooler, lock or no lock. "Would it help if you had the kitchen?"

"Had the kitchen?" Allie's forehead furrowed.

"If we processed the kitchen first, you could maybe get in there and clean up so you could use it later today. If you wanted to use it, that is."

"But what..." Allie shook her head. "Even if I could use the kitchen, I don't have any place to sell what we cook." She gestured at the sticky lake of jam in the middle of the floor, the cash register jutting out of the center like an island volcano. "I'll probably have to have a professional cleaning crew come in to take care of that. And I don't even know if the cash register is still working." Her lower lip began to tremble again.

"But if you had the kitchen, you could do your restaurant orders. And the orders for the B and B's." Kit put her arm around Allie's shoulders. "You could at least do something, Aunt Allie. And then you'd be ready to go once the cleaning crew took care of everything else."

"Oh god." Allie sighed. "Would you believe I forgot all about the restaurant orders? The B and B orders were delivered last night, but the restaurants pick up around nine or ten. I can't get anything to them today. I'll have to call them." She pressed a hand to her lips.

"It'll be all right," Kit soothed. "They've probably heard about it by now, the ones in town anyway. We'll call them, and you can give them something extra to make up for it once the kitchen is clear again."

"Clayton and I will get right on it, Allie," Nando said quickly. "Doesn't look like there's much damage in the kitchen. We'll do our best to get out of there by this afternoon."

Allie gave him a tremulous smile. "Thanks, Nando, I really appreciate it."

Nando started to smile back, then stopped. Kit watched him, her lips curving up ever so slightly. He blew out a breath. "That's okay. I'll let you know when we're done."

The corners of Kit's mouth moved up a bit farther. "Thanks, Officer."

Nando licked his lips. "You're welcome, ma'am."

He turned toward the kitchen just as the front door opened. Wonder Dentist stepped in, his thinning brown hair slightly windblown, his glasses crooked.

Allie looked up at him, narrowing her eyes dangerously as she wiped her nose with a tissue. "Steve, I swear to god, if you say anything sarcastic, I will brain you with the nearest soup pan."

Wonder blinked at her, then extended his arms. "Come here, baby, you look like you could use a hug."

Allie hiccupped another sob, then threw herself into his arms. Kit sniffed. Even Delaney looked a little bright eyed.

Nando sighed. "Come on, kid, let's see if we can finish going over this place before something else pops up."

Kit had considered staying home from work so that she could help Allie, but Allie herself had vetoed the idea.

"It's bad enough the Rose won't get any bread today," she reasoned. "I don't want them to be short a manager too. Besides there's nothing either of us can do here until Nando finishes. And after that it'll be mainly clean-up and prep work for tomorrow."

She managed to get to the hostess desk only a little later than usual, although it was still late enough to get a narrow-eyed look from Mabel. When Joe described the day's specials, he also explained the bread situation.

"Gee, should we tell the customers?" Elaine asked. "They might like to know."

"Tell them if they ask, but don't mention it up front. Allie Maldonado doesn't need any extra grief over this." Joe's eyes flicked to Kit and then back to his scribbled list of specials.

The lunch crowd was robust and largely happy, and apparently unconcerned about the origin of their bread. Kit couldn't decide whether that was good for Allie or not, but at least it was good for the Rose.

She'd meant to talk to Joe about what was going on at the bakery, but things were too busy in the restaurant for her to break away. She felt a little guilty about the way their "date" had turned out the night before. She wasn't sure what Deirdre and Clem were up to—or even that they were up to anything specific—but she definitely didn't want Joe to get caught in some weird situation with her and Nando.

Of course, in reality, there was no situation between her and Nando, weird or otherwise. He'd been good with Allie when she needed someone to reassure her. He'd seen how upset she was and done his best to help.

But she already knew he was a good cop. It was when he wasn't being a cop that they had problems. She closed her eyes for a moment, remembering.

Nando's body moving in the twilight shadows, the sound of cicadas in the trees, the scent of honeysuckle somewhere back in the woods.

"Are you sure this is safe?"

His smile flashing in the gathering darkness. "Trust me, babe, nobody comes to this side of the lake. And we've got the perfect cover."

The pattern of the live oak leaves against the darkening night sky as he leaned down, lips against her breast, warm breath on her nipple as it hardened to a tight bud.

Sighing, "Catarina, Catarina, you'll drive me crazy yet."

And Kit running her hands across his chest, feeling the smooth swell of muscle and bone beneath her palms, the warmth of his skin as she slid her hands down to cup him. "We'll go together then."

A confusion of voices drifted through the dining room door, couples heading her way. Kit jerked herself back to the present. Okay, they'd been hot back when they'd been together. Thinking about it didn't help her figure out where they were today. Or where she wanted them to be.

For the rest of the lunch rush, she threw herself into being a hostess-sommelier and part-time busboy, pouring water and tea, bringing bottles of wine, helping the ever-leering Gabriel clear tables. She resolutely set Nando Avrogado to the side.

Midway through the afternoon, Joe strolled through the tables, checking on the diners, smiling as he asked about their meals. Some of them knew him now, and he paused to talk to them.

Kit watched him. Olive skin, dark blue eyes, dark moustache and beard. The shaved head and gold ring in his ear gave him a slightly piratical look, as if he'd be collecting the ladies' jewelry on his next pass through the dining room.

Good-looking man. Leaking testosterone from every pore. And maybe interested in her, given the smile he had when his eyes followed her around the dining room. He was just what she needed. A fling, nothing serious, no drama.

He glanced up at her briefly, dark blue eyes dancing as he smiled.

She waited for the quick jolt of adrenaline in her belly, the sudden jump in her pulse. All those feelings she should have but didn't.

All those feelings she'd once had with Nando. *Once had?* The feelings hadn't exactly gone away, no matter how much she wanted to pretend otherwise.

Kit sighed. *Don't go there, Catarina, do* not *go there.* Joe LeBlanc was a nice guy, someone she could be interested in who didn't come with a lot of excess baggage. Now if she could only get her heart and the rest of her body to go along with it, maybe she could even do more than pretend that was the case.

Joe stepped into Clem's kitchen around two, after her lunch rush and long enough before dinner that he probably wouldn't seriously interrupt her preparations.

His own lunch rush had been interesting, given they had no bread for sandwiches. After a heads-up from both Allie and Kit, he'd sent Darcy to the nearest HEB to stock up on commercial hard rolls. The lunch crowd hadn't been happy about the absence of Allie's ciabatta bread, but it was the best he could do on short notice. At least Allie seemed to think she'd be able to fill the orders for tomorrow. As crises went, it was interesting. He usually had more trouble with his fishmonger than his baker.

He'd left his chef's coat back at the Rose when he'd decided to drive into Konigsburg, but he hadn't bothered to change out of the pants and shoes he used in the kitchen, which meant he entered the Faro in running shoes and a pair of loose black canvas pants with New Orleans Saints logos running up the seams. A couple of elderly ladies having chicken salad sandwiches and iced tea goggled slightly, but nobody else seemed to notice. He raised an eyebrow at Tom Ames behind the bar. "Clem back in the kitchen?"

Ames shrugged. "Far as I know." He went back to loading beer into his cooler.

Clem glanced up as the door swished closed behind him. She stood at her prep table surrounded by piles of chopped carrots, onions and peppers. A round, grey-haired woman stood next to her, while a middle-aged man with a sizeable beer gut loaded the dishwasher behind them. "Hey Joe. Don't you need to get ready for your lunch crowd tomorrow?"

He shrugged. "That's why the good lord made prep cooks. Thought I'd come in to talk over a couple of things. Need a hand?"

Clem shrugged. "Sure. You can do lettuce." She nodded toward a stack of red leaf and romaine on the other prep table, then turned to the gray-haired woman currently putting the finishing touches on a tray of handmade hamburger patties. "Put those into the freezer, then take a break, Margene. Tell Tom to give you some of that blackberry soda from Deirdre's shop."

Margene hefted the tray of patties toward the walk-in cooler at the side.

Clem glanced back at the man loading the dishwasher. "Beat it Leon. You can do the rest later."

Leon looked like he might protest, then thought better of it. He grabbed a broom from a rack beside the door and headed out into the bar.

Joe took a knife off the magnetic strip above Clem's table and pulled a head of lettuce onto the chopping board. "So what's on your menu for tonight?"

"Spaghetti Bolognese, shrimp tacos, and the usual: burgers and fries, salads, enchiladas, bar food. How about you?"

Joe gave her a dry smile. "Special tomorrow's PEI mussels with fennel cream sauce."

Clem shrugged. "Not much call for mussels around this place. So why are you here, aside from your crying need to get back into the food prep business?"

He split the head of romaine into quarters. "I want to know what was going on last night. How come my dinner with a good-looking, unattached woman suddenly became a dinner for four and a spirited discussion of appetizers."

Clem grinned at the onion she was chopping. "We came up with a nice menu, didn't we? Our advice was helpful."

"Your advice was fine. It's the timing I'm interested in." He gave another lettuce head a solid thump. "Along with the identity of the guy at the bar."

Clem's grin turned wry. "Noticed that, did you?"

"Noticed him. Who is he?"

"Nando Avrogado. He's one of the town cops. A good one."

"How does he fit into the picture with Kit Maldonado?"

Clem shrugged. "He's her former squeeze. I don't know much about it myself, didn't know either one of them when it was going on. But apparently it was hot and heavy for a while."

"When?"

"Year or so ago."

"So you and Deirdre decided they need to be back together?" Joe ripped the current head of romaine into a pile of chunks. "Thus your unexpected presence at the table last night?"

"I haven't entirely figured out how I feel about the two of them." She began chopping the onion into a tiny dice. "I think Deirdre would like it see them mend their differences. Nando's a friend of Tom's, and Deirdre's a hopeless romantic. But I sat down with you yesterday because I was curious about what kind of menu you'd come up with. On the other hand..."

"On the other hand," he prompted.

Clem shrugged again. "I like Nando. He's a good cop and a decent guy. And he seems hung up on Kit Maldonado. She could do worse."

Joe gave her a long look. "Does this mean you like him more than me?"

She threw her head back and guffawed. "Geez, just listen to yourself! 'Mama always liked him best.' Well, I like you both the same, how's that? Plus I'd be willing to bet that Nando's romanesca sauce can't lay a finger on yours."

"Damn straight." Joe grinned as he dismembered another head of red leaf. "I'm getting mixed messages here. Am I supposed to back off from Kit Maldonado?"

Clem shook her head. "Up to you, I guess. Kit's a big girl. She can make her own decisions. So can Nando, as far as that goes. If they're going to get together, my guess is you won't represent much of a hindrance. Might be a little battering for your ego, though."

He raised an eyebrow. "You don't rate my chances too high?"

She paused, laying her chef's knife on the prep table. "I don't rate your interest too high. Are you honestly telling me you'd fight with Nando over Kit, that you think she's the one true girl for you?"

Joe started piling lettuce chunks in a large stainless steel bowl. "Maybe not." He paused for a moment, then shook his head. "Probably not. Nice girl, though. Got a lot going for her."

"You think she's your kind of woman?"

He shrugged. "She could be. I might give it a try. Make the cop work for it. What's the harm?"

Clem narrowed her eyes. "So what happens to Kit while you guys are having your little *my dick's bigger than your dick* competition? How do you keep her from getting hurt? Suppose she starts thinking you're more serious than you are?"

Joe's smile was dry. "She might, but I'm not betting on it right now. I don't think either one of us is taking it all that seriously. I think it's a sort of wait and see kind of thing. How about you, Clemencia. Still seeing the lovely Lucinda?"

Clem gave him a lazy smile of her own. "Someday, Joseph, you'll find somebody who'll make you want to stop tomcatting around. At which time, you should only be as half as happy as Lu and me."

Joe laughed as he slid back onto an even keel again. "From your lips to God's ear, darlin', from your lips to God's ear."

Brody studied the small china bowl he'd taken from Allie Maldonado's bakery. He had no idea why he'd picked it up rather than smashing it against the wall. He'd dropped the rest of the loot in the abandoned dump outside Oltdorf, as he'd done with the stuff from the bookstore. He'd never understood the attraction of trophies for criminals, particularly since they made it so much easier for the cops to pin down guilt when they were found.

He didn't exactly consider himself a criminal anyway. Criminals were losers. He was someone who'd had a run of bad luck.

Still, he placed the china bowl inside his kitchen cabinet, next to the small silver box he'd lifted from Docia Kent's bookstore. That box had been even more satisfying. The symbolism there was clear—*I can take what's valuable to you and you can't do a damn thing to stop me.*

All in all the break-in at the bookstore had been much more fun than the one at the bakery, but that was how it had to be. Trashing the bookstore had settled some scores, but the bakery had established a pattern, made it all less personal. Now he could go on to hit a few more places, saving the biggest for last. With any luck, no one would make any connections. They'd just think it was some lunatic burglar who got off on breaking things up.

He knew what they'd be thinking now. Kids with too much time on their hands. Or dopers. Somebody out to destroy things for the fun of it or looking for money and too stoned not to realize they were in the wrong place. No one would see it for what it was—a strategy. It would divert attention, and suspicion, until he was long gone.

He'd have to be careful, of course. The new chief wasn't stupid, although he wasn't as smart as he thought he was. Things would have been much easier if that moron Ham Linklatter had gotten the chief's job, but you played with the cards you were dealt.

Brody didn't doubt for a moment that he'd succeed in the end. After all, they owed him. All of them. Every last citizen of Konigsburg owed him big time.

Chapter Ten

Toleffson called a meeting early the next morning so that Ham, who had night duty that week, could be around before he headed home for the day. He'd even brought in the two part-timers, Dawson Kirk and Rollie Martinez, who mostly worked weekends.

Helen passed around some of her more-than-adequate coffee and some cinnamon rolls from the supermarket that didn't begin to measure up to Allie Maldonado's scones. Nando felt annoyed all over again since Allie wouldn't be selling any of those scones for at least another couple of days, given that it was Friday and she'd stay closed for the weekend.

"Okay," Toleffson began, "let me summarize what we've got on this guy."

The chief's summaries were always complete and focused, a model for somebody like Ham who tended to ramble off the track. He outlined what little he'd gotten back so far from the forensics lab, the minimal physical evidence they'd been able to find in either the bookstore or the bakery, and the sum total of it all, which was basically squat.

"We sure it's the same guy both places?" Rollie asked.

Toleffson gave him a grim look. "As sure as we can be without any physical evidence at the bakery."

Ham snickered. "Too bad the guy didn't feel like taking another dump."

The others glanced at Nando a little nervously, but he managed to keep his expression bland.

Toleffson cleared his throat. "You're right. Too bad he didn't. It gave us DNA evidence from the first scene. That's a valuable commodity. If he'd left us some more, we wouldn't be wondering if it was the same guy." He gave Ham a long, cool look.

Ham flushed dirty pink, then faded back to his usual pale. "Just seems a little dumb, picking up pieces of shit."

Toleffson rubbed his eyes. "Ham, what part of DNA evidence don't you understand? If the guy's in the system, we can find him now, as soon as the lab gets the DNA report done. From our point of view, that would be a good thing."

Ham subsided into disgruntled silence.

The chief turned back to the rest of them. "Okay, we've got two ways to go with this. First is to start talking to people, see if anybody's heard anything. Somebody bragging, somebody who wasn't where they were supposed to be. You know the drill."

Delaney nodded quickly. The others looked slightly bored. They did indeed know the drill, which didn't make it any less monotonous. Plus it probably wouldn't get them much.

"The other thing is to start looking at the stores along Main a lot more closely when you're on night patrol. So far both places he's hit have been on Main Street. He may or may not stick with that. But from now on, spend a little more time checking there. He can't be doing this in total darkness—he's got to be using a flashlight at least. If you see any lights where you don't usually see them, find out what's going on. And don't forget to drive up the alleys. He's been going in from the back, so you may not see him if you just stay on Main. If you do see anything, call it in and get backup. For the next couple of weeks, Dawson and Rollie are going to alternate doing night patrol along with whichever one of you full-timers has the duty, so we'll always have somebody out there. Keep in contact with each other. Make sure you drive up Main at least every thirty minutes or so."

Helen narrowed her eyes. "You need me to stay on the desk at night?"

The chief shook his head. "The call forwarding we're using now should be enough, and the county 911 center. This hasn't turned into a crisis yet, just a serious nuisance."

"Do we know for sure yet what was taken from the bookstore or the bakery?" Nando asked.

Toleffson frowned. "The ebook readers and MP3 players from the bookstore. We've put out an alert to pawn shops, but we can't do much if he sells the stuff online. The only other thing Docia couldn't find was a silver box she used for miscellaneous things next to the cash register. And she's not sure when she saw it last—it could have been missing before the break-in."

"And Allie?"

"She's still sorting through the mess. Nothing is missing besides the copper bowls and the mixer, so far as she knows." The chief narrowed his eyes, watching Nando. "So?"

"So why's he doing this exactly?" Nando leaned back in his chair. "I mean it could be kids, somebody who just likes to smash things up. But if it's kids, we should hear about it—kids can't keep quiet, as a rule."

"Dope fiends," Ham said flatly.

The chief turned toward him. "Excuse me?"

"Dope fiends looking for money. And then trashing the place after they don't find any. That's what dope fiends do."

Nando thought about asking Ham how many dope fiends he'd met, but he decided the possible amusement wasn't worth it.

"But why would dopers knock over a bookstore and a bakery? Wouldn't they go for someplace that actually might have some money around, like a liquor store or a Stop 'n Go?" Delaney looked like he expected Ham to take that question seriously.

"Dope fiends don't think like that. Dope fiends don't think at all." Ham gave him a faintly condescending smile. "They're too hopped up on dope. They just break in places to steal stuff."

Toleffson pinched the bridge of his nose. Nando wondered if he ever regretted not firing Ham when he'd had the chance, back when the previous mayor had been dragged off by the Rangers for corruption. "While dope addicts are a possibility, I tend to agree with Clayton that they're not the most likely possibility we've got. So either this is somebody like teenagers who are vandalizing stores for fun or…" He paused.

"Or…" Nando prompted.

"Or somebody who's got his own agenda. Which we have yet to figure out."

As the meeting broke up, Nando caught the chief's eye. He assumed they were both thinking the same thing—figuring out what that agenda was would simplify figuring out who was smashing up the shops in the first place.

115

Kit came home around seven to find Allie slumped at the kitchen table. Wonder was standing at the stove, staring pensively at a frozen pizza.

Sighing, Kit removed it from his hands and turned on the oven. "Did you get into the kitchen in time to do any of tomorrow's baking?"

Allie nodded. "We got all the B and B stuff done, and a lot of the stuff for the restaurants is ready to go into the ovens first thing tomorrow. Since we couldn't cook anything for Sweet Thing, we had lots and lots of time." She lowered her head to her folded arms.

Wonder frowned as he watched Kit take the pizza out of the box. "I could have done that. I'm just shell-shocked from an afternoon spent defrosting blueberries. The whole damn state of Maine is down in that kitchen."

"They're Texas blueberries," Allie muttered. "Locally grown, if not exactly in season. We're nothing if not responsible."

Wonder turned to look at her, his frown transforming into concern. He raised one hand as if he wanted to pat her shoulder but didn't know exactly how well that would be received.

Kit sighed again. "Why don't you open a bottle of wine, Steve? And get yourself a beer. This should be ready in a few minutes." Once Wonder was on his way to the dining room, she sat down beside her aunt. "So tell me the rest of it—when do you open again?"

Allie shook her head without raising it from the table. "I've got a professional cleaning crew coming in tomorrow. I don't know how long it'll take them to clean up the mess in the bakery. I've also got insurance adjustors to deal with, and repair people for the cash register. I still hope we can open next week, though." She raised her head slightly, enough so that Kit could see her eyes above one arm. "I can't afford to stay closed too long, even if I can keep my restaurant and B and B customers."

Kit began to rub her shoulders. "There's no reason for you to lose the restaurants and B and B's. And all the other customers will come back as soon as you open—nobody else can do your scones. You should have a grand reopening party. Bake something special. I guarantee everybody in town will be there."

Allie groaned again, although she moved her back slightly to give Kit better access to her shoulders. "I can't think about that now, any of that. I'm too tired." She half-turned her head, looking back at Kit. "Tell me something that will make me happy."

"I sat down with Joe LeBlanc last night and worked out some menu possibilities. I think you'll really like them."

Allie stared, her eyes suddenly wide open. "Menu?"

Kit took a deep breath. "For the wedding. *Your* wedding. Joe's going to do the cooking himself. And Clem Rodriguez had some suggestions too. She'd be a great person to cater your shower."

"Shower?" Allie squeaked. "We have to plan a shower? Oh god, there's no time!"

"Allie, come on," Kit said firmly. "You don't do the shower, your friends do. And this is going to be a wonderful wedding. Everything's falling into place. You won't have to do anything about the food except finalize the menu, and it's a terrific menu, believe me. We got help from Deirdre and Clem."

Allie sat up, chewing on her lip. "I don't even know if I can afford Joe LeBlanc anymore. Not until I get the bill for the shop. Maybe we should postpone."

"*I* can afford Joe LeBlanc," Wonder said flatly, walking back from the dining room. He put a glass of red wine in front of Allie. "I'm paying for at least half of this shindig, and if it'll move things along I'll pay for the whole thing." He turned to Kit. "What's on the menu you worked out?"

"You can have a choice between redfish or smoked beef tenderloin. Or he said he could do chicken in Madeira sauce instead of one of those if you'd rather."

"Redfish and beef." Wonder nodded. "That'll take care of Calthorpe Toleffson, my non-red-meat-eating best man, and me, the red-meat-eating groom. What else?"

"Grilled asparagus," Kit counted off on her fingers. "Roasted fingerling potatoes. Wedge salads with some kind of special dressing that Joe didn't want to give too many details on, but I think it involves a balsamic reduction. Wedding cake and sorbet for dessert, with chocolates and mints for after. And then chipotle sliders and shrimp quesadillas at midnight if you plan on dancing until dawn."

"Oh." Allie chewed her lip again. "That sounds..."

"Delicious," Wonder snapped. "We'll take it."

Allie stared up at him, blinking.

He knelt beside her, taking her hands in his. "Sweetheart, this has dragged on for a long time already. If you really want to get married, let Kit do her thing."

Allie was still blinking nervously. "I do want to get married. Of course I want to get married. And Kit has taken a lot of the pressure off me." She raised her gaze to Kit. "What's left to get set up? Flowers? What about flowers?"

Kit shrugged. "The event center has a deal with a florist here in town, Clarice Baumgarten. I saw some pictures of her stuff and it looks okay."

Wonder shrugged. "Got an overbite she could use as a bottle opener."

Allie narrowed her eyes.

"I guess that's not relevant," he said quickly. "I'm sure her flowers are superb."

"What are your colors?"

Allie's eyes widened to that panicked look again. She pulled her hands away from Wonder. "Colors? I don't know. I didn't think."

"Orange and white," Wonder blurted. "Go Longhorns."

Allie stared at him open-mouthed. "No. That can't be right."

"Then pick two colors of your own," he said patiently.

"Lavender," she blurted. "And...silver."

"Lavender it is." Wonder winked at Kit over Allie's head. "What else you got?"

"Um..." Kit ran through her mental checklist a little desperately. "Who do you want to perform the ceremony?"

Wonder shrugged. "I'll get Judge Alaniz. He owes me. I came in on the weekend to fix his broken molar."

"You'll need to get the license."

"We can do that next week," he said quickly. "I'll put it on my calendar."

"I don't know if I can—" Allie began.

"You can," Wonder said flatly. "What else?"

"Okay. Attendants?" Kit checked back and forth between them.

Wonder nodded. "Already taken care of. Cal and Docia on lead, the rest of the Toleffsons on backup."

"Right. So they'll take care of the bachelor and bachelorette parties."

"Parties?" Allie gasped.

"They'll take care of them," Kit repeated more firmly. "You don't need to worry."

"Anything else?" Wonder raised an eyebrow.

"The wedding cake. And the groom's cake." Kit turned to Allie. "That's you, Aunt Allie. Nobody else would dare."

"Oh god," Allie whispered. "They've got to be perfect. When will I have time to plan it?"

"This weekend," Wonder said firmly.

Allie stared up at him.

"Think about it. The shop won't be open again until next week. Denny can oversee the bread for the restaurants and you've already done the stuff for the B and B's. You've got time to sit and design cakes while the cleaning crew takes care of whatever the hell that bastard did to Sweet Thing."

Allie blew out a long breath. "You've got a point."

"Of course I do." Wonder topped off her glass. "I've also got a lot more wine where this came from. Maybe by the time you've finished the bottle, I'll have convinced you that bride and groom statuettes based on *Battlestar Galactica* aren't really that weird. Plus I've got some definite ideas about that groom's cake."

"Oh Steve, not German chocolate," Allie groaned.

"I'm flexible." Wonder shrugged. "Black forest also works. C'mon, grab some pizza and we'll head over to my place."

Allie sighed, pushing herself to her feet. "Just let me get my drawing pad and we can go." She headed down the hall toward her office.

Wonder turned to Kit. "Nice going, kid. I'm beginning to believe this is actually going to happen. After the world's longest engagement."

"Look, I hate to bring this up, but does she actually have a wedding dress?" Kit murmured. "Or bridesmaid dresses?"

Wonder sighed. "I knew it was too good to last. I don't think she's actually done anything about that. Can't she just wear something she's got? I mean she's got all these dresses already—wouldn't one of them be okay as a wedding dress?"

Kit narrowed her eyes.

"No, no," he said hurriedly. "Of course not. I'll see if I can find a way to work the question in this weekend."

Allie's footsteps sounded in the hall as Kit shook her head. "Don't worry about it. I've got an idea. Leave it to me."

"Gladly." Wonder turned as Allie stepped back into the room again. "Come on, cupcake, let's head back to the ranch."

Allie sighed. "Don't call me cupcake, okay? Right now I feel more like a piece of flatbread." But she gave Kit a slightly tremulous smile as they headed out the front door.

Kent's Hill Country Books reopened on Saturday. Nando had to hand it to Docia—she'd found a way to make sure the place would be packed even if she wasn't serving cake and cookies. She'd landed a signing by an Austin historian who specialized in writing spicy chronicles of Texas. He had a new book about a notorious brothel located midway between Konigsburg and Marble Falls that was guaranteed to attract both locals and tourists, the tourists to read about the racy past and the locals to see if any of their relatives showed up in the anecdotes.

Janie Toleffson kept an eye on the book-signing table, while Docia ran the cash register. Nando saw a fair number of copies going out the door. Briefly, he wondered if he ought to pick up a copy for his mom, but then decided against it. His dad would probably scalp him if he did, given the number of Avrogados who undoubtedly studded the index.

He waited for a lull in the traffic at the register, then leaned against the wall beside it. "Looks like you've got a hit."

"Yeah, he's selling a lot of copies. Of course some people may try returning them when they find out Uncle Joe didn't make it into the list of the madame's customers." Docia flashed him a quick smile. "You want a copy, Nando? I'd even let you check the index first."

"Don't tempt me. My ancestors were probably regulars." He grinned in what he hoped was a reassuring way.

Apparently, it wasn't reassuring enough. Docia's smile faded slightly. "So what do you need to ask me? You're not in uniform, but I assume it's something to do with the break-in."

He sighed. "It's my day off. I talked to Janie last week, but I wanted to talk to you. Particularly now that Allie's been hit too."

Docia's jaw tightened. "I heard. You think it's the same person?"

"Seems likely. We haven't had a lot of vandalism around here up to now."

"So what do you want to know?"

"Mostly if you have any ideas about who could be behind this. Anybody who's got a grudge against you and Allie, say. Disgruntled customers, teenagers you threw out for messing up the merchandise, people who don't like your taste in books, former employees, anybody like that."

Docia shook her head. "I guess I've lived a pretty bland life. I mean Dub Tyler might be pissed over that map of his I gave to the historical society, but they decided it was possibly counterfeit anyway so it wasn't worth as much as he thought it was. Besides, he moved to Dripping Springs after that whole thing with Brody." She sighed. "That's the only scary thing that's every happened to me—the thing with Brody. And I don't know how it could have any connection to this. Sorry, Nando."

"Right." Nando nodded slowly. "I kind of figured it was a long-shot, but I thought I'd ask anyway. If anything occurs to you..."

"I'll tell you. Or Erik." She gave him a quick smile, then glanced at something over his shoulder, her eyes widening.

Nando turned. Kit was standing behind him. "Oh. Hi," he blurted.

"Hi." She licked her lips, then turned quickly. "Have you got a minute, Docia? I've got a favor to ask."

Docia gave her another smile. "Sure. But I have to stay here in case we get more people buying brothel books."

Kit blinked, then refocused. "Oh. Okay. I wanted to ask you if you'd give a shower for Allie."

"Sure." Docia shrugged. "I'd planned on it anyway. Is there some kind of problem?"

"Not exactly. But I had a sort of special shower in mind."

"Okay, now you've got my complete attention." Docia beckoned to

Janie, still standing near the historian's elbow, although he didn't appear to need any help. "Let's head back to the storeroom for a minute." She gave Nando a quick smile. "Unless you've got anything else you need to ask me."

He shook his head. "Not right now."

"Okay, then, lead on. This sounds like more fun than anything else I've talked about in a while."

He watched the two women walk away toward the door at the side, Docia's fiery red hair followed by Kit's sleek black curls. Something inside his chest tightened painfully. *Enough already.*

"Want a book, Nando? Guaranteed to hold your interest until you finish checking the index." Janie gave him a smile that seemed almost sympathetic.

He sighed, running a hand through his hair. "Not today, thanks. Maybe I'll give it to my dad for Christmas, as long as I've got a good head start."

He heard Janie's chuckle behind him as he headed out the door.

Chapter Eleven

Saturdays at the Woodrose were always hectic. The guests who came in for the three-day weekend packages were out trying to get their money's worth, soaking in the spa the inn had a contract with, playing nine holes of golf on the private course where the inn had privileges, and, of course, sampling the cuisine. The Rose had gotten a good review in the *Dallas Morning News* that brought a lot of people in from the surrounding motels as well as their own guests. Kit spent the morning answering the phone to take reservations in the restaurant for lunch, as well as dealing with minor emergencies in housekeeping that were usually Mabel's business. Mabel herself was apparently off supervising the set-up for a wedding in the event center. Kit wasn't sure when she'd become responsible for managing the inn when the real manager was missing, but everybody seemed to accept it as a given.

Around ten Mr. Didrikson, the gardener, waylaid her in the lobby, gray hair bristling. "Where's Morgenstern? I got a load of fertilizer I need her to sign off on."

"She's down at the event center until two," Kit explained. "Why don't you call her?"

"Tried that. She's not answering her phone."

Kit punched in the numbers for Mabel's cell without a lot of hope. If she was screening Didrikson's calls, she'd probably be even less likely to take Kit's. After five rings, Kit left a message on the voice mail, then turned back to the gardener. "I don't know what's going on. She's not answering me either."

"So? You can sign instead."

Kit shook her head. "I'm sorry. I don't have the authority to do that."

"Ah for Christ's sake," Didrikson growled. "Took me a week to get her to agree to the order. Now she won't pay? Pretty soon nobody's gonna deliver out here."

He was, of course, absolutely right, but that didn't mean she could get away with signing for an order. "Look, go down to the event center. Mabel's got to be there—there's a wedding going on. Just tell her to sign the invoice. She'll want to get you out of there, believe me." Considering Didrikson's grass-stained jeans and work shirt, Mabel would probably sign anything he shoved her way if it meant she could shoo him out the door.

Didrikson shot her a surprisingly sharp glance. "Might work. Thanks."

"Sure." Kit blew out a breath and went back to answering the phone.

Every table in the restaurant was full for lunch. Elaine was practically in tears. So were her customers. Philip's glares darkened to thunderous as the afternoon went on. The only thing that hadn't gotten the highest rating in the last review had been service, and Kit could see why. She poured, soothed, cleared, and brought orders from the kitchen in between crossing off reservations and refusing the not-very-subtle bribes she was offered to move people up the waiting list.

She gritted her teeth as she surveyed the room. Somehow she had to get Mabel to hire more wait staff. And soon.

By three the room was clear again and Gabriel ran the vacuum sweeper to gather up the last crumbs. Kit collapsed into a booth. At least the reservation pressure should die down since the Rose was closed on Sundays. On the other hand, she'd already begun to pick up some reservations for Monday. At least the food was a rousing success. After a moment, Joe thumped down across from her.

"Here," he said, extending a plate with a chicken Panini and a glass of tea, "eat."

She shook her head. "I'm too tired. I'll eat when I finish the reservations."

He narrowed his eyes, studying her, then shook his head. "Nope. Sorry, *too tired to eat* doesn't work for me." He took hold of her hand, pulling her up from the booth as he picked up the sandwich. "Come on. Bring the tea."

Kit didn't have the strength to argue. She followed him out the French doors to the patio where Didrikson or somebody else had set up a group of umbrella tables. Joe pulled out a chair for her, then plopped down beside her. "Now, take a breath, look at the view."

The green lawn that Didrikson had mowed into velvet rolled down to the white gravel road below. On the olive-colored hills across the valley she saw cattle grazing, moving slowly along the limestone outcroppings. Her shoulders seemed to loosen.

"Now—" Joe handed her the sandwich again, "—eat."

She did. The chicken was still faintly warm from the press. Slices of Emmentaler were melted against sliced pears. Kit closed her eyes. "This is heavenly."

"I don't know that I'd go that far, but it worked. At least we got Allie's bread today." Joe leaned back in his chair, staring out across the valley.

"She's got her kitchen back but nothing else is ready to open yet. The professionals are going to clean up this weekend. I think she said Tuesday for the reopening."

"Don't suppose they've figured out who the asshole was who did it?"

Kit shook her head. "Not that I've heard. And I would have heard—everybody would have." She took another bite, then managed to stop herself from gobbling, but it wasn't easy.

Joe grinned. "Take your time, darlin'. There's more where that came from, believe me."

"I didn't have much breakfast, and there wasn't time to grab anything during lunch today. It was a madhouse."

"Yeah." His face darkened. "You talk to Mabel about hiring more people?"

"I meant to, but I got sidetracked with the wedding and then the break-in. Plus she wasn't around all morning."

"Time to do it, then. I've seen the restaurant receipts. I'm pretty sure we can afford another waiter and a second busboy. Hell, we can afford more than that." He glanced down at her almost-empty plate. "What else can I do for you, darlin'?"

A quick shiver moved down her spine. "You mean food?"

He gave her a slow smile. "Sure. Food's a good start. Can't go wrong there. At least I usually don't."

She frowned, trying to remember how this game was played. Maybe she needed some practice. Except that she didn't feel like practicing with Joe. "Food is...fine. For now."

125

The French door swung open behind them, and Darcy leaned through. "Hey, chef, Jorge is claiming those scallops we ordered are for appetizers. Is that right?"

"Hell," Joe muttered. "Talk about your lousy timing. Okay, I'm coming." He pushed himself to his feet, throwing Kit one of his slow smiles. "Rain check, darlin'?"

Kit nodded. "Sure." She watched him head back toward the kitchen, wondering exactly what she'd just given him a rain check for.

Nando sat on his stool at the Faro wondering when his days off had become so monotonous. Laundry, grocery shopping, dry cleaners, hardware store. A regular social whirl.

He took another bite of Clem's enchiladas verdes. At least he hadn't had to cook tonight. He only hoped his mother didn't find out he'd been eating somebody else's enchiladas. She'd probably drag him home and stuff him full of home-cooked food. It had taken him and Esteban weeks to convince her not to come over and fill up the refrigerator with casseroles every Sunday.

He leaned back against the bar, watching Deirdre work the room. Apparently, Ames had relaxed his rules against her waiting tables, possibly because it was Saturday night and the Faro was swamped. A band was tuning up in the beer garden, and the patrons were beginning to drift out to the tables around the edge. From his seat, he could see some Toleffsons out there, Docia and her husband Cal, the vet, along with Janie and Pete. The chief might show up, but probably not. Nando thought he had night duty tonight.

It was always entertaining to watch the tourists' slack-jawed wonder when they caught sight of Deirdre. The locals had adjusted to having her around, although he figured nobody ever got entirely used to that kind of beauty. He wondered if Ames had, if waking up with Deirdre in the morning had taken some of the awesomeness away. He'd guess not. It never had with him.

Asleep, Kit's face always relaxed into the kind of smooth elegance that reminded him of fairytales. Sleeping beauty. Snow White in the forest. He used to lie awake on purpose sometimes just to look at her.

When her eyes opened, they'd still be shadowed by the thickness of her lashes. A sudden memory hit him like a flashback.

She raised one hand, running a finger slowly along the line of his jaw. "What are you looking at?"

"You."

"What do you see?"

"You. Just you."

He took her lips slowly, running one hand down to cup her breast, warm and soft in his palm. Her body trembled slightly beneath his fingers as she turned to press herself against him, then wound one long leg around his waist.

"You can do better than that," she whispered. "No more watching."

Nando took a long swallow of his beer. He needed to stop doing that, getting caught up in those memories. He'd managed not to be hung up on Kit Maldonado for two or three months now, and it had been a lot less painful than the year or so that had gone before. But as soon as she'd shown up in town again, he'd been thrown right back into it—all that pain he'd sworn he wouldn't feel again.

He blew out a breath. Time to move on. Maybe he'd find somebody tonight out on the dance floor, have a few beers, a little dirty dancing in the beer garden. If the woman was interested, maybe more than that. Of course, he'd supposedly sworn off that particular remedy for memories of Kit Maldonado. But what the hell—desperate times called for desperate measures. She was seeing other people. He should too. He grabbed his beer and pushed off the stool.

Deirdre stepped up beside him, gathering up his plate from the bar. "You heading to the beer garden?"

Nando shrugged. "Sure, why not? Who's the band tonight?"

"Somebody new, but they sound good. Save me a dance, okay?"

He grinned for probably the first time that evening. "Sure. Ready to ditch Ames for the excitement of an alpha male?"

Tom appeared at his other elbow. "You're alpha now? I was guessing beta. Possibly delta."

Nando pressed a hand to his heart. "Any time you want to exchange this omega here for the real thing, just say the word, sugar."

Deirdre cocked an eyebrow at both of them. "I'd be annoyed at the amount of crap the two of you are throwing around, but I'm too busy being impressed that you actually know the Greek alphabet."

"Between *Jeopardy* and Trivial Pursuit, I'm a regular font of

127

knowledge." Nando gave her a quick smile as he headed toward the beer garden. Too bad he'd been knee-deep in post-Kit depression when Deirdre had first shown up in Konigsburg. Now, of course, it was too late for anybody to make a play for her, given that Ames would turn them into throw rugs if they did. And given that Ames was his best friend, he wouldn't have tried that anyway.

He stepped into the crowded beer garden as the band launched into a spirited if not particularly inspired version of "Bar Light." Seats appeared to be at a premium, and he wedged himself against the fence at the side, watching couples swirl by. He searched the crowd for familiar faces, hoping he could find a table where he could pull up a chair.

Halfway around the garden, he found a very familiar face.

Kit was talking to Docia, her dark head leaning close to Docia's flaming red hair. Whatever they were discussing seemed to make them oblivious to everyone else in the garden, including him. His chest clenched so tight it was almost painful, and he considered heading back to the bar again. *A year.* He'd spent a year getting over her. He'd be damned if he'd dive back into it again, even if she'd let him.

He tried to make his feet move back to the door, then gave up. Apparently, she gave off some kind of magnetic attraction that kept him rooted to the spot.

He watched her, his heart heading for his shoes, unable to tear his gaze away from that fall of dark hair, her slender arm, her slim tapering fingers stretched across the table. If he got out of here now, if he pushed himself off the wall and headed back inside... Better yet if he went out the gate that led from the beer garden to the street before she saw him. He could be back in his car driving home in five minutes.

Where he could do what? Sort through the mail? Watch a game on ESPN? Play a hand of cribbage with Esteban? Scratch Guinevere's ears?

Where you could avoid having those hooks sunk in your gut again.

Yeah, well, that much was true. Or anyway, it was what he wanted to believe. But the truth was those hooks were already in place. They'd sunk deep the first time he'd seen her on the street. Now he could try to ignore the pain. Or he could do something about it.

He pushed himself off from the wall, dropping his empty beer glass on the outdoor bar as he went by.

Kit was aware that he was near before she saw him. Something about the way the people around her shifted, the way Docia glanced at her, the way the air moved.

The way the air moved? Get a grip.

She looked up then to see him standing in front of the table. Suddenly her throat felt so tight it was hard to breathe. He wore his jeans low on his hips, just the way he always had, with the same tooled leather belt with the silver buckle. His thumbs were hooked into the belt loops, a nervous habit, he'd told her once. The sleeves of his chambray shirt were rolled up below his elbows. A lock of dark hair strayed across his forehead, as if he'd run his fingers through it not long before he'd walked up to her.

She'd done that herself sometimes when they were together, coaxing those stray locks at the front down to his eyebrows, making him look less like a cop and more like an outlaw. An outlaw with the best moves in Konigsburg.

Not going there again. So not going there again.

She licked her lips. "Hi."

He nodded. "Hi." The line of his jaw looked tight. His hands flexed against his thighs. *Nervous?*

"Sit down with us," Docia said quickly. "Find a chair. Come on, Cal, slide over."

"That's all right." He looked back at Kit. "I just wanted to ask you to dance."

Kit licked her lips again. The band was playing something fast and safe. Something that wouldn't require them to get too close. "Sure."

She stood as he reached for her hand. For a moment she froze. They hadn't touched in over a year. Nando waited, hand extended, and she told herself to get it together. *Just a dance.*

She moved with him to the floor, sliding into a two-step around the outer edge. His hand rested, large and warm, against the middle of her back, leaving enough space between them for the steps. She let him move her around among the dancers, listening to the music behind her. After a few moments, her lips began to edge up into a smile.

She'd forgotten how good he was, how much fun it was to dance with him. They moved with the stream of people, her feet falling back into the familiar rhythm, quick quick, slow slow. The music buoyed underneath them, twirling them around the room. Quick quick... He looked down at her, his dark eyes alight with something that wasn't exactly mischief but was close.

She almost stumbled, but caught herself. Nando slowed slightly, letting her find her footing then pushing forward again.

Stupid, stupid. Never relax, never let your guard down. The minute she did, he'd slip inside, close to her, and then she'd have all that pain to go through again.

She was so busy berating herself she almost missed the way the music slowed, then stopped. She took a quick breath, letting her shoulders relax. Time to go back to the table and hide. She started to pull away, when the band began to play again.

Oh god, she recognized this one.

It wasn't *their* song. They didn't have a song, really. But she'd heard it enough when they were together. And they'd danced to it. All around them, couples moved in close, arms around each other. Nando stood poised, watching her. Then he moved slowly toward her, sliding his arm around her waist.

Her own arm went around his neck almost automatically, and their bodies were pressed together, shoulder to knee. He took her hand in his, folding their arms against his chest, then started to move forward slowly, his thighs pushing against her legs. She found herself moving with him, staring up into his face. His beautiful face.

"And anyone can tell, you think you know me well." The voice echoed over the PA system. "But you don't know me."

Oh god, oh god, oh god. But she did know him well, better than she knew a lot of the people in her own family. That's why she was here again in his arms, not that there had ever really been any question it would come to this eventually. Not with all there had once been between them. Not when she'd never really gotten over him.

Had he gotten over her? Would he be here if he had?

Part of her wanted to move back, put some space between them again, but somehow she couldn't manage it. Instead, his arm coaxed her closer still until she felt the hard muscles of his chest against her

130

breasts, the silver belt buckle brushing against her stomach, the swell of his arousal pressing hard against her own aching flesh. She took a deep breath, smelling his familiar scent again, that mixture of soap and sweat and Nando, and she was lost.

"And anyone can tell, you think you know me well. But you don't know me." Well, at least that proved the music gods had a sense of humor. He knew every inch of her, on one level anyway. On the other level, the most important level, he probably didn't know her at all. He sure didn't seem to know the Kit he held in his arms right now. She wasn't the same exactly, but she wasn't that different either.

What was he doing here anyway?

He could think of a dozen reasons not to do this. Hell, he'd already thought of them. He'd been thinking of them as he'd sat in the bar. But here he was again. Moth to the flame. Lemming to the cliff. Preying mantis waiting for that final blow.

Which was a hell of an image to have when he held her, all soft flesh and swirling hair. When he smelled that intoxicating scent again, spice and honey and faint tuberose.

The singer's voice followed them across the floor. "You don't know me."

He wanted to say something to her, something light and casual that would put this back in focus again, but his throat felt too dry for words all of a sudden.

The music began to swell toward the end, the final line, that final bit of heartbreak. "You'll never, ever know, the one who loves you so, cause you don't know me."

The dancers around them came to a stop, the buzz of conversation rising. *Say something. Say anything!* He stared down into her velvet eyes, his mind suddenly blank. His arms were still around her, her body still pressed against him.

Her eyes widened in something that might have been shock as she took a quick breath. "I should go."

After another moment he loosened his hold slightly. He couldn't stand there holding her forever, no matter how much he might want to. "Okay. Did you drive?"

She nodded silently, her gaze never leaving his face.

"Then I'll walk you to your car." He turned slightly, letting his arm rest across her shoulders as he took her back to her table.

Docia flashed them a quick speculative look as Kit grabbed her purse. "Done for the night?"

"Yeah." Kit gave her a slightly strained grin, then turned back toward the street entrance.

He followed her through the gate, wondering if he could risk putting his hand on her arm. She looked fragile all of a sudden, as if she might shatter with too much pressure.

At her car, she turned to face him. "Well..." she began.

He'd never know what she might have said—whatever it was, it didn't matter. Instead he slid his index finger under her chin, tipping it up slightly, so that he could bring his lips to hers.

The shock of it almost sent him to his knees. The taste, the feel, months stripped away, memories swamping him. And yet not the same exactly.

He wrapped his arms around her, one at her waist, one across her shoulders, holding her tight against him as he angled his mouth against hers, plunging his tongue deep inside.

After a moment, he felt her arms lock around his neck. And then she was kissing him back, hungrily, her tongue rasping against his. Her fingers dug into his shoulders, hips flat against his. He felt her rise to her tiptoes, bringing the V of her legs against him.

He turned, pushing her bottom alongside the car, pressing his aching arousal hard against her. The small portion of rationality he still had was screaming, telling him to back off, while his body screamed to take it as far as he could.

And then she was pushing on his shoulders, pulling back from the kiss, panting, her lips swollen, her eyes wide with panic. "Oh god, Nando," she gasped. "No. I can't. I can't do this again. It hurt too much. You don't know how much it hurt."

He rested his forehead against hers for a moment, fighting to get breath into his lungs. "I know," he whispered. "Christ. I know."

"You know?" She narrowed her eyes, her voice trembling. "You can't. How could you?"

"Because I hurt too." He bit off the words. "Because I'll hurt again if this goes south. I don't want to, but I will."

She stared at him for a long moment, her expression suddenly blank. Then she rubbed a hand across her forehead. "I should go home. I need to...think, I guess."

He leaned one arm against her car, half to get strength back in his knees and half to keep her from climbing into the driver's seat. "Have breakfast with me," he blurted.

"What?" At least he'd managed to surprise her, apparently.

"Have breakfast with me. I've got to work tomorrow night, but I want to see you. You're not working, right? The Rose doesn't open on Sunday?" She nodded. "Then give me the morning at least."

Kit was still watching him as if she expected him to abscond with the Sunday school funds. "Where?"

He hadn't thought that far ahead. Hell, Sweet Thing was closed and Deirdre didn't open on Sundays. Where the hell else could you get breakfast? "The Coffee Corral."

Kit took a deep breath. She looked like she was weighing a set of equally unattractive options. "What time?"

He had no idea what time Al Brosius opened, he just hoped it was early. "Nine?"

She closed her eyes for a moment, then shrugged. "Nine it is."

He backed up slightly to let her open the door, then stepped back onto the sidewalk. "I'll pick you up. See you then."

Kit gave him a tight smile. "I can drive."

"I'll pick you up," he repeated.

After a moment, she sighed. "All right." She climbed into her car and started the ignition. He watched her brake lights diminish as she headed toward the other end of Main.

He had a date with her, at least. What he was going to do with it, on the other hand, he hadn't a clue.

Chapter Twelve

Kit changed her outfit twice before eight thirty the next morning. She couldn't decide what look she was going for exactly. Strong, independent woman who really didn't need a man to feel complete? Gorgeous girl who got away (and aren't you sorry)? Exhausted restaurant hostess who hadn't gotten a lot of sleep?

That was probably the look she'd end up with whether she wanted to or not.

She'd lain awake most of the night, trying to figure out what it all meant. Nando had said he'd suffered like she had. Did she believe him? Or was it just another easy thing to say to a gullible woman? *Oh baby, it hurt so bad, believe me!*

Except it hadn't looked like it was easy for him to say it. It looked like the words were pulled out of him by force. And now he wanted to see her again. For what? Another of those "civilized" conversations where they showed how over each other they were? She swore if he tried that, she'd walk out of the Coffee Corral and never look at him again.

That was some comfort—that she felt strong enough to walk out and let him suffer for his own mistakes.

What she wouldn't think about—at all, under any circumstances—was the kiss. And, of course, saying that ensured that she wouldn't be able to stop thinking about it, no matter how hard she tried. She should have pushed him away. She'd intended to do just that. Except that when he'd kissed her, she'd been hit by a wave of longing so strong it almost knocked her flat. Suddenly, all she could do was hang on. And kiss him back.

She wondered if he'd felt something similar. Somehow she doubted that he had. Except maybe, just maybe...

What was that kiss supposed to mean, anyway? He wanted her right then? He wanted her for a quick roll in the hay? He wanted her, period?

Because wanting her wasn't enough. He had to feel something more. She did too. *And what would that something be, Catarina? Ready to put a name to it?* She closed her eyes, blocking it out. She wasn't ready for that yet.

She blew out a breath and went back to her closet, pulling out her favorite pair of jeans and a black cotton blouse. She took off the gypsy-size hoop earrings she'd been wearing and substituted a pair of pearl studs. *Screw it.* She was going to look like herself. Let him figure out what it all meant. She sure as hell couldn't.

She'd intended to walk over to the Coffee Corral. Arriving under her own power would send him a message about how this thing between them—whatever it was—was going to go. Nobody in charge of anybody else. But while she was gathering her purse, someone knocked. She had a feeling she knew who it was before she opened the door.

"Morning," Nando said, leaning one hand against the doorframe. He was wearing the same clothes he'd worn the day before, or maybe they just looked the same. Kit felt like sighing. Nobody should look that good in a pair of jeans. It wasn't fair.

She gave him her coolest smile. "Hi. I was just getting ready to walk to the Corral."

His car was parked out front, but he shrugged. "I'll walk with you, then. Nice morning. Allie still asleep?"

"She's off at Wonder's house." Kit took a breath and headed down the front steps after locking the door, resolutely not looking at Nando walking at her side. *Just a walk. You can do this.*

As they turned down Firewheel, he took her hand in his. She had a quick impulse to jerk away from him, but she stifled it. Holding hands was nothing in the great scheme of things. Kids held hands, and it didn't mean they were thinking about anything romantic.

He laced his fingers through hers, and she swallowed hard. Not kids. Not by a long shot.

The Corral was doing a brisk business, which wasn't surprising since it was one of the few cafés that was open on Sunday morning. Carol Brosius was behind the counter taking orders as Al fried up bacon and eggs at the grill. Her eyes might have widened slightly when she saw them, but her smile was bland. "Hey Nando, Kit, what can I get for y'all this morning?"

"Couple of bacon and egg tacos and some coffee for me." Nando turned to her. "What would you like?"

Kit pretended she had to make up her mind, although she'd known what she was going to have from the moment he'd mentioned the Coffee Corral last night. She didn't want to sound too eager, after all. "I think huevos rancheros, Carol. Maybe with a side of tortillas."

They found a booth at the side, sipping their coffee while carefully not looking at each other. Kit took a breath. She wasn't going to sit here in strained silence until her eggs arrived. "Well..."

He gave her a questioning look. "Well?"

"Why are we here exactly?"

Very good question, Ms. Maldonado. Nando only wished he had a good answer on the tip of his tongue. Other than the one he wanted to give her: *Because you drive me crazy and I need to know why that is. And I also need to know if there's any chance we could have anything together again.*

"I don't suppose you'd accept that I just wanted to have breakfast with you." He took a sip of his coffee.

Kit shook her head. "Not a chance. We told each other to go to hell eighteen months ago. Then last night we...didn't. So what's happening here? How did we end up almost jumping each other in the parking lot after not having anything to do with each other for months?"

"We needed..." He paused, watching a small boy energetically coloring his placemat two tables over. "*I* needed to know if there was anything still between us. And there was. There is. So I guess the answer to your question is that we're here to see what else is still between us besides just the jumping each other part."

Kit looked like she might have something more to say about that, but just then Carol showed up with their breakfasts. Gratefully, Nando managed to occupy himself with applying salsa to his tacos.

"So how did you plan to go about this?" Kit said after she'd had time to sample her *huevos.*

He shrugged. "Tell me about your life. What's been happening to you during the last eighteen months since you told me to go to hell."

"We told each other to go to hell," she corrected. "I finished my coursework at UTSA, did an internship at a downtown hotel, and graduated."

"But you're here now. You said once you were going to work in San Antonio, at your family's place." In fact, she'd said it when she'd told him to go to hell, which meant he remembered it very well.

She shrugged. "That didn't work out. Aunt Allie said I could come and stay with her, so I did. I figured there'd be more opportunities here."

Given the difference in population size between Konigsburg and San Antonio, that statement was pretty much bullshit. He waited for her to go on, but she turned back to her *huevos*. After a moment, she looked up at him again. "How about you? How's the cop shop?"

He gave her a dry grin. After all, that's what he'd called it back when they were together. "Toleffson's a great chief. I'm assistant chief now, which means I make a little more money and have a lot more paperwork. I still moonlight a little when someplace like the fairgrounds needs extra security, but I don't have to do it as often as I used to."

"Do you still have the same people? Ham and Helen and, what was his name, Kurt?"

"Curtis. Curtis Peavey, and he just retired. Ham and Helen are still there, plus we've got a new kid, Clayton Delaney. Just started a couple of weeks ago."

She smiled slightly. "The pool player. I heard Chico say he was whipping asses regularly."

"Steinbruner asses, anyway. But I guess that counts." He took another bite of his taco, trying to decide if he should tell her anything else. She hadn't exactly been forthcoming with details herself.

Carol Brosius stopped by their table with a coffee pot, topping off his cup. "You want anything else while I'm here? Al's doing pancakes."

Kit shook her head. "No thanks. This is already more breakfast than I've had in weeks."

Carol gave her a critical look. "You could stand a little more meat on your bones, Ms. Maldonado. Doesn't that fancy chef at the Rose give you any food, for Pete's sake?"

Kit grinned. "His food's terrific, but I don't have time to eat much. Just like you guys at lunch time, I imagine."

"Yeah, only our customers don't show up in Mercedes," Carol said dryly. "If you want anything else, just holler."

Nando watched her walk back toward the front counter where her son was currently taking orders. "So how's working at the Rose?"

"It's great." She gave him a smile that he didn't believe for a moment was real. "Business is booming. It's a wonderful restaurant."

She cut off a piece of egg with a vicious swipe of her fork. He wondered briefly what the egg had done to deserve it.

After a moment spent stirring his coffee, he looked up at her again. "You know, if this is going to work at all, this finding out about us again, we have to stop lying to each other." He took a quick sip. "Like with me—I do love my job, I'm not lying about that. But right now I'm walking a tightrope at work and it's not fun. I've been hitting the Faro a little more than I probably should as a result."

Kit gave him a mutinous look, then subsided back into her chair. "Okay. The job at the Rose has all kinds of potential, but right now it sucks a lot of the time. The restaurant is terrific, I wasn't lying about that. And Joe LeBlanc is a pro. But the manager at the inn is borderline competent, and her idea of making the restaurant profitable is to hire inexperienced staff she can pay next to nothing. And not even enough of those. I'm being run off my feet out there trying to make up for all the people the restaurant needs and doesn't have. Joe's trying his best, but unless Mabel gets her act together, the restaurant's new rep is going to burn out fast."

"Mabel?" He raised an eyebrow.

"Ms. Mabel Morgenstern, manager of the Woodrose Inn. Although if Resorts Consolidated ever finds out what a lousy job she's doing with their newest acquisition, she could be out on the street. Or at least I devoutly hope so."

Nando frowned. "I didn't know the Woodrose had been bought out."

"A few months ago. I heard about it in San Antonio. RC is a British company trying to break into the upscale trade in the region. The Woodrose was a major purchase." She picked up her coffee cup. "So how about you? What's this tightrope that's got you drowning your sorrows in craft beer."

He shrugged. "The job's not bad, not by a long shot. Toleffson's the best chief the town's ever had, and he's got the department running a lot better than it used to. We could still use more people, but we're getting along with four full time and two part time, which is a lot better than two full and four part like it used to be."

Kit gave him a slight smile. "But?"

He grimaced. "But I'm on probation with the City Council for the assistant chief position. And not everybody is okay with that. Ham Linklatter in particular."

She put down her cup. "Nobody in their right mind would appoint Ham to anything in authority. Everybody agreed on that when he didn't get the chief's job. How can there be any serious question now?"

He narrowed his eyes, studying the far wall. "If it was just Toleffson's decision, there probably wouldn't be any question. But there's some sentiment in favor of Ham."

Kit leaned forward in her chair. "This is Ham Linklatter we're talking about, right? The guy you never want answering your 911 call? The closest thing we've got to a village idiot? How can there be any question about him being assistant chief?"

Nando sighed. "You remember when the council hired Toleffson instead of Ham to be chief?"

"To the resounding applause of everybody in town, as I recall."

"Right." He nodded. "Nobody wanted Ham in that position. But some people feel like his feelings got hurt when he didn't get chosen, and they're kind of sorry for him. And they might be in favor of giving him this job as a consolation prize."

Kit gave him an incredulous look. "That makes no sense at all. Ham's barely competent doing what he's doing now. How can they seriously want to bump him up to something more demanding?"

"My guess is they figure Toleffson's going to be in charge and he can keep Ham from screwing up too much, so it wouldn't be like he'd be a danger to the town."

"Except when Chief Toleffson's not around to keep track of him."

"Right." Nando rubbed a hand across his face. "If Ham takes over this job, everybody in town had better pray that Toleffson doesn't take too many vacations."

"But he won't take it over, will he? I mean if you've already got the position, not even people who feel sorry for him would take it away and give it to him. They'd want to keep you there."

He shook his head. "It's not automatic. I'm supposed to be supercop for a few weeks just to reassure the citizens that everything is okay."

"Still." She shrugged. "I wouldn't think there'd be much problem. You're really good at your job. Between you and Ham, any sane person would stick with you."

He grimaced. "That assumes the city council is sane. I'm not entirely sure."

"Have you done any campaigning?"

He shook his head. "Just tried to keep my head down. With middling success."

"What happened?"

"Just...I found some DNA evidence in the bookstore after it was vandalized, but the story got a little twisted." He stared down at his coffee, hoping his ears weren't actually turning red.

Kit stared at him. "Oh my god," she said finally. "The poop. I heard about that."

"Yeah, so did everybody else, thanks to Ham."

"But that was a good thing. DNA evidence. That could help you find the guy who's doing this."

"Right." He sighed. "And I guess a lot of people understand that by now. The problem is the boys locker room factor. It sounds funny. And Ham's been riding it for all it's worth. He's made me look sort of like a moron. Or a pervert. A crap collector."

"But that's crazy." Kit sat straighter in her chair. "You're a great cop, and everybody knows it. Ham's an idiot, and everybody knows that too. They can't possibly give him the job. I think you're worrying about something you don't need to worry about. Hell, we're all smarter than that, Nando."

Nando watched her, listening to the note of outrage in her voice. He hadn't told anybody about the whole thing with Ham until now, not even Esteban. It was the first time anybody had been irate on his behalf. And it felt really...good.

"Thanks," he said slowly.

"You're welcome." The corners of her mouth edged up. "Listen, I was thinking of going out to the state park this afternoon—I haven't been there since I've been back. Want to come?"

140

He found himself grinning for no particular reason. The state park had a lake where they'd spent a lot of time. That probably wasn't what she had in mind. Still... "Sure. I'll even drive."

They spent a lazy morning at the lake, neither of them acknowledging the time they'd spent there before or what they'd done then, although Kit thought she could identify at least three places on the shore where they'd made love. They skipped rocks and walked the paths through the live oaks and finally found a picnic table in the shade. And talked. A lot of talking, as it turned out. More talking than she'd done in eighteen months. But then she hadn't had him to talk to until now.

He asked her why she hadn't gone to work for her father, and she told him about the restaurant sale. It was the first time she'd told anyone all the details, even Allie.

"I had this dream about managing the restaurant ever since I was a kid, in fact. In the front of the house, not the kitchen or the dining room. So I told my dad I wanted to go back to work there after I graduated, that I thought the things I'd learned in hospitality management could be useful. He didn't say much at the time, just sort of nodded and let me hostess in the afternoons for a while."

Nando ran a piece of rye grass between his fingers. "Did he tell you he was thinking about selling?"

Kit shook her head. "Not at first. I think he was still sort of mulling over the offer."

"Then what happened?"

She took a deep breath. "He called us all together, the three of us who were still in town, that is. Me, my brother Art and my sister Juana. He told us he'd had a good offer and was thinking of selling, but he'd pass the restaurant on to us if that's what we wanted. Juana said no right off the bat—she's a social worker and she's got no interest in switching to food service. Art's an accountant. We talked about it, he and I, but it would have been mainly me doing all the work in the restaurant—the ordering, the menus, the hiring, the day-to-day management. All of it."

Nando's forehead furrowed. "But wasn't that what you were looking for?"

141

Kit stared down at her hands. "Yes, but... It was the family restaurant. If I blew it, I'd be blowing all my father's work, his reputation. And I'd always know everybody was watching me, waiting to see if I could handle it. Papi had had years to build the place up, and I'd have to try to keep it going the way he had."

"And you were afraid you couldn't do it," he said quietly.

She nodded slowly. "I had my chance. And I flinched. Papi understood. He knew how I felt, how scared I was. But the thing is, I should have had the guts to do it. I should have believed in myself and gone ahead. I just...didn't."

Nando ran his fingers gently up and down her arm. "I'm sorry."

Kit sighed, telling herself to knock it off. Whatever she should have done, she had to live with what she *had* done. "I could have looked for something else in San Antonio, and I'd probably have found a job—Papi could have helped me find something in the restaurant business there. But I couldn't stay around and watch strangers take over Antonio's instead of me. I called Aunt Allie, and she said to come on up."

"Did you tell her what happened?"

"Some of it."

"Did you want to work at Sweet Thing?"

Kit shook her head. "Allie doesn't need anybody in the front of the house either. She runs everything, and she's got the kitchen operation down to a science. Unlike Mabel Morgenstern, she hires the right staff and then she holds onto them, although she'd probably have given me a job running the cash register or something if I'd asked."

Nando tossed a piece of bark toward the lake, watching it bounce off a rock before sinking. "She's a good person to be connected to around here. Everybody loves her." With the exception of the asshole who'd broken in and trashed her restaurant, of course.

Kit shrugged. "So how's your family?"

"Same as usual. Esteban's the assistant wine master, but Cliff Barrett doesn't leave him a whole lot to do. Dad's still running the vineyards. Mom's still driving everybody crazy. My sister Blanca is still living in Albuquerque and refusing to come home for Thanksgiving, which drives Mom crazy so it sort of evens out."

She turned to look out over the lake. "Do they still want you to quit the police force and come to work at the winery?"

"Sure. They'll never believe I could be happy doing anything except making wine." Nando shook his head. "Secretly, I think they're sort of proud of me, but they'll never admit it to my face."

"They're good people," She said slowly. "I like them."

"So do I, but they still make me nuts."

Kit shrugged. "That's their job. They love you."

Nando picked another piece of rye grass

"Speaking of Sweet Thing, as we were not that long ago, want to go see if we can grab some iced tea and ham sandwiches there for lunch?"

He frowned. "I thought Allie was still closed down."

"She is, but she's got the kitchen open, thanks to you. She's making bread for all her regulars, plus she's always got some ham around."

He pushed himself off the picnic table. "You've got a deal."

To her everlasting credit, Allie didn't blink when she saw them together. And she was willing to sacrifice a fresh loaf of seven grain, along with some Virginia ham and cheddar cheese, for sandwiches. They sat at one of the unused tables on the restaurant patio, leaning back in their Adirondack chairs to bask in the sun.

"I don't suppose you've got any new ideas about who messed up the restaurant," Kit asked. The cleaning crew had made some inroads in the lake of jam and honey still hardening in the middle of the bakery floor, but it looked like the floor might need refinishing. She only hoped the crew could loosen the rest of the mess without dynamite.

Nando shook his head. "He didn't leave any samples this time, which is a good thing, I guess, since this is a restaurant."

"Right." She blew out a breath. "Allie found something else missing, by the way, although I don't know how important it is."

"Anything's potentially important." He leaned toward her. "What was it?"

"A little china bowl she kept near the cash register. I don't think it's worth anything. I mean she got it at a flea market."

"What does it look like?"

Kit held her fingers together in a circle. "About so round. White

143

with purple flowers. It had pennies for change."

"Did he take the pennies too?"

She frowned. "I'm not sure. I'll ask. Does it mean anything?"

Nando shrugged. "Not yet. But it will when we find him. If he kept it, it could tie him to the burglary."

"Why would he keep it?"

He shrugged again. "I don't know. Sometimes crooks keep souvenirs, don't ask me why. Maybe we'll figure it out when we find out who he is." He leaned forward, pushing himself up from the chair. "I'd probably better get home. I've got night duty this week, and I need to get changed before I head to the station."

Kit glanced at her watch and discovered the afternoon was almost over. They'd spent most of the day together. Funny—it hadn't seemed that long while it was happening. She followed him to the back gate. "Thanks for breakfast."

"Thanks for lunch."

He smiled down at her and her heart suddenly kicked up a notch. She'd managed to push all her thoughts about what this day meant to the back of her mind while it was happening. Now they threatened to come tumbling back to the front again.

Nando ran his fingers down the slope of her nose, his smile narrowing slightly. "I'd like to see you again, Catarina. Would that be okay with you?"

Her heart gave another thump. She was surprised he couldn't hear it. "Yes. I think so."

"Of course I'm working nights all this week." He sighed. "And I assume you're working days like usual."

She nodded. "Start at ten, get off around six."

"When's your day off?"

Kit's smile turned dry. "This is it. Remember what I said about not enough staff?"

"I might be off on Wednesday." He shrugged. "We could meet at the Faro after you get off work."

Kit cast a quick glance back toward the kitchen, lowering her voice slightly. "Wednesday is supposed to be Allie's super secret shower. I'm going to try to get off early so I can meet Docia."

"Shower?" His eyebrows went up. "The wedding's coming up that soon? Hell, I had August in the office pool."

"The wedding's definitely bearing down on us." She gave him a better smile this time. "I'll make sure you get an invitation."

"Well, then, Ms. Maldonado, shall we say next Sunday?" He leaned down slightly, brushing his lips across hers, then wrapping his arms more tightly around her waist as the kiss deepened.

Kit leaned against him, feeling the same warmth descending to her toes. The same ache in her core. The same everything, just like before.

No. Not like before. They still hadn't discussed what had happened between them the first time. She leaned back, touching his cheek for a moment, trying to find something in those black magic eyes that would give her a clue about what was going on.

"Next Sunday, Officer," she whispered finally. "Count on it."

Chapter Thirteen

Kit spent two days working very hard and not thinking about Nando Avrogado. Or actually trying not to think about Nando because every time she did, she ended up confused. What were they doing together anyway? What was happening between them? She hadn't talked that much to anyone for a long time. Around eighteen months, in fact. And she'd never told anybody else how miserable the end of Antonio's had been for her in San Antonio.

She'd always been able to talk to him when they were together. He still listened better than anyone she knew except maybe her sister Juana. Were they getting back together again? Or were they turning into friends? But she didn't usually feel like jumping her friends no matter how close they were. And she definitely felt like jumping Nando whenever she spent more than five minutes around him.

Friends with benefits? Kit shuddered. Nothing like turning into a cliché as you aged. And they still hadn't talked about all the things that had come between them the first time. Until they did, she had a feeling they'd never be able to trust each other again.

Allie's shower was scheduled to begin at eight o'clock on Wednesday evening. It was also supposed to be a complete and total surprise, which meant everybody Kit had talked to had been sworn to absolute cross-your-heart secrecy. Allie still turned pale every time she heard the word *wedding*. Kit had a feeling her aunt would have taken off for an extended buying trip to Dallas if she'd known a shower was coming up. Particularly the kind of shower she and Docia had in mind.

She'd managed to get Mabel Morgenstern to agree to let her leave the Rose an hour early by promising to come in an hour early the next day, and also promising to straighten out another mess with the Woodrose's software, this time the scheduling software Mabel used herself. She wasn't sure who was going to handle the reservations after she left for the day, but Joe told her not to worry about it and she decided to take him at his word.

And that was another problem she knew she'd have to deal with eventually: Joe LeBlanc. It wasn't like they had a real romantic relationship exactly. But they had something. And it was something she needed to straighten out. If it was just a passing flirtation, she could probably move it to a somewhat less serious plateau. But if, as she suspected, their friendship had a serious side, she'd have to decide if her relationship with Nando made it impossible to have a friendship with Joe.

That was, of course, assuming that she actually had a relationship with Nando. Or that she knew what that relationship was. *Screw it! I'm not going to think about this anymore.*

At five thirty, she tossed her purse and a couple of sacks of Darcy's custom-made tortilla chips into her car and headed toward town. Docia had been tasked with bringing Allie to the shower location without letting her know what was going on. Kit wasn't sure how she'd manage it, but she had a feeling Docia could cope with subterfuge better than most people.

She parked in the lot behind the Lucky Lady dress shop, then waited until Mrs. Dupree unlocked the back door. Janie's mother had worked there for almost twenty years, and Kit figured not much fazed her in terms of clothes-buying ideas. Particularly given that Janie was now a Toleffson and unusual things seemed to happen around them with great regularity.

Kit stepped inside the shop at six and blinked—Docia was setting up a couple of ice buckets with champagne near a circle of chairs at the center of the shop. A low coffee table held a variety of snacks that Kit recognized from the Faro. So Clem had gotten her catering job after all. A strategically arranged rack of dresses concealed the table and chairs from the plate-glass window at the front of the store.

She hurried forward. "Where's Aunt Allie? Is she already here? Did I miss it?"

Docia put her hand on her arm. "It's okay. Janie's bringing her instead of me. I figured it wouldn't seem as weird if Janie said she needed to come here to see her mom, assuming she can come up with a good excuse for why she'd be working late." She nodded at Mrs. Dupree, who regarded the shop with a critical eye.

"Are we going to need to clear more space?" she asked. "Are y'all going to be doing games?"

Docia shook her head. "No games. Well, no organized games, anyway." She grinned at Mrs. Dupree. "Didn't Janie explain what this is all about?"

Mrs. Dupree frowned slightly. "Well, yes. I mean she told me what you were planning to do. But surely that won't take the whole evening, will it? I mean, I've got everything pretty much organized the way you said. If you want to do something fun, though, I've got a good shower game where you tear napkins into the shape of brides."

Docia regarded the ice chest at the side of the room with narrowed eyes. "I think by the time we've gone through all the champagne I brought we won't be up to tearing anything—at least not on purpose. Fortunately, we've all got designated drivers."

Kit frowned. "I don't." She wondered what Nando would think if she called him at the station for a ride home.

Docia grinned. "Don't worry about it. Wonder said he could transport you and Allie both back to her place. Your car will be safe in the lot until tomorrow."

"Wonder's on chauffeur duty? He never seemed to be all that enthusiastic about ferrying people around before."

"Believe me, anything that will get Allie closer to marching down the aisle is fine with him. And if worse comes to worst, we can call on the entire Toleffson brotherhood. Cal's got the SUV with seats for six."

Kit glanced up as someone rapped on the back door and Mrs. Dupree let Jess Toleffson and Morgan Toleffson in. Jess carried a couple of boxes wrapped in silver paper, and Morgan had a bottle under each arm, her dark brown curls floating around her head.

"I brought some wine from Cedar Creek," she said. "Allie always likes the Morgan's Blend." She caught sight of Kit and grinned. "Hey, stranger, when are you coming out to the winery to say hi?"

Kit blew out a breath. "Maybe sometime when I get a spare millisecond." Going to Cedar Creek had been low on her list of priorities since it always reminded her of Nando. But then again, maybe that wasn't as much of a problem anymore.

Docia glanced at Jess. "Is Lars okay with giving people rides home?"

"Lars is babysitting," Morgan said. "Erik said he'd be available if we needed any extra drivers."

Kit sighed, wondering just how embarrassing it would be to have the Chief of Police drive her home if she was too tipsy to walk.

Mrs. Dupree opened the back door again to admit Deirdre and Clem, along with a pleasantly rounded woman Kit recognized as Bethany Rankin, the mayor's wife.

"We saw Janie and Allie down the block, headed this way," Deirdre said breathlessly. "They should be here any minute."

"I just brought the rest of the buffet." Clem put two more plates down on the table. "I'll slip out the back way."

Docia shook her head. "Stick around. The more the merrier. Besides, we may need another vote on some of these dresses."

Clem frowned. "Vote? I've got dinner to fix."

"Have a seat. Margene can take care of the kitchen for a night. I already talked to Tom about it." Deirdre gestured toward the chairs. "Clem's great on makeovers. Absolutely great."

Clem narrowed her eyes, but went back to arranging her platters.

Mrs. Dupree glanced toward the front of the store. "I'll go out there and wait." She licked her lips. "My, I hope I don't give everything away as soon as she looks at me."

"Ssh, everybody," Docia whispered.

That inspired a round of giggles from everybody except Clem, who was inspecting her appetizers critically. "I should have made more quesadillas. Whose chips are those?"

"Ssh," Docia hissed more urgently.

Mrs. Dupree's voice from the front of the store sounded incredibly artificial. "Why Janie, sweetheart. And Allie Maldonado. What a nice surprise!"

Docia rolled her eyes. "Okay everybody, showtime. Get out there before Allie heads back out the door."

"Surprise," Jess and Morgan chorused together.

Bethany Rankin slipped by them, taking a firm grip on Allie's arm before she could turn around. "Come on, Allie, it's shower time. No escape."

Allie cast a narrow-eyed glance at Kit over Deirdre's shoulder. "Was this your idea?"

"This was everybody's idea," Docia said firmly. "Now sit down.

149

Have a quesadilla. Clem made them and they're terrific."

Clem smiled, dipping one of Darcy's chips into some green tomato salsa. "Bet your ass they are."

Morgan began pouring champagne into flutes, passing them around quickly, as Docia dropped into a chair beside Allie.

"Here," she said, handing Allie a glass. "Take a swallow."

Allie sipped. She looked a little like someone who'd just been given a nice cup of hemlock. "You know I hate showers."

Docia shook her head. "Horseshit. You and Janie and Bethany gave me the best shower ever, even though I fought you tooth and nail. We're now going to return the favor. This is going to be the second best shower ever, and we're all going to have a great time."

"Assuming we can remember it afterward," Deirdre muttered, glancing at the bottles of champagne in the cooler.

"Are you going to give me the same kind of gifts we gave you?" Allie asked suspiciously. "I really don't need any sexy lingerie or bedroom toys."

"Nope. This is a very special kind of shower." Docia glanced at Kit. "Tell her."

Kit took a deep breath. "This is a wedding dress shower, Aunt Allie. Also bridesmaid dresses. Mrs. Dupree found you all kinds of great things to choose from. We're going to help you pick."

Allie gave her a look of sheer horror. "No!"

"Yes." Docia gestured toward the glass in Allie's hand. "Drink up. Now."

"But no, I mean, I'm not ready..."

"Goddamn it, Allie." Docia sighed. "It's time for you to be ready. You're just afraid things at your wedding won't be perfect. Well here's a news flash—they won't be. Weddings never are. Remember everything that happened at mine? You've got a way to go before you beat that, toots. But it's going to be wonderful anyway. And now we're going to have a great time finding you the right dress for the Woodrose event center."

Allie's eyes looked very bright all of a sudden. Her hands gripped the chair so tightly that her knuckles turned white. Her lower lip trembled dangerously. "But..."

"Okay," Bethany announced loudly, "I propose a new drinking

game. Every time Allie says 'but' everybody has to drink."

"But..." Allie stammered.

Everyone raised their champagne flutes. "This could be quite a party," Clem muttered.

It took another ten minutes—and lots of sipping—before Allie finally settled down enough to look at the dresses. Mrs. Dupree licked her lips. "Now I was told that you didn't want an actual wedding gown, the full-length type."

"Oh, I don't," Allie said quickly. "That is, I don't think so." She gave Kit a beseeching glance.

"You don't," Kit said flatly. "You told me that several times." *Before you lost you mind and your ability to make a decision, that is.*

"So," Mrs. Dupree went on, "I found several of what you might call special occasion dresses." She pulled out a rack of white and cream and ivory dresses, with a couple of peach and pink thrown in.

Allie took a deep breath. "Oh. So many. I don't..."

"Drink," Docia commanded. Everyone took a quick swallow.

"Docia," Allie said as she set her glass down on the table, "what happens if I end up choosing something while I'm plastered. What if I get something with pink polka dots."

"Mamie here is pledged to sobriety," Docia said, nodding at Janie's mother. "She'll make sure you don't do anything absolutely stupid. Plus she's already eliminated all the pink polka dot numbers."

Morgan and Janie flipped through the dresses, oohing and aahing appropriately. "Oh, my, Allie, look," Janie cooed, holding up a strapless empire column with a strip of silver embroidery under the bust.

Allie shook her head. "If there's one thing I don't need, it's something to emphasize my boobs. Believe me, there's enough there without ribbons."

Kit checked her glass. It looked like Allie had emptied it in record time.

Docia poured her more champagne. "Next."

"How about this?" Morgan held up a soft pleated jersey in ivory. The neckline dipped to a low V.

Allie narrowed her eyes. "Not bad. Not bad at all."

"Put it on the possibles rack," Mrs. Dupree said quickly, pushing a group of hangers to the side.

After thirty minutes, they had a selection of possibles, all of them soft and flowing, two of them strapless. Allie seemed to have settled into a rosy glow.

"Now," Docia said, rubbing her hands together briskly, "we do the fashion show."

Allie blanched. "I'm not wearing the right underwear."

"Not a problem. Mamie has everything you need, I promise."

"But I'm not..." Allie sputtered

Everyone drank.

Allie closed her eyes, as if to gather her strength. "Okay. Lead me to 'em. But keep in mind—mine is a figure that laughs at Spanx."

"You don't want to wear a girdle at your wedding," Bethany said. "You want to have a good time. Hell, we're all beyond the Cinderella stage by now, aren't we?"

"Hear, hear." Docia opened another bottle of champagne.

Kit glanced down at her glass. When had it emptied?

After a few minutes in the dressing room, Allie stepped out in the jersey dress. The soft folds fell around her knees. The V-neck dipped down to show a sizeable amount of cleavage. The ivory color made Allie's skin glow. The shower guests seemed to sigh in unison.

Allie stepped in front of the mirror. "It's not bad, is it?"

"It's gorgeous," Kit murmured. "As far as I'm concerned you can stop right there."

"No she can't," Docia corrected. "Let's see 'em all. Then we'll go for the bridesmaids' outfits." She lounged back in her chair, munching on a quesadilla.

Kit sighed, settling down in the chair beside her. It looked like they were all in for a long evening.

Nando turned the cruiser down Fifteenth Street, ready to make his third run through town. After this one, he'd head back to the station to catch up on paperwork for a half hour or so, then drive through town another two or three times before morning. They'd already decided they needed to patrol at irregular intervals so the perp

152

couldn't predict when they'd be by. Rollie would take over patrolling while Nando was at the station, then they'd switch again later in the night.

So far he hadn't seen anything more interesting than some unexpected lights at the Lucky Lady clothing store. But he'd also seen Janie Toleffson heading in the front door with Allie Maldonado, plus the place was fully lighted with shadows passing back and forth across the windows, so he figured whatever was going on was okay. It probably had something to do with Allie's mystery shower. And he had no intention of going to a dress store that was liable to be full of women doing something he probably didn't want to know about.

He hadn't seen Kit since Sunday, but he hadn't really expected to. The only people he saw when he was on night duty were customers staggering out of the Faro or the Dew Drop Inn or the Silver Spur. And his main job in that case was to make sure they didn't stagger into the driver's seat and out onto the road.

He sighed. Maybe it was just as well he'd ended up doing night duty this week after all. Maybe he and Kit both needed a little time to process what was going on between them, or what wasn't.

Their last fight before she'd left for San Antonio that fall had been a screamer. As he recalled, Kit had thrown him out of her life in no uncertain terms. To be fair, he'd done about the same to her. And then he'd sealed the deal by picking up Lizzie Farraday at the Dew Drop in front of half the town.

It seemed like one minute they'd been fine, more than fine. Good in bed, good everywhere else. And then, bam, they'd blown sky high. At the time, he'd blamed it all on Kit since he hadn't particularly wanted to blame it on himself and since the whole thing seemed to come out of nowhere. But once he'd screwed up with the Lizzie Farraday thing, he'd been willing to admit she hadn't been the only one at fault.

What he mainly remembered about the last few days before the blowup that summer was being scared shitless. Scared that Kit would leave. Scared that she'd stay. Scared that he'd have to decide which thing he wanted more.

He turned down Spicewood, checking the dark windows at the bookstore. He doubted the vandal would be dumb enough to hit it twice, but given that they had no idea why he'd done it the first time, Nando wasn't inclined to risk it.

He looped into the alley, heading the other direction from the bookstore and traveling slowly. There was no way to be absolutely silent in a car as heavy as the cruiser on a gravel surface like the alley, but he tried to keep the engine noise down as much as he could, rolling through the ruts using only his parking lights.

The buildings were all dark except, of course, for the Lucky Lady. He thought he could hear a quick sputter of female laughter coming from inside. Okay, he definitely wanted to avoid the Lucky Lady at all costs. Whatever was going on in there was nothing he or any other male needed to see.

He counted off the other shops as he rolled slowly along the backside of the block: the candle store, Ivy Merkel's gift store, the fudge shop, Beaman's antiques, Margaret Hastings' angel store, the card and stationery place.

Something flashed at the edge of his vision. He slowed even more, bringing the cruiser to a stop as he turned to check again. All the shop windows were dark, the security light over Beaman's back entrance casting long shadows on either side. Nando held his breath, measuring seconds.

A light flashed again behind one of the back windows—faint, almost a reflection. Probably it *was* a reflection. But he had to check. He counted off the stores again: Margaret Hastings' place.

Nando felt like groaning. Of all the stores on the block, Margaret's would be the worst to check out in the dark. It was full of hanging things, tinkling things, angelic things with flat shiny surfaces that could reflect the street lights. Trying to figure out whether someone was really inside shining a light would be a bitch and a half.

He switched off the engine and the dome light, then slid out the door of the cruiser as quietly as he could. If somebody was there, he definitely didn't want them to have advance warning that the law was on the way.

Chapter Fourteen

By nine thirty, they'd managed to get Allie's wedding dress chosen and tucked away where she couldn't change her mind. It was, in fact, the same flowing jersey she'd tried on first, but Docia was right—trying on lots of other dresses had helped cement Allie's choice in her mind and had convinced her that the shower was actually a perfectly splendid idea. That, plus a really amazing amount of champagne.

Kit had discovered she herself had a champagne limit, even for very good champagne like the stuff Docia was pouring. After two glasses, she'd switched to bottled water, although only Janie's mother seemed to notice, giving her a sympathetic nod.

Now they were working on the bridesmaid dresses, and a raucous lot the attendants and kibitzers had turned out to be. Jess, Janie and Morgan were all bridesmaids. Docia was matron of honor. Allie had wanted Kit to be a bridesmaid, too, but she'd gently refused since she couldn't possibly keep track of all the things she needed to keep track of at the wedding and also march up the aisle. That left her, along with the other non-bridesmaids—Deirdre, Bethany, and Clem—to offer totally unsolicited advice, passing judgment on the rack of dresses Mrs. Dupree had managed to scare up as the various bridesmaids tried them on in various combinations.

"That gun-metal satin looks terrific on Jess," Clem commented, taking a hearty sip of her champagne.

Deirdre shook her head. "Won't work for Janie. It'll make her skin look too sallow."

"Janie looks lovely in that pale pink." Mrs. Dupree gave her a look of maternal approval that had Janie blushing.

Docia paused, fluffing her bright red hair. "No pale pink for me, please."

Kit frowned. "It's going to be really hard to find a single color for all of you. Unless you all wear something unimaginative like black. Do you all have to match?"

"We could probably do different colors if they were all the same style, assuming Mom could order them for us," Janie said helpfully.

Mrs. Dupree smiled very brightly, but Kit could see the panic in her eyes. "Well, we could certainly try. Some of them might be available in several colors and sizes. Of course, we do only have a few weeks until the ceremony."

"Who says they have to match?" Allie asked from the throne-like chair they'd set up for her in the middle of the room.

"Well..." Mrs. Dupree looked slightly nonplussed. "I mean, it's sort of traditional, isn't it?"

"Why?" Allie's eyes had taken on a certain dreaminess. "Why should I have to have a matched set? I mean it's not like they're carriage horses or something."

Janie snickered, then wiped her face clean of expression when her mother glared.

Allie was warming to her subject. "After all, if I wanted them all to match, I could put them all in chef's pants and jackets for Pete's sake."

"Wow, great idea," Morgan enthused. "We could really work with that."

"Dibs on the ones with the chilies," Docia added quickly.

"And beanies," Clem threw in from the audience. "You could all wear chef's beanies. Fantastic for bad hair days."

"No!" Allie slapped her hand down on the arm of her chair. "It was just a rhetoric...rhetorish...*rhetorical* example. You will not wear chef's beanies at my wedding."

Clem shrugged. "Your choice, Al. Personally, I'm going to consider it seriously if Lu and I ever decide to tie the knot."

"Anyway," Allie continued, with a quelling glance at the audience, "I want you each to choose the prettiest dress for yourself. And then we'll tell you whether or not we agree. And then we'll see how they all fit together. If they're like, harmonious."

It took another forty-five minutes of trying on dresses, complaining about dresses, commenting on dresses, and finally, amazingly, reaching consensus on dresses. Jess wore the gun-metal gray satin that Deirdre had picked out for her, and she looked stunning. Janie wore pale pink that made her complexion glow and her dark eyes snap. Pete Toleffson was going to be a very happy man, Kit reflected. Morgan found a full-skirted silk dress the color of burgundy that was wildly appropriate for the marketing director of Cedar Creek Winery. And Docia settled on a magnificent emerald green that somehow managed to make her red hair even redder.

Allie chewed her lip as she stared at them. "Oh my, you're all absolutely gorgeous. I should have thought of that. Nobody's going to notice me with the four of you standing around."

Bethany blew a raspberry that sounded way too unruly for the mayor's wife. "Allie, honey, nobody ever notices anybody except the bride at a wedding. Believe me, once you walk down that aisle, it'll be just like nobody else is even there."

Allie sniffed loudly and took another sip of her champagne.

"Okay, now that we've found the dresses, let's get back into our civvies for the rest of the evening." Docia headed toward the dressing rooms, followed by her fellow bridesmaids.

"I think they're gorgeous. I think everybody's gorgeous." Deirdre watched them go with a smile that seemed slightly off center. Kit was suddenly very glad they had those designated drivers.

She bustled around the room, handing out food to try to compensate for all the champagne they'd consumed, until the bridesmaids returned, clad once again in their normal jeans and T-shirts.

"Okay, now it's time for the presents." Janie bent down behind another rack of clothes, emerging with a brightly colored gift sack.

"Presents?" Allie looked confused. "I thought this was a clothes shower?"

Deirdre shrugged. "Well, now that the clothes have all been taken care of, we've got other things to contribute."

Allie narrowed her eyes. "Other things like what?"

"Like this." Docia handed her a small package wrapped in silver striped paper. "Open it, Toots."

Allie pulled off the wrappings, then stared. "Chocolate-flavored body paint?"

Behind them, Mrs. Dupree turned bright pink. "I'll just get those dresses ready for you all." She headed out of the room with considerable speed.

"This is actually a culinary shower," Docia purred. "Or rather a shower that's geared toward eating, drinking and licking."

Nando approached the back windows of Margaret Hastings' shop cautiously. If it was laid out like all the other shops on Main, the back would be a storeroom, closed off from the main part. He slid his flashlight from his belt, cupping the front in his hand as he leaned toward the back windows but waiting to turn it on until he was sure he needed to. Behind the screens, he could see vague shapes of furniture and boxes. Storage, as he'd suspected.

He crouched in the darkened yard, letting his eyes adjust to the lack of light, waiting to see if the flash would come again.

Probably just a reflection. A headlight in the street, catching one of Margaret's mobiles with the glass angels or the Christmas tree ornaments with the glass angels or the wind chimes with the glass angels. Margaret loved glass angels, and they were everywhere around the freakin' store.

He moved carefully along the side of the building in the narrow space between Margaret's store and Beaman's antiques. If their boy was looking for something valuable to smash, Beaman's would be a much better bet, but Beaman was a lot more likely to invest in an alarm system than Margaret was.

The movement in the store was so subtle he almost missed it. A mini-flashlight of some kind pointed downward so that the light couldn't be seen from the street. He watched the shadow move across the floor, trying to gauge size—if it was kids, he'd head straight for them. If it was a man, he'd have to be more careful.

He moved back the way he'd come, trying to see how the intruder had gotten in. An unlocked door would be handy, but he could use an open window if he had to, since calling Margaret to come down and unlock her shop didn't seem like much of an option.

He paused at the back door that led into the storeroom, turning the knob. It moved in his hand, proving that either the intruder was good with a lock pick or Margaret was incredibly careless about security. Either one could be true, given Margaret's level of competence. The woman was dating Ham, after all.

He slid his flashlight back into the loop on his belt, unsnapping his holster, then slipped through the door into the darkened shop. Now that he was inside, he could hear the faint sounds of the intruder at work, the thump of objects hitting the floor, the slight shuffling sound of his feet as he moved around the store. Nando stepped carefully down the short hall leading to the interior, patting his holster once just to reassure himself that the gun was there and ready. He could see shapes now, dark against slightly less dark, silhouetted against the glow from the streetlights down the block.

He measured his steps more carefully as he approached the entrance to the main room. The noises the intruder made seemed to mean he had no idea anyone was in the shop with him, and Nando wanted to keep it that way.

Slipping around the corner into the back of the shop, he started to step forward again when his feet suddenly jerked out from under him. It took him a moment to realize his boots were tangled in a piece of cloth hanging from a rocking chair at the side. A rocking chair that toppled over sideways as he jerked his feet away, trying to kick the cloth loose.

In the room ahead of him, the intruder froze and then moved quickly toward the front door. Nando threw the cloth away from his boots and pushed himself to his feet. "Stop where you are! Konigsburg Police," he yelled, without a hope in hell that the intruder would pay any attention to him.

The man threw the front door open and burst out onto the street. Nando managed to jerk his service revolver from his holster as he dashed after him, trying to avoid the jungle of dangling angels on all sides. He ran out the entrance, only to see the intruder sprinting down the street toward the Lucky Lady. A man. Maybe six feet tall but hard to tell in the dim light reflected in front of him. No weapons that he could see.

"Hold it," he yelled again, holding the gun loosely at his side as he raced after him.

Ahead of him the door to the Lucky Lady opened and light poured into the street, along with several vaguely familiar female shapes. The running man dodged around and behind them, keeping the women between himself and Nando as he ran.

"Out of the way," Nando yelled frantically. "Get back inside. Now!"

The women froze, staring at him open-mouthed. Docia, Deirdre, Allie, Jess, Clem—Jesus, hadn't anyone stayed home tonight? "Move," he yelled. "Please!"

Docia grabbed hold of the women closest to her, pulling them back out of his way as he sped up again. He could hear the sound of the man's footsteps echoing down Spicewood. He probably didn't have a prayer of catching him now, given that he'd had to detour around what seemed to be a every woman in Konigsburg, but he had to try.

He turned up the street, pounding along the sidewalk, but by the time he reached the next corner he knew it was no use. He jerked his cell phone off his belt, punching in the number savagely. "Rollie, we've had another one. Margaret Hastings' place. And the perp is still on the loose. I need backup. Now."

Toleffson wasn't pleased, but then neither was Nando. They'd searched every yard and vacant lot for a square mile around the place where the intruder had disappeared, but none of them had much hope that they'd find him. Instead they found a lot of semi-awake, semi-hysterical Konigsburg citizens, many of whom were waving their favorite weapons. Toleffson managed to get everyone calmed down, while Nando circled back to Angels Unaware again.

The damage at Margaret Hastings' store wasn't as extensive as it had been at Docia's or Allie's. Apparently, the intruder had just gotten started when Nando found him. Margaret was, however, very unhappy about the woven throw that Nando had managed to trample and the upended rocking chair, even though the chair had been for display rather than something she was trying to sell.

"It's a genuine tapestry," she told him, her blonde curls trembling in indignation. "From China."

It looked like junk to him, but he wasn't feeling exactly charitable about it. By that point, he didn't give a shit what Margaret Hastings was upset about. He was too busy being upset with himself for letting the bastard get away.

He didn't need to be told this was another black mark against him with the city council. First it was the whole poop policeman thing. Now, more seriously, he was the cop who'd let the thief get away—the cop who'd blown their best chance to get the bastard. Ham would ride it for all it was worth, and the city council might well agree with him.

When they all met back at the station house, Ham's solution was simple. "You should've shot him."

Nando blew out a breath, willing himself not to kick Ham's ass. "When should I have shot him, Ham? When I was running after him? When he was dodging around the crowd of women outside the Lucky Lady? When would you have shot him?"

"I'd've taken the bastard out soon as I walked into the store," Ham grumbled. "Should have yelled *police* and then blasted him."

Toleffson pinched the bridge of his nose. "Suppose Avrogado had started firing and it turned out to be Margaret rearranging her stock? What does he say then—Oops? Have you ever bothered to read the Use Of Force Guidelines, Ham? They might be real useful to you in a situation like this."

Nando sighed. "I was trying to get a clear shot at him when the women came out of the Lucky Lady. After that it wasn't possible."

"Damn fool women," Ham muttered. "Should've been home where they belonged."

Toleffson gave him a cold, silent stare, his eyes narrowed. Nando wondered just how long it would take Ham to remember that those particular women included the chief's wife and sisters-in-law.

After a few seconds, Ham flushed the usual dull pink and started examining the pile of papers on the desk in front of him.

Toleffson turned back to Nando. "Did you manage to get a look at him at least?"

He sighed again. "Not in the light, no. He was tall, around six feet. Not too heavy, maybe one fifty or so."

"Did he run like a young man?"

Nando paused, thinking. "Hard to say. He was fast over the short distance, but since I didn't get a chance to run him down, I couldn't say what his stamina was. He wasn't a teenager, but I can't give you much on his age beyond that."

"What was he wearing?" Delaney asked, jotting notes on his legal pad. Ham gave him a poisonous look; Nando didn't think he'd ever seen Ham jot down anything in his entire police career.

"Dark shirt and pants—looked like jeans. Baseball cap. He had it pulled down low, and he ducked his face away from the light."

Toleffson stared off in the distance. "That's interesting."

"What was?" Delaney's pen paused over his pad. The others sat up a little straighter.

161

"Sounds like he didn't want anyone to see his face. Maybe he thought someone would recognize him. Seems like a casual thief would have just kept running and not worried about being recognized until later on."

"So we've got an adult male whom somebody might recognize." Nando rubbed the back of his neck. "Maybe the women saw him more clearly. They were closer to him than I was when he ran by."

Toleffson pinched his nose again. "We need to question them. See what they remember."

Nobody groaned, but everybody looked like they wanted to. Eye witnesses could be a royal pain in the posterior since none of them ever seemed to see exactly the same thing.

"I took statements last night," Rollie said. "They were all pretty shook up, though. And they'd had a lot to drink. Nobody could describe him."

"They've had some time to think about it now," Toleffson mused. "And they've had time to sober up. They might have remembered something they didn't think about when it happened. Who was out there in front of the store?"

Rollie pulled out his notes. "Docia Toleffson, Allie Maldonado, Jess Toleffson, Janie Toleffson, Morgan Toleffson, and Deirdre Brandenburg." He flipped a page. "And Kit Maldonado. The others were in the doorway, but they said they weren't close enough to see what was going on."

Toleffson nodded. "Right. I'll go over it with my wife and Janie and Jess since they all live in the neighborhood. Nando, you talk to Docia and Allie and Deirdre. And Kit. Linklatter, you and Delaney go over Margaret Hastings' place again. See if we missed anything. Do it soon—she'll want to open up today."

Ham tucked his pen back in his pocket as he got to his feet. He gave Nando a look that was close to a smirk before heading out the door. Nando's jaw clenched tight. No chance the town wouldn't know he'd screwed up. The news would probably be all over the Coffee Corral by noon.

Toleffson turned toward the two part-timers. "Rollie, you and Dawson do a door-to-door on the houses around where he took off. See if anybody noticed anything since the last time we asked."

Rollie groaned, rubbing his eyes. "Can I get some shut-eye for a couple hours first? I been on duty since six last night."

Toleffson's jaw tensed, but he shrugged. "Okay. Take a couple of hours, and then come back. Dawson, you do as much as you can on your own."

Nando felt like pointing out that he'd been on duty now for close to ten hours himself and was dead on his feet, but he decided to let it go. He was already in enough shit for letting the son of a bitch get away. He pushed himself to his feet as the others headed out to the parking lot.

"You all right?" Toleffson asked.

He shrugged. "Sure. Just tired."

The chief narrowed his eyes. "You played it right. The only thing you should have done that you didn't was call Rollie so he could back you up before you went into the shop."

"Yeah." Nando blew out a breath. "In retrospect, I sure as hell should have done that."

"Shooting at him on Main Street wouldn't have been a good idea," Toleffson said slowly. "Even if the women hadn't been there, there's too many people around and too much risk of damage. It wasn't an option."

"I know."

But as he headed for his car, Nando had a sinking feeling the rest of Konigsburg wouldn't see it that way. They'd want to know why he hadn't drilled the bastard and asked questions while his body cooled in the dirt.

Brody worked to rein in his anger. Angry people made mistakes, and he couldn't afford any. Not when he was so close to his goal.

He tossed a package of microwave popcorn into the machine and punched the buttons with more force than necessary. A beer would be good, but he'd stick to soda. Beer would only increase his fury, and he needed to keep a clear head.

He hadn't expected the Konigsburg cops to be that much on the ball. They never had in the past, as he had good reason to know. He'd been careless, and he'd almost gotten caught because of it.

In the future, he'd take nothing for granted. He'd need to find out exactly how many opponents he had—how many men were on night duty, and how they were assigned. And he'd have to come up with ways to avoid them, which might involve learning something about their personal habits. It was annoying, a waste of his time, but clearly something that had to be done.

Not that it would slow him down. His plan was still in force, and still workable. He had no intention of turning back now. He'd decided to speed up his timetable, though, heading for the final, most important stop.

And if the Konigsburg police got in the way, he'd deal with them. He always had before.

Chapter Fifteen

Docia looked very tired the next morning and, unless Nando missed his guess, very hung over. She offered him a cup of coffee as she slumped into a chair at her kitchen table. Cal Toleffson wandered around behind her, fixing breakfast while he bounced their baby son on his shoulder. The kid was already the size of the average two-year-old, and he wasn't even walking yet. Apparently, when both parents topped six feet, they produced babies who resembled Paul Bunyan.

"It all happened so fast," Docia groaned. "We heard you yelling in the street and we heard someone running. I guess I just automatically opened the door without even wondering if it might be dangerous."

Behind her back, Cal looked as if he'd tasted something sour, but he said nothing.

"Did you get a look at him as he ran by?" Nando asked.

Docia started to shake her head, then paused. "I guess I did, in a way. I mean, he was right there. But he was moving so fast and we didn't know what was happening exactly."

"Tell me what you can remember about him."

She massaged her forehead. "He was tall. Not Toleffson tall exactly—" she threw a quick glance at her six-foot-six husband, "—but tall by normal standards, around my height. He had on dark clothes. I didn't see his face when he ran by: he turned his head away when we stepped out."

"Hair color?"

She shook her head. "He had on a baseball cap. I couldn't see."

"Was he a young guy? Older? How did he strike you?"

Docia sighed again. "I don't know. He wasn't a teenager, but more than that I couldn't say."

Nando managed to keep his frustration to himself. It wasn't like he'd expected anything more from her.

"He seemed..." She paused for a moment, massaging her forehead again.

"Seemed?"

"Familiar." She grimaced. "I don't know what I mean by that exactly. I didn't recognize him but I felt like I'd seen him before. Does that make sense?"

"Maybe." Nando leaned back in his chair. "Did he maybe remind you of somebody?"

Docia shook her head. "I don't know. It was just this fleeting impression. That he was someone I knew. Or used to know." She blew out a breath. "That's all. And I know it's not much help. Sorry."

He flipped his notebook closed. "That's okay. I didn't think any of you were able to see much. But if you do think of anything more..."

"I'll let you know," Docia finished for him. "So was that the guy who smashed up my store?"

He shrugged. It wasn't like it was any secret. "Probably. He managed to do some damage to Margaret Hastings' place before I got to him. Not as much as what he'd done to your place or Allie's, fortunately."

"Margaret Hastings?" Cal said. "I didn't know she was involved in this."

"Her store was. That's where the guy was when I found him."

"That's...strange." Cal frowned. "Docia and now Margaret."

Nando flipped a new page in his notebook. "Strange how?"

"Well, they were both involved in the Brody thing, Docia and Margaret."

"But Allie wasn't involved with Brody at all," Docia said slowly. "What could these burglaries have to do with Brody anyway? We're all members of the Merchants Association too, Allie and Margaret and me. It's just as likely to be something that happened there. Hell we might all have had the same nutball customer who went off the deep end."

Cal shrugged. "Probably coincidence."

"Probably." Docia rubbed her forehead again. "I'm sorry, Nando. That's really all I can remember."

"That's okay." He flipped his notebook closed. "Thanks for your help."

"Yeah." Docia gave him a dry smile. "I might have been even more help if I'd stayed inside the Lucky Lady instead of walking out into the middle of your chase last night."

Nando gave her a tight smile. She was absolutely right, of course. "Don't worry about it. We'll catch him." Now all he had to do was make that statement come true.

Kit figured Allie was lucky to have an assistant who could do the morning baking for her as well as open the café. Allie herself looked like she'd rather spend the day in bed in a darkened room with cotton in her ears to keep the noise down.

"Why did you let me have that much champagne?" she croaked after inhaling a cup of coffee. Wonder cut her a piece of coffeecake that she regarded with distaste.

"It seemed like a good idea at the time." Kit checked her watch. She needed to get to the Woodrose early enough to satisfy Mabel.

"Have the police been around?"

She shook her head. "Not yet. I don't know what I could tell them anyway. I didn't see more than a blur."

"Me neither. Exciting finish for the evening, though."

"It was that," Kit agreed.

Allie's eyes widened. "Oh my god, did anybody think to get the dresses? Did we leave them in the store after all that commotion? Will Janie's mom remember whose is whose?"

Kit sighed. "Allie, your dress is hanging in your closet where I put it when we got home last night. Everybody else's dresses went home with them too. Trust me, we're good to go." She checked her watch again. "Speaking of going, I've got to get out to the Woodrose before Mabel decides to dock my pay."

Allie frowned. "We need to get you a better job someplace else—you're way too good to be working for that screw-up. I'll ask around and see if anyone else is hiring."

Kit felt an odd pang. Could she actually feel some loyalty to Mabel? She blew out a breath. Not Mabel, but surprisingly enough, she found she felt a lot of loyalty to the Rose. Her restaurant, for better or worse. "It's not such a bad place, Allie."

The lunch crowd at the Rose was no better or worse than usual.

167

Lots of women in tennis outfits, and men who looked like they'd either spent time on the golf course or wanted people to think that they had. They were drawing more and more groups of shoppers who were having a day in the Hill Country and had come to the Woodrose to have a bowl of Joe's shrimp bisque and the Cobb salad he'd added after heavy pressure from Mabel. Of course, since it was Joe's Cobb salad, it featured local goat cheese and toasted pecans. Kit only hoped the shoppers had someone to drive them back to wherever they'd come from since they probably wouldn't be in any shape to do it themselves, judging from the number of wine bottles she was opening.

Mabel came to the hostess station around one thirty, when the rush was beginning to die down and the late stragglers had slowed to a trickle. "Did you get the scheduling software straightened out this morning, Kit dear? I need to start entering information."

"It's almost ready. Just a few more tweaks in the settings." Settings that Mabel could probably have figured out for herself if she'd taken the time. Kit gritted her teeth—at least she was now square with Mabel after taking time off for the shower.

"You can go work on it now," Mabel said briskly. "I need it ASAP."

"But we've still got a few people coming in for lunch."

Mabel waved a vague hand. "Oh, I can handle the hostess station. The software is more important, believe me."

That was, of course, a matter of opinion, but Kit wasn't really sorry to spend the rest of the afternoon sitting in front of a computer. Her arches had already begun to ache.

After Elaine had dropped off a third order, without a single one from Phillip, Joe stepped out into the dining room to see what the hell was going on. As he'd suspected, he found Elaine's station was almost full, while Philip leaned against the wall, muttering, probably about the empty tables that surrounded him.

Mabel Morgenstern was standing at the hostess station. As far as Joe could tell, she was spending more time on her BlackBerry than on taking care of anything in the dining room. Elaine was trying desperately to keep water and iced tea flowing.

"Where's Kit?" he snapped. He'd found that Mabel responded more promptly to bluntness, which was fine with him since she pissed him off so thoroughly most of the time that it was hard not to snarl at her.

Mabel patted her smooth chignon. "She's doing some work for me on the scheduling software. Why? Do you need her for something?"

Joe gritted his teeth. "I need her to manage the damn restaurant. I thought that was her job."

"I'm the one who decides what her job is, and today I needed her to fix the software." Mabel gave him the usual sunny smile that didn't extend any farther than her lips.

"And you're taking over as the restaurant hostess?"

Mabel raised an eyebrow. "Why would you have a problem with that?"

"I don't, in general. Only the part about you screwing the seating up, which is, in fact, most of the goddamn job. You've got all the customers on one station. The most experienced waiter is just standing around while the novice is being run off her feet."

Mabel shrugged. "I put the people at the tables by the windows so they could have the view. You can just tell the waiters to split the tables up. Seems simple enough."

"That's why we have the damn stations, Mabel. They're supposed to divide up the work so the waiters can take care of all the customers. It only seems simple to you because don't know what the fuck you're doing."

Mabel's mouth tightened to a thin line. "Listen, Joseph, I don't care how wonderful a chef you think you are, you can still be fired. Just like anybody else. At my discretion."

Joe gave her his best lazy grin. "You gonna try to fire me, Mabel? Even though you didn't hire me in the first place? Even though you aren't my boss in any way except technically? You want to try explaining to Mauritz why you felt it necessary to fire the chef who got them back their four-star rating because I didn't work and play well with you? Good luck, darlin'. But if I was you, I wouldn't push it."

Mabel's eyes burned bright as diamonds. For a moment, he thought she might actually let loose with a few obscenities, which would have suited his mood exactly. Instead she blew out a breath in an exaggerated sigh. "Anything else?"

"Nope." He shook his head. "But if anybody else comes in, send them over to the empty section. I don't want to have to deal with a waiter rebellion when lunch is over."

She gave him a blood-chilling look. "I'll consider it."

"You do that, darlin'." He started to head back to the kitchen, then decided not to. In his current mood he was liable to pick a fight with one of his line cooks, and he needed to keep them happy. Maybe he'd see if he could find Kit. He'd been planning to ask her out again anyway and doing it now would definitely improve his mood.

Unfortunately, his mood took another turn south when he saw the cop from the Faro walk in the front door of the inn as he crossed the lobby. Joe paused, folding his arms across his chest. Maybe he could pick a fight with him instead of the cooks. That might be entertaining. Of course, it might also be painful. "Can I help you?"

Apparently, judging by his narrowed eyes and his tightened jaw, the cop recognized him too. "I'm looking for Kit Maldonado."

Joe allowed himself a slightly curved lip. "Well now. Don't tell me the beauteous Ms. Maldonado is in trouble with the law. I'd hate to lose one of the few competent employees the Woodrose has."

The cop's eyes narrowed still further. "Ms. Maldonado isn't in any trouble, and I need to talk to her. Can you tell me where she is, or should I start opening doors at random?"

Joe grinned in spite of himself. "Nice one. If Mabel was out here on duty, she'd probably be cowering." He stuck out his hand. "Don't believe we've met formally. I'm Joe LeBlanc. I work with Kit."

The cop looked like he was considering whether he wanted to shake hands or not, but apparently his mama had raised him with the same set of manners Mama LeBlanc had used on her nearest and dearest. He gave Joe's hand a half-hearted shake. "Fernando Avrogado. Now where's Kit?"

For a moment, Joe considered jerking him around a little more since it was the most fun he'd had all day. On the other hand, a dustup in the lobby would give Mabel an actual reason to fire him, one that would probably stand up with Bert Mauritz, the head of Resorts Consolidated's U.S. branch. "She's in the manager's office." He pointed down the hall. "Third door on the left."

Avrogado nodded curtly. "Thanks." He walked past him toward the door.

Joe felt like sighing all of a sudden. The chances of hooking up with Kit Maldonado were looking more and more remote. Which made this the capper on an already shitty day.

He decided to head back to the kitchen. Hell, there had to be something in there that needed chopping.

When Kit heard the door open behind her, she assumed it was Mabel. She'd already been back to check on her progress three times. Of course being checked on every fifteen minutes hadn't made the work go any more quickly, but that apparently didn't bother Mabel as much as it did Kit.

"Look, Mabel, I'm almost done," she muttered. "I'll call you when it's finished."

"Fine by me," a masculine voice rumbled behind her. "Of course, I don't exactly know what you're talking about."

Kit swiveled the desk chair around with a frantic squeak. Nando stood in the doorway. "What are you doing here?" she blurted.

He shrugged, his smile turning dry. "I'm on the job, as it turns out. I needed to ask you some questions about last night. Can you give me ten minutes?"

Kit managed a quick smile of her own. "Sure, of course. I'm sorry, that was pretty rude. I wasn't expecting anybody except my boss back here."

He pulled up the visitor chair from beside the desk. "That's okay. Shouldn't take long. I just wanted to find out what you remembered about the chase last night."

Kit shook her head. "Not much. I was at the back of the crowd and the guy ran by at light speed. I didn't really see him."

"Any idea of height and weight?" Somehow a notebook had materialized in Nando's hand.

She shrugged. "Nothing much, really. I mean he was taller than most of us, but except for Docia we're all pretty much average size. And I've never been able to estimate weight anyway."

"How about clothes?"

Kit closed her eyes, trying to remember. "Dark. That's about all I can tell you. Shirt and pants. And baseball hat. All I really saw was his back." She tried to visualize it again, then opened her eyes, frowning.

171

Meg Benjamin

"What?"

"Now that I think about it, I'd swear I've seen him somewhere before. But I don't know where or when. It's just...I've seen that back. Doing something."

Nando sat very still, his hand poised over his notebook. "Take your time."

Kit waited for a moment longer, trying to push at the faint tickle at the back of her mind. Then she sighed, grimacing. "No, sorry. I don't know what I'm thinking of exactly. But I'd swear the guy was from around here somewhere. I guess that's not much help, though, is it?"

Nando shrugged again. "It's some help. If we put it together with what other people remember, we might get somewhere with it." He yawned, then rubbed his eyes, grimacing.

Kit studied the deepening lines around his mouth. He looked a couple of years older than he had the last time she'd seen him. "Are you okay?"

"Just tired. I haven't been to bed yet."

She shook her head. "You've been up since last night?"

"Yeah, and I'm back on duty again at six. I'm hoping I can grab a couple of hours of sleep before then." He slid the notebook back into this pocket.

"That's..." she shook her head again, searching for an adjective that was dire enough.

"It's okay. It's just work. I've done it before." The corners of his lips turned up slightly. "Have dinner with me Saturday night."

She blinked at him. "Saturday night?"

"My first day off night duty. And I'm off again on Sunday." His grin became more pronounced. "It'll give me something to look forward to."

Kit blew out a breath. "Okay, I'll have dinner with you. Now go home and get some rest."

"I'll do that." He pushed himself to his feet, then looked back again. "And now I'll have pleasant dreams."

Kit resisted the urge to fan herself as she watched him walk away. It really wasn't that hot in the office.

*

172

The last customer took off at two when Joe emerged from the kitchen again. He'd already managed to soothe the waiter rebellion by reminding them that Kit would be back on tomorrow, and she at least knew what she was doing. Now he wanted to make sure that was the case.

Mabel ignored him elaborately as he walked through the lobby. He thought about leaning on the desk and exchanging a few words, but he no longer felt like it. Besides, harassing Mabel about her incompetence was like shooting fish in a barrel.

He headed for the office, then paused in the doorway. Kit was leaning back in her chair as she looked out the window. She wore a faint smile, her eyes slightly unfocussed, as if she were daydreaming. She looked even more gorgeous than usual. Unfortunately, he had a pretty good idea who'd put that dreamy smile on her face.

Well, shit.

"Did the cop find you?" he asked, as if the answer weren't obvious.

"Nando? Yeah. He just had some questions about what happened last night."

"Last night?" Joe frowned, trying to remember if he'd heard anything about last night. The only thing that sprang to mind was a screwed-up produce order.

"What happened downtown last night. I was there."

"Downtown?" He wasn't usually this slow on the uptake. He wondered just how many brain cells he'd sacrificed in New Orleans.

Kit shook her head. "You haven't heard about all of this, have you? There have been some burglaries downtown, with vandalism. You know—Allie's bakery was one of the places that got hit."

Joe nodded, happy to be back on solid ground. "Right, sure. I remember now. Took off with some kitchen equipment."

"That's the one. He hit another store last night, only Nando saw him and chased him down Main."

"And you were there?" Joe frowned, envisioning a number of unpleasant scenarios involving hostages. If this was what Avrogado did on dates, maybe he still had a chance.

"I was there by accident. We were having a shower for Allie in a store down the street and the shower guests walked into the middle of the chase. If it hadn't been for us, Nando might have been able to catch the so-and-so." Kit sighed. "It's going to take us a few weeks to live that down."

"Did you see the guy?"

She shook her head. "It all happened too fast. I think he's a local, though. His back looked familiar."

Joe grinned. "You an aficionado of backs, darlin'?"

Kit flushed pink. "Not especially. It just...I thought I'd seen him somewhere before."

"Ah well." He let his grin slide into something lazier. "There's a new place opened up in Johnson City. Chef used to work in Houston. Want to check it out with me after the lunch rush Saturday?"

She licked her lips, her cheeks still faintly flushed. "That sounds nice, but I'm busy Saturday. Sorry."

Joe gritted his teeth. *A day late and a dollar short—foiled again.* "Maybe next time, darlin'." Although he sincerely doubted there'd be a next time, given the effect the cop had had on Kit. Maybe he should start checking out the talent at the Faro. There had to be some interesting unattached females in this town.

Although he figured none of them would be quite as interesting at Kit Maldonado. Unfortunately.

Chapter Sixteen

Toleffson called another meeting for six, after Nando had managed to catch a couple of hours of sleep. He wasn't exactly groggy, but he hoped to hell nobody decided to knock over the bank tonight—his reflexes weren't exactly first rate.

He sipped a cup of Helen's coffee, which was a lot like mainlining caffeine. Helen herself had stuck around after her shift ended, a clear indication of just how dire the situation was becoming since Helen rarely stayed at the station any longer than she had to.

Ham and Delaney had gone over Margaret's store, but hadn't found any more evidence to speak of, although Ham had taken lots of fingerprints. Judging by the state of his clothes, he'd left a fine dusting of fingerprint powder everywhere he'd gone. Nando was guessing Margaret wasn't pleased.

"So what did he get this time?" Toleffson asked.

Delaney shrugged. "Ms. Hastings said she didn't think he took anything, but she'll double-check once she finishes cleaning the place up. I guess he smashed some figurines. Plus she kept talking about some 'throw' that got all messed up. I don't even know what a throw is."

"It's like a blanket," the chief explained, carefully not looking at Nando.

"Well, anyway, this throw thing and the figurines are the only real damage. He tossed some stuff around, so he was maybe looking for something else to take, but I guess he didn't have time to find anything good."

Toleffson turned to Rollie and Dawson. "Anybody on the block see anything?"

Rollie grimaced. "Sure. They all saw the boogeyman coming down the chimney." He flipped open his notebook. "One guy said he saw, and I quote, 'some big Mexican dude' climbing over his back fence." Rollie himself was a sort of big Mexican-American dude, but the witness might not have noticed. "Another one saw somebody running down the sidewalk with a shotgun. He ran back inside and got *his* shotgun out of the closet, but he said when he got back, they were gone."

"Fortunately," Nando muttered.

Dawson nodded. "Got that right. Last thing we need is everybody blasting away in the dark. Two or three other people thought they might have seen somebody in their backyard, but nobody had a description. If he was around that block, he got away clean."

Helen shook her head. "Nobody's gonna see anything over there. People over on that block probably go to bed at nine. Mostly retired folks, one or two families with young kids. You must have woke 'em up. They're not gonna remember nothin'."

Toelffson pinched the bridge of his nose. "So that's a wash. I talked to my wife, along with Janie and Jess Toleffson. None of them saw much. Said he wore black and moved fast. How about you?" He turned to Nando.

Nando sighed. "Allie and Deirdre said they didn't see a thing. Both of them were too far back in the group. But Docia and Kit both said he looked familiar."

The chief frowned, leaning forward slightly. "Familiar how?"

"Neither of them could explain it. But they were both fairly sure they'd seen him before."

"So they saw his face?"

Nando shook his head. "Nope. Just general impressions."

Rollie blew out a derisive breath. "Yeah. Like the big Mexican dude who was absolutely and for sure going over the guy's back fence."

"No." Nando shook his head again. "Neither of them claimed they actually recognized him, and they were both sort of apologetic about bringing it up. But both of them thought there was something familiar about the guy. We just don't know what it was."

The chief glanced at Helen. "Any gossip floating around about this? Anybody on the radar?"

She shook her head. "Lotta people talkin' about it, but nobody who's the favorite candidate yet."

Toleffson leaned back in his chair again, sighing. "Okay, then, basically we've got nothing. No prints, no physical evidence, no solid descriptions."

Delaney shrugged. "Maybe he'll take off now. He almost got caught this time, and he didn't get away with anything. The stuff he's taken so far isn't worth much. Maybe he'll decide to cut his losses."

"Maybe. But I wouldn't count on it." The chief turned to Dawson and Rollie. "I've got authorization from Rankin to keep up the double patrols until we catch this SOB. You guys can alternate—two nights on, two nights off."

The two nodded. Rollie yawned so widely his jaw cracked.

Toleffson glanced at Nando. "You good for tonight?"

"Yeah. Tomorrow's the last night of my shift. I can do it." He rubbed his eyes.

"Okay, who takes over this weekend?"

"Me," Dawson said.

"And me." Delaney raised his hand tentatively. "My first time on nights."

Toleffson sighed. "Well, kid, at least now you know what to look for. Everybody who's not on duty go home and get some sleep. Let's hope somebody other than the perp gets a brilliant idea overnight."

Nando settled his Stetson on his head as he headed out the front door. The only brilliant idea he had currently involved bribing Tom Ames to brew him up a cup of Deirdre's dark roast, size humongous. Helen's coffee had given his brain a jumpstart. Now he needed something to keep it functioning for the rest of the evening.

Saturday dawned clear and warm, with honey-colored sunlight pouring over the bluebonnets and primroses blooming on the borders of the smoothly rolling lawn at the Woodrose. Not for the first time, Kit wished she were a guest at the inn rather than an employee.

She watched the gardener, Mr. Didrikson, circle the riding mower back and forth across the grass, careful to leave the margins of wildflowers at the side. He might be a hell of a gardener, but so far she'd never seen him do anything but mow the lawns. He seemed to have one of the easier jobs around the property.

She wondered if he'd gotten around to putting out the fertilizer he'd ordered. It would be just her luck if he decided to do it the weekend of Allie's wedding.

Kit closed her eyes, massaging her temples as she went over her mental wedding checklist. Her physical checklist was back on the whiteboard in Allie's kitchen, but by now she had it memorized. The flowers and decorations for the ceremony had been ordered through Mabel, using one of the florists who usually worked at the event center. They had a DJ for dancing at the reception, since Wonder and Allie couldn't agree on which band to hire. Joe had the menu for the dinner and she assumed he was working on it, or would be when the time was right.

She blew out a quick breath. Had Wonder nailed down the judge to officiate? She'd forgotten to ask him. On the other hand, Wonder had been writing checks left and right, and making sure Allie kept on task. She had a feeling he'd do whatever it took to get the wedding underway on time, up to and including ordaining one of the Toleffsons, if that became necessary.

They'd been addressing invitations for a week, and should be able to drop them in the mail on Monday. Kit had known they'd have a lot of relatives to invite, given the size of the extended Maldonado family, but she was surprised at how many other people were on the list, including a couple of celebrity chefs whose names made her blink.

"Do you think they'll actually come?" she'd asked Allie.

Allie had shrugged. "I went to their weddings. Hell, I baked the cakes for their weddings. I assume they'll be there unless they're cooking for the White House or something."

Kit rolled her shoulders to relax them. So there were famous people coming to the wedding, so what? Maybe they'd stay at the inn. Mabel would be ecstatic. And the important thing was that the wedding took place and everyone had a good time.

Including her. Which was why she'd invited both Nando and Joe. She figured one or the other of them would dance with her.

Thinking of Joe, she watched him make his circuit of the dining room, smiling at the regulars, stopping to check with newcomers. Just like her father, although there was nothing particularly fatherly about him. Still, her father had done the same thing for twenty years, talking to people, smiling at people, while a succession of cooks turned out the recipes he'd gotten from various members of the family. Antonio's Fine Mexican Cuisine had run like a finely tuned engine—she'd just begun to understand how much work that had taken. No wonder her father wanted to retire.

Her father and Joe LeBlanc. Both of them pros. Who knew? She waited for the same feeling of loss that she usually felt whenever she ruminated about Antonio's Fine Mexican Cuisine. It was still there, but maybe not as strong as it had been once. At least her father had taught her how a good restaurant should be run. And now, little by little, she was applying those lessons at the Rose, whenever she could find a way to work around Mabel Morgenstern.

Joe leaned against the other side of the hostess stand. "What's up with Phillip?"

Kit squinted in his direction. Philip was giving the people at his station a remarkably surly look. Which was pretty much the same look he wore every day. "Nothing I know of. He's leaving early, though."

"Today?" Joe scowled. "He's leaving early on one of the busiest days of the week?"

"I told him I'd cover for him. I'll give some of his tables to Elaine. She said she could use the tip money. I can pick up any slack."

"Still." Joe grimaced. "I talked to Mabel about more wait staff last week. Haven't heard anything back, though."

Given that when he spoke to Mabel he usually sounded like he was lecturing a not particularly bright five-year-old, Kit couldn't say she was too surprised. "I'll remind her. If I tell her I'll take care of the hiring end, she might be more willing to go through with advertising it." Especially if Kit emphasized that the new wait staff would increase revenue. She'd be careful to avoid mentioning Joe's name in the conversation.

"Thanks, darlin'." Joe grinned, dark blue eyes dancing. "You sure you got a date tonight? I hear that restaurant over in Johnson City rocks."

Kit gave him a cautious smile. "I'm sorry, I'm sure it's great, but I've definitely got a date." In fact, the thought of that date made her heart rate speed up slightly, although she didn't really want it to.

"If I believed you really were sorry about it, darlin', I might try a little harder. But I guess I'll take your word for it." He glanced back at the rapidly filling dining room. "Don't let 'em run you ragged. Remember, you're not getting paid enough."

True that. Kit prepared to run some credit cards for Elaine, trying to put the thought of Nando Avrogado onto the back burner where it belonged.

Nando fell into his bed at seven on Saturday morning, and didn't emerge until five in the afternoon. Normally when he switched from night shift to days, he tried not to sleep the day away since it made for difficulties adjusting to the different hours. But he was going out with Kit that night, and he wanted to be ready.

He wasn't sure what exactly he was going to be ready for. Anything fate dished out, probably.

Guinevere was sitting on the kitchen table again, admiring the world outside the window. "Get down, Bozo," Nando growled.

Guinevere ignored him. She usually did unless she wanted her ears scratched.

Esteban was setting the microwave to nuke his fried chicken dinner. If their mother ever found out they were eating frozen crap, she'd skin both of them before supplying their freezer with enough casseroles to keep them fed for the rest of the millennium—a fate neither of them wanted.

"The dead are reborn," Esteban commented, glancing Nando's way as he hit the power button. "Hallelujah."

Nando leaned against the counter, rubbing his face. "Any coffee around?"

"I haven't washed the pot yet. If you don't mind cold and stale, it's available."

He sighed and opened the refrigerator. At least there was iced tea. "You going out tonight?"

Esteban shrugged. "Maybe. Junior Bonner's at the Faro. I thought I might swing by. How about you?"

"Thinking about it." He took a swallow of tea. "I'm going out with Kit."

Esteban turned to stare at him for a long moment, folding his arms across his chest.

Briefly, Nando was sorry he'd mentioned it. If his brother said anything sarcastic, he might end up punching him.

"That right?" he said finally.

"Yeah." Nando took another swallow. "I thought I might show her this place, if that's all right with you."

Esteban said nothing for a while, then he nodded. "Okay with me. I'm going out to see the folks tonight. Might not be back."

Nando stayed silent, waiting to see if he'd say anything else—anything that would require retaliation. He didn't. "Okay," he said finally. "Tell 'em hello for me."

"I'll do that. My best to Kit."

"Right." He watched Esteban lift his dinner out of the microwave, pouring some tea down his throat so he wouldn't say anything else.

It wasn't until he started to change his clothes that his nerves really began to kick in. He'd told Kit he'd pick her up at her house when she got off work, which she'd said would probably be around six. He stared at his closet, trying to decide where he wanted to go with this.

He could take Kit to Brenner's, the best restaurant in town and a place he could only afford once every couple of months or so. But she might be sick of gourmet food, given that she probably ate it on a daily basis, thanks to LeBlanc. He could take her to the Faro, where Clem's stuff was terrific without being too highfalutin, but the Faro on a Saturday night could be a zoo, particularly when they had a band playing in the beer garden as they would tonight. He ran through a list of other restaurants—the Silver Spur, the Coffee Corral, Mi Ranchito. None of them seemed right for what he had in mind.

Not that he was too clear on what he had in mind right then, but he thought he had an idea or two. He sighed, gazing around the apartment. It was in decent shape for once since Esteban had actually done some sweeping and run the dishwasher.

Suddenly he had a vision of the perfect dinner—a large pizza from Athenos with sausage for him and sliced tomatoes for Kit, sitting in the middle of his kitchen table. Along with one of those bottles of red wine Esteban always had lying around.

Of course, Kit would figure he had some kind of ulterior motive in mind if he suggested it. She'd also be right, and he didn't think that was necessarily a bad idea. Nando closed his eyes for a moment and tried to think of the right way to phrase the request. He had a feeling he might have to do some persuading.

Assuming, of course, he made it a request. It might be just as easy if he went ahead and ordered the pizza before he went to pick her up. Persuading after the fact could be a lot easier than trying to set the stage beforehand.

And hell, once upon a time he'd been the prince of persuaders. That was, of course, before Kit Maldonado stepped into his life and turned it upside down. Now he needed to summon up what was left of his former persuasive skills.

And hope that the sight of her didn't turn his brain to mush the way it usually did.

Working Philip's section for part of the afternoon had had one great effect. Kit hadn't had time to feel nervous about going out with Nando again. At least she hadn't until she was in her car headed for home. Even then, she told herself it was no big deal, nothing to get jittery about. She'd change out of her work clothes but not put on anything fancy. Just jeans and maybe a T-shirt. Or no, maybe that lavender silk shirt that made her skin look so creamy. And were her best jeans clean, or had she thrown them in the laundry?

When her sweaty palms slipped on her steering wheel, she knew she was lying to herself about the nervous thing. But she'd always been a lot better at lying to herself than to anyone else. After all, who knew better what she wanted to believe?

She trotted inside the house, tossing her purse on the couch and noting, gratefully, that Allie wasn't home. She hadn't told her she was going out with Nando yet. She wasn't sure she would, either.

Kit stripped off her navy suit and flowered blouse, locating the lavender shirt and the good jeans in her closet. She turned to study herself in the mirror briefly. *Okay, not cotton underwear. Maybe the red lace.*

Her heart gave a mighty thud, and she grasped the edge of the dresser. What the hell was she thinking of? Why would her underwear matter?

Oh please. Like you don't know.

She closed her eyes for a moment, taking a series of deep breaths. *You don't have to do this. You don't have to go through with it. You can tell him you're tired.*

She felt an ache then, somewhere below her heart. True enough—

she could break the date, which would probably end whatever it was that was stirring between them again. That would be sharp, simple and effective. And it would break her heart all over again.

For better or worse, she was going out with Nando. And for better or worse, she was changing her underwear.

Five minutes later she heard his car in the driveway. She gave one last look at herself in the mirror, checking to make sure her mascara hadn't run and her lip gloss hadn't smeared onto her teeth.

She headed for the door as she heard his step on the porch, then paused to wipe her suddenly damp hands on her jeans.

Showtime, baby, showtime.

Chapter Seventeen

She looked glorious. It was the first thought that jumped into his brain when she opened the door. The lavender shirt made her dark eyes glow, and her hair fell across her shoulders like water. Even the faint sheen of perspiration on her forehead made her look delectable, like she should undo a few buttons and fan herself.

Or maybe let him do the fanning. And the unbuttoning.

He ushered her to the car, trying to jumpstart his brain enough to at least think of something halfway intelligent to say. But every time he looked at her, his mind went blank. All he really wanted to do was pull her into his arms. So much for his persuasive skills.

"Are you hungry?" he managed finally. "Do they give you dinner out there at the Rose?"

"No, just lunch." Her lips moved up in a small grin. "They call it 'family meal' in most restaurants, and you get whatever's the cheapest thing on the menu, or whatever was left over from yesterday. Joe's pretty good about it, though. If he wants the waiters to push something to the customers, he makes sure he has some available for them to taste before they start serving."

"Oh." Nando really didn't want to talk about Joe LeBlanc and his goodness. "I felt like a pizza, so I called in an order to Athenos." He gestured toward the backseat where the pizza box sat giving off some of the most delectable scents known to man. "It's got tomatoes."

Kit's smile turned slightly wary. "You remembered I like tomatoes on my pizza?"

He glanced at her, then turned back to watch the road. "Among other things."

There was a moment of silence while he cursed himself. *Not the time to remind her about the past, moron.*

"If you don't want any food, I can always save the pizza for later," he said quickly. Although it would almost kill him to do that since he hadn't had anything besides a glass of tea since he woke up.

"Pizza sounds good," Kit said a little stiffly. "Where are we going to eat it?"

At my house, my kitchen table, with my bedroom right down the hall. Except that would be pretty much guaranteed to send her out the door. And he wanted—*needed*—this to work.

"How about the city park?" He turned up Third Street. Neutral ground since the park was probably still full of families and charcoal grills.

She seemed to relax slightly. "That sounds good. I haven't been there since I came back."

He pulled into a space at the side of the picnic grounds, handing her the pizza box. "I'll bring the wine and the cups."

Kit frowned, balancing the box on the tips of her fingers as she looked for an empty picnic table. "Is that legal, Officer? Drinking wine in the park, I mean."

He shrugged, heading for a table tucked beneath a couple of pecan trees. "Sort of semi-legal. You can drink in the park as long as you keep it out of sight. The ordinance says something like *No openly displayed alcoholic beverages.* I figure it was the Germans making sure they could drink beer as long as they kept it in their buckets. Another one of those Konigsburg compromises with sin."

She smiled, more relaxed now. "Let's hear it for compromises."

He checked the surrounding area as he used the corkscrew on the wine. One older couple at the table to the left, finishing their meal. A family packing up after a couple of kids at a table a little farther on. They should be gone soon too. He covered the wine bottle in a paper sack and grabbed the two plastic glasses he'd picked up before he left the house.

"What are we drinking?" Kit asked.

"Bored Ducks." Nando shrugged. "Esteban had a couple of bottles sitting around the house. Hope that's okay."

Kit's smile softened. "I remember when they released that wine. Did it do as well as Morgan hoped it would?"

"It's a big seller, I guess." He handed her the glass. "I don't keep track of that kind of stuff usually. That's my dad's thing."

She sighed. "I miss that place. I really enjoyed it, even with all the

185

drama that summer."

He managed not to grimace. Some of that drama had involved the two of them and their breakup-to-end-all-breakups. "Did you check around out there when you were looking for a job? Morgan might have something available."

Kit stared down into her glass. "No. That was then, this is now. I wanted to try working someplace different."

Which probably meant she hadn't wanted to go someplace that was tied up with him and his family. He did grimace this time, but he hid it by opening the pizza box. "You like working at the Rose?"

Her brow furrowed as if she had to think about it. "The pay sucks," she said slowly. "My boss is incompetent. I'm run off my feet most days. But…"

"But?" he prompted.

"But it's a wonderful place." She shrugged. "Or it can be. *Will* be if we can make Mabel see reason. I feel like I'm in on the beginning of a great restaurant. And I'm making a difference in what happens there."

He gave her a questioning look. "How?"

Her smile turned dry. "It turns out I actually know a hell of a lot about running a restaurant. More than I realized. I've been training the wait staff, or trying to anyway. And I've been sort of bowled over by how many things I understand about orders and promoting, to say nothing of customer flow. Joe says I've got the Rose almost up to where it should be. All we need to do now is push Mabel to let us order everything else we need."

"So I guess Joe's good." He took a sip of wine to clear the sour taste out of his mouth.

She shrugged. "He's a great chef. He sucks with personnel."

Nando managed a half smile. "So you're the go-between? He probably appreciates that."

Her eyes were dark in the gathering twilight. "He's my friend, Nando. I respect him. That's about it."

He felt an absurd jolt of relief which he promptly suppressed. *Keep it light, moron.* "So how's the wedding coming?" he picked up another slice of pizza. "I got my invitation, by the way."

The wedding conversation took them through half the pizza and most of the wine. The older couple left with their picnic basket. The

186

family left with one kid asleep on his father's shoulder and the other whining as his mother pulled him along toward the car.

Nando leaned forward on his elbows, watching Kit's face in the darkness. Shadows from the overhead lights along the park paths picked out the hollows beneath her cheek bones. She turned to look at him, her eyes dark in the dim light, and he realized they'd been silent for few moments. For the life of him, he couldn't remember what she'd been saying before that. He'd been lost in the wonder of her face.

He swallowed hard. "More pizza?"

She shook her head, smiling faintly. "I've had all I can eat tonight."

"Well..." He rubbed his jaw. "We could go dancing—there's a band at the Faro."

"We could," Kit agreed. She didn't sound too enthusiastic. "I've been on my feet all day, though."

"Or we could stick around here at the park..." he began.

A group of teenagers clattered to a table a few feet away. They watched as the boys set up speakers leading to an iPod dock and then turned up the volume.

Kit grimaced. "Or not."

Nando didn't recognize the music that began to play at near-sonic levels, but he hated it instantly. He considered arresting the little pissants for violating the noise ordinance, but it would have meant leaving Kit and doing paperwork at the office. He leaned across the table so that their heads were close enough to let him be heard without bellowing. "Want to go to my place?"

Kit stared at him for a beat, and his heart began to ache in anticipation. Then the corners of her mouth edged up in another faint smile. "Mine's closer."

What are you doing? What the hell are you doing? The voice of her rational self almost drowned out the thumping of Kit's heart.

We're just going to the house. It doesn't mean we're going to do anything. I can stop this anytime I want.

Do you want to stop?

She'd rushed home from work. She'd put on her red lace lingerie. Clearly, she'd already been thinking about doing this. And stopping didn't seem to fit into her plans. Kit took another in a series of deep breaths. *We're going to do this. We're going to do this now. Even without the Lizzie Farraday conversation we need to have.*

She glanced at Nando's profile in the streetlights as they cruised up Firewheel—his jaw was set, his dark eyes fixed on the road ahead, his hair slightly mussed from the breeze. He looked like he'd focused every particle of his consciousness on getting them to her house as quickly as possible without breaking any of the relevant traffic laws.

If he focused that kind of attention on her, she'd probably be dragging him into her bedroom five minutes after they got in the front door, assuming they made it that far. She closed her eyes. *Dangerous. Really, really dangerous.*

Oh hell, what's life without a little risk? We can always talk later. And we will.

Nando pulled into the driveway and turned off the ignition. "Is Allie around? Will I need to move the car?"

Kit shook her head. "Allie's off playing with Wonder."

He glanced at her, grinning. "That sounds like a song title."

"Yeah, well, it may be the only way Steve Kleinschmidt qualifies as poetic." She sighed. "If you bring the wine and pizza, I can give you a piece of Tupperware or something to put it into."

He nodded, gathering up the bottle and box from the backseat as she dug into her purse for her keys. She was annoyed to feel her fingers trembling. *Knock it off, Catarina. It's just a date. With Nando. That's heading inside toward the bedroom.*

Fortunately, he was so busy juggling the pizza and wine he didn't seem to notice how many tries it took her to get the key in the lock. She stood in the front hall, watching him slide the pizza into the refrigerator, wondering if she should ask him to sit down, maybe search out some glasses for the wine, maybe put on some music.

He sauntered back from the kitchen, looping one arm around her waist as he stared down at her lips.

Maybe not.

Now that it was happening, or maybe about to happen, he had a sudden attack of nerves. Maybe she didn't want this. Maybe she'd tell him no. Maybe...

Kit stared up at him for a long moment, then wrapped her arms around his neck, pulling his mouth down to hers. He felt the press of her teeth against his lower lip, the tip of her tongue sweeping along the edge. And suddenly he was pulling her tight, feeling her breasts soft against his chest, her mouth opening beneath his as his tongue plunged deep. He angled his head again, one hand buried in her hair, his palm cupping the back of her head as he deepened the kiss.

His blood roared in his ears as his groin ached with arousal. His pulse seemed to have become a constant beat, *now, now, now.* Now up against the wall. Now on the floor. Now on the kitchen table only a few steps away. But now, somewhere now.

He raised his head, panting, trying to get his brain to function again. She stared up at him with whiskey-dark eyes, her lips full and bruised with his kisses. He could feel the puff of her breath on his chin, see the quick rise and fall of her breasts.

He covered one breast with his hand, feeling the warm weight against his palm. *Now, now, now.*

"Kit..." he managed to gasp.

"No," she said, pulling his mouth down again. "No talking. No."

His brain was rapidly turning to mush, but he had just enough wit left to know that he didn't want to do this against a wall or on the floor. He didn't want to do it anywhere that would let her think she'd made a mistake in doing it at all. He started to pull her down the hall that opened off the kitchen. There were a lot of doors ahead—one of them was probably hers.

Kit slowed and pushed one of the doors open, pulling him in behind her, then slamming the door after him.

He turned and looked down at her again. Moonlight poured through the window next to the bed—her bed, he assumed. Her dark eyes stared back up at him, like dusky pools in the dimness of the room. Her nipples peaked hard against the silk of her blouse.

That was the first thing he needed to do—get that blouse off her. He needed—really needed—to touch her skin. His fingers fumbled at the buttons, finally managing to push them through openings that seemed way too small for the purpose. Then he was pushing the blouse away from her shoulders and down her arms, onto the floor.

His breath sounded loud in the silence of the room, his fingers fumbling again at the opening of her bra. Kit leaned forward, pushing his T-shirt up his chest, running her hands down his body, her thumbs scratching quickly across his nipples.

He was making a mess of the clasp, his fingers twisting the fabric. God, why didn't lingerie manufacturers think of this when they made the damn things?

She pushed his hands away, lightly, then unfastened the bra and dropped it to the floor with her blouse.

He stared at her, his mouth suddenly so dry he wasn't sure he could speak, didn't know what he'd say even if he could. *You are the most glorious thing I've ever seen. Please don't let it be a dream this time. Or if it is, please don't let me wake up.*

He moved toward her again, cupping her breasts in his hands, then bending down to take a nipple in his mouth. He sucked hard, drawing it up against his teeth, feeling it pebble against his tongue. Kit's breath hissed in a gasp of what he devoutly hoped was pleasure.

His fingers moved to the snap on her jeans, then the zipper pull, pushing them down her hips and then watching as she kicked them aside. He took a moment, just a moment, to look at her, her slender body half in moon shadow. The memory of her as she'd been eighteen months ago, silver in the moonlight, blended with the now.

She was here. Finally, she was here with him as she should be, as he needed her to be. His heart gave a mighty thump. *Please, please don't let me screw this up.*

He touched her hip, running his hand slowly down the slim column of her thigh. Her skin beneath his hand was cool, soft, almost too delicate for his own calloused palm to touch. Slowly, slowly, he let his hand drift around, cupping the warm mounds of her buttocks, feeling them flex beneath his palm. She gasped again, her body trembling beneath his hand.

And then she leaned forward, her fingers stabbing into his hair, her mouth devouring him, teeth, tongue, startled hot wetness. She slid her lips down the side of his throat, leaving a trail of warmth and sensation, then nipped at his collarbone. Immediately, he was granite from the waist down, so tight he wasn't sure he could lower his zipper without causing permanent injury.

She leaned forward again, her lips brushing against his ear. "Nando," she whispered, "let's get you naked."

In some distant corner of her mind, Kit was terrified. She'd never felt like this with anyone before, not even with him—like she had to get him inside her within the next five minutes or die here in the middle of her bedroom. He had way too much power over her all of a sudden, but she didn't know how to stop him. And, of course, she didn't really want to.

Nando, Nando, Nando. The name kept pounding in her brain, echoing through her body. Eighteen months she'd been without him, telling herself she didn't care. Now her body was telling her the whole not-caring part had been a lie.

I can do this. I don't need explanations to do this. I'll think about that later.

He pulled off his shirt, then began working on his belt, but she stilled his hands. She stood for a moment, looking up at him, the smooth slabs of muscle over his chest, the slender hips, the flat circles of his nipples beneath the slight dusting of dark hair. "Let me," she whispered and reached for his belt buckle.

He dropped his hands to his sides for a moment as she unfastened the buckle, then reached up again to clasp her shoulders, as if he couldn't stop touching her.

He wants me as much as I want him. The knowledge sped through her like brandy in her blood, warming, thrilling. She reached for his zipper.

"Um..." He narrowed his eyes, taking hold of her hand. "Better let me." He struggled for a moment, pulling the zipper carefully over the swell of his arousal, then jerking his jeans and underwear down and kicking them away.

Kit stared at him again, the lean body with its ropes of muscle. The solid length of him jutted free, painfully erect. Her breath caught in her throat for a moment, and then she moved forward again, pressing herself against him from shoulder to knee. His erection pulsed against her belly, the sound of his breath loud in her ear. He fisted his hands in her hair, pulling her back gently until his mouth

191

found hers again.

It wasn't a kiss so much as a claiming. He nibbled on her lips, then plunged deep into her mouth, his hands cupping her face now, holding her steady.

She slid her hands down his sides, feeling the points of his hip bones, the slight indentation at the top of his thighs. She slid down further to cup him gently, hearing the quick hiss of breath as his mouth dropped away from hers.

He took hold of her shoulders, pushing her back until she felt the edge of the bed against the backs of her knees. And then she was sliding down gently, with Nando's hands guiding her to the mattress.

He fumbled at his jeans on the floor, pulling the foil packet loose from the pocket. She didn't stop to wonder how he'd known it would end like this. He'd just known. So had she. And then he was kissing the side of her neck, running a hand down her stomach to cup her, one finger dipping inside to send something like an electric shock through her abdomen.

She gasped at the suddenness of the feeling that washed across her.

Nando pushed himself up on one elbow. "Okay?"

She nodded, chewing her lip. "More than okay. Way more than okay."

His teeth flashed in the darkness before he ripped open the foil, sheathing himself quickly. "Sorry, babe, I can't be slow this time. I'll make it up to you."

"I don't want slow," she growled. "I want you. Now. As hard and fast as you can make it."

He pushed her back against the mattress, spreading her knees wide. And then he was sliding in, impossibly large, stretching her more than she could bear but so much what she wanted. She wrapped her legs around him as he plunged deep, then fought the urge to moan in protest as he moved back again.

"Oh Christ, Kit," he muttered. "Sweet Christ. I forgot how good it feels to be inside you."

She wrapped her arms more tightly around his waist to hold on, arms and legs both locked around his body. All of a sudden she felt as if she might fly apart without an anchor to hold her in place. The feel of him deep inside, the thrust against her inner muscles made her whimper with need. Pressure began to build within her, carrying her up.

He slid his hand between them, rubbing his thumb against her, and she cried out, digging her fingers into his shoulder blades as she spiraled upward toward a starburst of sensation.

"Open your eyes," he whispered. "Look at me, Catarina. Look at me now. I need to see you feel it."

She squinted, fighting for breath as the starburst took her, then stared up into the infinite darkness of his gaze. The muscles of his face were taut, his mouth pulled tight across his teeth. "Look at me," he gasped. "Now."

She brought her hands down to cup him, closing her fingers around the root, and he shattered, plunging deep inside as he threw his head back and shouted. Kit brought her heels tight against him holding him in, the breath whistling in her throat.

In another moment he dropped down beside her again, rubbing his face against her shoulder, one hand moving to cup her breast. "Ah, Catarina," he whispered. "Catarina. I've missed you so much."

Kit swallowed hard. She felt as if her heart had missed a beat. *Careful, for Christ's sake be careful!*

"Me too," she whispered so softly she wasn't sure he could hear. "Oh, me too."

Chapter Eighteen

Clayton Delaney took one more turn down Main Street. People were still coming and going at the bars and a couple of the restaurants like Brenner's that stayed open late. It was Saturday night in Konigsburg, and both tourists and locals were taking advantage of the balmy weather, even if it was the end of March when it could start raining at any moment.

On the whole, Clayton got a kick out of Konigsburg, a lot more than he had out of Johnson City where he'd grown up and where his parents still lived. He was looking for an in-town apartment in his price range, but he hadn't found one yet. As soon as he did, he'd be moving out of his parents' house and into his own place. It wasn't that Johnson City didn't have its own attractions, but everybody there knew him. And his parents. And his grandparents. And his uncles, aunts and assorted cousins. Some people in Johnson City could probably draw up an entire family tree for a couple of generations of the Delaneys with no trouble at all. And when they saw him, they probably remembered every half-assed thing he'd ever done, all the way back to grade school. It was no way for a cop to live.

No, Konigsburg was definitely better for him. He liked the town, he liked the people, he liked the other cops. Well, he liked most of the other cops. Ham Linklatter was an asshole, but Clayton figured most police departments had one or two assholes running around. It sort of went with the territory.

The other people were outstanding, though. Chief Toleffson was already legendary in the county, the guy who'd personally caught the crooked mayor and a woman who'd tried to kidnap a baby. Clayton thought he was probably as good as most big city chiefs of police, and he figured Konigsburg was lucky to have him, particularly since he had family in the area and would probably stick around for the long haul.

He respected Nando too. Like Toleffson, he was a lot better than some of the small town cops Clayton had encountered while he was growing up in the Hill Country. And Helen Kretschmer was the most terrifying woman he'd ever seen, which was actually a plus for a dispatcher. She was very good at her job too.

Watching Nando and Toleffson work was an education in itself, almost as helpful as the Criminal Justice classes he'd taken at Austin Community College. He wanted to finish his associate's degree, and Toleffson had said they might be able to adjust his hours so he could take a few more classes on line this summer.

Clayton ran an assessing glance over the lower end of Main. It was still early for the burglar to be out and around. In reality, he thought the creep had probably taken off by now. They'd almost caught him last time, and he hadn't taken anything that was worth shit in either of the other break-ins. He'd probably figure he should cut his losses and maybe move on to someplace like Marble Falls.

Still, if Clayton had learned anything in his short law enforcement career, it was that crooks didn't always think things through. If the perp was local, he might want to stick around—he might not even think about moving on to someplace that wasn't familiar. And if he decided to stick around, it was going to be a lot easier to catch him. Because sooner or later his luck would run out. Sooner or later his own stupidity would help them get a line on him.

Clayton smiled. He really, really wanted to be the one who did that. He'd started cruising Main in the evenings, even when he wasn't on duty. He figured if he saw anything suspicious, he could always call the station and be forwarded to whoever was patrolling that night. Nailing this particular SOB would help him to move from being the New Guy to being someone the others knew they could depend on. He didn't figure it would happen overnight, but he figured it would happen a lot quicker if he could catch the burglar, or at least see something that would help somebody else catch the burglar.

And tonight, he was officially the guy on patrol. Well, he was one of the guys, along with Dawson Kirk. But if he saw anything tonight, he'd be the one who led the charge—although he'd be careful to call for backup, having learned from Nando's experience that it was a good idea to have someone else around before taking the perp down.

Clayton took one more careful survey of the darkened shops. He didn't see any lights or any movement. He'd already been up the alley once, and he'd make another sweep there when he came back after he'd gone to the station. Kirk was there doing paperwork, and they'd switch over on the half hour. But he'd head out again himself soon after that. The chief had said he wanted both men on patrol at night with minimal breaks. That worked for Clayton—he hated paperwork and he hated sitting around the station waiting for something to happen.

He checked his watch again. Maybe five minutes more. Enough time for one more pass up Main on his way back to the station. His hands tightened on the steering wheel as he swept a quick glance across the shop windows, looking for a light. He really, really wanted to be the one who caught this guy.

The second time they'd made love, Kit had straddled him, riding him slowly, her hands braced on his chest so that she could stare down into his eyes until they'd both come undone. Nando had been glad Allie didn't have any close neighbors. He figured they'd made enough noise to warrant somebody banging on the door if they'd been back at his apartment.

Now Kit lay dozing in his arms, her breath light against his shoulder, while he stared at the ceiling, trying to remember exactly what he'd said when they'd made love the first time. Eighteen months ago he'd sworn he'd never let himself be that vulnerable again, never let her close enough to wound him. He didn't exactly feel that way anymore. Still, he wanted to make sure he hadn't said anything that would let her know just how much power she still had over him.

He remembered telling her how good she felt, but he didn't think that was too revealing. He also sort of remembered telling her how much he'd missed her, which was a lot more dangerous. But he thought he'd heard her say she missed him, too, although her voice was so soft he wasn't entirely sure.

He knew for sure he hadn't said he loved her. And he was pretty sure he wouldn't. At least not yet. Of course, he'd already told her that before, and it hadn't made any difference. But that might have been because he'd said it in one of those voice mail messages she'd never answered. And then there was the way he'd said it.

Do you want me to say I love you? Is that what you want? Okay, I love you. Is that enough? Does that take care of it?

He winced slightly. Jesus, that had been a godawful time. He still felt bruised when he thought about it. He knew he'd deserved her

196

anger after Lizzie, but he hadn't expected her to shut him off completely. To not even talk to him for eighteen months. Why had they both tried to hurt each other—and accomplished it so expertly? He'd loved her. How could he have done what he'd done to her?

He'd loved her. The tense was wrong. He loved her. Now. Still. But he sure as hell didn't want to end up slashed to pieces and bleeding again. He didn't want to think about how long the recovery might take this time.

"Nando?" Kit moved against him sleepily. "Are you okay?"

He ran his hand down the silk of her hair. "Sure. Go back to sleep."

She pushed herself up on one elbow, running a finger down his throat. "What's wrong?"

"Nothing." He caught her hand, bringing it to his lips. "Nothing, *chica.* Everything's working right as far as I can see."

Her lips turned up in that faint smile, but her eyes looked troubled. Or maybe just wary. "Are you hungry? We've still got all that pizza."

"Maybe we can finish the wine. I'll get it." He pushed himself up, grabbing his underwear from the floor.

He found the bottle where he'd left it on the kitchen table, then scrounged a couple of juice glasses out of the cupboard, ignoring the hallway where they'd almost had sex on the first available flat surface. Something about Kit Maldonado stripped away every last particle of good sense he'd ever had. Which was how he'd ended up behaving like the village idiot last time and being kicked in the gut as a result.

He heard a step behind him and turned to see her standing in the doorway, watching him in the moonlight that spilled through the kitchen window. She was wearing his T-shirt and nothing else so far as he could tell. He'd forgotten just how long her legs were, and now he had a terrific view of almost their entire length.

He concentrated on pulling the cork out of the bottle as he felt himself harden again. He hadn't been this randy since high school, and even then it seemed like his recovery time had been longer than this.

"Here." She took the glasses he'd found and put them back on the shelf, then brought back two wine glasses. "Bored Ducks deserves better than that. Bored Ducks deserves the best."

197

"So do you," he blurted.

Holy crap, he'd just sworn he wouldn't say anything like that. Whatever happened to caution? His higher brain functions seemed to go on vacation whenever she walked into his range of vision.

Kit put the wine glasses on the table, then took the bottle out of his hands and poured them each a healthy shot. "Thanks," she murmured. "You do too."

He closed his eyes, sipping his wine and fighting not to pull her back into his embrace again. Just a few months ago, he'd been wishing for this, longing for this. Just this kind of night with her. Now he was scared witless that he'd lose it all again. *Be careful what you wish for, cholo. You just might get it.*

Helen Kretschmer parked her Mustang on the street beside the station. She didn't use the station parking lot because she didn't trust those cowboys who drove the cruisers not to put a dent in her baby. She'd only had it for a year, and she wasn't ready to abandon it to Ham Linklatter's driving skills.

She extracted the key for the back door of the station from the inner pocket of her billfold. Chief Toleffson had given it to her last year, when he'd moved her from being a civilian employee to being an actual police officer. At the time, he'd said he considered Helen the only one likely to be able to remember where the spare key was kept. Helen agreed with him.

On the whole, she liked Toleffson. She'd been with the department a hell of a lot longer than any of the others, even Linklatter, who'd come on duty when Brody had been chief. Brody had hired her, too, but he hadn't ever considered her more than a glorified receptionist. Helen had thought about asking him if she could take the training necessary to become an officer, but once she'd gotten to know him, she figured it wasn't something he'd be likely to approve. When Brody hired his police officers, he seemed to look for crooks or fools exclusively, and Helen didn't fall into either category.

Olema had come in after Brody had fled the area, but he hadn't been much better as a chief. Helen hadn't asked him about becoming an officer either, mainly because she figured he wouldn't last long. Brody was a crook, but Brody was smart, even if it was a mean kind of smartness. Olema was honest enough, but he was also dumb as a rock, although not as dumb as Linklatter, who'd somehow managed to survive both police chiefs.

Toleffson was neither dumb nor crooked, and he'd been the one to suggest that Helen might like to take the Texas Commission on Law Enforcement basic licensing course at Austin Community College and then apply to become an actual police officer. Once she'd completed the course, he promised he'd promote her. And he had. One thing about Toleffson, if he promised you something, he did it.

Helen relocked the back door behind her. It opened off Lamar rather than the parking lot, and using it saved her having to walk around the building. It also gave her a reputation for mysterious appearances and disappearances that she enjoyed, mainly because it seemed to scare the crap out of Linklatter. Given Linklatter's brainpower, it didn't take much to do that, but she enjoyed it anyway.

Now she walked into the main room and saw the new kid, Delaney, working at one of the computers at the side. He glanced up when he heard her footstep, his hand jerking toward his baton. "Jesus, Helen, you scared the life out of me." His ears turned slightly pink. "I mean...sorry. I didn't mean to swear in front of you."

She gave him a dry look. "Kid, you can't say anything I haven't already heard. In fact, I'll be glad to give you a few new words to use if you want."

Delaney blushed again. From what she'd seen, he had the makings of a good cop, but the blushing thing had to go if he wanted to survive on the mean streets of Konigsburg. "What are you doing here? I thought you were patrolling."

"I was. I mean, I am. Dawson and I are alternating on who stays here and who hits the streets. I'll head out in another ten minutes or so, then he'll come back here after that."

Helen shook her head. "You don't need to stick around here. I've got some work to do—I'll run the station. You head out on patrol. The longer you and Kirk drive around, the more chance you've got of catching that son of a bitch in action."

"Okay." He pushed his chair back. "I didn't realize you were on duty tonight. If you're going to be here, I'll stay out longer."

"Do that." She gave him a brisk nod. Technically, she wasn't on duty, at least not paid duty. Toleffson hadn't told her to come in. But when she weighed how much she wanted to sit around the house watching the Spurs play the Nuggets, she decided she'd be more useful at the station. Besides, a few hours when she didn't have to keep track of Linklatter would give her a chance to bring her spreadsheets up to date.

"Go on ahead," she told Delaney. "I'll turn off the call forwarding and catch anything that comes in after I tell Kirk I'm here. You might want to keep an eye on the Silver Spur. Last time I drove by it was sounding a little loud. And the Dew Drop. Faro looks okay, though."

Delaney nodded. "Right. I'll head up there now." He settled his buff-colored Stetson on his head and opened the door.

Helen fought back the urge to say *Be careful out there.* The kid could probably figure that out for himself.

Kit watched Nando sip his wine as he lay across her bed. He was naked, or mostly naked anyway. She'd almost forgotten how beautiful he was without any clothes. Actually, she'd made a major effort to forget that, telling herself he hadn't been as gorgeous as she'd thought he was. That it was all exaggerated by memory.

Only it wasn't. He was just as gorgeous as ever. Also nervous, if she could still read him right. He wasn't looking at her. Instead, he stared down into his glass or down at the sheets or down at his toes. Anywhere, in other words, rather than up at her face.

With anyone else, she'd think he was trying to avoid her, maybe trying to think of an excuse to duck out early and head for the hills, even though they'd just spent a couple of hours having the most amazing sex of her life. But somehow she didn't think that was it.

The one time he'd looked at her directly, what she'd seen had looked like fear. The kind of fear that came from thinking something was too good to be true. She knew how that felt. She was feeling it herself. In fact, she wondered if the two of them would ever stop feeling it, if it would keep them from pushing over the last few barriers that were left between them.

She took a deep breath. "You were right, you know."

He looked up at her then, his eyes immediately wary. "Have to be some of the time, I guess. Which time are you thinking of?"

"When you said I'd be back. That last fight before I left."

"Oh." He blew out a breath. "Yeah, well, I didn't exactly mean it that way, but okay, I guess in the long run I was right. Here you are."

She nodded. "Here I am."

The corners of his mouth edged up slightly. "How do you feel about that?"

She raised her head to gaze at him directly, holding the moment. "Good. Overall, good."

His smile became wider. "Glad to hear it."

She licked her lips. Maybe it was time to go a little further than that. "You were right about that. But you were wrong about some other things."

His smile dropped away again and he stared down again. "I know."

"I always wondered what happened. What kicked off that last fight and...everything."

He stared down for a long moment, then up again, his gaze bleak. "Not yet," he said softly. "Please, *chica*."

Kit's chest tightened slightly. He wasn't going to talk about it. Or maybe he just wasn't going to talk about it now. Maybe she just needed to wait.

Nando looked up at her again, then sighed. He took hold of her hand, pulling her across the bed until she was nestled in his arms again, rubbing her face against his shoulder. "Sometime, I promise," he murmured. "But not now."

His mouth touched the side of her throat again, sliding down toward her collarbone. In another moment, they'd be beyond talking. She had to decide if this was enough, if she needed more from him than that.

His fingers closed around her nipple, pulling gently until it pebbled beneath his thumb.

Screw it. It's enough for tonight.

She skimmed her lips along the edge of his jaw, and then his mouth, taking him in again. She'd worry about it tomorrow. Maybe.

Helen worked for an hour entering data and answering the occasional call. Most of them were minor. Complaints about noise (the college boys living over on Milam were kicking up their heels again). A lost dog, although what the woman thought the police could do about it was anybody's guess. A possible prowler complaint she passed on to Kirk, although he hadn't found anybody when he got there.

It wasn't their guy anyway. Helen was actually hoping the call came in for that asshole while she was on the desk. It would make her night, even if she wouldn't get to go out and drag him back to the cell herself. She had a baton, but Toleffson hadn't yet issued her a gun, although she was pretty sure he would once he saw the results from her last round of marksmanship tests. Helen hadn't grown up in hunting country for nothing.

She leaned back in her chair, rubbing her tired eyes. She'd been staring at the computer screen for about thirty minutes straight, which was close to her limit, particularly with the low res monitors the city bought. She'd already turned off most of the lights in the main room. No reason to waste electricity, given the city's budgeting problems. The overtime they were spending trying to catch the burglar was already enough of a strain.

Helen pushed herself to her feet, sliding her desk chair back in place, then began a slow stroll through what passed for a bullpen.

Each of the officers had his own desk, but they shared computers, all of which were linked into the city's intranet. Nando's desk was piled high with bulletins from the Rangers, along with printouts of information on whatever case he was working on. Delaney's desk was clear except for a couple of legal pads, but that was because Delaney hadn't been around long—give him a couple of months, and he'd be as loaded down as Nando. Linklatter's desk had a half-eaten candy bar and an unwashed coffee cup, along with takeout menus from the Chinese restaurant on the highway and the Coffee Corral.

Helen felt like sighing, but Linklatter wasn't her problem. Or rather he *was* her problem, but only because he was everybody's problem.

She turned up the hall toward the bathroom opposite Toleffson's office. At least he'd hired a cleaning service. Under Brody and Olema, cleaning the johns had been Helen's duty only because nobody else would do it and she wasn't willing to live with that kind of filth.

She paused at the end of the hall, listening. Nothing. For a moment, she'd thought she'd heard noises coming from Toleffson's office, but it was probably just the spring wind picking up.

She started down the hall again, walking more quietly this time. Outside Toleffson's office, she paused, watching the dark line underneath the door. She knew for a fact nobody was supposed to be there, certainly not Toleffson himself, who spent the nights he wasn't on duty at home with his wife. After a moment, she saw it. Just a glimmer. A light moving across the floor.

Helen stood very still, her hand resting on the end of her baton. *Son of a bitch!* The asshole had actually come to the station. And she was the only one here. She wondered for a moment if there was any way she could get into the weapons locker for a Glock, but she knew there wasn't. Toleffson kept that key himself.

Anyway, she didn't need one. She'd been waiting for something like this for years, a chance to show them all that she was the equal of any of those assholes. And she was, damn it! She could shoot better than most of them, and she'd already put in her time behind the desk. This was a chance for her.

Except she didn't have a weapon beyond her baton. For just a moment, she thought about calling Delaney, or even Nando Avrogado, although he was off duty tonight. But the guy might hear her make the call and cut out before she could stop him.

And she'd stop him. No question.

She took hold of the door knob carefully, turning it as slowly as she could and then cracking the door to peek inside. Good thing the chief didn't lock his office, not that there was anything in there worth stealing. A fact the burglar apparently didn't know. She stood still, surveying the room through the crack in the door, trying to see him. She could hear a faint thumping from the far side. After a moment, she identified it as the sound of the desk drawer bumping against the lock as someone jerked on it. Although the chief didn't lock his office door, he apparently locked his desk.

Helen shifted her position slightly so that she could see the man at the side of the room. The darkness in the office made it impossible to see his face, but he held a mini flashlight in his mouth so that he could use both his hands to try to jimmy the lock on the drawer. The open window across the room showed just how he'd managed to get in. The chief would *not* be pleased.

She watched the burglar struggle for a few moments longer, then eased the door wider as she pulled her baton from her belt. Once again, she wished she had a gun, but she'd had hand-to-hand training. And she'd been known to take down men who were twice her size. And there was no sign the perp was carrying a weapon. The sound of the desk drawer rattling covered any sounds she made as she stepped into the room. The guy was taller than she'd anticipated. She held her baton at the ready. He'd probably run, but she could stop him if he did.

"Hey," she barked, "what do you think you're doing?"

The man jerked upright, staring at her, and Helen's throat clenched in shock. "What the hell?" she muttered. "What are you doing here?"

She realized her mistake almost instantly, but by then it was too late. He'd reached her before she could bring her baton to block him, the heavy bookend from the chief's desk clutched in his hand.

After that she remembered nothing at all.

Chapter Nineteen

The call woke Nando at five forty-five. He grabbed his cell, glancing at the number as he stepped out into the hall so he wouldn't wake Kit. Too late he remembered he was in Allie's house, and he hadn't taken time to grab his underwear. If Allie walked in the front door, she'd be in for a shock.

"Yeah?" he muttered, trying to keep the exasperation out of his voice. He was off today, and he had some plans for the rest of the morning since Kit was off too. He hoped to god nobody had called in sick.

Five minutes later he was back in the bedroom pulling on his clothes as quickly and quietly as he could. Kit stirred in the bed, turning toward him with sleepy eyes as she pushed her hair away from her face. "What's up?"

"I've got to go," he muttered. "I'm sorry." Looking at her, warm and luscious among the rumpled sheets, he realized how sorry he really was.

"What?" She sat up now, the sheet pooling in her lap to show her truly remarkable breasts. "Why?"

He sighed, trying to decide how much he could tell her. Hell, the news would probably be all over town in a couple of hours anyway. "That SOB we've been chasing for the last month broke into the station last night. This time someone got hurt."

"Into the station?" Kit was fully awake now. "Why on earth would a burglar break into a police station?"

Nando shook his head as he zipped up his pants. "You got me— it's not something the average burglar would do, that's for sure."

"Hurt?" She was focusing now. "Who? Who got hurt? How badly?"

He buttoned his shirt. "Helen. And I don't know how badly yet. She's in the hospital."

"My god." She shook her head slowly. "This is really serious, isn't it?"

"Yes ma'am, it really is." He leaned down, sliding an arm around her neck, tasting those wonderful lips one more time. "Sorry, *chica*. I wanted more time with you today."

"That's okay." Her lips turned up slightly. "I'll be here if you get a break."

"I'll do my best," he murmured. Jerking his brain back into cop mode was going to be tougher than usual today.

He got to the station a few minutes before Ham. Delaney was already sitting in the bullpen nursing a cup of convenience store coffee, his face the color of dirty milk. Kirk was sitting behind him, looking like he'd been dragged through the nearest knothole.

Toleffson stood behind Helen's desk, talking on the phone—which was weird since he usually did his phoning in his office. Nando glanced down the hall and saw the yellow crime scene tape stretched across the chief's office door.

"What the hell?" He dropped into a chair next to Delaney. "What happened?"

Delaney shook his head slowly. "I don't know exactly. I came back here around four o'clock. Found Helen on the floor in the chief's office. Somebody broke in there. Window was open. Bushes trampled outside. I called the hospital and got an ambulance to come get her. Don't know how she is yet." He took another swallow of coffee.

Linklatter plunked down at his desk, dropping a McDonald's sack on the blotter. He sighed loudly. "Don't usually come in this early on a Sunday."

Nando ignored him. "Why was Helen here alone anyway? She doesn't work nights usually, unless she's got extra paperwork to get through."

Delaney shrugged. "She came in around nine. Said she'd run the station so Dawson and I could do more patrolling. She turned off the call forward, so we didn't hear anything from the station. I didn't see her when I checked back for a bathroom break—I thought she'd gone home. Then next time I saw the light in the chief's office and found her."

"You should've sent her back home. Rules are rules. She shouldn't have been in here." Linklatter sounded vaguely like a middle school vice principal. Nando didn't like to think about the probable result if Delaney had tried to make Helen go home again.

"Helen came in around nine?" he asked. "And you were out the rest of the night?"

"About that. Like I said, I came back for a bathroom break once, and I guess Dawson did too." He glanced back at Kirk, who nodded, then he stared down at his cup again. "We had a lot going on. There were some drunks at the Silver Spur and some problems at the Dew Drop. I talked to the Silver Spur guys and found somebody to drive them home so they wouldn't be driving themselves. We had a couple of noise complaints and a woman over at the Lone Oak said there was a coyote hanging around but I couldn't find it. I guess Dawson had some prowler calls out at the edge of town, and some kids messing around the high school. Sort of a busy night." He rubbed his eyes. "I just...Helen said to stay out on patrol, so we did."

Nando thought about telling him to go home and get some rest, but he figured that was Toleffson's call. He watched the chief hang up, then walk toward them.

"County Crime Lab's on the way. They'll go over the office, then we can break it down after that."

Nando took a breath. "How's Helen?"

"Concussion," the chief said tersely. "Still unconscious. Bastard used one of my stone bookends on her."

Nando's right hand curled into a fist. The burglar had moved up to assault. He only hoped he got a piece of the son of a bitch before the chief got to him. "What was he looking for in your office? There's nothing in there that's worth anything."

Belatedly he realized that might not have been the most politic thing to say about Toleffson's office, but the chief shook his head. "Damn if I know. Maybe he thought I kept money or drugs in there."

"Who breaks into a police station anyway?" Delaney said dully. "I never heard of that happening before."

"Could be he was after guns," Ham suggested.

"Except the guns are in the gun safe down the hall, not the chief's office And I didn't see any sign he'd tried to get into any other room in the station." Delaney sounded beyond tired.

"Well, this guy hasn't exactly been logical up until now either." Toleffson sighed. "We need to find this asshole. Soon. With any luck,

Meg Benjamin

Helen saw him and she'll remember what he looks like. Maybe she'll even know him. She knows everybody in town."

"If she wakes up," Linklatter said helpfully. He reached into the sack on his desk, pulling out an Egg McMuffin.

All five men stared at him. Toleffson's eyes took on a malevolent gleam. "*When* she wakes up, Linklatter."

Ham shrugged. "Sure."

Nando glanced longingly at Delaney's coffee. He should have thought to grab a cup for himself on his way in. "Shouldn't we have somebody at the hospital? To talk to her when she comes to?"

Toleffson nodded. "Yeah. I just talked to the doctor who's treating her. He said she could wake up any time, but it may be a while. One of us should be there with her until she does." He turned toward Ham, narrowing his eyes. "You can take first shift, Ham."

Ham chewed his muffin glumly. "You want me to just sit there? Until she comes around?"

"Yep." The chief's mouth edged into a dry smile. "You can take a book."

Nando doubted that Ham owned a book, let alone wanted to read one.

"Seems like a waste of time," he grumbled.

The chief's smile disappeared. "Don't worry about wasting your time, just do it. When she comes around, ask her what she remembers—ask her who the guy was."

"I could spell you," Delaney said hesitantly. "Let me get a few hours of sleep, then I could take over this afternoon before my shift begins."

Toleffson looked like he might disagree. Nando figured he really liked the idea of leaving Ham at the hospital all day. But then he shrugged. "Okay. Then one of us can come in for the evening, assuming she's still unconscious."

"I can take over for Delaney," Nando said slowly. "Unless you want us all out on the street."

The chief shrugged. "Hold off for now. She may be awake by then. I want you to help me take that office apart after the crime lab guys get finished."

"Thought it was Avrogado's day off," Ham said around a bite of

208

muffin.

"There are no days off, Ham. Not until we finish this. We need to get this guy—*now*. We've got an officer down, and we don't let that happen." Toleffson's voice sounded like a whip crack in the silence of the office.

"You mean Helen?" Ham looked slightly confused.

"Helen is an officer in the Konigsburg Police Department," Toleffson's jaw was tight. "She was assaulted in the line of duty. Are you clear on that?"

Ham licked his lips. "Yessir. Guess I am."

"Good. Now get on it. Delaney and Kirk, go home and get some sleep. Linklatter, go to the hospital. Rollie, you're on patrol. Nando, stick around until the county guys are done. That's probably them in the parking lot," he said as a white county van pulled in.

Nando squared his shoulders. Whoever the burglar was, he'd just become the target of every cop in the Hill Country.

For once Kit was glad she had the wedding to worry about. The news about Helen Kretschmer had spread around town with the usual wildfire speed. Allie had come back with Wonder, full of questions that Kit couldn't answer, and then had gone off to Docia and Cal's house, hoping they'd heard some news from Chief Toleffson.

She had around ten days left before the ceremony, and all the major tasks on the professional wedding planner's checklist had been taken care of. Her last big job had been to find a photographer, but fortunately Wonder had a patient who was in the business. Or who wanted to be in the business. The guy looked to be around twenty, but Kit had seen his work and he seemed to know what he was doing. Just because he didn't have a studio outside of his parents' garage didn't mean he couldn't function. And besides, none of the professional photographers were available on the day of the wedding.

She spread out the seating chart for the reception on the table in front of her. Allie had given her the usual vague suggestions. She was trying to fit people together based on shared interests or the likelihood of their having long-standing friendships or feuds.

They'd sent out the invitations and received a surprising number of RSVP cards by return mail. Apparently, Allie's friends and family felt the same way Kit did about the necessity of getting the whole thing wrapped up quickly before Allie decided to back out again. Given her rigid training in the Maldonado family's code of conduct, Allie was much less likely to disappoint people who'd made travel plans.

She and Wonder hadn't taken the time to register for gifts anywhere. She argued that since they'd both been living on their own for a long time and since they both had completely furnished houses, they didn't need anything more. If anything, they needed a lot less. Still, gifts had begun to arrive. Kit was piling them on a table in the study.

She glanced around Allie's cozy living room. The Craftsman cottage she'd bought after Sweet Thing had become a success was a jewel. Even though Allie seemed to have decided to live at Wonder's house after they were married, she still hadn't made any move to put her own place on the market. Kit only hoped she wouldn't sell it immediately. Finding a place for herself that she could afford on her Woodrose salary wasn't a prospect she looked forward to.

She went back to the checklist again. Rings and license were Wonder's problem. If he couldn't drag Allie to the county clerk's office and the jewelry store, they might as well just give up. Cakes were Allie's department, thank god. It seemed to be the only thing she was working on, but at least she'd done the planning and started doing some test runs.

She glanced at the next item. Rehearsal dinner. *Crap.* Kit pinched the bridge of her nose. The groom's family were supposed to take care of it, but Wonder's mom lived in an assisted care facility in Dripping Springs, so she probably wasn't eager to do any planning for her son. Kit would have to remember to ask Wonder himself what he wanted to do and where. They could probably set up something in one of the meeting rooms at the inn, which would be convenient since the rehearsal itself would be taking place at the event center. Kit made a note to herself to check the Rose's calendar. There shouldn't be too many events during the middle of the week, but she'd need to reserve the room as soon as possible. Probably she should just go ahead and do it. Chances were Wonder didn't have any strong feelings one way or the other, and it would be another thing checked off.

Kit blew out a breath. This wasn't exactly the way she'd planned on spending her Sunday. Almost immediately she felt a quick pinch of guilt. It probably wasn't the way Helen Kretschmer had meant to spend her Sunday either. It wasn't exactly Nando's fault that he'd had to take off first thing in the morning.

Still. She rubbed her tired eyes. Would he have stayed if he'd had the chance? He'd said he wanted to, but did she believe him? Of course, not believing him hadn't gotten her very far in the past either.

They still hadn't talked about the past. He hadn't said how he felt about her. He hadn't really told her before either, but she'd thought she knew. Still, that was then. This, Kit reminded herself, was now.

They were circling each other like a pair of wary cats, each afraid of letting down their guard so that the other could slash.

Taken all in all, she had no idea where they stood or what was ahead for them. A smart woman might cut her losses and pull back, or at the very least take things more slowly to make sure she wasn't going to get crushed again.

But then again, when it came to Nando, had she ever been smart?

The county lab techs were very thorough, which meant they were also very slow. Nando sat at his desk shuffling through some paperwork until his eyes gave out and he dropped his head onto his arms. He should be doing the paperwork—hell, he should always be doing paperwork. But he didn't feel like it, and napping was better than calling the hospital again to check on Helen.

Toleffson stood watching the techs, asking the occasional question and, judging from his expression, not getting the kind of answers he wanted. When the techs finally headed out the door, carrying their bags of equipment with them, Toleffson walked back into the bullpen.

"Anything?" Nando asked.

Toleffson shook his head. "Some fingerprints on the window, but they're probably mine. In fact, mine are all over the place. They picked up some other prints, but my guess is they'll turn out to be the cleaning service or you guys. This asshole has worn gloves every other place he's hit. Too much to hope that he'd go barehanded here." He glanced back at Helen's desk, his jaw firming. "Come on. Let's take that damn office apart and see if we can figure out what he was looking for."

Nando pushed himself to his feet. "That assumes the guy was looking for something in particular. Maybe he was just going through the first room he saw after he climbed in the window."

"Then why didn't he stop when he figured out nothing was in there? If it was all random, why didn't he just keep going through the station until he found something that was open or something that was worth taking? Why did he stay in here?"

Nando frowned as he circled the desk behind Toleffson. "That would mean he deliberately broke into this office, looking for something specific. That was either incredibly stupid or reasonably well planned."

The chief narrowed his eyes. "Okay. Why?"

"Because I figure he thought the station was empty. No burglar in his right mind would have broken into a cop shop if there were any cops around. He must have figured nobody was here."

"But Helen was sitting up front." Toleffson scowled. "Why didn't he see her?"

"Helen doesn't park in the parking lot, and she comes in the back way most times. Plus when she's here at night, she turns off most of the lights except for her desk light. She's always complaining about wasted electricity."

"So you're thinking this perp was watching the station? That he saw Delaney and Kirk take off?"

Nando shrugged. "It's possible. Or maybe he just checked the parking lot and saw that both cruisers were out. Put that together with most of the lights being turned off, and he could have figured it was all clear."

"It's possible," Toleffson said slowly. "Doesn't help much, though. Chances are if he was watching, he did it from a car or someplace nobody would see. If he was standing out front, somebody on the street could have seen him. And we still don't know why he broke in here at all." He looked around his office, eyes narrowed. "Start with the filing cabinets. That's the first thing he'd see. Nothing interesting in 'em so far as I know, but maybe he thought different. Stack the stuff there." He pointed to a folding table he'd set up at the side of the room.

Nando narrowed his eyes, studying the cabinet. "What's in here? Case files?"

The chief shook his head. "Budgeting stuff mainly. Plus some older files from Olema and Brody. I should have cleaned the damn thing out a long time ago." He pulled one of the side desk drawers open, lifting out some legal pads, paperclips and a stapler.

Nando scanned the folder tabs on the first file drawer, mostly travel vouchers and receipts. "Not much here. Nothing I'd want to steal anyway."

"Damn straight," the chief growled. "I don't keep anything important here. I lock any case files in the evidence room, whatever I don't keep on my computer, and I take my laptop home at night. The only thing left is the dock." He nodded toward the computer dock at the side.

"Doesn't look like he was interested in it." Nando pulled out the next file drawer and found more of the same of the same, along with some antiquated computer disks and a stray thumb drive. "Could he be looking for something like this?" He held up the drive. "Maybe trying to find some computer files?"

The chief shrugged. "If he was, he doesn't know much about police procedure around here. My files are backed up at the county. I don't keep external copies. I don't think anybody does anymore."

"Could be something old, from back before the county started backing files up."

Toleffson sighed. "Possibly. Seems like a stretch, but pull out those disks. Maybe they're labeled."

Nando stacked the disks on the table, then pulled out the final drawer and found office supplies: pads, pens, paperclips, scissors and a paper punch. "That's it?"

Toleffson nodded. "Like I said, I don't keep anything valuable in my office. The only thing that makes sense was that he was just looking around for anything he could find. Maybe he thought there'd be a computer here. Maybe he was looking for money. Maybe Ham was right for once and he thought he'd find drugs or guns in here."

"But he took the time to case the joint," Nando said slowly. "And he broke the window lock so he could get into this office. If it was just an impulse, wouldn't he have opened the first unlocked window he found?"

The chief sighed. "Okay, let's go through the desk and see if there's something worth taking. Not that I keep anything in there either."

A couple of hours later, the desk drawers and file drawers were stacked on the floor as Toleffson turned them around to check the sides and bottoms. Nando ran his fingers along the inside of the file cabinet, feeling slightly like an idiot, then did the same thing to the underside of the desktop. He crawled beneath the shell of the desk and ran his fingers over the inside surfaces, trying to see if anything had been taped there. All he found was dust and a couple of splinters. He backed out in time to see Toleffson toss the last drawer to the floor in frustration.

"Goddamn it," he snapped. "If there's anything in this freakin' office, it sure as hell isn't obvious. Or even hidden in places where you'd expect it to be."

Nando leaned back against the wall, staring at the contents of the desk drawers and the file cabinet that were piled on the table. There was nothing in the pile that he didn't keep in his own desk, as well as every other desk he'd ever seen. He couldn't for the life of him figure out why anybody would go to the risk of breaking into a police station just to grab stuff he could have found at any office supply store. He shook his head, sighing. "Why did he hit her?"

Toleffson squinted at him. "She found him in the office. He was trying to get away."

"He could have just gone back through the window and run down the street the way he did when I found him at Margaret Hastings' place. Why hit Helen? Why take it from burglary to assault?"

The chief paused, thinking. "Maybe he lost it. He didn't expect there to be anybody else here besides him. Maybe she startled him."

"But he used a bookend from the bookcase. If he was startled, wouldn't he grab the first thing that came to hand on the desk?"

Toleffson's expression darkened. "Her baton was next to her. It was the only weapon she had with since she hadn't gotten her service revolver yet. Maybe he thought she was threatening him."

"Knowing Helen, she probably was." Nando grimaced. Only Helen would consider holding off a perp with a baton. But under normal circumstances, she probably could have done it. "She must have been distracted. I mean, normally I'd take odds on Helen in just about any fight. She's one tough broad."

Toleffson stared at him for a long moment, then blew out a breath. "She knew him."

As soon as he heard it, Nando knew he was right. "Which is why he had to hit her."

"And why he got the drop on her in the first place. She must have heard someone in the office and grabbed her baton. But she was surprised to see him—that particular guy. Which gave him a chance to grab the bookend and hit her."

Toleffson's jaw was set, one large hand resting on the side of the desk. Nando had a feeling the perp would be very sorry he'd hit Helen Kretschmer once Toleffson got hold of him.

"But that doesn't help us much," he said slowly. "I mean, like you said, Helen knows everybody in town."

The chief shrugged. "It means the guy isn't a stranger, that he's somebody from around here. But I agree—that just limits it to a few hundred citizens of Konigsburg."

Nando checked his watch. "I better go relieve Delaney at the hospital so he can go home before he's on patrol. I don't guess the perp's going to try anything else tonight, but who knows? He hasn't exactly followed the rules up to now either."

Toleffson nodded grimly. "Go on. I'll stay here a while longer. Maybe something will turn up."

"Maybe," Nando agreed. But he didn't figure they should count on it.

Brody sat in the broken-down recliner that was part of the furnishings in his room and tried to think. His anger made it difficult to think clearly, and clear thinking was essential at the moment. He stared down at the shot glass full of tequila in his left hand. Getting drunk right now would be very dangerous, but alcohol helped to deaden the burning fury in his gut.

What the hell had Kretschmer been doing there anyway? Nobody was supposed to have been around. He'd kept careful watch throughout the evening, keeping track of the cruisers, when they came and went. He figured they'd stepped up the patrols after the near miss the previous week. Probably using some kind of call forwarding system to route the incoming calls. The damn place was supposed to have been empty. He'd seen the last cop take off at eleven. And still he'd waited another ten minutes before breaking the flimsy window lock and climbing in.

Yet Kretschmer was there. Where she absolutely shouldn't have been.

It was her own fault. He knew that. But it still rankled. He'd been so close, and then she'd come bursting through the door, pretending to be a cop. Well, she'd found out the price of pretending. With any luck she wouldn't wake up until he was gone. Hell, with any luck, she wouldn't wake up at all.

He weighed his options again. He could cut his losses and get out now. All he would have given up would be time spent in a job he despised. He'd still have his freedom. It was a risk to stay around. Kretschmer could still wake up, and if she did, she might remember what she'd seen. They wouldn't find him immediately, even then. But they'd know who to look for.

But if he left now, he wouldn't have much to show for the weeks he'd spent in Konigsburg. His future would still be as dim as it had first seemed when he'd decided to come back.

He hadn't found what he was looking for, but he hadn't seen anything to show him that anybody else had found it either. And as long as it was there, he'd have a chance for better times. Much better times.

He'd fought for that chance. He deserved that chance. He was going to get that chance.

He tossed back the contents of his shot glass and went to bed.

Chapter Twenty

Helen's hospital room was so small Nando felt like he was in danger of kicking over her water pitcher every time he moved his feet. It was his second tour of duty as her bodyguard and he still wasn't used to the room.

He'd expected Helen to look shrunken and vulnerable, like his grandmother had when she'd gone to the hospital the last time. But Helen mainly reminded him of one of those effigies on the top of warriors' tombs. Give her a broadsword and she'd be set to take out an enemy battalion single-handed as soon as she woke up.

He tried to settle himself into the singularly uncomfortable visitor's chair. No wonder Delaney had looked so miserable when he'd relieved him first thing this morning. The kid had been sitting in the chair for a large part of his night shift, after Toleffson had sent him over. He'd probably lost all feeling in his butt by the time Nando got there.

Nando had smuggled in a cup of Deirdre's coffee and a blueberry muffin that he'd grabbed in the middle of the breakfast rush. It was still early, and he needed that shot of caffeine. He wasn't going to take the chance that Helen might wake up and find him drowsing.

Not that there was much possibility he could sleep in that chair. Maybe that was the point—use the chair torture device to keep visitors from staying too long and exhausting the patient. He slumped down far enough to rest on his shoulders, then opened his paperback, setting his coffee cup on the bedside table. Maybe Kathy Reichs could keep him entertained until Toleffson showed up at noon to relieve him.

An hour later he'd finished the coffee and was still fighting off yawns. The dull hum of the monitors that were attached to Helen seemed to have a drugging effect, in spite of the fact that his ass was bristling with pins and needles. He wondered if he could switch on the television set, or if that was off-limits for unconscious patients. On the other hand, it wasn't like Helen needed more sleep. Maybe the noise would help to wake her up.

He rummaged around the bedside table, trying to find the remote without knocking over his coffee cup. "Goddamn it," he muttered. "Don't tell me there's no remote."

"On the TV," someone said.

Nando froze, staring down at the cool gray eyes that gazed back at him from the bed. He swallowed. "Hi Helen. How do you feel?"

Helen turned her head slightly so he could see her better. He wasn't sure she was fully awake yet—those eyes seemed a little unfocused. "Thirsty," she muttered finally.

"I'll call somebody." He grabbed the call device and jabbed at the button for the nurse down the hall. Then he remembered suddenly what he was supposed to ask when Helen woke up. "Who was it who did this to you, Helen? Do you remember?"

She pursed her lips, squinting slightly as if she were confused by the memory. Nando thought about telling her to forget it, they'd talk later. But they really needed to know, and they needed to know now.

Finally, she muttered something he couldn't hear. Nando leaned closer. "Say it again please."

"Brody," she croaked. "It was Chief Brody."

Kit surveyed the dining room, fighting down panic. They still had a few minutes before the lunch crowd showed up. Maybe something would happen, hopefully something good as opposed to the current disaster.

Joe pushed open the kitchen door to lean into the dining room. "You want any lunch, or you want me to save you some for after the rush?"

She shook her head. "I'm not hungry."

He let the kitchen door swing closed as he walked toward her. "What's up, darlin'? You don't look like life's treating you right."

"Philip's missing." Her hands clenched into fists. "He hasn't come to work, and he hasn't called. I've been trying to reach him, but he hasn't been answering his phone. I don't have time to go check on him now. That leaves me and Elaine, assuming I can get Mabel to come run the hostess station."

Joe's eyes narrowed. "Mabel's the worst hostess in the history of hostessing."

"What do you suggest?" Kit snapped. "Should I just let Elaine take care of all the tables, even though that would probably make her quit by the end of her shift?"

"Take it easy, darlin'." Joe put a hand on her arm. "I'll send one of the line cooks to check on ol' Phil—he doesn't live that far from here. You get Mabel to the hostess stand, and we'll cope. Hell, Darcy could probably run the hostess station if it comes to that. I could juggle things around in the kitchen so we could get by without her."

Kit tried to picture Darcy, whose highlights were currently magenta and whose more visible piercings probably set off every airport security device known to man, running the hostess station at the ever-elegant Rose. "I'll go get Mabel," she said quickly.

Mabel glanced up from her computer as soon as Kit trotted into her office. "Did you reserve one of the party rooms, dear? I saw the name Maldonado but no first initial."

Kit nodded hurriedly. "It's for my aunt's rehearsal dinner. I've already cleared it with Joe."

Mabel grimaced. "Joseph really doesn't have anything to do with reserving rooms. Next time talk to me first, please. That's one of our bigger rooms. I like to keep it available in case we have any last minute requests."

Kit thought of all the arguments she could make—that no one else had reserved it and that it stood empty more often than any of the other rooms, but decided to let it go. "All right, I'll remember that in the future. We've got a bit of a crisis at the moment, though."

"A crisis with the meeting rooms?" Mabel's brow furrowed. "I should be the first one to hear about that. I'm in charge of scheduling, you know. If I don't hear about things, I can't make sure everything is functioning the way it's supposed to."

Kit fought the impulse to close her eyes and count to ten. "No, not about the meeting rooms. We're missing one of our waiters and lunch service will start in fifteen minutes. I can take over the waiter's station, but we'll need you to run the hostess stand."

Mabel's brow stayed pleated. "Oh dear. I don't know if I can take the time to do that. I'm really, really busy today..."

"Yes, well, the lunch service only lasts a couple of hours. And it's

219

our biggest moneymaker. We really can't do without a waiter or a hostess." Kit balled her hands into fists to keep from drumming them on Mabel's desk. What on earth was wrong with the woman?

"Kit, dear, I'm sorry, but if this is another one of those ploys to get me to hire more wait staff..." Mabel began.

Kit grimaced. "It's not a ploy, Mabel. It's a fact. One of the waiters didn't show up, and the one who's there can't possibly take care of the whole restaurant. And of course we can't run the dining room without staff. We do, in fact, need more wait staff. Desperately. But that's a conversation for another time."

Mabel shook her head sorrowfully. "Oh my. If we go on having these kinds of problems, we may have to consider cutting back on meal service. Perhaps even closing the restaurant altogether. We can't have part of the inn siphoning off money and personnel from all our other activities."

Kit blinked. "Close the restaurant? What do you mean? We're pulling in so many customers we have waiting lists on reservations. We've been written up in newspapers all over the state. We're making a profit, even though we're only open for lunch. How could you consider closing it down?"

"Oh it may not come to that." Mabel patted her arm. "We can probably find some ways to take care of the money problems. I'm not at all sure we need to be open six days a week, for example. Although, of course, you're doing excellent work there." Mabel gave her another quick pat.

Kit took a deep breath. She'd get all of this sorted out later. "Mabel, could we discuss this another time? I really do need your help right now."

Mabel sighed. "Oh well, if I must. Let me close down my computer. I'll meet you at the hostess stand."

Lunch wasn't exactly a nightmare, just close. By the end of her shift, Elaine was verging on hysteria. Only the amount of money she'd collected in tips seemed to make up from the abuse she'd gotten from some of the customers. Mabel had to be reminded repeatedly about sending guests equally to both stations, a concept she apparently found too confusing to bother with.

Kit herself was trying to ignore her aching feet. As she hurried to get her orders in and to keep Gabriel moving, she avoided thinking about what Mabel had said. The Rose was wildly popular. It was becoming one of the premier restaurants in Konigsburg, thanks to the combined efforts of Joe's superb kitchen and her own blossoming management skills. Surely Resorts Consolidated wouldn't consider closing it down, no matter how expensive it was to run.

Of course, if the inn itself wasn't doing well, they might decide to retrench. She wondered what Joe's salary was, then decided not to worry about it. No luxury hotel chain would want to lose a famous chef if they could help it.

At one thirty, she took over the hostess station again, sending Mabel back to her office. She checked the reservations for the next day while she massaged her toes. She was pretty sure she was developing a couple of world-class blisters. She hadn't come to work dressed for waiting tables.

Joe sauntered through the restaurant, nodding at customers he recognized. "Here," he said, pushing a plate in front of her.

Kit sighed and picked up the cheeseburger. "Thanks. I realized how hungry I was after the adrenaline wore off."

"I sent Jorge over to Philip's place in Johnson City, but he wasn't there. Jorge didn't see his bike either."

She raised an eyebrow. "Bike?"

"He rides an old Kawasaki. Usually has it locked up in the garage out back when he's working. Jorge said he pounded on the door at his apartment, but nobody answered."

Kit sighed, rubbing her eyes. "Great. Sounds like he may have taken off without giving notice. I'll check with his landlord if I can find him."

"So tell Mabel she needs to hire new waiters ASAP. Hell, if she doesn't know that by now, she hasn't been listening."

Kit paused, trying to decide whether she should tell him about Mabel's threats concerning the Rose. If she did, he'd probably head for Mabel's office now, which would probably produce one godawful fight. And they'd need Mabel to run the hostess stand tomorrow unless Phillip had a miraculous change of heart. "I'll tell her," she said finally. "Later."

Joe gave her a dry smile. "Trying to put off the explosion, darlin'?"

"As long as I can." She managed a smile. "Great burger, by the way."

Joe shook his head. "This staffing problem had better get straightened out, Ms. Maldonado, or the restaurant's going straight down the tubes."

Kit felt a quick drip of ice water down her spine. If the restaurant went down the tubes, Mabel wouldn't have much trouble convincing Resorts Consolidated to close it. Particularly after the disaster the last chef had caused at the inn. "I'll work it out," she promised. "Tomorrow at the latest."

"I'll look forward to it. Meanwhile, you might want to go back home and get yourself some sneakers." He nodded toward her sandals. "Those are gonna rip your feet to shreds if you're waiting tables."

Kit closed her eyes for a moment, massaging her toes again. "Tell me about it."

"Brody." Toleffson narrowed his eyes.

Nando nodded.

"Chief Brody? The guy who swindled the city out of several thousand dollars while he was extorting conventioneers? The guy who tried to steal an antique map and ended up almost killing my sister-in-law?" His jaw tightened.

"That's the only Brody I know about."

"Did she actually *say* 'Chief Brody'?"

Nando nodded, staring around the half-empty hospital parking lot. They'd already had an abbreviated version of this conversation over the phone, but Toleffson had headed over immediately and dragged him down here where they were less likely to be overheard, at least theoretically. "She said 'Brody' and then she closed her eyes. And then she said 'Chief Brody'. The nurse said she'd probably be in and out of consciousness now, but eventually she'll be fully awake."

Toleffson leaned back against the side of his truck, sighing. "This makes no sense. You know that. If Brody was back, somebody in town would have recognized him. It's not like he left all that long ago."

Nando shrugged. "Maybe he looks different now. He's been on the run for a few years. Hell, maybe he's dyed his hair or shaved it off." He had a momentary mental image of Joe LeBlanc but dismissed it. The guy was way too young anyway.

"Still." The chief kicked a piece of gravel across the parking lot. "If he's here, where the hell has he been hiding for the past month? He can't have been out in the open that much—he couldn't take the risk of somebody recognizing him. And if he was holed up somewhere in town, there'd be gossip about the strange guy who didn't come out of his room."

"I don't know. I've been thinking about this since Helen woke up." In point of fact, he hadn't been thinking about much of anything else since Helen woke up. "He could be living in someplace like Johnson City or Mable Falls, but even if he was actually living here in town, most people probably wouldn't notice. I mean, if I knew Brody was around, I might recognize him. But if I didn't expect to see him, I probably wouldn't. Especially if he's lost weight or dyed his hair."

"You mean you wouldn't see him or you wouldn't recognize him?"

Nando shrugged. "Both. The guy was in his forties when he took off. There are a lot of men in that age group around here. And I always saw Brody in uniform—everybody did. Seeing him in civilian clothes might be like camouflage. To tell you the truth, the SOB could walk right by me now in the right getup and I'd likely not know it was him unless I was looking close."

Toleffson stared down at his boots for a moment, then glanced back at him. "You said you wouldn't recognize him if you didn't expect to see him. But what if you knew he was here?"

Nando shrugged. "Then all bets are off. From now on, I'll be checking out every middle-aged man I see, trying to make sure it isn't Brody. From now on, I'll be looking for him." And hoping he'd be the one who found the bastard.

The chief blew out a long breath, staring back toward the hospital entrance. "I don't suppose we've got any pictures of Brody around the station."

Nando shook his head. "Not that I've seen. They used to have a portrait of the chief hanging up there, but they took Brody's down when he ran off, and then Olema wasn't around long enough to rate a picture of his own." He glanced at Toleffson, frowning. "Anybody ask for one of you?"

Toleffson gave him a dry grin. "Nah. Maybe they decided not to spring for another picture, seeing as how they'd had so much turnover.

223

I like Al's cartoon over at the Coffee Corral better anyway."

"We can look around the station. That old portrait might be stored someplace."

"That would be real helpful since I don't have a clue what this asshole looks like." He shrugged. "Maybe there's something on line."

"Lots of people in town might recognize him if they knew he was around," Nando said slowly. "Are you going to let everybody know?"

Toleffson stared down at his feet again for a long moment, then shook his head. "No. You know how that would be. All of a sudden everybody in town would start seeing him everywhere they looked. They'd have us running all over creation checking out false sightings. We need to be the ones doing the looking."

"But the only cops who know what he looks like are me and Ham. And Helen once she comes back. Rollie moved here after you did, Dawson's been here for less time than that and Delaney's the newest of us all."

The chief shrugged. "Which is why we need a picture of him."

"So we don't tell anybody?" Nando tried to keep the worry out of his voice.

Toleffson shook his head. "Wait until Helen's talking. Maybe we can get some more information from her. Meanwhile, we'll keep doing patrol. And we'll tell the boys to keep quiet about it."

"And Ham?"

The chief sighed. "Him too. I'll brief him on it. And tell him to keep his mouth shut, which we both know he won't do. Hell."

"Maybe we should just let the news leak," Nando said carefully. "No big announcement, but let people in town find out. They need to know what's going on. Brody's always been a loose cannon, and now he may be desperate."

Toleffson stared back at him, his eyes dark. "Look, I've got family concerns here too. I don't think it was an accident that he went after Docia's shop. Or Margaret Hastings' place. They were the two women he attacked before. Maybe he was getting a little payback while he threw us off the scent."

"What about Allie?"

The chief shrugged. "She's Docia's friend. And maybe he thought it would be too obvious if Docia and Margaret were the only ones he hit."

Nando's jaw set. "Look chief, I think Docia needs to know. Margaret too. And Allie. If this gets out and we didn't tell them, they're going to be pissed. And they're going to be scared. And they'll have a right to be. We don't know what's on Brody's agenda, but it's not likely to be anything good."

Toleffson rubbed a hand across his jaw, narrowing his eyes. Then he shrugged. "Okay, you've got a point. I'll call Docia and Cal. Ham can talk to Margaret. You can talk to Allie or Kit, assuming she'll tell Allie herself." He gave Nando another dry smile. "They'll undoubtedly tell other people, like Wonder, so it'll be all around town in a couple of days, but at least we'll have a head start."

Nando nodded. "Okay. I'll get on it."

"And we'll need to keep somebody at the station from now on, particularly at night, in case he decides to come back for whatever it was he was trying to get the first time."

"You don't think he got it?"

The chief shook his head. "I'd bank on him not getting anything. He's dangerous but he's not stupid. After he hit Helen he must have taken off. He had no way of knowing if anybody else was around." He pushed off from his truck. "I'll call the county crime lab too. Chances are they have some of Brody's DNA on file already—they could compare it against the sample we found in Docia's shop. It wouldn't hurt to have some concrete confirmation for whatever Helen saw."

Nando nodded. "It wouldn't at that."

Chapter Twenty-One

Nando waited until evening to head over to Allie's place. He hoped Kit would be there by herself after she'd gotten off work. He had a feeling it would be easier to explain the whole Brody situation without a lot of other people around, and Allie and Wonder together constituted a lot of people.

At first, when he saw Allie's darkened house, he was afraid Kit wasn't there at all, but then he saw her battered Civic at the side. He took a deep breath and climbed the steps to her front door.

Kit opened it before he could knock. Her smile started an ache in his groin that he knew was going to last for a while, probably until he could get her underneath him, no matter how long that took.

"Hi," she said softly. "I didn't know if you'd be working tonight."

"I'm on days this week." He tried unsuccessfully to keep his mouth from sliding into an idiot grin. "Can I come in?"

She stepped back to let him pass into the cool dimness of the house. "I just got home a few minutes ago. You want some wine? I'm having a glass."

"Sure."

He followed her into Allie's dining room. The subdued light from overhead cast shadows around the corners, emphasizing the sculpted planes of her face. She reached up to the top shelf of the china cabinet to get him a glass, pulling the fabric of her knit top tight against her breasts.

His groin gave another throb. He took another deep breath.

"It's Australian shiraz," Kit said as she poured red wine into the glass. "It's okay, but not as good as Cedar Creek."

He took a sip. "Tastes all right to me. Not that I'd recognize the difference."

"You don't like wine? Even though your family makes it?"

He shrugged. "I like it well enough. I just avoided learning too much about it whenever my dad tried to teach me. Call it my version of youthful rebellion." He managed a grin that he hoped was a step above idiot grade.

Her lips edged up slightly. "So what brings you here?"

He took another of those deep breaths, then set the glass back on the table. "You, mainly." He slid one arm around her waist, pulling her close enough to smell that slight mixture of floral scent and musk. *Ah, Kit.*

Her lips tasted of wine, and he took his time, exploring her, letting one palm slide down the curve of her side. The bottom of her shirt pulled free at her waist, and he slipped his hand underneath, feeling the weight of her breast, the slight roughness of her lace bra.

After a while, Kit leaned back to look at him, her eyes smoky. "Mainly?"

He gritted his teeth—he'd really hoped she hadn't been listening that closely. On the other hand, maybe if he got this over with quickly they could go back to more interesting things. "I've got some news. About the burglar."

She brought her fingertips to her mouth, her eyes suddenly wide. "Oh my god, Helen. I forgot. Is she all right?"

"She will be. She was out for a while, but she woke up this afternoon. The doctor thinks she'll be okay."

"Good. Allie said she'd bring her some scones when she was up to eating them."

"My guess is that would be any time now." By the time he'd left that afternoon, Helen had been close to her usual prickly self. He figured she'd be more than ready for scones and decent coffee tomorrow, particularly if they made her spend another day in the hospital.

"So what's this about the burglar?" Kit raised one elegant eyebrow.

Nando felt another jolt and willed his loins to calm down. "Helen saw him, and she recognized him." He paused for a moment, trying to decide how to tell her the rest without just blurting it out.

"And?"

"It was Brody," he blurted. "Chief Brody. Ex-Chief Brody." He blew out a breath. Not really the way he'd planned on telling her.

Kit's eyes widened in shock. "The one who ran away? The fugitive?"

"That's the one."

"Oh my god," she said again. She moved into one of the dining table chairs. "Why didn't anybody recognize him?"

Nando didn't particularly want to rehash his entire conversation with Toleffson. He stuck to the short version. "He's been away for a while. People may have forgotten him by now. And he probably looks different."

"I saw him," she said slowly.

His pulse accelerated. "When? Where?"

She shook her head impatiently. "Not now. Back when he was here before. I was in town that summer when it all happened, when he ran away. My sister and I were staying with Allie."

He dropped into a chair beside her. "Do you remember him?"

"Vaguely." She shrugged. "Mainly I remember his uniform and his size. And his voice."

"His voice?" He frowned. "What about it?"

"Very deep and macho." She shook her head. "But maybe he was putting that on. He turned out to be a hollow man at the end. He looked great as a police chief, but that just shows you can't judge character based on how great somebody looks."

"Right." He wondered how he could get her back into his arms again. She didn't look like she needed comforting, unfortunately.

She frowned. "Does everybody know? Does Allie?"

He shook his head. "We're telling the people he burglarized, or probably burglarized—Docia and Margaret and Allie. But not the whole town. We figured they'd find out soon enough."

"But you haven't told Allie yet?"

He shook his head again. "I thought maybe she'd be here." Of course, he'd also hoped she wouldn't be.

"She's at Wonder's place." Kit's forehead furrowed. "We should call her. She needs to know."

Nando felt like groaning. If they called her, she'd probably come home, which would pretty much screw up his plans for the evening. *You're the one who said she needed to be told.* Indeed he had, which just demonstrated the perils of being conscientious.

He sighed. "Go ahead and call. I can talk to her if you want."

Allie got home within fifteen minutes, not enough time for much besides some incendiary kisses on the couch that left him so hard he felt like putting a pillow in his lap.

Fortunately, Allie had other things on her mind besides the state of his arousal. "Brody? Brody's back?"

"Apparently." Nando shifted on the couch trying to find a more comfortable position. He avoided looking at Wonder since he had a feeling the man was grinning. "We don't have any hard evidence yet, but Helen was sure."

"She should be sure. The man tried to kill her." Allie dropped into one of the wing chairs opposite the couch. "Why did he break into my bakery?"

Nando shrugged. "Why did he do any of those burglaries? He must have been after something, but so far we don't know what."

"Did he leave anything behind at the station when he took off the first time, after he tried to kill Docia and steal Dub's map?" Wonder moved beside Allie, rubbing a hand across her shoulder.

"Probably almost everything." Nando narrowed his eyes, thinking. "He ran before the Rangers could find him, once he figured they knew about what he'd done after they arrested his accomplice. And he never came back to town after he kidnapped Docia, so he probably didn't have a chance to grab anything from the station. That didn't give him much time to pack things up. He had to leave with what he had."

Allie shuddered. "He tried to kill two women the last time he was here. Now he's tried to kill another one. He's definitely not the kind of guy you want around."

Nando was still caught up thinking about what Brody could have left behind, but he knew he was supposed to be the one who offered comfort here. "He may not be around anymore, Allie. He must know Helen recognized him."

"He might figure she wouldn't remember—she had a head injury," Wonder said helpfully. "And besides, he's come this far. He probably doesn't want to stop until he gets what he came for."

Nando gave him a dark look. He could have a point, but he sure as hell wasn't making Nando's job any easier. "Still, he has no reason to come after you, Allie. You didn't see him. He's already been through your bakery, so anything he wanted from there he could have taken. My guess is you were just sort of a 'target of opportunity'. The burglary at your bakery was supposed to distract us from whatever he was really after."

"Great," Allie said dryly. "That makes me feel so much better about those cleaning bills I had after taking care of the mess he left behind." She sighed. "Does Docia know?"

Nando nodded. "The chief was going to tell her."

"Well, that's something. She's someone he might have a grudge against. Her and Margaret." Allie paused as she got up again. "Docia and Margaret. I didn't even think of it until now. They're the ones who found out what he was up to before. That's why he hit both their stores, isn't it?"

"Probably."

"Anybody want coffee? I've got some date-walnut loaf from yesterday."

Nando watched her walk toward the kitchen. Apparently she was going to settle in, which meant no more playtime with Kit. *Ah, well.*

Kit leaned against him for a moment, running a hand over his arm. "You know," she murmured, "you never did show me your place."

"That's right." He smiled down at her. "Want to see my place, *chica?*"

"I thought you'd never ask." Her hand moved from his arm to slide across his chest, and suddenly every nerve in his body was on fire.

"Then let's see how many speed records we can break getting there," he croaked, pulling her to her feet.

Halfway to Nando's apartment, Kit remembered that he lived with his brother. She had a few minutes to wonder just what she'd say to Esteban when she saw him. She had a feeling there wouldn't be much time for polite conversation before she disappeared behind Nando's bedroom door. Not that she was complaining about that, necessarily.

Fortunately, nobody seemed to be home at Casa Avrogado when they got there. She had a few moments to glimpse a slightly messy but attractive living room and small kitchen, with a large black and gray cat squarely in the middle of the table, before Nando whisked her down the hall.

He closed the bedroom door behind her, pulling her into his arms immediately, his mouth hot upon her throat. She heard the click of a lock behind him.

"Are you worried about Esteban coming in?"

"Not Esteban."

Outside the door there was a quick scratch of claws and an unmistakably disgruntled "Mrrowr!"

Kit managed to swallow her giggle. Moonlight spilled through the open window behind them.

"Maybe we should pull the blinds shut?" she whispered.

"Nobody out there. Just a patio."

His hands closed on her waist, soft and warm, pushing aside the bottom of her T-shirt. When she glanced up at his face, his eyes had darkened to the color of slate in the moonlight. She raised her hands to his chest, sliding them beneath his shirt to place her palms over his nipples, feeling his shiver of response. His gaze dropped to her mouth, and he pulled her tighter against his body. Her legs wrapped around his, her lips parting, then he bent his head to cover her mouth with his own.

His lips were hard upon hers, slanting slightly to take the kiss deeper, then pressing firm as she opened to him. Her body danced with heat, her pulse thundering in her ears, while his arms tightened, pulling her even closer against him. The hard swell of his arousal pressed into the V of her legs, making her ache with need. She shuddered, her hips arching up, her arms looping around his neck to draw the kiss deeper. His tongue curved around hers, and he sucked relentlessly.

His thighs pushed against hers, pressing her backward until she felt the bedroom wall against her back. His hands reached down to cup her buttocks, pulling her up until her softness met the hard ridge of his erection. He rubbed against her, groaning deep in his throat.

Then he was fumbling at the snap on her jeans, jerking them down along with her thong. The wall felt cool against her bare buttocks. She heard a vague ripping sound and hoped it was the thong rather than her jeans. Nando wrapped his arm around her hips, yanking her up so that her thighs fell apart. He jerked his own zipper

231

down, freeing and sheathing his erection, and then guided himself into her depths in a single hard thrust.

She dug her fingernails into his shoulders, holding on tight as he began to move.

"Jesus," he breathed into her ear. "Holy Christ."

The sounds that came from her throat had no relation to words, no relation to any sound she could ever remember making before. She caught her breath, her chest aching. "Ah, Nando," she gasped. "Nando."

He was thrusting deep now, long, slow movements that made her shudder with need, each one setting off that starburst of pleasure in her muscles. He grasped her buttocks harder, settling her so that he rubbed against her burning core, opening her folds still further.

The pleasure seemed to swell inside her, the tension coiling deep down, then spiraling up. Dimly she heard him groaning again as she dug her fingernails into his shoulders. His head dropped forward as he plunged more quickly.

And then she was shattering, exploding in light, the flood of pleasure taking her up with him. She cried out once and then again, her body shuddering hard against him as he reached his own climax.

He thrust deep a few more times, then pulled her into his arms, resting his forehead against hers. "God, Kit," he whispered. "My god. I'll never recover from you."

She brought her hand to his cheek, running her fingers across the soft skin, feeling warm and drowsy and sated. "Do you want to?"

He shook his head. "No. Not now."

She caught her breath. Suddenly she was wide awake. *I'll never recover from you.* Was this the right time to push it, to open up the past? Would there ever be a right time? Could she wait until there was? "Not now?"

Nando grasped her hand, bringing it to his lips. "I mean it."

She licked her lips. "What you said?"

"Yes. I mean it."

Her mind raced through all the options, all the words she could say, all the ways they could move forward from this. And she came up absolutely dry. "Okay," she stammered finally.

Okay? Okay? Eighteen months and that's all you can think of?

Okay?

He stared at her for a moment, his lips inching up in a dry smile. "Okay then." He reached down, gathering her up in his arms, then carried her the few steps to his bed, lowering her onto the mattress and lying down beside her.

Kit licked her lips, trying desperately to find a way to backtrack. "I mean... I'm trying... I want..." She sighed, shaking her head as she pushed her hair out of her eyes. "Damn it. I don't know how to say anything all of a sudden."

Nando brushed his fingers across her cheekbone. "It's okay, Catarina. Don't worry about it. We've got time."

Do we? Will we? She closed her eyes again, feeling the faint rasp of his fingertips across her skin. *Enough. Just let it go.*

She slid her arms around him, resting her cheek against his chest, then pulled back to look at him again. "Nando?"

"Hmmm?"

"You still have your clothes on."

He narrowed his eyes, glancing down at his open shirt and unzipped jeans. "So I do. I lost track."

She ran her fingers down his chest, lightly. "Don't you think it might be better if you didn't have them on?"

She saw his grin flash in the dark as he pulled her back against him again. "Yeah, *chica.* I'd say it would be a lot better."

Chapter Twenty-Two

Nando spent the next few days in a state of sleep deprivation. Not that he minded. He spent his nights with Kit, sometimes at his place and sometimes at hers. They slept only when they couldn't manage to stay awake any longer. He figured Deirdre's dark roast was the only thing keeping him from falling into a coma.

Caffeine was also the best way to deal with the dozens of hysterical people who kept calling the station. Toleffson had been right about the citizens of Konigsburg seeing Brody behind every bush. So many sightings came in that they started taking them in batches, each patrol covering three or four in a single drive-by. Needless to say, none of them resulted in anything more than several tall, gray-haired, male Konigsburgers delivering colorful obscenities concerning their neighbors' eyesight.

Helen had insisted on coming back to work after two days in the hospital and another at home. Even though she still looked a little shaky, she'd been invaluable on the phones. As Nando came in, he heard her sighing. "Maxine are you sure it was Brody and not Harlan Somers? You know Harlan's over at that garage all the time and they're about the same size."

Nando sighed too, taking another swallow of dark roast. He'd probably be heading to that particular garage sometime during his shift. Wonder's question about what Brody had left behind in the station still nagged at him. He and Delaney had already been through the building from one end to the other, but they hadn't found much other than the original portrait of Brody that had been tucked away in the same broom closet where they kept the cleaning supplies. He placed his coffee cup on his desk and carried the portrait into Toleffson's office.

The chief squinted at it. "Sort of average-looking, isn't he?"

Nando nodded. "I never thought about it while he was here, but yeah, he's one of those people who'd blend into a crowd. So long as he wasn't wearing a uniform."

"Which we assume he isn't at the moment," Toleffson said dryly.

Nando glanced around the chief's office again. "How much of this stuff on the walls was here when you came?"

"Pretty much all of it. Olema had a bunch of his hunting trophies around, but he took those with him. The rest of it was left over."

One wall had an engraving of the old Lutheran church downtown, while another had somebody's watercolor of the Guadalupe River.

"You see anything interesting about this stuff?" the chief asked.

Nando shook his head. "Nah. But last time the map Brody was after was hanging on the wall at the bookstore."

"I don't think either of these has much value." Toleffson lifted the engraving down, turning it over and opening the paper covering on the back. "And it looks like this is the only thing in the frame."

Nando checked the watercolor. "Same here. Another dead end. Unless the artist is somebody famous."

"It wouldn't be something on the walls anyway," Toleffson mused. "He could have lifted that down and taken off before Helen came in here. She said he was trying to get into the desk."

"So how much of the stuff in the desk did you inherit from Brody?"

The chief sighed, staring at the contents of the desk they had spread out on the folding table. "I don't know exactly. Some of it was probably Olema's, and some of it may even date back to whoever was chief before Brody." He prodded a calcified stick of gum with his index finger. "I wouldn't try chewing this, for example. It looks like it belongs in the junk food museum."

Nando narrowed his eyes. "Is there a junk food museum?"

Toleffson shrugged. "If there isn't, somebody in town will probably start one eventually."

"Nobody cleaned out the desk before you moved in?"

He shook his head. "Nope. I added the desk calendar and a couple of legal pads. And some working pens. Most of the ones in here were drained."

"What about stuff you took out of the desk?"

Toleffson frowned. "What do you mean?"

"I mean stuff you put somewhere else. You said you don't keep files in the desk, but Olema never struck me as that careful. Maybe Brody wasn't either. Were there files or log books or something that you took out of the desk and put someplace else when you moved in?"

The chief rubbed the back of his neck, thinking. "Olema kept the duty rosters in the desk, but I moved them out to the bullpen where people could see them." He frowned, staring down at his desktop. "There were some case files here too. I remember because it struck me as a damn fool thing to do, keeping current files in a desk drawer instead of the file cabinet. Or better yet on line."

"You remember what cases?"

Toleffson shrugged. "No. It's too far back. The names didn't mean anything to me."

"Could one of them have been Brody's file?"

They stared at each other for a long moment. Then the chief blew out a breath. "I wish I could say yes, but I don't know for sure. All I can say is maybe."

He headed across the hall toward the evidence room where they kept the file cabinets, along with some spare equipment that had been stowed out of the way. The Konigsburg Police Department didn't have enough spare rooms to devote one to files and evidence alone. Toleffson pulled out one of the drawers, leafing through it until he found the file folder. "I just looked at this yesterday, but I wasn't thinking of it as anything Brody might want."

He brought the file back into the office, dropping it onto the desk. Nando watched as he flipped through the pages. "Docia's statement, Margaret Hastings' statement, duplicates of the Rangers' reports. And the original report on the investigation at the bookstore." He glanced at the signature on the second page. "Ham?"

Nando shrugged. "He was the only one left. Brody and the other full-time guy, Clete Morris, were in on the criminal conspiracy. Ham ran the investigation at this end until the sheriff took over temporarily."

Toleffson grimaced. "Which probably explains the quality of the work. You see anything in this file that Brody could be after?"

Nando shook his head. "I suppose it could be something technical. I mean, the forensic accountants tracked down most of his bank accounts, including the ones overseas, and he might be after something in their reports. But I don't know why since you'd think he'd already have all that information himself."

"He might not have had the account numbers with him, but they wouldn't do him any good now anyway. They've been shut down." The chief sighed. "Back to square one. He left something behind, but we don't know what and we don't know where."

"And we don't know where he is either. A trifecta."

Toleffson snorted. "Go patrol, Nando. Maybe you'll get lucky and arrest him for jaywalking."

Kit was dividing her time between the wedding and her job at the Rose. And Nando, but at least she was with him after hours. She rubbed a hand across her face. The combination of the three was wearing her to a frazzle, but at least the wedding would be over after the weekend. The Nando part would last longer than that. Or so she devoutly hoped.

They were still treading carefully around talking about the past, but there didn't seem to be any question about how they felt in the present. Of course, neither of them had said anything specific about that either.

Kit sighed. Thinking about it gave her a headache.

The wedding rehearsal would be tonight, the wedding itself tomorrow night. She'd already shifted her hours around to cover the wedding, although she'd probably have to run back and forth between the event center and the party room to get set up for the rehearsal dinner tonight. Theoretically, Wonder was handling everything, but these days Wonder seemed to be operating at less than peak efficiency.

She and Joe together had finally browbeaten Mabel into hiring a new server since Philip was apparently gone for good. Kit had driven by his apartment one morning to see if he'd come back, but nobody had seen him for several days. His landlord was on the verge of clearing out what remained of his stuff and renting the place to someone else. She wondered if she should be worried about what had become of him but decided after a while to let it go. She had enough to worry about as it was.

Now Joe leaned against the hostess desk, flipping through the thin stack of waiter applications. After a moment he paused, staring at one. "This guy works at Brenner's?"

Kit nodded. "Bryson Mitchell. I talked to him this morning. He's my top pick."

Joe shook his head. "He'll never come here. He's got to be making more at Brenner's than we'd pay him."

"I thought about that." She stared down at the application. "I told him the job was for a head waiter. And I boosted the pay by a buck fifty an hour."

The corners of his mouth quirked up. "Did Mabel okay that?"

"Not yet. But I'll make sure she does." Actually Kit wasn't all that sure about how Mabel would react, but it was the best idea she'd come up with.

His jaw tightened. "You tell her I okayed it. I'm in charge of the goddamn restaurant, not her. If she doesn't stop screwing around with this place, I'll string that bitch up by her toenails."

Kit put a hand on his arm. "You can do whatever you want to her—she probably deserves it. Only please, please, please wait until after the wedding. I've got too much on my plate right now. I can't deal with another crisis." She managed to keep the panic out of her voice, but it wasn't easy.

Joe glanced at her, then shrugged, grimacing. "Okay, darlin', I'll leave her alone until after you're done. But you tell me what she says. If she doesn't come through on this, we're gonna have words, her and me."

"Oh good," she muttered as she watched him stalk back to his kitchen. "Something else to look forward to." She checked the dining room, confirming that the last few customers were getting ready to go, then headed up the hall toward the office.

Mabel didn't look particularly delighted to see her, but that wasn't any surprise. She shuffled a stack of papers on her desk. "What is it, dear? I'm really swamped this afternoon."

Kit gave her a slightly rigid smile. "I just wanted to let you know I've found another waiter. He's very experienced, currently with Brenner's. He'll be just what we need in the dining room."

Mabel shrugged. "Fine. Have him fill out the paperwork and drop it off whenever he starts."

Kit licked her lips. *Now for the fun part.* "Since he's experienced, I offered him a slightly higher salary than the one we were paying Phillip. He can serve as head waiter, which means he could double on the hostess stand in an emergency."

Mabel narrowed her eyes, all pretense of a smile sliding away. "How much higher?"

"A dollar fifty an hour. It's on par with what the other fine dining restaurants in town are paying." She felt like crossing her fingers since she had no way to prove that was true. But it didn't sound unreasonable.

Mabel drummed her fingers on her desk for a moment, her gaze remarkably flinty. "I suppose that will be acceptable for the time being. We'll review it when we review the Rose's operation next month."

"Review?" Kit felt the familiar drip of ice water down her spine. "Review what exactly?"

"Expenses." Mabel shrugged. "I've already mentioned the Rose's high operating expenses. I believe it's dragging the rest of the inn's earnings down. We'll need to find ways to economize if we're to keep the Rose open at all."

Kit blinked, her chest tightening. "You'd really close the Rose?"

Mabel shrugged again. "It may not come to that. It probably won't. But it's a possibility I'll explore with the inn's management. Now, if that's all?"

Kit managed to push her lips into a tight smile, then turned and headed for the event center. At least she could make sure the wedding went smoothly, even if her own job was apparently hanging by a thread.

She spent the afternoon checking with the florist and decorator to see that the event center was set up for the rehearsal, while keeping tabs on tomorrow's reservations with call forwarding and frequent checks on her laptop. Sooner or later she'd have to tell Joe what Mabel had said, but given her choice, she'd opt for later. She had a feeling the battle would be long, bloody and loud. And she wasn't sure who'd win in the end.

Just get through the wedding. Just get through the wedding.

Wonder was supposedly bringing the judge with him and Allie, and Kit figured the rest of the wedding party could find their own way to the Woodrose. The family wasn't due in until tomorrow, even though her father was giving Allie away. They'd find someone to stand in for

Papi at the rehearsal, sort of a substitute Dad.

She blew out a breath. Just as well. She still hadn't decided what to say to Papi exactly about her job at the Rose. Or whether she was going to introduce Nando.

At four, she looked up to see Allie wandering through the rose garden outside the event center. She frowned—her aunt wasn't due until five and Wonder was supposed to bring her. After a moment to smooth her hair, she headed into the garden herself.

"Hi Aunt Allie," she chirped. *Geez could you sound any phonier?*

Allie glanced at her, and Kit caught her breath. Her aunt's face seemed drawn tight, her eyes shadowed, deep lines etched around her mouth as if she hadn't slept for a couple of nights. "Allie," she said quietly, "are you okay?"

"Sure," Allie replied quickly, then paused, rubbing a hand across her mouth. "Well, sort of, I guess. I'm just tired. Really, really tired."

Kit put a hand on her arm. "Come here. Sit down in the shade." She maneuvered her onto a stone bench under a spreading pecan. "Now tell me what's wrong."

"Nothing," Allie said stubbornly, but she closed her eyes. After a moment, she shook her head. "He wants me to sell the house."

"Steve? Your house?" Kit licked her lips, trying to decide what to say. She'd sort of taken it as a given that Allie would want to sell her house. "You don't want to?"

"It's my house," Allie said softly. "When I bought it, I knew I'd finally made a home in Konigsburg. Finally gotten where I wanted to go."

"But..." Kit took another breath. "Steve's house is nice too."

"Steve's house is great. But it's not my house." Allie's voice sounded like a mechanical toy that was wound a bit too tight. "I don't want to give up my house."

"Allie." Kit leaned forward, resting her hand on her aunt's knee. "You don't have to think about this now. You can work it out after you and Steve get back from your honeymoon. You've got enough things to worry about at the moment."

Allie nodded. "I do have a lot of things to worry about. This is one of them."

"Let me get you some tea," Kit said quickly. "Why don't you come inside the event center? I think we've got some of Joe's appetizers left over from lunch."

"I'll come inside in a little while. Right now I want to walk." Allie stared out at the roses, not looking at her.

Kit licked her lips again. "Aunt Allie..."

"I'll be all right. But I need to be by myself for a while." Allie pushed herself to her feet. "Don't worry about me. Just go on doing whatever you were doing before." She stepped away from the bench, then headed toward the inn, her back a rigid line against the blooming rose arbor.

"Crap," Kit whispered as she watched her walk away. "Crap, crap, crap."

Allie wandered along the graveled garden path, not really paying any attention to where she was going. She'd have to tell him. Now. Before the rehearsal. Because, of course, there was no point in having a rehearsal for something that wasn't going to take place. She'd have to tell him she couldn't marry him before this went any further.

Her heart seemed to contract, almost as if someone were pulling it tighter with a string. *Steve.* She caught her breath in a gasp.

She loved him. She'd loved him for years, ever since he'd taken her to the Liddy Brenner Festival the first time. She knew all his faults, all the reasons she shouldn't love him, but it didn't seem to matter. The sarcasm. The thinning hair. The hornrims. The slightly pot belly that would probably turn into a true gut by the time he was fifty, given his affection for German beer. None of it bothered her. She knew the character underneath it all, the kindness, the intelligence, the loyalty.

She loved him. She did. And she couldn't marry him.

Breathing was becoming more difficult. Her throat seemed to have closed up. Her jaws ached. She wanted nothing so much as to find a quiet corner somewhere and cry her eyes out.

She'd suspected for a while that she couldn't do it, couldn't carry off a wedding, but she'd always managed to talk herself out of it before. Now suddenly the whole thing seemed to be landing on her shoulders with a crunch. Maybe she could write him a note and just leave town for a while.

Meg Benjamin

She pressed her hand across her mouth, fighting back a sob. How could she not marry him? He'd be so hurt. But how could she marry him? How could she give away everything she'd worked for? How could she give away herself?

Everything will change. All the things I worked for will slip away. My house will be gone. And then I'll be gone. I won't know myself anymore.

She took another shuddering breath and sank down on another stone bench. Somewhere nearby she heard the sound of garden shears snipping.

Great. I'm going to embarrass myself in front of the groundskeeper.

She took another breath, raising her head in what she feared was a very shaky imitation of normal.

The snipping came closer. A man in a gray uniform was silhouetted briefly against the rose bushes where he was clipping off deadheads. The nametag on his shirt read "Didrikson." He paused when he caught sight of her. "Something I can help you with, ma'am?"

Why yes. Could you go tell my fiancé I can't marry him? Allie pulled herself upright. "No, that's all right. I'm just enjoying your garden."

The gardener stepped closer, clipping another rose from the bush. "Enjoy away."

She sat very still, staring at him as he put down the clippers to gather the dried flowers into a trash bag. Something about that voice. Deep. Gravelly. The body was familiar, too, now that she thought about it. There was something about the set of the shoulders. And the uniform. Something about the uniform.

She squinted at him again. The face. She knew the face.

She pushed herself a bit shakily to her feet. "You have lovely roses," she said in a voice that sounded totally artificial even to her.

The gardener watched her carefully, letting the trash bag with the dried roses slip through his fingers to the ground.

Allie licked her lips, giving him another shaky smile. "Well, thank you for...your beautiful garden. I've got a wedding rehearsal to get to. I guess I'll just head back to the event center now."

Almost before she knew what was happening, the gardener grasped her arm, yanking her toward him. "I guess you won't."

"I..." She was appalled to hear her voice shake. *Pull it together.* "What are you doing? Let me go. Right now." She jerked back hard, trying to pull free of that iron grasp.

"What am I doing? I'm saving my life." He gave her a smile that was more like a grimace. "And my freedom, Ms. Maldonado." He wrapped one arm around her waist like a vice, pulling her tight against him as she struggled.

Allie dug in her heels, drawing a breath to scream. But he slapped his hand across her mouth, his other arm still tight around her waist. "No screaming now. We can both still get out of this alive if you stay smart. You could actually prove useful." He began to drag her backward, half carrying her toward a service door.

Allie struggled against his arm, trying and failing to jerk her head free. He cuffed the side of her head, sharply. "Knock it off, Maldonado. I don't want to hurt you, but I know how."

For a moment, her head swam. She heard his shoulder hit the door behind her, heard the swish of the door itself opening, then felt the coolness of air conditioning washing across her skin as the sunlight dimmed. She closed her eyes, shaking her head limply, trying to dig her heels into the slick surface of the floor as he dragged her back up the hall.

Damn! Oh damn, damn, damn! This was worse than wedding nerves. So much worse. And it was her own fault. She'd been the one who'd wandered off to the rose garden instead of staying where she should have been.

Because she'd been off sulking in the garden when she should have been meeting Steve, she'd just been kidnapped by Chief Brody.

And then the door slammed shut behind them.

Chapter Twenty-Three

Nando took one last look at the file open on the desk in front of him. The Rangers' report on Brody didn't tell him much he didn't already know. He'd been hoping they might have included details about Brody's various bank accounts, information that Brody himself might possibly have needed or wanted to find. But a cursory read had confirmed that the accountants were much too smart to put that kind of data in a report anybody could read. There probably was a report with greater detail somewhere, but he doubted it was in Konigsburg.

He shook his head, leaning back in his chair. Whatever Brody had been searching for was at the heart of this. Somehow it had to be. But he hadn't a clue as to what that something was.

He glanced around the station. Helen had gone home early at Toleffson's urging. Ham was patrolling with a new sense of importance since he was one of the few people in the office who claimed he could recognize Brody on sight. Toleffson was off at the wedding rehearsal. Nando was supposed to be doing his eternal paperwork, but in fact he was playing Sherlock Holmes. Badly.

He'd clicked to Google on the office computer, trying to find more information about Brody's escape, when the phone on Helen's desk rang. He pushed himself to his feet and ambled over. Whatever minor crisis somebody was having might at least give him something else to think about.

He picked up the receiver. "Konigsburg police."

"Let me speak to your chief," a man's voice said abruptly.

"The chief isn't here right now. Can I take a message?"

"Who are you?"

Frowning, Nando managed to keep from snarling back. "I'm Assistant Chief Avrogado. What can I do for you?"

"Assistant Chief Avrogado?" The man said. His voice seemed faintly mocking, as if he found Nando's title absurd.

Nando stiffened. "What can I do for you?" he repeated through clenched teeth.

"Well, Officer, I've got a hostage here. She's all right at the moment. She'll stay that way if you do exactly what I say."

Nando grasped the phone so tightly his fingers ached. "What? Who the hell is this?"

"Keep it down, Officer," the man snapped. "You don't want to involve anybody else in this, not if you want her to stay healthy. And you know who I am. Or you should if you think about it."

Nando leaned a hand on the desk. Brody. Had to be. "Yeah. I know who you are, you crooked son of a bitch. Who's your hostage?"

"Easy, Officer Avrogado. You don't want to piss me off. My hostage is Ms. Maldonado," Brody said.

Nando's breath caught in his throat. "Kit," he choked out.

There was a pause at the other end, then Brody was back. "No. Allie Maldonado. Still want to save her?"

Nando thought he heard a noise in the background, maybe a gasp. *God damn it to hell!* "What do you want?"

"Here's what you're going to do," Brody said calmly. "I want the contents of the chief's desk. All of it. Every drawer. Put it in a sack and bring it to the Woodrose. I'll have Ms. Maldonado in the Damask Meeting Room. Once I have the sack, I'll give her back to you. Come alone, Officer, and don't tell anybody else. You've got twenty minutes before she starts getting hurt."

This time the gasp was definite. "Twenty minutes isn't enough time," Nando said hurriedly.

"Maybe. But it's all the time you've got. Better get moving."

The phone went dead in his ear.

Kit stood in the back of the event center, studying the decorations. They weren't great. If she'd had a few weeks longer she might have been able to find people who'd have done a better job. Still, they weren't awful. They'd do.

The silver swags along the benches glowed in the late afternoon shadows. The pale pink roses with sprigs of lavender were charming and besides they smelled great. The lavender roses at the front were maybe a little over the top, but not so far over that they'd upset Allie.

Allie. She frowned quickly. Shouldn't she have come back by now? Even if she was having yet another crisis of confidence, she should at least get back here in time for the rehearsal. It wasn't like Allie to keep other people waiting, no matter how upset she was.

Members of the wedding had already begun to straggle in. Cal Toleffson stood up front with Docia and his brother Erik, the chief of police. She could see Jess and Lars heading down the gravel walk from the parking lot. Maybe it was time to go looking for Allie.

"Where is she?" The voice at her elbow made her jump. She hadn't seen Wonder come in.

"She went for a walk," Kit explained, pressing a hand to her heart.

Wonder's forehead was furrowed, his jaw set. He looked like he was going through a mild crisis of his own. "Was she still upset?"

Kit nodded. "A little."

"Damn it. All I did was ask her if she'd listed her place with a realtor yet. How does that qualify as pressure?"

"She's just nervous. I think the whole wedding thing is getting to her." And, of course, to everybody else. For the hundredth time, Kit gave thanks that the whole thing was almost over.

"Where did she go walking?" Wonder glanced around the parking lot. "I'll see if I can find her."

"She's in the rose garden. I'll come with you." Kit walked purposefully toward the main entrance. If she was with Wonder, it might cut down on the chances that Allie would do anything to disappoint everybody. At this stage, she was willing to use any strategy she could think of to keep everything running on track.

After a moment, she heard Wonder trailing after her. "She doesn't have to sell her house," he muttered. "She doesn't have to do anything she doesn't want to. Hell, we can live there if that's what she wants. She keeps getting worked up over everything."

"She's just nervous," Kit repeated absently. "Don't worry. It'll be okay."

Of course, right now the problem was that she didn't see Allie anywhere in the rose garden, where she'd supposedly been walking. She felt the first faint stirrings of panic. Allie wouldn't really bolt, would she? Leaving her favorite niece holding the bag?

"I don't see her," Wonder said from behind her.

"I don't either. Maybe she went into the inn." Kit turned up the path that led back to the lower inn entrance, then paused. A flash of something bright had caught her eye. She leaned down, pushing aside a rose bush.

Allie's purse sat half-propped against a floribunda, the gold clasp shining in the sun. A pair of garden clippers lay on the ground nearby along with a trash bag full of dead roses.

"What the hell?" Wonder stopped behind her. "Isn't that Allie's? Where would she go without her purse?"

Kit nodded slowly. "And Mr. Didrikson's stuff. Why would either of them leave these things here?"

Suddenly she had a flash of memory—Didrikson on his mower, riding back and forth across the lawn, his broad back straight above the seat.

His broad back. *I'd swear I've seen him somewhere before. But I don't know where or when. It's just...I've seen that back. Doing something.* Her chest clenched tight. Suddenly it hurt to breathe.

"Christ," she breathed. "Oh Christ. Brody. He's Brody. And he must have taken Allie with him. That's why she left her purse. He grabbed her."

"What?" Wonder glanced around the garden, his head swiveling like a turret gunner. "Brody? Where? That doesn't make any sense. Why would he take Allie?"

Kit pressed a hand to her pounding heart. "I don't know." *Think!* "Maybe for a hostage. Maybe he's kidnapped her to help him get away." *Please let that be it. Please don't let him hurt her.*

"A hostage?" Wonder shook his head slowly. "That's nuts. She probably just went inside the inn. Maybe she was so frazzled she forgot her purse." He turned toward the rear entrance.

Kit pulled back on his arm, holding tight. "Listen to me. Please, Steve! Go get Erik. I'll call Nando. If I'm wrong, it'll be just another false sighting. You can all laugh at me. But if I'm right, we need them. Now!"

Wonder stared down at her, blinking. "Erik?"

"Please. He's in the event center. Just do it!" She pushed him in the direction of the building.

He stared back at her for a moment longer, then began trotting back up the path.

Kit pulled her phone from her pocket, running toward the rear entrance to the inn. There was no way she was going to stand outside waiting while somebody threatened her aunt. Particularly not when they had a wedding tomorrow.

Nando took one frantic glance around the station. Helen and Ham were gone. Toleffson was gone. The night shift wouldn't be in for an hour.

And he had less than twenty minutes to pick up the stuff and drive to the Woodrose.

He pulled a large plastic trash sack from behind Helen's desk and headed for the chief's office. The desk and file cabinet contents lay where they'd left it earlier, spread out on the folding table. Nando grabbed handfuls and threw them into the sack, not taking the time to look at them. He checked his watch.

Seventeen minutes.

He pulled the drawstring at the top of the sack and ran for the parking lot, locking the door behind him, although a fat lot of good that would do. His truck was parked next to the cruiser. After a moment's hesitation, he unlocked it and climbed in. The less attention he drew the better, and taking the cruiser to the Woodrose would definitely draw attention.

The highway into town was clogged with weekend tourists, but fortunately he was headed the other direction. One part of his brain kept track of the time while the other tried to figure out what to do. Brody would want to hang onto Allie as his hostage. He had to figure out a way to keep him from taking her with him when he left. If only Toleffson...

Nando blew out a quick breath, remembering suddenly just where Toleffson was tonight. The wedding rehearsal. At the event center behind the Woodrose. But there was no time to go and get him before the twenty minutes was up. Nando punched the button on his automatic dial, praying the chief would pick up.

He wouldn't, of course. He was in the middle of a wedding rehearsal, and he'd probably turned his phone off. The voice mail message came on as Nando turned into the drive leading to the Inn. "Brody's got Allie," he barked. "He's holding her in the Damask Room at the Woodrose. I'm supposed to go alone and bring everything from your desk. I'm almost there. Don't let him see you when you come over there. He says he'll kill her. I'm going there directly. Maybe you can find a back way in."

He snapped the phone closed and tossed it onto the seat, then pulled the truck into the parking lot at the back of the inn, heading for the rear entrance at a dead run.

He looked at his watch. Four minutes.

It would help if he knew which room the Damask Room was, but he couldn't take the time to ask, and besides, he didn't see anyone to ask anyway. He headed down the hall that led to the ballroom, noting the names of the other rooms along the way. Floribunda, Bourbon, Gallica.

Jesus. He had no idea what those names meant or if he was even in the right hall. They didn't look to be arranged alphabetically, unfortunately.

Ahead of him, he saw a card on an easel standing next to one of the doors. *Maldonado-Kleinschmidt Rehearsal Dinner,* it said. Behind it, he saw the room plaque. *Damask.*

He took a deep breath, then knocked on the closed door.

"Nando?" Allie's voice sounded shaky.

"Yeah," he muttered.

The door opened and he was looking down at Allie's pale face. "He's right behind me," she said.

"I've got the sack. Let me in."

She stepped to the side, letting him slide past. A tall man with silvery hair and a weathered face stood behind her holding a Walther PPK aimed at the middle of her back.

"Cutting it close, Officer," he said. "I wasn't sure you'd make it."

"I'm here," Nando said through clenched teeth. "Here's your stuff. Take it and get out—I won't stop you."

"Of course you won't. You can't, as long as I have Ms. Maldonado here. Take the sack, Ms. Maldonado."

Allie reached for the sack he held loosely in his hand. As their fingers touched briefly, he felt the coldness of her skin.

She swallowed hard. "Here," she said, holding the sack toward Brody.

"Open it," he said.

She blinked. "Me?"

"You. Let's make sure the officer hasn't decided to do something supremely stupid, like dropping in a couple of dye packs."

Nando's jaw tightened. If he'd had more time, he might actually have done that, assuming they had any dye packs at the station. "It's clean," he snapped.

"Open it," Brody repeated. "Tell me what you see."

Allie pulled the top of the sack open, peering inside. "It's just office stuff."

"Tell me what's in there." Brody's voice was sharp. "Now."

She licked her lips, then looked inside again. "I see a couple of legal pads, a lot of pens and pencils, some gum, some file folders with papers inside, some old computer disks, some energy bars, a bunch of paperclips and rubber bands, some spare change, some envelopes and stamps and some stationery. Do you want me to dig through it?"

Brody's lips spread into the ghost of a smile. "No. That's enough." He stepped beside her, taking hold of her upper arm. "We're going into the parking lot now. Hold onto that sack. You'll stay here, Officer."

"Take me," Nando said quickly. "Leave her here. She's got nothing to do with this."

"Oh, I don't think so." Brody folded the sack under his arm. "Ms. Maldonado is a lot safer hostage than you would be."

"If she gets hurt..." Nando said through gritted teeth.

"If she gets hurt, it's your fault. All I want to do is get out of here."

Brody moved the hand with the gun into his pants pocket. Nando could see the outline of the pistol still pointed at Allie. "Move, Ms. Maldonado. The sooner we get out of here, the sooner this will be over."

She cast an anguished glance at Nando. "It's all right," he murmured, his chest clenching tight. "It'll be all right."

Brody nodded toward the far corner of the room. "Get over to the far side and stay there, Officer. Ms. Maldonado will lock the door when we leave. If you start yelling too soon, she's likely to get hurt. Am I clear?"

250

"Crystal," he muttered.

Kit stood in the hallway, her gaze fastened on the door to the Damask Room. Nando had gone in carrying a sack and for just a moment she was sure she'd seen Allie's white face when she'd opened the door. Which meant that either Nando was in cahoots with Brody or Brody was forcing him to do something by using Allie as a hostage. Since the first possibility was absurd, the second must be fact.

She wiped her palms on her thighs. At least that explained why she hadn't been able to get Nando on the phone. She could try to run back to find Wonder and Erik, but who knew how long Brody would stay in that room? Yet if she didn't go for help, what could she do? She didn't have any weapons and she wouldn't have known how to use them if she had.

She walked quickly back up the hall again, her hands trembling. *Think, damn it, think! It's not just Allie, he's got Nando.*

"Hey darlin'." Joe stood at the end of the hallway, holding a large cake in his hands. "Got Ms. Allie's groom's cake here. Work of art, I'm telling you."

Kit stood rooted in the spot for a moment then started trotting down the hall toward him. "Give it to me."

Joe peered at her doubtfully. "To you? I was just going to put it in the kitchen with the wedding cake."

"Give it to me now. Don't argue, Joe, for god's sake. Lives are at stake." She slid her hands under the large platter, taking the considerable weight on her forearms.

"Lives at stake?" Joe's forehead furrowed. "Look, Kit, I know this whole wedding thing has been a strain..."

She turned, moving back up the hall. "Go to the event center. Find Wonder and the chief. Tell them he's in the Damask Room. Hurry! Please, Joe."

She had no idea whether he did as she asked. Her whole concentration was on the door to the Damask Room, which was slowly opening.

Allie stepped through first, grasping the black plastic garbage sack in both hands. Behind her, Brody-Didrikson looked deceptively bored. His gray groundskeeper's uniform was stained around the knees, his hair squashed down where he'd worn his cap. He looked annoyingly ordinary—just your average gardener taking a break. Except for the hand jammed in his pants pocket that probably held a gun pointed at his hostage.

Kit took a breath. "Aunt Allie," she called, forcing her voice into the kind of hearty cheerfulness she figured she should be using on the day before the wedding. "Look! Joe had your groom's cake."

She pattered up the hall, hoping her grin was sunny enough. "Oh hi, Mr. Didrikson. I didn't see you there. Look at Allie's groom's cake. Isn't it super?"

Didrikson narrowed his eyes as she stopped in front of him, probably trying to decide if she was serious.

"It's German chocolate, isn't it?" Kit babbled. "And look at the detail in the frosting."

Brody shifted his gaze to the cake for an instant.

Kit put all the strength she'd managed to build up from weeks of carrying laden trays and full pitchers of tea into her forearms, pushing the cake up to smash it into his face.

Several things happened at once. Allie screamed. Nando almost leaped out the door of the Damask Room, jerking Brody's hand out of his pants pocket and bringing his knee up hard in his groin. Brody dropped to his knees, groaning, as Nando pulled the gun free.

Kit had flattened herself against the wall, staring wide-eyed as Brody pulled into the fetal position on the floor in front of them, icing and cake dripping from his face.

From further down the hall somebody muttered "Ouch." Kit turned to see Joe standing at the bend in the hallway. He shrugged. "They're on their way."

Nando jerked the handcuffs from his belt, pulling Brody's hands behind him none too gently. "You have the right to remain silent," he droned. "Anything you say can and will be used against you in a court of law. You have the right to speak to an attorney. If you cannot afford an attorney, one will be appointed to you. Do you understand these rights as they have been repeated to you, you asshole son of a bitch?"

Brody groaned again.

"I'll take that as a yes." Nando looked like he felt an almost overwhelming desire to kick him again, but restrained himself when he glanced at Allie.

"Are you all right?"

She nodded, pressing her fingers to her lips. "I was so scared," she whispered. "I've never been so scared before. I didn't know if I'd ever make it back to the event center."

"Allie!" Wonder ran across the hall, his thin hair on end, his glasses slightly askew on his nose. "Allie, sweetheart. Are you okay?"

Before she could answer he pulled her into his arms, hugging her tight. "Oh, sweetheart, sweetheart, I'm sorry. You can keep the house. You can have anything you want. All you have to do is ask."

Allie leaned her forehead against his chest, and burst into noisy tears.

Nando stared at Kit where she stood huddled against the wall. After a moment he stepped across Brody's prone form, dodging around the remains of the groom's cake that littered the floor, until he stood in front of her. His eyes were burning, his hands trembled. She suddenly realized he was furious. "What the hell did you think you were doing?" he growled.

"I wanted to stop him," she managed, voice shaking. "It was all I could think of."

"You could have been killed. He had a gun." He took a deep shuddering breath, then reached for her, pulling her tight against his chest. "Don't ever do that again," he murmured against her hair.

Kit closed her eyes, letting herself sink against him. "I can pretty much promise I won't."

"I almost hate to break this up, but somebody's got to take this asshole to town."

Kit glanced up. Chief Toleffson stood beside the wall a couple of feet away. He wore civilian clothes, khakis and a knit shirt, but he was holding a gun in his hand. He sighed as he walked toward them. "Got your message, Avrogado. And yours." He nodded toward Kit, then narrowed his eyes. "You do know what you just did was unbelievably dumb."

Kit managed a shaky shrug. "Seemed like a good idea at the time. Of course, Allie's probably going to have a new fit of hysterics when she actually realizes what happened to her groom's cake."

Toleffson stepped over a lump of cream-colored frosting to reach Brody, taking him by the elbow to pull him to his feet. "Former Chief Brody, I assume, somewhere under all that goop. I've wanted to meet you for a while. You tried to kill my sister-in-law, as I recall. And then you did the same thing to my dispatcher." He gave Brody a very unsettling smile.

Brody blinked at him. "Business," he muttered.

"Uh huh. I don't supposed you'd care to tell us just what you were after in my office?"

"Fuck you," Brody wheezed.

"Right." The chief turned back toward Kit for a moment. "Sorry about this. Looks like I'm going to miss the rehearsal. Morgan can fill me in later." He turned back to Brody again, giving him what looked like a slight shove, although it almost made Brody lose his footing. "Let's take it downtown. I'm sure Helen will be very glad to see you again."

Kit wasn't entirely sure, but she thought Brody paled slightly as he stumbled toward the parking lot entrance.

Across the hall, Allie raised her head from Wonder's chest. "Thank you. Both of you. He could have killed me."

"That's okay, Aunt Allie. We weren't going to let him take you away." Kit took another deep breath, surveying the fragments of pastry strewn around the floor of the hall. "I'm so sorry about your beautiful groom's cake."

Allie stirred in Wonder's arms, staring down at the smashed bits of cake on the floor in front of her for the first time. "Who cares about a damn cake," she murmured. "It's the groom who matters." She slid her arm around Wonder's waist, leaning her head against his chest as they headed back up the hall toward the event center. "Come on," she murmured. "Let's go get married."

Kit sighed. "And that's my cue to head back to the rehearsal. At least, there's going to be a rehearsal. And a wedding. This will probably all hit me somewhere around the toasts at dinner tonight. See you later, Officer?"

Nando tipped her chin up with his thumb, giving her a fierce kiss that left her lips almost numb. "Count on it, ma'am."

Chapter Twenty-Four

Allie still claimed she wasn't upset about the cake, even though her lip trembled when she said it. She insisted on staying for the rehearsal dinner after Nando took her brief statement. He had the feeling she was running on fumes but not yet willing to give up.

So was Kit as far as he could tell. He made her promise to call him rather than trying to drive back to town herself—he didn't want her behind the wheel once the adrenaline wore off.

He headed back to the station with the sack of stuff from the chief's desk, fairly certain that he'd be walking into chaos once he got there. He was right.

The parking lot was full of police cars from various jurisdictions. He saw the circular insignia of the Texas Rangers on one, the county sheriff's gold shield on another two. The Konigsburg cruiser was in the lot, along with a few civilian cars. Nando parked on the street.

Inside, there were at least six men in unfamiliar uniforms, along with the entire Konigsburg force, including the part-timers and Helen. She sat behind her dispatcher's desk, looking slightly pale but absolutely determined. Nando decided he wouldn't even bother suggesting she sit this one out.

He pulled up a chair beside Delaney's desk. "What's happening?"

Delaney glanced at him, then grinned. "Hey, the chief told us what you did out there. Nice work."

"Thanks. I had help," he said shortly. "What's going on now?"

"Deciding where to send Brody first, I guess. Rangers want him for official corruption; Friesenhahn wants him for attempted murder and assault. Friesenhahn's got a court order to take him. Rangers will probably get him for major crimes eventually, but I'm guessing he's headed for the county jail right now."

Nando grimaced. "Hell, we've got a solid claim on him for burglary and assault. Don't we even get to question him? The son of a bitch broke into our station."

"The chief did question him, but I guess he didn't say much of anything. Maybe we'll get another chance later."

There was a flurry of voices from the hall leading to the cells, and then Brody emerged, his ankles and wrists shackled. Sheriff Friesenhahn held one elbow while a Ranger held the other. Nando managed to hide his grin. Maybe they'd split Brody up the middle, Solomon style.

Brody's gaze flitted across the faces of the cops watching him, pausing momentarily at Nando, then at Helen. His mouth tightened.

Helen gave him a basilisk glare that should have turned him to stone.

Friesenhahn gave him a slight shove forward. "Move, jerk-off. You got no friends here."

Nando stared at Brody's hunched back as he shuffled out the door. What Friesenhahn had said was manifestly true. He figured every cop in the place would like to nail Brody's hide to the wall, not only for his most recent crimes but also for the way his activities had made the civilian population doubt the rest of them.

After the entire procession had cleared the parking lot, Nando pushed himself to his feet again, grabbing the sack as he headed toward the chief's office. "This was what he told me to bring out to the Woodrose when he had Kit—the contents of the desk. But I don't know what part of it he wanted."

"Leave it on the table." Toleffson was pulling on his uniform shirt. "I'm going over to the County to sit in when they question the SOB. We'll see what he has to say about breaking in here."

Nando was guessing he wouldn't say much. "Do you want me to check through this stuff again?"

The chief shook his head. "Leave it for now. Go on back to the Woodrose and pick up your girlfriend. At least one of us ought to get a chance for a decent meal tonight." He gave Nando a dry grin, then headed back up the hall toward the parking lot.

Allie kept insisting she was so happy that Kit had saved her and Wonder was marrying her that nothing else mattered. But Kit still felt guilty about the globs of frosting and crumbs on the floor from the shattered groom's cake. She hurried back and forth between the Damask Room and the event center, grateful that the maintenance staff had been able to clean up the last remnants of cake from the rug before the guests arrived. She wasn't sure Allie would have been so forgiving if she'd had to walk on the crumbs to get to the rehearsal dinner.

Her reaction finally began to set in as the rehearsal crowd finished their meal and broke into smaller groups around the room. They showed no signs of wanting to go home.

She sank into a chair behind the hostess desk at the Rose, suddenly so tired she was afraid her knees wouldn't hold her up any longer. Technically the rehearsal dinner was Mabel's responsibility since it was a private event. She shouldn't have had to make sure they left on time or that the housekeeping staff took care of the room before tomorrow. But Mabel didn't seem to be around. Apparently, she'd left Kit in charge without telling her and gone home for the night.

Eventually, Kit knew she'd have to ask around for someone to take her home, too, but she wasn't entirely sure her feet would carry her that far. She definitely couldn't drive herself, and she had a feeling Nando would still be busy with the aftermath of Brody's arrest. Maybe she'd just find an empty room at the inn, if there was one. If there wasn't, maybe she'd just sleep on one of the banquettes in the dining room. She didn't think she could stay awake for the trip home, even if it was only ten minutes or so.

"Hey, darlin', you okay?" Joe squinted down at her with narrowed eyes. He looked like he was doing a quick assessment of her sobriety.

"I'm okay," she murmured. "Just tired. Really, really tired."

He raised an eyebrow. "Want me to drive you home?"

A couple of weeks ago, she'd probably have said yes. Now... "That's okay. I'll ride with Allie." Kit frowned. There was something she was supposed to tell Joe. After a moment, her sluggish brain kicked into gear again. "I talked to Mabel about hiring Bryson. She okayed it."

He frowned slightly. "Without a fight?"

"She said..." Kit searched her memory, trying to unearth the right facts. "She said she was going to 'review' the Rose. The expenses. Next month. She said we were spending more money than we were taking in."

"What the fuck? Spending more than we're making? Since when?" Joe brought the flat of his hand down on the hostess stand with a solid thwack.

Suddenly Kit was wide away again. "You promised," she said weakly. "You're not going to go after her until after the wedding tomorrow night."

Joe's hands were clenched on the edge of the hostess stand, his eyes like lasers. After a moment, he nodded. "I promise I won't do anything to upset Allie's wedding," he said slowly. He pushed himself away from the stand and stalked back toward his kitchen.

It was another moment before her sluggish brain understood that he hadn't exactly promised to do nothing at all.

"Oh great," she muttered. "Just great."

"Kit?"

She peeped around the side of the hostess stand. Nando stood in the doorway, peering around the room. He still wore his rumpled Konigsburg police uniform.

"Nando?"

He walked toward the hostess stand, his mouth stretching into a grin. The band of tension across her shoulders began to relax again, marginally.

"Hi." He stepped beside her, then ran the back of his hand along her cheek. "How are you holding up?"

"I'm not, really. I don't think I've ever felt so tired in my life."

He nodded, his smile softening. "It's reaction. You had a shock. You should have driven home and gone to bed after they took him away."

She shook her head. "I couldn't. I had too much to do out here. After tomorrow, I can relax."

"Why didn't you call?"

She shrugged. "I figured you'd be busy with Brody. I was just trying to get up the energy to go find Allie."

"I told you to call me. I can take you home." He moved his hand to the nape of her neck, his fingers kneading lightly. "I'm off duty now."

"Did they...is he gone?" Her stomach gave a quick lurch.

Nando nodded. "They took him to the county jail. My guess is they'll take him to Austin tomorrow."

"Will Allie have to testify?"

He grimaced. "Possibly. But it won't be soon. This particular episode is likely to be pretty far down the list of Brody's crimes."

She leaned forward, pressing her forehead against him. "I'll think about it tomorrow, okay?"

"Okay by me."

A gust of laughter sounded from the hall where the rehearsal dinner was still in progress. Allie and Wonder ambled toward them. "Kit," Allie called. "Come on, you're missing the dinner."

Kit gave her a ghost of a smile. "I'm just resting right now, Aunt Allie. You go ahead."

Allie leaned against Wonder. She looked almost as tired as Kit felt. "Sweetheart, are you all right?"

"I'm okay. Honestly." Kit closed her eyes for a moment. "What about you?"

Allie pressed a hand against Wonder's chest. "I'm going back to town with Steve. Would you like us to drop you off at my place?"

"No," she said resolutely. "Don't worry about me. I'll take care of myself."

"I'll take her home," Nando said.

"Oh." Allie turned to look at him. "That's nice of you, Nando. I'll be there later."

Wonder cleared his throat.

Allie narrowed her eyes at him. "I'm not coming home with you tonight, Steve. I told you that already. You can't see me before the wedding. I'm going to sleep at my house and then head back here tomorrow afternoon. Eloise is going to run Sweet Thing."

Wonder's face looked like a mask of tragedy all of a sudden.

"Oh for pity's sake," Allie muttered. "It's just one night."

"I don't want to be away from you. Even if it is just one night," Wonder said mournfully. "I don't want to be away from you any more than I have to. Not after today. Not ever."

Allie stood up slowly, her eyes suspiciously bright. "Steve Kleinschmidt. That is one of the most beautiful things you've ever said to me." She slid her arms around Wonder's waist, pressing her face

259

against his chest.

Wonder leaned his head against hers. "It's the truth."

Allie looked back at Kit, smiling tearfully. "Okay, I'll see you later I guess." She turned back to Wonder. "I'm still not going home with you."

"We can negotiate," he said.

The two of them walked side by side toward the Damask Room. Or tried to walk, anyway—the fact that they were holding onto each other so tightly apparently made it a little difficult.

Kit felt her own eyes stinging slightly. Wonder the Romantic. Who knew?

Nando sighed. "C'mon, sweetheart. You need to get some rest before things get any crazier."

She fell asleep almost as soon as she sank into the front seat of his truck. She was dimly aware that her cheek was resting on his shoulder, but not much more than that.

"Kit, wake up," he murmured after the truck pulled to a stop. "We're here."

She leaned forward, discovering that the truck door beside her was open and he was standing outside waiting for her. Another moment, and she was scooped up in his arms. "I feel a lot better after that nap. I can walk."

"I know you can. Indulge me. Close your eyes."

She was dimly aware of a door opening and lights. And then a faintly surprised masculine voice. "Kit?"

Her eyes popped open. Esteban Avrogado stood in the doorway to the kitchen, wearing a UT T-shirt, battered running shorts, and flip-flops. He looked almost as shocked to see her as she was to see him. She grabbed Nando's arms, staring around the room. "This isn't Allie's place."

"Nope." He grinned down at her. "I said I was taking you home. I didn't specify whose home I was taking you to."

"Is she okay?" Esteban's voice sounded dubious.

"I think so." Nando was still grinning. "Are you okay? My brother wants to know."

"I'm...okay." Kit blew out a breath. "I can walk. Really."

"Take it easy. You had a shock." He glanced at Esteban. "Brody tried to take Allie hostage. Kit fought him off. With a cake."

Esteban blinked. "I'm sure that will make sense eventually, right?"

"I wouldn't count on it." Nando grinned again, shifting her in his arms as he turned down the hall toward his bedroom, then glancing back briefly. "Can you convince Guinevere to stay with you tonight?"

Kit thought she heard some feline grumbling from the direction of the kitchen table.

"I don't know." Esteban sounded like he was grinning too. "You're breaking her heart here."

"She'll get over it." He hit the door with his shoulder, moving into the bedroom.

She felt her face flush hot. "God, this isn't fair to Esteban. It's his house too."

"Right, well, we both live here. And he's a big boy." Nando flipped the latch on the door.

"Nando, I really…I mean I should probably be home tonight." She fought down a quick pinch of guilt. Allie might need her to keep things moving tomorrow morning.

He let her slide to her feet slowly, so that she felt the hard reassurance of his body against hers. "I want you to stay here. I need you to. I could have lost you this afternoon, Catarina. And I've got some things to say."

Kit was suddenly wide awake. "What things?"

He sighed. "We've wasted way too much time pretending that we know what each of us is thinking, when neither of us really has a clue."

She narrowed her eyes. "Huh?"

"You know what I mean, even if I didn't say it right. You walked out eighteen months ago because you thought you knew what I was thinking. I also thought I knew what I was thinking. It turns out we were dead wrong on both counts. From now on, I'm going to be as clear as I know how to be."

"Okay." She sank down on the bed, leaning back on her elbows. "Go ahead."

He licked his lips, folding his arms as he looked down at her. "I love you, Catarina. I've loved you since I first knew you. I walked out

261

on you because I was pissed off, and it almost took me down. You hurt me, and I wanted to hurt you back. So I did it in the stupidest way possible—with Lizzie Farraday. I didn't care about her, and she didn't care about me. But god knows I cared about you, and I knew it was wrong as soon as I did it. I ended up damn near killing both of us. I'm sorry, *chica*. I know that's not enough, but I'll say it anyway. I was a fucking idiot, and I'm sorry."

Kit swallowed hard, staring up at him. What was she supposed to say now? What could she say?

But he wasn't finished.

"I told you I loved you eighteen months ago, although you might not have heard it at the time. That hasn't changed." He ran his fingertip lightly down her nose. "I loved you when we had that last knockdown, drag-out fight. I loved you when I acted like a damn fool. I loved you when you left. I loved you all the time you were gone. And god knows, I love you now that you're back. If you walk out now, I'll go on loving you. I won't want to, and it'll hurt like hell, but that's the way it is for me."

He cupped his palm around her cheek, slowly leaning down beside her to leave a line of whispering kisses along her throat. "I didn't stop loving you even when I thought you hated me. And believe me, I didn't want to then. But I couldn't help it."

For a moment her throat felt too tight to say anything. "It was mutual," she mumbled finally, snuggling under his arm.

"We were afraid. That's what I think anyway."

She turned to look at him again. "When?"

"Eighteen months ago. When we had the fight to end all fights that didn't seem to be about anything in particular except fighting. When you told me to go to hell. And I went. When I did the stupidest thing I've ever done in my life, and regretted it the minute it happened."

"Oh." She sighed. "That."

"Yeah, that. I was scared shitless myself. I'd guess you felt sort of similar."

She closed her eyes. "Maybe."

"Maybe?"

She felt him moving so that he could look down at her again.

"Okay, probably. Maybe even certainly. It was a very scary time."

"I don't know why exactly." He tipped her chin up, gently. "What were you—we—afraid of?"

"This." She nodded toward him. "What's happening now. It means changing all our plans. Back then neither of us was ready to do that yet."

"And now?" One eyebrow arched up.

She sighed again. "I knew you were going to ask that. And I don't have any answer. I also don't have any plans beyond getting Allie down the aisle tomorrow. Can we just live in this moment, please? It feels so good."

He touched his lips to her forehead. "It is good. Living in the moment works for me right now."

She closed her eyes, leaning against him.

"You're dead on your feet, *chica*. You need to sleep."

She nodded, sighing. His body felt so good against hers. "But I don't have anything to wear tomorrow."

"We'll worry about that tomorrow."

"But..." She knew there was something else she should be worrying about. She just couldn't remember exactly what it was.

"Hush, Catarina," he whispered. "Let it go. You scared me half to death this afternoon. Let me hold you tonight. Let me know that you're safe."

Suddenly she couldn't remember why she'd thought that wasn't a good idea. The best idea she'd ever heard. "Yes," she mumbled. "Let's do that."

Chapter Twenty-Five

Kit awoke with sun in her eyes and Nando nibbling on her ear. "Hmmm." She burrowed deeper into the bed beside him. "Fifteen more minutes please. Just let me sleep fifteen more."

He sighed, moving his palm along the side of her hip. "I'd love to let you, babe, but you told me to get you up at seven."

She squinted in the sunlight, then opened her eyes all the way. "Oh, hell. The wedding."

"Yes, ma'am." He kissed the sensitive area behind her ear, his breath warm on her throat.

"Oh, don't," she whispered. "I've really got to get up."

"You will. I promise." She heard the smile in his voice. "Both of us will. Eventually."

She curved her spine against him, soaking up the warmth of his body against hers. "Okay," she murmured, "fifteen more minutes. No more."

Nando chuckled against her ear. "Ah, woman, I do love a challenge."

An hour later she was on her way to Allie's house to make sure everything about the wedding was on schedule, feeling warm, sated and almost ready to face the total chaos that she feared the day was going to slide into. Nando had promised to try to make it to the reception, assuming he could get someone to cover for him at work.

She found Allie sitting at her kitchen table, her eyes slightly glassy, staring with dismay at the plate of scrambled eggs on the table in front of her.

Kit took a deep breath. "You okay, Auntie?"

"I'm fine. Perfectly, absolutely fine. Really." She took a swallow of coffee. "Of course, I'm feeling a little nauseous but that's understandable, right?"

Kit poured herself a glass of orange juice and dropped into the chair across from her. "Do you need a pep talk? It's going to be wonderful, Allie, I promise. Everything is going to fall into place today." She restrained herself from rapping her knuckles on the wooden kitchen table.

Allie glanced up at her, smiling slightly. "It's all right. I'm not going to run. Yesterday I confirmed that I love Steve right down to his socks. And once we're married, I can always buy him new ones."

Kit snickered. "Do you want any help getting ready?"

"No. Docia and Janie are supposed to come over to do my hair and makeup. Although what they think they're going to do with this escapes me." She gestured toward her short black bob.

"It'll be beautiful, regardless." Kit pushed up from the table. "Okay, enough conversation. I need to get my wedding clothes together and get out to the Woodrose to make sure everything does, in fact, fall into place out there. I'm working lunch, but I'm off afterward."

"Kit…" Allie stretched across the table and took her hand. "I haven't thanked you enough for all this. I know I wasn't much help. And I know you basically saved my wedding and my butt."

Kit felt the quick sting of tears. She had a hunch that would be happening a lot today. "No problem, Aunt Allie. You've saved my butt more times than I can count. Including this time around when I showed up on your doorstep with no job and no idea of what I was going to do up here."

Allie pushed herself to her feet, wrapping her arms around Kit's shoulders for a quick hug. "I was glad to do it, sweetheart. But I've got one more favor to ask."

"What's that?" Kit frowned, her shoulders tightening.

"It's about the house. I'll be moving in with Steve when we get back from the honeymoon. But I'm not ready to sell this place yet. It means too much to me." Allie's eyes took on a misty look. "And Steve says it's okay if I keep it. Would you maybe consider staying on here until I decide what to do? I promise I won't charge you much rent, just enough to cover my mortgage payment and utilities."

Kit felt the first of what would probably be a lot of nervous churning in her stomach. "I'd love to, Aunt Allie. We can set it up after the honeymoon."

Allie sighed. "Okay. We'll talk about it when Steve and I get back from Cancun."

The front door opened behind them and Janie's voice echoed down the hall. "Where's the bride? We're here to work our magic. And we've got champagne."

Allie rolled her eyes. "Oh groovy. A drunk wedding."

Joe did a quick survey of his kitchen. Since the restaurant was closed after the lunch service, they could concentrate on Allie's reception, which, given the high profile the wedding had in the foodie community, was probably a very good thing. Not that he had any real worries. He'd planned the menu to show off the local produce, and to show what he could do for a crowd.

The appetizers were sitting in the cooler, although some would have to be heated before they were served. The cases of wine and champagne were stacked in the cellar, waiting to be transferred to the bar in the event center. The tenderloins were sitting in their bath of salt and spice rub. The redfish was waiting to be dressed. Jorge, the faster of the two line cooks, was dealing with the baskets of asparagus. Leo, the slower, was working on the potatoes. And Allie's wedding cake sat in solitary splendor at the side of the kitchen. He'd get Jorge and Leo to carry it to the restaurant when Gabriel had cleared out after the lunch rush.

He sighed. Allie Maldonado was the greatest baker he'd ever worked with. Watching Kit smash her groom's cake had been a major trauma. If anyone other than Allie herself had been at risk, he might have tried to come up with an alternative, like shooting the asshole. Allie had been pretty nice about it, given that he'd basically allowed the culinary equivalent of a Picasso to be destroyed.

He checked his watch, then headed down the hall. He still had a good half hour before Kit was due for the lunch crowd, and he needed to do this when she wasn't around to dither. No time like the present.

Mabel glanced up as he walked in her office door. It was probably tough to transform her initial scowl into her usual artificially sunny smile, but she managed it. "Joseph, how nice to see you so early in the morning. I wouldn't be here myself if it wasn't for the Maldonado wedding. And how are the preparations going for the reception?"

Joe leaned forward, placing his fists upon the edge of her desk. "What's this bullshit about closing the restaurant, Mabel?"

Mabel's smile contracted to a grimace. "Oh dear, I'd hoped you wouldn't hear any gossip about that. Nothing has been decided yet. It's still very possible that the restaurant will only need to close for one more day a week rather than closing altogether." She gave him a rueful smile. "I know I should have brought this up with you before, but we've all been so busy, haven't we? And so much drama!"

"Cut the crap, Mabel." Joe straightened. "What are you trying to pull?"

Her eyes hardened, but her smile stayed firmly in place. The woman was obviously a pro. "Well, to be blunt the restaurant is too expensive for the inn. It's pulling down the rest of our profits. I'm going to propose three alternatives to Mauritz—cutting back on the days we're open, closing the restaurant altogether or firing you." She gave him a flint-eyed smile. "Your salary accounts for a major part of the restaurant's expenses right now."

"All of that would make sense if the restaurant wasn't paying for itself." He gave her a humorless smile of his own. "In fact, of course, it's more than paying for itself. And has been for the past two months."

Mabel's smile didn't waver. "I'm sure you wish that was the case. Unfortunately, it isn't."

"Oh but it is." Joe broadened his smile slightly to show more teeth. "You see, when we had our first conversation, way back before Kit Maldonado was hired, when you said you couldn't afford to hire more wait staff or a professional hostess, and the wait staff you brought in was clearly incompetent, I started keeping track of the daily receipts in the restaurant. And I made copies for myself going back a few months."

He wasn't entirely sure, but Mabel might have paled slightly. She managed a quick shake of the head, along with another patronizing smile. "Unfortunately, receipts don't tell the whole story, Joseph. As I said, your salary is a major expense. So is the overhead in the restaurant—wait staff, maintenance, laundry, the cost of food, even the cost for printing menus. All of it adds up, and it undercuts the restaurant's success."

"Yeah, I figured the restaurant's expenses would probably be your excuse. So I kept track of the Rose's expenses too. I contacted the vendors directly, and I made copies of everything. You forget, Mabel, I've been in this business for a lot of years. Sometimes in places where I was in charge of the front of the house as well as the back."

267

Mabel swallowed, her smile curdling. Her hand contracted to a fist on the desktop. "Nonetheless, I keep the books. I'm only too aware of how expensive the Rose has become. And I'll be sending the records to Resorts Consolidated at the end of the month. They'll make the final decision, of course."

Joe shrugged. "I really wouldn't do that if I were you, but of course it's your call. I've already taken the liberty of sending a couple of spreadsheets to Mauritz. I wanted to get his input on the hiring situation for the restaurant. I also recommended we start dinner service and a Sunday brunch. We'll switch the closed day to Monday since Sunday is a big day for dining out. As I understand it, he's all in favor."

"You don't have the complete figures," she snapped. "All the expenses. You can't. I'm the only one who has them."

"Yeah, that's true. That's why I broke into your office a few times over the past couple of weeks. You really need a better lock on that door, and you sure as hell need better security on your computer."

Mabel's eyes widened. He could hear the rasp of her breathing.

"I wanted to find the figures you were looking at. The real figures, that is." His smile disappeared. "Not the ones where you charged off the event center's expenses to the restaurant." He shook his head. "Sloppy, Mabel. Very sloppy. Running the event center at a loss is a really bad idea, by the way. My guess is Mauritz will think so too. And if he and his accountants should happen to find a certain amount of rake-off going on with your suppliers, they'd be very, very unhappy."

"I didn't..." Mabel took a quick breath, folding her hands in front of her. "It hasn't been running at a loss. And I haven't been raking off anything. I may have accepted a few gifts from our suppliers, but that's standard in this business. And it's standard accounting practice to spread the expenses around the entire facility."

"Right. That's a standard accounting practice called juggling the books where you secretly switch expenses from one part of the inn to another. Makes it look like the event center's a champ rather than a loss leader. Particularly interesting since that center used to be very profitable from what I understand. Mauritz is likely to hold you responsible for taking it down, Mabel. He won't be pleased."

She licked her lips, staring up at him, her brown eyes suddenly sharp. "What are you going to do?"

"You mean who am I going to tell? Nobody. As long as you don't send in those juggled figures to the head office." He rested his fists on the desk again. "That means hands off the restaurant, Mabel. Sooner or later the auditors are going to catch up with you, you know. I'd recommend sending in the real figures and taking your lumps, but that's up to you. They probably won't fire you for letting the event center go to hell. Just reassign you someplace else." Like their resort in Alberta. According to Joe's sources, it was snowed in for a large part of the year. Mabel should have plenty of time to work on her promotional skills.

"I'll take that under advisement." She sounded like she was gritting her teeth.

"You do that. Incidentally, Kit will be hiring more staff over the next two weeks. And she should be taking over the management for the restaurant, including all the ordering, given that she's better at it than you are. You're lucky to have her. We need a couple more waiters and busboys, plus I could use a pastry chef, particularly if we start doing a brunch. Although we might be able to work something out with Allie Maldonado. Assuming she's happy with her reception this afternoon." He gave Mabel a lazy smile. "Speaking of that, I'd better get back to my kitchen."

He started for the door, then paused. "Do we have an understanding, Mabel?"

She stared down at her desk for a long moment, then looked up at him with a ghost of her former smile. "Of course. I'm so glad we had this talk, Joseph."

"Oh me too." Joe grinned at her. "Definitely."

Nando came back to the station after lunch. With any luck he'd get a large chunk of the Brody paperwork out of the way this afternoon so he could spend the evening with Kit. He felt a brief clenching in his chest as he thought of her and wondered how long it would be until that feeling went away. Probably until he could forget the look in her eyes as she'd confronted Brody with the cake. In other words, a very long time.

Helen glanced up as he came in, then turned back to her screen. "Chief wants to see you."

"Is he in his office?"

"Last time I looked."

Oh well, he could do paperwork some other time. He headed up the hall.

Toleffson was sitting next to the folding table, his chin in his hand, staring at the contents of the trash sack that was spread out in front of him again. "Come on in." He gestured toward the chair on the other side of the table. "Help me make some sense of this."

Nando sank into his seat, frowning down at the pile of objects. "Making sense sounds kind of optimistic. I'm assuming Brody didn't tell anybody anything."

Toleffson shook his head. "He's being a hardass. Maybe he still thinks he'll manage to get back here and grab it. Do we know for sure whatever he was searching for was in this stuff? Did he look at it?"

Nando shrugged. "He didn't look through it, but he had Allie open the bag and tell him what was inside, and he looked satisfied when she did." His jaw tightened as he remembered. *Smug son of a bitch.*

Toleffson sighed. "I've been picking through this junk for a couple of hours now, and I still don't see what he was after."

Nando sorted idly through the rubber bands and postage stamps. "Most of these are out of date. You got some twenty-nine centers here."

"Anything look rare and valuable? Worth coming back for?"

Nando shook his head. "I remember most of these stamps, and I ain't that old." He picked up the legal pads, stacking them at the side of the table. "Let me clear away some of the stuff that can't be what he was after so we can look at the rest of it. I mean, no way I can see legal pads being worth all that much, even if they were antique which these aren't."

Toleffson watched him for a moment then shook each pad carefully, fluttering the pages. "And nothing's hidden in here."

Nando made a new pile of stationery and envelopes, checking each to make sure they were empty. "This stationery was printed up after Brody took off, so it can't be anything."

The chief squinted at the rubber bands and paper clips. "Those can probably go. Unless he melted down something valuable and made it into a paperclip."

Nando stared down at the paperclips for a moment, then stepped over to the file cabinet, removing a calendar in a magnetized plastic frame. He held the back of the calendar over the paper clips, then watched them all attach themselves to the magnet. "Looks like run-of-the-mill paperclips to me."

"Right."

Toleffson sorted through the ancient computer disks. "Most of these are fiscal year data, assuming the labels are right. I don't know where we'd find a computer drive that would run these disks anyway."

"What about the thumb drive?"

The chief shook his head. "It's mine. I checked it, but nothing on it is earlier than last year."

Nando nudged a stray penny with his finger. "These coins yours too, Chief?"

Toleffson shrugged. "Most of them. If I've got extra change in my pocket after lunch, sometimes I toss it in there."

"I do that too. Get rid of the small stuff." He studied the spill of coins on the table. Pennies, nickels, dimes, a couple of quarters. He leaned closer, sorting swiftly through them.

"See anything?" Toleffson leaned down next to him.

"I'm not sure." He stared at the coins spread out in front of him, copper, silver, some dull, some bright.

"That's a strange-looking quarter," the chief murmured.

They both leaned closer. The coin was dull silver. It seemed smaller than the other quarters, more worn.

Toleffson placed his index finger on it, pulling it apart from the others so that he could study it. "Seated Liberty instead of George Washington," he said, staring down at the coin. "That makes it nineteenth century, I think."

Nando squinted at the somewhat worn image. "Worth anything?"

"Bound to be, but I don't know how much." Toleffson picked up the coin, peering at the date. "1878."

"So do you think this is it? Is this what he wanted?"

"Could be." The chief studied it again. "It's the first thing we've found that makes any sense. When he asked Allie to tell him what was in the bag, did she mention the coins?"

Nando closed his eyes, trying to remember. "Yeah. I'm pretty sure she did—along with everything else."

Toleffson nodded slowly. "So there's a chance that this is it. Maybe a very good chance." He picked up one of the envelopes and dropped the coin inside.

"It fits with Brody, sort of. He had a thing for valuable historic stuff, judging from the map he tried to steal from Dub Tyler."

"Which means he might have stolen this too." Toleffson blew out a breath. "If he did, there might be a police report somewhere."

"He stole a valuable coin and then tossed it in his desk?" Nando shook his head. "Why would he do that?"

"Best place to hide it, in a way." Toleffson leaned back in his chair. "Safe deposit boxes can be opened with a court order, plus they're not great if you need to get at something quick. Houses and vehicles can be searched. But who looks through the junk in a desk drawer?"

"He outsmarted himself again. He couldn't get the map from Docia and he couldn't get the coin this time."

"So maybe when his luck ran out after he ran away, he decided to come back here and pick this up. Commit some petty burglaries to make us think this was just one more in a string. Then take his coin and head for the hills again."

"And it might have worked except for Helen."

Toleffson shrugged. "I'd like to say we'd have caught him anyway, but who knows? Right now I've got to get home and change for Allie's wedding, but I might make a couple of calls before I go. You going to be at the wedding too?" He raised an eyebrow at Nando.

He gave him a dry grin. "Wouldn't miss it. The reception anyway."

Kit stood in the back of the room at the event center, studying the decorations. She still didn't think much of them, but the place smelled great and the swags of lavender and silver chiffon looked elegant along the sides. The chairs were already filled for the most part. The people on the groom's side were almost all from Konigsburg, with a couple of women who must have been relatives, given their unfortunate resemblance to Wonder. The bride's side had a full complement of Maldonados, all of them grinning and waving at Kit whenever they caught her eye. There were also three or four faces she recognized from the Food Network and Bravo, along with a lot of other people who looked like they spent time in kitchens. Kit blew out a quick breath, hoping that Joe had the food under control. He'd have a lot of people eating his stuff who knew the difference between morels and baby bellas.

"Catarina?"

Kit jumped, swiveling to stare behind her. Her father was standing in the doorway. "Your mother's looking for you."

"Oh." She rubbed a hand across the back of her neck. "I'll see if I can find her in a few minutes. I need to make sure the bridesmaids and groomsmen get set up."

He nodded slowly. "Alicia said you were the one who'd designed the wedding for her. Probably wouldn't have happened if you hadn't stepped in when you think how long she's been stalling."

"Oh well, I was glad to help." Kit licked her lips, surprised at how nervous she felt all of a sudden. "So how's South Padre?"

Her father shrugged. "Seems fine. Your mother's happy. She's got the grandkids to spoil. You should come visit."

She smiled. "I'll try to when I get a spare weekend."

"So you're working here now?" He gestured back up the hill toward the inn.

She nodded. "I'm managing the restaurant. It's been...interesting."

"Kind of different from San Antonio, I guess."

Kit took a breath. "Yeah, very. The restaurant was floundering when I got here, although they have a wonderful chef. It's doing better now, but we're still not out of the woods."

His forehead furrowed slightly. "What was the problem?"

"Inexperienced staff and not enough of it. Problems with figuring out who was in charge of what. And they hadn't computerized the reservations yet."

"And you had to take care of all that?" He frowned. "Sounds like a lot of work."

"It was. I'm still working on the staff issues. But we're doing better than we did before." She gave him a tentative smile. "Between my coursework at UTSA and a lifetime of watching how a really good restaurant functions, I figured out what they needed pretty quickly.

Thanks for teaching me the right way to run a restaurant, Papi. It's been a lifesaver."

Her father stared at her for a long moment, then he swallowed hard. "You always were a good student, Catarina. So are you happy here?"

She sighed. "Overall, yes I am. I'm learning a lot, Papi."

He gave her a slightly crafty smile. "Lots of restaurants in South Padre, you know. Places you could work if you wanted to try somewhere else. In fact—" her father leaned forward, "—there's this little taqueria down near the beach. Just a counter and a few tables. Great location. I've been talking to the manager. I could see maybe a Mexican seafood grill. Fish tacos. Snapper Vera Cruz. Camarones Diablo. That kind of stuff."

Kit blinked. "You're opening another restaurant?"

He shrugged. "Maybe. Thinking about it. I mean, a man can only play so much golf, Catarina."

"Oh, Papi." She shook her head. "You're hopeless. Have you mentioned this to Mami?"

"Not yet. Have to work out the details. I could use a good manager." His smile widened. "Interested?"

She shook her head again. "I'm committed here. They need me. And you need to break the news to Mami before you go any further."

Her father rubbed his chin. "Good idea. I'll wait until she's all teary over Alicia, give her a couple of glasses of champagne. Keep it in mind, *chica*. I meant what I said."

Kit felt the familiar prickling of tears. *"Gracias, Papi."*

"De nada, querida."

"Antonio," Allie's voice sounded from down the hall, slightly tinged with panic. "Where are you?"

Her father gave her a dry smile. "Time to go get the bride ready for her long walk. I'll talk to you later, *chica*."

"Right." Kit turned toward the sound of feet as the bridesmaids and groomsmen trooped her way.

The three Toleffson wives who were bridesmaids seemed to shimmer in the late afternoon light, their dresses glistening around them like jewels. Their husbands stood beside them, looking like tuxedo-clad lumberjacks. They also looked as if they'd all prefer to be doing other things with their brides that evening rather than standing around the event center in formal clothes.

Pete Toleffson squinted toward the room, running a finger around the collar of his tuxedo shirt. "We got a full house?"

"Looks like it." Kit fluffed Janie's skirt where it had gotten slightly crushed, then helped Jess smooth the ribbons on her bouquet.

"Wonder looks like he's going to pass out," Lars Toleffson muttered.

"He wouldn't dare." Janie peered toward the front of the room. "He's not going to give Allie any excuse to postpone the wedding again."

Kit glanced toward where the groom stood with the judge who was going to conduct the ceremony. Wonder looked more pale than she'd ever seen him look before, and considering that he was already one of the palest men she knew, that was saying something. Cal Toleffson, his best man, was standing close enough to catch him if worse came to worst. Of course, Kit reflected, if Wonder really did faint, the worst for him would be the merciless ribbing he'd take about it after the ceremony was over, assuming he could be revived for long enough to repeat his vows.

She heard a step behind her and saw Allie and Docia walk into the hall, along with her father. Allie held tightly onto her brother's arm as she chewed on her lower lip. Kit's father gave his baby sister a slightly patronizing smile. He had, after all, been married for over thirty years now.

Kit took a quick breath. "Ready?"

Allie nodded. She looked gorgeous in her soft flowing jersey, a circlet of white roses in her short dark hair. She also looked almost as nervous as Wonder. Papi smiled down at her, then glanced at Kit, his gaze suddenly bright again.

No, no, no. No tears, damn it. I don't have time. Kit turned back toward the room and raised her hand to the string quartet at the front. The Toleffsons, male and female, began to proceed down the aisle to the strains of Vivaldi. Docia winked at her, fluffing out her matron of honor bouquet. "Courage, kid," she whispered. "It's almost over."

It's almost over. Unexpectedly, Kit's eyes pricked with tears again. The wedding had taken up a lot of her waking energy for the last few weeks. She had no idea what would take its place.

Maybe Nando. She pushed that thought ruthlessly from her mind.

Meg Benjamin

Maybe later. Or maybe not. *One problem at a time, Catarina.*

Docia paced decorously down the aisle by herself, grinning widely. Aunt Allie and Papi stepped forward as Docia reached the front of the room. Papi glanced Kit's way again just for a moment, his eyes warm, and then they began their own procession. The audience stood as they walked down the aisle, and Kit smiled. Allie really did look lovely. And the wedding really was going to take place.

And that was all she was going to think about. For now.

Chapter Twenty-Six

Nando had juggled a lot of schedules to do it, but he got to the Woodrose around seven. Theoretically, he was still on duty until six, but he'd talked Delaney into starting his shift early so he could change and get to the inn. He hadn't been able to make it for the ceremony, but he could at least make it to the reception.

He wanted to dance with Kit. He also wanted to tell her he loved her and wanted her to stay with him. The *I love you* part was easy. He figured the *Stay with me* part would be the killer.

He fingered his tie nervously. He hated wearing suits because he suspected they made him look like a twelve-year-old heading for communion. Still, if wearing a suit and tie was what it took to get Kit to take him seriously, he'd wear suits and ties for the rest of his life.

For the first few moments after he stepped into the Rose, he didn't see her. He hadn't realized they were using the restaurant for the reception until he got there, maybe an indication of the importance Joe LeBlanc and the kitchen staff put on the whole event. The room was full of people—some he knew but many he didn't. They lounged in the banquettes and at the linen-covered tables. The buffet included some of the most tantalizing food he'd ever seen, plus a spectacular wedding cake. Even he had to admit it—LeBlanc was good, and so was Allie.

He glanced around the room, trying to find Kit. Konigsburgers were everywhere, along with a lot of people who had to be related to Allie and Kit. He even recognized a couple of faces from television cooking shows. The Toleffson brothers, including the chief, loomed over most of the other guests, like mile markers, while their wives flitted around the room like jewel-toned butterflies. He took a deep breath. He'd never met Kit's parents; now was probably the right time.

The chief caught his eye, motioning with his head toward the side of the room.

Nando approached him cautiously. He hoped this wouldn't be a conversation about why he was at the Rose instead of driving the cruiser around the streets of Konigsburg. And he hoped the chief hadn't found anything new for him to do right now.

Toleffson turned away from the rest of the guests, pitching his voice so that only Nando could hear. "I made a couple of phone calls and got lucky. One of the Rangers is a coin collector."

"What did he say?"

"He thinks it may be an 1878-S Seated Liberty. Less than a hundred in circulation."

Nando narrowed his eyes. "Worth how much?"

"One went for $185,000 at auction a few years ago."

He blew out a quick breath. "How the hell did Brody get hold of one?"

The chief shrugged. "Brody's not talking, but according to the Ranger, one was reported stolen in Dallas a few years ago. Owner collected on his insurance too."

"You think he and Brody had a scam going?"

"Either that or Brody stole it. Or lifted it from the original thief." Toleffson grimaced. "Anything's possible with Brody. Let's just say he probably didn't come by it honestly."

"Must have pissed him off to leave it when he took off the last time."

"Must have. But he did leave it. Until he ran out of money after the Rangers closed out his accounts."

"And then he got dumb." He pictured Brody again, aiming his pistol at Allie, ready to run back to whatever rock he'd been hiding under.

"That he did." Toleffson's lips spread in a slow grin. "Nice job you did with this, Nando. I'd say nobody's going to have any questions about you being assistant chief now."

"Thanks." Nando took another surreptitious glance around the room.

"Enjoy the reception." Toleffson gave him a quick nod before he walked back to where his wife was standing with her sisters-in-law. The smile she gave him could have lit the room without benefit of chandeliers. The chief was clearly going to enjoy the reception himself, no matter what happened to Nando.

He turned back, looking for Kit again. Allie sat at the front table, resplendent in her white dress. Beside her, Wonder looked a little woozy, but someone had found him a Spaten. At least he wasn't drinking champagne. With any luck, one of the Toleffsons would drive him and Allie to wherever they were going tonight.

Nando did a quick survey of the rest of the crowd and stopped.

Kit was talking to Joe LeBlanc next to the buffet table. She wore a dress the color of an evening sky, her midnight hair hanging down to brush her shoulders, her earrings glittering like stars against the darkness. LeBlanc said something that made her laugh, and Nando began to work his way across the room.

Not that he thought LeBlanc would try anything. On the other hand...

Before he could reach her, Kit turned and walked through a door at the side of the room, waving to a waiter. Nando gritted his teeth in frustration.

LeBlanc glanced at him as he came alongside, his lips spreading in a dry grin. "She just went to check on the wine supplies. I told her we had plenty but she wanted to see for herself. She'll be back."

Nando blew out a breath. "Thanks. I'll wait for her."

"Shouldn't be long. The DJ's due to start playing music in a few minutes back in the Damask Room, and she said she needed to check his play list." LeBlanc narrowed his eyes. "I've been meaning to ask this for a while, but I'm going to do it now because we're in the middle of a crowd and because Kit's going to be back in the room any minute. I figure you can't take a swing at me right here."

Nando stared at him. "What?"

LeBlanc narrowed his eyes. "Are you serious about her?"

Nando blinked. "What the hell business is it of yours?"

"None." LeBlanc shrugged. "Except she's a friend. And if you're not serious about her, you're likely to hurt her. And if you hurt her, I'd have to hurt you and you might punch my lights out if I tried it. I just want to make sure my insurance will cover that."

Nando stared a moment longer, then gave up and shook his head. "I'm as serious as a coma. I don't supposed you've asked her if she's serious about me."

"I don't have to. Here she comes. Just take a look."

Nando watched her face for a moment, the rush of light when she saw him standing there. Assuming she was looking at him rather than LeBlanc.

Screw that.

He knew where she was looking, and it simultaneously warmed him to his toes and scared the life out of him. He was responsible for that. All that. He had to live up to it somehow. He only hoped he could.

LeBlanc wasn't the only one who'd go after him if he hurt her. Hell, he'd beat himself up if he did.

"Hey," Kit said softly as she stepped to his side. "You made it."

"Excuse me." LeBlanc gave them both a faintly sour smile. "I think my presence is urgently needed in the kitchen."

Nando was only dimly aware that he was no longer at his elbow. "You look amazing."

"Thanks." Kit's smile widened. "You look pretty terrific yourself. Can you stay?"

"Stay?" He frowned, trying to process whatever she was asking. "Oh, you mean stay here. Sure. Delaney's taking over."

Behind them music began to play, some eighties power band that he only vaguely remembered. "Damn," Kit muttered, "I didn't get a chance to check his set list."

"Hey." He ran his index finger along the line of her jaw. "You're off duty now. You got them to the altar. Now you can relax, right?" He moved his hands to her waist. "Dance with me."

She stared up at him, her eyes like dark seas. "I can do that," she whispered.

She moved her hands to his shoulders, feeling the press of his palms against her hip bones along with a rush of delight she had no business feeling. In his black suit and burgundy tie he seemed dark and dangerous, like a high-stakes gambler looking for a game. The stakes between them could hardly be higher, but it wasn't a game exactly, at least she didn't think so.

The DJ had switched to something disco, with a thumping beat. Nando ignored the new music, sliding his arms tighter around her, pressing his cheek against her hair. She could smell the faint cinnamon spice of his aftershave. They swayed gently at the side of the room while other people moved past them to get to the dance floor.

"Nando?" Kit whispered after a moment.

"Mmm?"

"Let's get out of here."

He stared down at her, his eyes darkening. "Where did you have in mind?"

She felt a jolt of heat all the way to her knees. *Steady, Catarina.* "Just the terrace for now."

"Okay." He turned to unlatch the French doors behind them, then took her hand as they stepped out to the flagstone terrace facing the green hills. The lawn rolled down to the distant white graveled drive. For a moment, she found herself wondering who'd take care of it now that Mr. Didrikson no longer existed.

A few people were scattered here and there in lawn chairs, one or two couples cuddled together in the wrought iron chaises, ignoring the effect of twisted ironwork on the human body.

"Where are we going?" Nando asked.

Kit slowed, glancing around the rolling green lawn. "To tell you the truth, I'm not sure. I just knew if I stayed in there, I'd go on being a wedding planner, and I was ready to stop." She smiled up at him, then away, not ready to get the full force of those dark eyes again quite yet.

Nando took a quick survey of the lawn, then started to walk toward the edge of the golf course. There was a small pavilion at the top of one of the hills just beyond the garden, its peaked roof barely visible over the tops of the ornamental trees. The latticed sides were shaded by rose bushes. Kit followed him up the stairs, hoping fervently that they weren't about to interrupt someone's garden tête-à-tête.

Fortunately no one else seemed to be looking for a secluded spot at the moment. Nando dropped down on one of the upholstered benches that ran around the edge, pulling her down beside him. He smiled, brushing her hair back from her forehead. "You did good work with that wedding, *chica*. I know it was a pain in the ass while you were doing it, but it looks like it all came together in the end."

"It did, didn't it?" She smiled. "Maybe I'm not as bad at event planning as I thought."

"I'd say you were a champ." He glanced back at the restaurant terrace. "Damn. We should have snagged a bottle of champagne before we took off."

She shook her head, sighing. "I'm sick of champagne. I've been drinking it all week. If I never see another bottle, I'll be a happy woman."

He stared out at the green hills for a long moment, then turned back to her, his dark gaze meeting hers again. "Yeah, well, I'm hoping you'll move out of this anti-champagne phase."

"Why?" She felt a jitter of nerves. Something about his expression made her feel wary all of a sudden.

"Because I'd like to serve it at our wedding."

Kit's heart was suddenly thumping so hard she thought he must be able to hear it. Her stomach clenched, something between terror and delight. "Are you proposing?"

He watched her for a moment. "Are you ready for me to do that?"

She blinked, feeling the slight clench of anxiety in her chest. "I'm not sure."

He shook his head. "Then not yet. If you're not ready to hear a proposal, I don't want to scare you off. I just wanted you to know the thought is there, with me."

"The thought." She licked her lips. "Okay, the thought's in my head too."

He frowned. "Meaning?"

"Meaning I love you." She took a deep breath, staring at her toes, her hands clenching beside her. *All or nothing, Catarina. Time to step off the edge.* "I've loved you since I met you, since you walked into Cedar Creek Winery while I was pouring wine for a bunch of tourists. And I still do. And if I were to marry anyone I want it to be you. It *will* be you as far as I'm concerned."

"Okay. Good to know." He nodded slowly, sliding his arm around her shoulders and pulling her against his side.

She could feel the warmth of his skin through his shirt, the thumping of his heart beneath the hand she pressed against his chest. She leaned back against him. "So now what? I mean, I think we're both kind of tiptoeing around here, like we're afraid something will blow up."

He nodded. "That's about right. I want this so much. I want *you* so much. I'm afraid I'll jinx it if I say the wrong thing." He took a breath. "I'll make you a deal. From now on, I'll tell you what I want and how I feel. If you're pissed at me because of it, you'll tell me. And we'll move on from there. Together."

Kit closed her eyes, feeling the rush of giddiness like wine in her blood. "Fair enough."

"Okay," he repeated, taking another deep breath. "Here's what I want, then. I want to be with you. Spend time with you. If you're not ready to get married yet, I can live with that. But I don't want to be apart while you're deciding when we'll do it."

She cleared her throat, trying to slow her thumping pulse. "Being together would work." She leaned back to look at him, letting her lips edge up into a grin. "I just agreed to rent Allie's place until she's ready to sell. Knowing Allie, that could be a while. Maybe by then I could buy it myself."

His forehead furrowed. "Allie's not going to sell the house after she moves in with Wonder?"

She shrugged. "Not right away. We're supposed to talk about things like rent when she comes back from her honeymoon."

He narrowed his eyes. "So you've got a house of your own?"

Kit managed to ignore the clenching in her chest. "Looks like it. For a while anyway."

He nodded slowly. "It's a nice house. I wouldn't mind living there. And I get a little salary boost with the assistant chief job. I can definitely cover the rent."

She stared at him blankly. "You mean the two of us? Living together?" She felt another rush of terror and delight somewhere around her stomach.

"There or at the apartment," he said slowly. "Or in a tent. Or in the backseat of a fifty-seven Mercury. I just want to be with you, Catarina, wherever you want."

"Okay." She ran her fingertips across his cheek. "I want that too. Aunt Allie's would work. We'll figure it out."

He pulled her closer, one hand cupping the back of her head as he stared down at her. "I love you, Catarina. Now, then, always. Okay?"

She closed her eyes, turning her mouth up to his for a kiss. She tasted sweetness, spice, warmth. Nando. Her Nando. Now, then, always. *Yes.*

For a moment, they clung together, arms wrapped tight. And then he pulled back again. "Okay?"

"Okay." She smiled. "Very okay. The most okay thing that's happened to me for at least the last month. Maybe ever." She glanced back toward the terrace. More couples had moved outside to the grass now, dancing to the music that echoed softly through the French doors. She leaned her forehead against his shoulder again. "Maybe we should go back inside."

He grimaced. "So you can be a wedding planner again?"

She smiled up at him, running her fingers along the side of his face. "No. So I can dance with you. And introduce you to my folks."

He straightened. "Lead me to them."

They walked slowly back toward the patio, his fingers interlaced with hers. The music sounded faintly from inside the restaurant. "Here," he said, moving carefully across the lawn toward the edge of the terrace. "Dance with me."

Inside, the DJ flipped on "You Don't Know Me".

Nando groaned. "I swear I didn't request it."

Kit rested her forehead on his shoulder for a moment. "Doesn't matter. It no longer applies to us. I think I do know you now. I know you know me."

He tightened his arms around her waist, pulling her closer until she looped her arms around him too.

"Just dance, sweetheart," he whispered. "Just dance."

About the Author

Meg Benjamin is the author of the Konigsburg series for Samhain Publishing: *Venus In Blue Jeans, Wedding Bell Blues, Be My Baby, Long Time Gone, Brand New Me,* and now *Don't Forget Me.* Meg lives in Colorado with her DH and two rather large Maine coon kitties (well, partly Maine coon anyway). Her Web site is www.MegBenjamin.com. You can follow her on Facebook (meg.benjamin1) and Twitter (@megbenj1). Meg loves to hear from readers—contact her at meg@megbenjamin.com.

If any man wants more than a dance with her,
they'll have to get past him...

Brand New Me
© 2010 Meg Benjamin
Konigsberg, Texas, Book 5

Deirdre Brandenburg has an MBA and a dream to become the coffee supplier for Konigsburg's growing restaurant industry. What she doesn't have is money, courtesy of her billionaire father's scheme to make her come home. All she needs is three months until her trust fund kicks in. Until then, she needs a job.

Hiring the new girl next door is a no-brainer for ex-gambler Tom Ames. He's already succeeded in making his bar, The Faro, a growing tourist draw. Deirdre's beauty will pull in the locals—particularly every red-blooded male in the Hill Country. As he watches her transform from tentative business wonk to confident, sassy barmaid, he realizes he wants first crack at her heart.

When Big John Brandenburg sends Deirdre's ex-boyfriend to drag her home, the plan backfires, leaving Tom's bar in shambles and Deirdre kidnapped by a band of loony Texas secessionists.

Things are looking pretty bleak—except the good people of Konigsburg have no intention of giving Deirdre up, either. Even if it takes every Faro employee, every last Toleffson, and one cranky iguana to give the honky-tonk lovebirds a chance at forever.

Warning: Contains dirty dancing, hot summer sex, a honky-tonk makeover, and one nippy iguana.

Available now in ebook and print from Samhain Publishing.

9 781609 288150